A V O N

An Imprint of HarperCollins*Publishers*

AVON BOOKS
An Imprint of HarperCollins*Publishers*
10 East 53rd Street
New York, New York 10022-5299

Copyright © 2011 by Karen L. King
ISBN 978-0-06-201735-2
www.avonromance.com

First Avon Books mass market printing: November 2011

Avon Trademark Reg. U.S. Pat. Off. and in Other Countries, Marca Registrada, Hecho en U.S.A.
HarperCollins® is a registered trademark of HarperCollins Publishers.

Printed in the U.S.A.

10 9 8 7 6 5 4 3 2 1

All About
Seduction

Chapter 1

What was so important as to require the privacy of the study? Stifling her impatience, Caroline Broadhurst folded her hands in her lap and waited for her husband's pronouncement. They'd spent a great deal of time together at the mill and then shared dinner, but after telling her he wished to speak to her about a certain matter, he had turned taciturn. Whatever he had to say, he hadn't wanted either the clerks or the servants to overhear.

The setting sun cast an orange glow over his solemn features. Everything Mr. Broadhurst did was slow these days. His spotted hands shook as the whiskey decanter clinked against his glass. He poured out a generous dollop then shuffled to sit gingerly behind his desk. Taking a hearty swig, he gulped, loudly shattering the silence. Moisture pooled at the edges of his mouth.

Did he feel the need for liquid fortification?

He set the tumbler down, frowned, then shifted ledgers and papers to the side of his blotter as if he could not go on until everything was in order.

He picked up the tumbler and drank. He didn't offer her a glass, but then ladies didn't drink whiskey. He'd married her because she had the kind of breeding and connections to society that even his money could not buy. He could buy entrée, but welcome was beyond his reach. Yet with her by his side, he was tolerated in polite circles.

"I want a child," said Mr. Broadhurst, startling her. "A son."

A jagged pang ripped through her, tearing open a hard truth she'd thought she had accepted. Her prayers for a child had fallen on deaf ears. Caroline choked then coughed.

After enduring her husband's twice a week visits to her bedroom for fifteen years of marriage, she no longer believed she would be blessed with children. No matter how she longed to count little fingers and toes, to cradle a child to her breast, to worry if a baby was too hot or too cold like mothers do, those joys would never be hers.

Shifting, she murmured an apology. She couldn't have said if it was for her coughing or her failure to conceive.

What did he expect her to do at this point? She fought to lock the yearning for a child into a dark corner of her mind, where it wouldn't drag her into melancholy. Nothing could be done about her desire for a child or his. Or was his case less hopeless? Her thoughts chased their tails in circles. If he meant to take a new wife . . .

"What is your meaning?" she squeaked out.

His gaze slid away from hers, and he twisted the glass in a slow circle on the letter blotter. "I want a son to leave the mill to." His words were even and measured, as if he were discussing a load of cotton or ordering new machinery.

This couldn't be happening. Her chest squeezed and she wanted to push his glass back to his lips before the next words spilled out of his mouth. If he divorced her, she'd be an outcast. Being married to a man in trade was bad enough, but to be put aside by a man whose only recommendation was his wealth would make her a pariah. No one would ever take her seriously in the business world, let alone in society.

Caroline clenched her skirt of brown worsted. Would he even be able to perform with another woman? The last few times Mr. Broadhurst had come to her bedroom, he'd suffered embarrassing failures. She had tried to reassure him, he was just tired or working too much. Celebrating the end of that part of her marriage was wrong, but after so long, the hope of pregnancy was only a crushing burden that was cruelly dashed each month. At least without his attentions, she knew to expect her courses.

Perhaps he would buy himself a beautiful young wife. Perhaps he could find a wife who did not find congress between a man and a woman so distasteful. Perhaps he could perform with a younger, prettier, more passionate woman.

Mr. Broadhurst stood and shuffled over to the credenza to pour another drink.

"Should you have another?" she asked before she could censor the concern he would take as an attack on his health or his age.

"I do not think it will kill me just yet." Mr. Broadhurst raised his glass in a mock toast. "This is not a criticism of you, my dear wife."

His words were only marginally reassuring. Caroline looked down and forced her hands to relax. A lady did not fidget so. "Sir?"

"I have always been grateful that you have not behaved as your sisters have." He studied her. "But, regrettably, it has put us in a fix."

Her face heated. Even though her sisters, with the help of Mr. Broadhurst's money, had married in their own class, none of their marriages were any more of a love match than hers. Funny, at one time she'd envied them their philandering husbands and gaiety in London society.

Mr. Broadhurst cleared his throat. "I am not getting any younger."

"None of us are, sir," said Caroline. But while she approached thirty, he was well over seventy now.

He sat again in his chair, his glass thumping on the heavy oak desktop. He fiddled with the drink for long seconds, sloshing the amber liquid back and forth. He raised the whiskey, took a sip, and then wiped his mouth with the back of his hand.

Containing her wince, Caroline knew he had a handkerchief. Every morning before they left for the mill office she made certain he was properly pressed and dressed like a gentleman, with a fresh handkerchief tucked in his pocket.

"I need to make arrangements for the mill before I die."

Caroline started to protest that day was surely far distant, but she knew it wasn't. Her husband had outlived most of his contemporaries.

"I could run the mill well enough," she said. Her husband did not have any relatives to leave his massive wealth, and he'd insisted she learn the operations years ago. She expected to run the mill. Why had he been training her, if not to take over?

Years ago he had caught her hiding a novel under the ledgers she was supposed to study. He'd sat her down and told her that she needed to learn the business so she could watch over it while their children grew old enough to take it over. He was not a young man. Feeling guilty for her rebellious attitude, Caroline had applied herself to learning.

"You are a woman," he said. "And too softhearted to run a business for long."

Caroline leaned forward on her chair. Not that she had any doubt of her abilities, but to placate her husband's fears, she said, "I would hire a man to oversee the running of the mill, and I would just—"

Mr. Broadhurst held up his hand, stopping her. "That would be enough if you were holding it for a son. But what good is building the Broadhurst name if there is no one to carry on?"

She knew the operation inside and out, but the children hadn't come. If she was not to run the mill, what was she to do—spend all her days idly reading or sewing or, God forbid, collecting birds and cats as if they could substitute for the children she should have produced? Her hands curled and she had to concentrate to stretch out her fingers.

No, the mill was to be hers. She hadn't spent all these years docilely standing by him to be relegated to a cipher.

"I do not know what to say. I always wanted children. I would have given you a son if I could." She clasped her hands tightly together to keep from twisting them. She would have been thrilled to give him a dozen children, boys, girls. Even one child to kiss good-night, to teach how to be a good and compassionate steward to the mill and its workers, and to give all the love she held in her heart, would have been a heaven sent miracle, but she had proved barren.

"I hope you mean that." He looked at her so intently she felt bound to offer a solution.

"If you would like to adopt a boy, little Danny Carter is an orphan and he is very good at ciphering. I think his grandmother would be relieved to . . .

Mr. Broadhurst's lowered brows over glaring eyes stopped her.

"We could raise him to take over the mill," explained Caroline. Certainly it was not an ideal situation, but it was done. Flutters in her chest suggested a fairy bearing hope had spread excitement with a tiny wand. A child would give her a reason to want to get out of bed each morning.

"You are not suggesting naming a mill child as my son." Mr. Broadhurst's tone was derisive. "He would suffer the same exclusions from society that I do."

With his innate intelligence and unflappable confidence, she thought he would have found acceptance if he had tried harder, but he had come to rely on her for smoothing the way with people—which was almost laughable, as she was the least sociable creature in the world.

"What does that matter?" The hope flitted away. She'd never understood why her husband so desperately desired the acceptance of society. He found little pleasure in their frivolous pursuits and had a bourgeois distaste for the lack of morality among the elite. They'd seemed ideally suited for each other in that respect.

"I married you to be sure that my children would be accepted everywhere. That *my name* would be *welcomed* in the highest of circles."

Caroline lowered her head and gazed at her lap. The back of her throat grew dry. She swallowed several times, to no avail. She always knew her bloodline had been a commodity exchanged for money. Only she had failed to deliver her side of the bargain.

Her husband stood and shuffled over to the window. Her eyes narrowed, but she fought to find the numb place that allowed her to get through each day. To allow the disappointment to rule her only left a bitter taste in her mouth. Nothing could change her barrenness.

"You are my third wife without issue, and your sisters have all produced children. The fault does not lie with you."

Her ears rang as if they had been clapped soundly. As

long as a man could do his part, the failure to conceive was always blamed on the woman. Her mouth worked, but she couldn't force out the demurral she should voice.

He swallowed a shaky gulp. "I consulted with a London physician some time ago, and he told me I am sterile."

Caroline gasped. "How could he know?"

Mr. Broadhurst's shoulders stooped forward and his head bowed. He cleared his throat several times and coughed into his sleeve. "He looked at my fluid under a microscope. He said I had no seed."

She didn't want to know that much detail. Her face burned, yet her hands felt like they'd been submerged in the coldest of well water. *It wasn't her fault?* She'd been shouldering the blame for years—believing that the failure to conceive was some infirmity of hers or her inability to happily tolerate the necessary union. But the fault was all along her husband's?

How long had he known? Tightness boiled in her chest. How long had she suffered the indignity of his nighttime visits after he learned he could not father a child? Hoping the twilight masked the heady emotions tumbling through her, she looked away.

"I have written to your brother and he has agreed to bring a few of his friends for a hunting party."

"What?" Caroline half rose from her seat. Her husband had never cared for her brother, and to invite him and his cronies to invade their quiet home was unnerving. She could guess what he wanted, but it didn't comport with their weekly hours in church, with the moral man she thought her husband was.

"Any child born of your loins would by law be mine and would carry my name. I would claim a son as a miracle God has granted in my last years."

Her heart thumped erratically as her legs turned to pudding. She sank back down onto her seat. No, this couldn't be happening.

He was sanctioning an affair, but she recoiled, with every fiber tightening in protest. Duty required that she submit to her husband, but never to any other man.

"I have already told the housekeeper to stock extra provisions. The men will arrive a week hence."

"No," whispered Caroline, her throat too tight to allow out more than the faintest breath.

"If there is any particular friend of your brother's you want invited, send word."

Unbidden, the faces of the men her brother comported himself with flashed in her mind's eye, and quickly she rejected each one. Between his portly political friends or his sporting cronies, not a single man was the least bit interesting to her, let alone one she would consider in that manner. "I do not wish for them to come."

Stars above, what had Mr. Broadhurst told her brother?

"They will be robust young men, men of your ilk. All you must do is lie with one of them and conceive a child. I know that my age has been disagreeable to you."

A memory of a millworker with too-long dark hair her fingers always itched to brush off his forehead flashed in her mind. She shook her head, willing the completely unsuitable image away. Dear God, what was wrong with her? The whole idea was preposterous, crass and utterly unthinkable.

"No!" Caroline popped out of her chair, no longer able to sit. The act of conception was disgusting. To endure it when it was not an obligation of marriage—well, it was a gross indignity.

"Mrs. Broadhurst, please."

Mr. Broadhurst never asked, never used the word please.

He was always in command of his business, his household, and even her. Staring at him as if he were a foreign creature, she shook her head while backing toward the door. Her heart tried to pound out of her chest and she couldn't catch her breath. She needed to lie down or loosen her stays before she swooned.

"Mrs. Broadhur—Caroline, I'm begging you." Mr. Broadhurst took a step toward her.

Caroline felt for the doorknob behind her back. "It would be a sin."

He thrust out his chin and glared at her. "You did not come to me with so much religion. I only ask you to behave as your sisters have. Have I ever asked anything else of you?"

She had been a perfect wife, caring, modest, and always a lady in every way, and this was how she was repaid? No gentleman would ask this of her, but then Mr. Broadhurst was not a gentleman other than by money. Perhaps he didn't understand the magnitude of what he was asking. Her sisters with their faithless marriages must have given him a distorted view of what was acceptable in aristocratic circles.

"Sir, no one could think this a reasonable demand." Her whole body shook. Her fingers closed around the doorknob, and for a second she feared she was locked in with the madman who had replaced her husband. Finally, she twisted the knob and opened the door.

"Caroline, you will do this. I will brook no disobedience." Mr. Broadhurst's tone had turned stentorian. For a moment he resembled the hard man who had come from a crofter's hut and built an empire.

She had never dared to defy him so openly before. A lady didn't argue with her husband, raise her voice to him, or refuse him. "No, I shall not."

Shaking her head, Caroline backed out the door. She'd

taken great pride in always behaving as a lady ought, but this was too much.

Her legs barely held her as she stood quivering in the hall. The always silent hall. The house always echoed with too much silence. Once, she'd believed the rooms would resound with the laughter and playful shouts of her children. Instead the silence mocked her.

Gulping a couple of breaths that did nothing to calm her, Caroline fled to her bedroom. She could not believe what her husband had asked of her. She would not lie with another man.

Ever.

Jack Applegate backed against the loft ladder as the chaos of the morning exploded around him. After a week away, the household seemed frenetic, loud, and pressing him down. This had been his home for twenty-eight years, but choosing to leave permanently was the right decision.

As usual, his brothers and sisters pushed and shoved to get a turn at the pitcher and basin. The baby howled, while the two-year-old banged a spoon on the table. His fourteen-year-old sister stood at the stove stirring a pot of gruel so thin it looked blue.

His stepmother, Martha, set the kettle back and pushed at escaping strands of her fading hair, then tried to still the banging spoon. She closed her eyes. Likely the babe in her belly was giving her fits this morning.

One of the boys bumped against the ladder, while trying to pull on boots without sitting. Jack steadied his brother. The main room barely contained the lot of them, and didn't offer enough places for everyone to sit at one time. In a few minutes all but the youngest would leave for work.

Jack's father shuffled out of the bedroom, stooped and

crooked and leaning heavily on his cane. Lines of permanent pain had carved deep grooves in his face, and Jack hated that he was about to add to them.

One of the girls popped out of their father's chair at the table and pulled it out for him.

"Weather's changing," he grunted as he gingerly sat.

"You hear your father. Mind you take sweaters." Martha stood at the stove, filling bowls. "Jack, would you—"

"Mine has holes," complained a middle child before Martha could finish, but the caterwauling from the cradle drowned out anything else.

Jack picked up the baby and lifted him high in the air until the cries turned to gurgles of laughter.

"I was going to ask you to fetch milk," said Martha.

If he walked to the dairy to get milk, he'd have to pay for it. This last month alone he'd already bought new boots for Beth—the hand-me-downs no longer mendable—stove blacking for the stove Martha claimed was past repair, and a new doorknob to replace the one the middle boys had managed to break. The family always had needs. He could spend all his money and it wouldn't make a dent. "I have to talk to Da this morning."

Jack stopped swinging the baby and cradled the tot against his chest. But the cries quickly returned and the boy gnawed at Jack's collar.

Martha shouldered past him and plunked bowls of steaming gruel on the bare wood planks of the table. "I would think someone who could afford to take a train trip could manage to buy a bit of milk to help out the family."

"I'll fetch milk at the dinner break," conceded Jack.

He'd have to buy a chunk of cheese if he expected anything to eat for his noonday meal, because payday was too long ago and little food was left to go in the lunch pails. The haunch of beef and the bakery bread hadn't gone as far as Martha hoped when she bought them after getting paid last month. Too many mouths to feed, and he was the only one in the house earning a man's wages.

Martha should have bought flour for bread, but she kept saying the stove wouldn't bake right. Jack suspected this pregnancy so close on the last one was draining her and she was too tired when she got home from the mill to cook.

He nudged a sibling off the table bench and took the seat closest to his father.

His father turned jaundiced eyes on him. "What is it? You planning another trip?"

Perhaps this would be easy. "For good. I'm moving to London." Jack adjusted the baby on his knee, put a bit of gruel on the end of his spoon and took it to the little lips. The baby attacked the spoon, his head shaking left and right, getting gruel more on his face than in his mouth.

Only as Jack was trying to scrape the food back onto the spoon did he realize that the room had gone silent, as silent as the middle of the night—assuming none of the little ones were fussing.

He looked up. Martha pressed her hand against her chest.

His father's watery eyes fastened on him. "Now is not a good time, son."

"It's never a good time." Jack's spine tightened, but he strove to sound calm.

Twice before he'd been ready to leave. When he was twenty he hadn't had a real plan, but when his mother died giving birth to one of the middle boys, he decided to wait. Later, after his father remarried and all seemed well, Jack renewed plans to leave. Then his father injured his back and Jack postponed leaving again. This time he had thought out the smallest of details. His plans were solid, he'd saved enough money, and he was going no matter what.

"I talked to a man about my equipment designs. I've an appointment to see the company owner about a job in a fortnight." Jack had done more than talk. He'd bought a secondhand suit so he didn't look like a hayseed. He'd paid a university student to label his drawings with fine penmanship. He'd found the company that made the machinery the Broadhurst mill used and approached the shop manager all in the space of his four actual days in the city.

If he wanted success in life, he had to act now. He'd been worried no one in London would listen to him, take him seriously, or—as the stories went—would rob him blind. But as he found his way about the vibrant bustling city, nothing in his life had ever felt so right or so liberating.

Ever since he returned late the night before, the walls had felt close, as if they were squeezing him. He'd woken to find three of the little ones curled on his mattress in the corner of the attic he curtained off to make his own room. He loved his family, but they would suck him dry if he didn't venture out and make his mark in the world.

"You need to hold my mechanic's position until I get back to work," said Jack's father. "Too many men let go from Granger's mills are looking for work to let a good job go vacant."

"I need a new stove," muttered Martha.

Jack ignored her and swallowed hard against the tug of duty and obligation. "I have been *holding* your job for nigh on four years. If you aren't able to take it back now, you never will be."

Frankly, he didn't know if his father would ever be able to work again.

Jack's father put a hand on his arm. "Son, this restlessness will go away if you just take a wife. You can move her in here. This house will be yours one day."

Jack stopped himself from making a sour face. He was older than most to remain a bachelor, but it was his choice. Most men his age had their own homes, their own wives, and their own children, but he'd stayed at his father's house long past the time when he should have left.

Besides, there was only one woman who interested him—and she was far out of reach. He might have caught her eye a few times, but she always looked away. For all he liked to watch the graceful way she moved, or catch sight of her pale arched neck under the heavy knot of gleaming dark hair, she always looked a little startled and unnerved by his interest. Of course, he had no business thinking that way about the mill owner's wife. She was a lady and he was a laborer.

But if he could make his way in the world and have success, maybe a woman like her would be possible in the future.

Martha pressed her lips together, while two of his sisters nudged each other and mouthed the name of the girl he was stepping out with. But she was not the woman he envisioned as a future wife, and he'd told her he wouldn't be marrying her—more than once. "I'm not ready for a wife and family."

"You're long past due. We can build you a proper room on the back."

And lose the last of the garden space. And by "we" his father no doubt meant Jack and his brothers who could be trusted with a hammer.

"Or bump out a dormer upstairs," said Martha.

And who would pay for the lumber and nails? Jack took his time feeding the baby another bite and carefully scraping the spoon around his lips. As the oldest son, he would inherit one day, but along with the rickety house and mortgage would be the responsibility of his siblings, which appeared year after year without fail. One day he hoped to support his own children, but not like this. Not with scrimping and scraping by, spending every shilling on bare necessities. "I don't want this house, Da."

"You think you can do better?" sneered Martha.

"He wants the Broadhurst house. He's always staring at it," said his brother David.

How could he not look at the mansion when it was visible from every corner of the village? Although nearby, the towering pompous reminder of the Broadhurst wealth was far enough removed from the laborer's houses so as to not sully its white stone facade.

Sighing, Jack fed the baby another bite. He didn't want the Broadhurst house specifically, but one like it with a woman like Mrs. Broadhurst to welcome him home.

"You'll never have a house half that big," said Martha.

"We'll see," said Jack. Hell, if he had a house half that big, Martha and his father would be first in line to move in with him.

"This is a fine house," objected his father. "David, bring me the bottle. My back is killing me."

David brought over the gin bottle, and his father took a healthy swig. Jack fought the boil of anger. No milk for the babies, but there was gin for his father's back pain. Jack rubbed his forehead. He no longer knew if the pain was an excuse for the gin or the gin was an excuse for the pain. What he did know was that if his father couldn't put his family's needs above his own, then he shouldn't have to either.

"What is wrong with you, Jack? Can't you see we need you around here?" demanded Martha.

Jack knew the strain of a rough pregnancy, and the fear that everything would fall apart made her lash out. After having walked over fifteen miles yesterday to make it home, he too was tired and irritable, and he couldn't miss another day of work to rest.

Holding the baby around his waist, Jack stood. "I'm not your husband. He is." He pointed to his father. "And you two should give having baby after baby a rest."

He wanted to call the words back as soon as they left his mouth.

"What makes you think you're any better than the rest of us?" hissed Martha.

"I'm not better than you. I just want a better life." And he'd put it off for far too long, but now was determined to get the hell out of this mill town before he was trapped here forever.

Chapter 2

In spite of Caroline's protests, the hunting party was due to arrive later in the day. Her brother had ridden in late the night before, but she hadn't spoken to him. His collusion in this base plan of Mr. Broadhurst's robbed her of any joy she might have taken in the rare treat of seeing one of her family.

After another night spent tossing and turning while the hope she fought so hard to suppress kept whispering, *You could have a baby to love,* she had gone into the mill office instead of waiting for Robert to rise.

Mr. Broadhurst and Robert could welcome their "guests." She had at least had the satisfaction of telling Mr. Broadhurst that he must be present when the members of the party arrived and would have to leave the running of the mill to her. After all, for a purported hunting party and a gathering of gentlemen, a host was expected, not so much a hostess. But in his absence, she would show him she could run the mill as well or better than him.

She spread out on her desk the shipping manifests. Making neat notes, she determined exactly how much cotton Mr. Broadhurst had bought this season. Taking over vital decisions, such as the purchase arrangements for next year, would show her husband she was more than capable. She would convince him to leave the mill to her care, son or no son.

The door opened and her brother swept into the office, bringing the scent of horseflesh and autumn air with him. He strode across the floor, his boots clomping heavily against the bare wood.

The clerks all stopped in the midst of their endeavors. Robert had never been in the mill before. He scarcely looked at his surroundings as his gaze fastened on her. She rose to greet him.

"Caro, there you are. Your housekeeper said I would find you here, but I scarcely could credit it. You must come back to the house before the others arrive." He stopped in front of her, caught her forearms and bent to brush his muttonchop whiskers against her cheek.

She bit back her retort that someone must run the mill while he and her husband spun useless schemes. Instead she greeted him civilly, "Hello, my lord. Allow me to introduce you to the office staff." She turned to the others in the large room filled with desks piled with ledgers and papers. "This is Mr. Smythe, our shipping clerk . . . my brother, Lord Nesham, and—"

"Hello everyone," Robert interrupted, and briskly nodded to the occupants of the room. Returning his attention to Caroline, he searched her face. "We need to talk. I have spent the morning closeted with Broadhurst." He looked around the open room. "Is there no private office?"

Only thin clapboard separated the private office from the main one. Conversations could easily be overheard. If her husband wished privacy for business, he brought people to the house. The house was the last place she wanted to be right now.

"Perhaps we should take a stroll." Caroline held her hand out toward the door. Robert was the sibling who closest resembled her, with his dark hair and blue eyes, but the resemblance was fading. Whereas age had sharpened her features, it had dulled his. His skin was pasty and his frame had turned stout. He looked as if he had aged a decade since she'd seen him at their father's funeral a year and a half ago.

"What an ugly place," said Robert as soon as the door closed behind them.

The three-story red brick building was built for function, not aesthetics. The bricks had been left bare both inside and out. Mr. Broadhurst did not believe in sparing expenses for comfort. Nonetheless there was a beauty in its starkness. "Mr. Broadhurst would say it's a mill, not our home."

"I see," said Robert, huffing alongside her.

A horse was tied to a bush near the door. Even though the crisp fall weather seemed ideal for walking from the house, Robert must not have thought so. Her husband had made the ten-minute trek daily for most of his life. Only in the last few months had he taken to ordering the gig brought around.

"Would you like a tour?" Caroline offered. Even if Robert didn't see the merits of the place, she was proud of the mill.

"I have no desire to see the workings, but we can walk along these paths," he said. "Are you not curious about whom I have invited?"

"No." She stepped onto a path leading to the canal providing power for the mill.

"I invited Tremont, he is a favorite with the ladies." Robert twisted around, looking every which way except at what was probably a sour expression of distaste on her face. His voice dropped lower. "He has fathered at least one lady's child. Whitton is said to have a half dozen by-blows. Berkley's wife passed during childbirth."

Caroline's spine tightened as Robert listed the men he'd invited as if he were offering her a particularly delectable array of virile sweetmeats. "These are not your usual cronies."

"No, I went to great length to invite men who might appeal to you, which was difficult enough. We hardly know you anymore, Caro."

He should have known she wouldn't have an affair. Her heart thumped oddly. Mr. Broadhurst had her brother the viscount acting the roll of procurer. She would have laughed at the absurdity of the situation were it not for the seriousness of it.

"You have only to let me know if you take a liking to any particular gentleman, and I will facilitate an alliance."

Caroline stopped walking. The cold air burned her heated cheeks. "You are laboring under a misunderstanding. I have no intention of forming an alliance with any of the men you've invited."

"You have another man in mind?"

"Of course not." Barely restraining a sniff of impatience, Caroline resumed walking. Ahead of her a few millworkers filed out, swinging their dinner pails. As far as bloodlines went, one of them would be much closer to Mr. Broadhurst. She scanned for a particular man who always caught her eye. A heavy sigh left her when she didn't see him. He'd been absent last week too. She hoped he wasn't ill.

She lowered her voice. "I shall not do this. I *will* not. Mr. Broadhurst is mad to speak of it."

Robert blinked once, then twice. "He assured me you wanted a child—that you were in agreement . . ."

She had wanted a child, she'd said so many times. It was the only thing that allowed her to get through nights with her husband without turning into a bedlamite. But it was not to be. "Not this way."

"But you sent that letter saying that while you were overjoyed by the birth of Sarah's latest, you couldn't help but feel melancholic that you had not been so blessed."

Caroline's breath snagged. Mr. Broadhurst must have retrieved the sheets on which she'd poured out her anguish then tossed in the dustbin. She'd written a proper note expressing her felicitations, and not her disappointment. "I did not send that."

Robert jerked her to a stop. "Did you write it?"

Knowing he had read the letter felt a bit like he'd pried open her deepest secrets and exposed them. A pang in her chest stole her breath as she shrugged away striving for nonchalance. "I wrote it, but I copied the parts I wanted to say in another letter. I threw that version away." Months ago. How long had this scheme been in the works?

"I should have known the letter was not your usual fare, but I thought you were finally revealing your innermost feelings." Robert rubbed his face and his shoulders slumped. "Hell, any feelings."

Caroline stiffened, her nails biting into her palms. "Just because I am reserved, does not mean I am without feelings."

But if she poured out her private thoughts in letters, she would just give everyone a case of the doldrums. A lady didn't complain about her circumstance, her loneliness, her isolation, or the lack of affection in her life. What good would complaints have done? So she wrote of inconsequential things like the weather and asked after her nieces and nephews.

"I thought it strange you commented twice on Sarah's baby and the pages had the look of being pressed out after being crumpled. But I took it as your way of expressing your willingness to go along with Broadhurst's plan," said Robert.

"I may have had a moment of weakness when I wrote that, but I did not send it. Mr. Broadhurst must have." She should have shredded the stupid missive or burned it. She stroked her index finger with her opposite thumb. "I want no part in his scheme. I am resigned to my condition. I just want the mill."

"Caro. He wants a child, and you must want one too. Even if you did not mean for me to see that letter, I saw yearning in every word you wrote."

Blackness ate at her insides. Was her brother to gang up on her too? "I will not speak of it anymore."

Didn't he understand it tore her apart to even think of a child? If she dwelt on how much she wanted a baby of her own, she wouldn't be able to return to work. And the work fulfilled her. Robert wouldn't understand, but running the mill was what got her out of bed every day.

She had thrown herself into learning the mill to fill the empty hours of her days, and perhaps a bit of her husband's ambition had transferred to her. Her family would never understand her fascination with the manufactory.

She'd been raised to believe that people of quality did not sully their hands with industry, but such a foolish attitude was part of what brought her father to insolvency and forced him to trade one daughter for the funds to marry off the rest.

"We have to have this conversation, Caro, whether you will it or no." Robert's voice dropped low. "Broadhurst has not asked you to do anything so terrible."

Caroline laughed, but it sounded more like glass breaking and she broke off midway. "No?"

"He wants a son and an heir. Is that so much to ask?"

"I have been a dutiful wife, but to command me to

commit adultery is beyond the pale." She folded her arms, proper deportment be damned. She'd never given her husband a reason to regret marrying her—other than not giving him children. And if the fault lay with him . . . she should not suffer for it.

Robert rubbed his face. "You have to, Caroline, we need his money. Papa . . . Papa mortgaged everything. Without the Broadhurst funds I would not survive. Nor would Mama. Sarah, Amelia, and the twins' husbands all expect their payments."

Were all her family members leeches to her marriage? Caroline's throat constricted. She fought for the equanimity to deal with this too.

All her adult life had been filled with silent mantras about how a lady behaved. She did not shout, she did not rail, she pushed down any violent emotion until it no longer threatened her sanity. She'd been stifling her feelings so long, it was odd she couldn't manage to now.

"You will not survive? Or will all of you have to stop going to Brighton in the summers, Newmarket in the fall, and London for the social season?" Her voice trembled under the strain of suppressing a shout. What kind of family did she have that they demanded again and again that she sacrifice for their comfort? "Mama will have to stay at inns in the Riviera instead of the best hotels? Amelia will have to settle for only ten new ball gowns?"

Robert blinked and took a step back. "Since Papa died, I alone have been to London to take my seat in Parliament. I let the London house and take rooms in Cheapside. Mama hasn't been back to the continent. My wife complains that she and the children have nothing to wear." He lifted his hand, patting the air. "Besides, our sisters know nothing of this arrangement. Hell's bells, *I* knew nothing of it before inheriting. But there are loans on top of loans . . . mortgages on everything. I was counting on the payments to sort this out."

"I should have thought the bride price Mr. Broadhurst paid for me would have taken care of the family finances." Caroline's anger curled tightly into a black ball in her stomach.

"God knows it should have. We all thought it did. If I had any idea Papa was spending so beyond the estate income, I would have curtailed my expenditures years ago. But I am obligated to make payments on all the loans to family and others. Papa . . ." Robert's shoulders slumped. "Papa all but ruined us. In the end only family would loan him money."

Resigned, but not surprised, she asked, "Mr. Broadhurst is still paying?"

"Yes, of course. It was part of the settlement. The second settlement." Robert's brow furled. "I don't know if Papa recorded why there are two settlements, and I haven't made it through all the paperwork yet. I should have read it all, but I thought you were in agreement with this plan."

"No, I never agreed to such an abomination."

Robert pensively studied her. "We . . . Papa never thought your husband would live so long. No one thought you should be stuck in North Country for more than a half-dozen years. We all expected you would be a wealthy young widow, and that would make up for any comparison you might suffer if you were brought out with any of our sisters."

Caroline cast about for a place to look. The trampled brown grass at her feet offered no comfort. Her brother's assessment of her lack of attributes in comparison to her accomplished sisters stung. Even though she'd never been thrust in the fishbowl of the marriage mart where her plainness and inability to carry a tune would matter, the thought that no man would want her when one of her sisters was available still cut like a knife.

Long before leaving the schoolroom, she'd heard her parents' worried conversations about how she would fare in London. She was too bookish, too plain, too retiring, while her older sisters Sarah and Amelia were beautiful, accomplished in the arts, and vivacious. Their youngest siblings had taken after Sarah and Amelia, not her. With five daughters to see settled, their parents expected her to be a huge burden. Instead she'd been the first to marry.

It was silly. She didn't want another husband and had never found the endless rounds of festivities in London enjoyable. The throngs of people overwhelmed her. And marriage was something she wanted no part of ever again. When Mr. Broadhurst passed, freedom would come . . .

"Broadhurst married you for our bloodline."

Caroline swiveled on her brother. "Then let Sarah or Amy or one of the twins produce another baby. I'll stuff a pillow under my dress. Let one of them throw herself on the Broadhurst money altar. Why am I the only lamb put out for slaughter?" Caroline winced. She didn't really think of herself as the sacrificial lamb. She preferred a quiet life. Mr. Broadhurst had given her that. Until her husband's demand, she would have considered herself content to wait until she was a woman of independent means.

The blood drained from Robert's face. "That's not fair. We've all done things, Caro. I promised my vote on bills I cannot like to gain alliances with at least three of the men I invited. And I have done my best to further your husband's interests. I've secured contracts to supply cloth for the military. Sarah, Amelia, beyond declaring the best fabrics come only from Broadhurst mills, have always insisted he be accepted in polite company when you've come to town. Fortunately, you have not availed yourselves of our hospitality so much. You do not know how our reputation suffers. He makes everyone so uncomfortable."

Fighting for calm, Caroline closed her eyes. They had done nothing compared to what she'd done. They hadn't had to lie with an old man pawing them and poking them. They hadn't had to go through years of not feeling welcome outside her home. But she drew the line at this base manipulation.

She took in a couple of slow breaths. With the letter pouring out her personal heartbreak, Robert had likely been acting under the assumption that she wanted a child badly enough to have an affair. She could hardly fault him for providing what he *thought* she wanted, no matter how wrong he was. And she didn't want to spend her time arguing with him, when Mr. Broadhurst was truly the cause of their contention. "You have not told any of these gentlemen of this plan, have you?"

"I have hinted to one or two you are lonely. But I didn't think it would do to tell *all* of them. It would not do to have them lining up at your bedroom door."

As if that would happen. She'd be lucky if any of them were interested in her. "Perhaps Mr. Broadhurst should pay one a stud fee," she mused.

"He offered," said Robert dryly. "I did not think that would be the best course or necessary."

Caroline scarcely had a second to decide if she was mortified that her husband thought her so lacking in wiles that he thought he had to pay a man, or if he had just decided it might be expedient.

"Caro," said Robert in a quiet voice. "I suppose you will marry again after Broadhurst passes, but consider, your choices will be so much better with Broadhurst wealth."

A shudder ran down her spine. The last thing she wanted was to allow another man the right to use her body at will. "I cannot conceive of a prospect more unpleasant."

"You don't wish to marry again?" Robert's brow knit. "You have always told us you were content in your marriage."

He truly didn't know her. "No. Are you saying I couldn't return home to Nesham Hall? Hasn't my husband's contribution to the family coffers earned me a place there?" She didn't exactly want to return home as a widow either, but she couldn't imagine living so close to the mill if it were no longer hers. She would have to purchase another house, perhaps close to her family.

Robert tilted his head to the side. "Of course you can come home. I just thought you'd want a child. Don't you want a baby?"

"If God did not grant me one through my marriage, then I don't wish to commit adultery to have one." Therein was the crux. "I want the mill, Robert. I know how to run it."

Besides, who else could Mr. Broadhurst leave it to? He had no one else.

One of the millworkers joined the others and settled his hands on his hips while watching her. His unbleached muslin shirt puffed around his braces. Recognition jolted her. She always noticed him when she entered the mill. Worse yet, he always seemed aware when she looked in his direction.

The chill wind ruffled his dark hair, which had been neatly barbered. More used to his hair being too long and unruly, she stared at him. Where had he been? He smiled at a comment a young woman tossed in his direction. The man's attention shifted back to Caroline and his eyes tightened.

Catching herself, she resisted the urge to change her direction and go toward him. It wasn't as if he'd beckoned to her. He didn't watch her because she was beautiful like her sisters. He probably watched her with the wariness of a man who suspected she could end his employment with a snap of the fingers. Her fascination with him was entirely misplaced.

His family worked at the mill, except she'd decreed that no child under nine could work. She remembered the man standing to the side as she told the middle-aged woman who answered the door that the youngest children should attend school. The woman protested, but he had quietly said it was best they learned as much as they could, while they could. Caroline had been pleased he understood the value of education even if the woman did not.

As far as sacrifices for family went, Caroline could have had it worse. Mr. Broadhurst always made certain she had fashionable clothes, beautiful jewelry, and the latest books. She hadn't been put to work in a mill at the age of five. Her duties to her husband were mild compared to the life the millworkers led.

"Sarah said you might make use of her husband, if needs must."

"For Pete's sake, does everyone know?" she exclaimed.

The millworker squinted over his shoulder as if asking if she needed assistance.

Her mind spinning, she shook her head, silently rebuffing the worker's concern. She deliberately dropped her arms.

The worker gave one last questing tilt of his head before entering the mill. Heart pounding, Caroline swung away from the sanctity of the brick building, where once again she'd drawn that man's attention.

For pity's sake, if she were to do this, he would be just as good a potential sire as any other. He at least appeared concerned about her.

"I consulted with Sarah and Amelia," her brother said, "because I thought Broadhurst might have been trying to secure you a second husband. Besides, Amy said you would object to married men."

"I object to all men."

"If you were to form a *tendre* . . . oh never mind." Robert waved off the thought. "I did not realize that Broadhurst had been made a widower twice before. I thought he had been building his wealth and only married late in life."

Caroline rubbed her forearm. "Why would you have known? You were only sixteen when I married him." Little more than a year older than she'd been, but they'd both been so young. She hadn't known her husband had been married twice before until he told her in his study a week ago. He'd always rebuffed her inquiries into his life before her. "Did you know he asked for Sarah's hand first and then Amelia's?"

Papa had decided that if the daughters were interchangeable, he might as well offer up the one daughter who would be hard to marry.

"Caro, none of us had anything to do with Papa's decision for you to marry Broadhurst. I'm certain if Sarah or Amy had been told to marry him, they would have." He furled his forehead again. "He has shown me his will. Your entire inheritance is contingent on having a son to inherit."

Her gut knotted. She must have misheard. Just because he didn't want to leave the mill in her hands didn't mean he would will away all his wealth. "He doesn't intend to leave me penniless, does he?"

"Yes. Broadhurst has entirely cut you out of his will." Robert reached out.

She recoiled. Her ears buzzed and her fingernails cut into her palms. This was how she was repaid for being an obedient wife? Her insides blackened and curled like paper tossed in a fire. How could he do this to her?

Her brother softened his tone. "If you do not give birth, everything will pass to a man named Granger."

Her spine tightened as if a knife had been thrust in it. Granger? That man made Mr. Broadhurst look like a saint. Granger's mills ate up workers, spit them out broken, and left them to the poorhouse or an early death.

"We could sue for your widow's portion, but it might take years. And if Papa did not properly secure it in the marriage contract, who knows if you will ever get more than a pittance. Bloody hell, Papa made such a mess of things."

Robert's earnest expression made her insides churn.

"I don't know what I can do to make sure his wealth stays with you if you don't want a child."

Caroline stared at the mill. She'd put years into learning the operation. The idea of it being snatched away from her left her feeling cheated, but Mr. Broadhurst's plan to leave her destitute was like the ground turning to liquid under her feet.

A knot fisted in her chest. She'd tried so hard to be a good wife, a perfect lady, and to keep alive her hope of independence she had to commit adultery.

"Caro . . ." Robert rubbed his hand over his face. "You don't have to do anything you don't want to do . . . but—"

A horrible grinding screech and thump emanated from the mill. Caroline's shoulders came up, while Robert jerked.

Shrill screaming rent the air. Shouts and cries followed. Picking up her skirts, Caroline ran, as no proper lady ever should, toward the brick building.

Chapter 3

Before Caroline reached the side door of the mill, a man stumbled out, dropped to his knees and wretched in the grass beside the door. Oh, God, what had happened? Her heart in her throat, she raced inside. A group clustered around an ominously silent machine with its big gears and massive drum. The room was chock full of gears, shafts, and belts that powered all the machinery required to take cotton to material.

An ignored blood-spattered child stood sobbing. Dread pouring coldly through her veins, Caroline ran to the little girl and dropped to her knees. "Where are you hurt?"

The tiny waif closed her mouth, hiding her milk teeth, and shook her head as big tears leaked out of her eyes. Caroline ran her hands over the child but didn't find any source for the blood. Thank God, the little one was unhurt. She gathered the child to her and smoothed back the girl's flyaway blond hair.

Her relief at not finding injuries made her hug the girl too tight. She was a tiny thing, her arms scarcely bigger around than a string bean. The warm sweet smell of the child tugged at a yearning deep inside her.

Caroline picked up the child and turned toward several

men working to turn the massive cogs. At their feet a man lay on the floor. He must be the source of the blood. Her relief at finding the girl unharmed flitted away, leaving a sick churning behind. Feeling as if she were forcing her steps through thick mud, she walked closer. The crowd parted in deference to her. She held her breath.

The injured man lay on the floorboards, his right ankle smashed between two massive gears. How could it even fit there? Thickness rose in her throat, and she shielded the girl's eyes from the growing pool of blood. As the workers let her through, the man's unbleached muslin shirt with the left sleeve shredded and bloody came into sight, then the newly barbered dark hair. Her lungs ached for air and her head spun. Oh God, it was him, the man who'd been watching her outside.

He opened his eyes. His gaze turned on Caroline than moved to the child cradled in her arms. "Is she all right?"

Caroline took a step back, half surprised he was conscious. "She's fine."

A tall lanky man scurried through the crowd with a long metal bar and braced it on the gear trapping the young man. Together with a heavier man, he leaned against the pole, trying to turn the giant metal cog. The trapped worker's face twisted but he did not cry out.

"I don't know as we can get him out, ma'am," said the foreman, sidling up beside Caroline.

"Do whatever you have to," she said.

"Might have to take off that leg." The foreman twisted his cap in his hands.

The injured man glared in their direction. "No."

Her stomach turned. That hadn't been what she meant by doing whatever was needed. She had to take charge. Pulling command from a hollow hole in her chest, she instructed, "Dismantle the gears."

"Iffen he dies, we'll just cut off the leg," said the foreman. "Reckon we can crank it out the other side. Mr. Broadhurst don't hold with taking apart the machinery."

"Mr. Broadhurst is not here. I am in charge of the mill today." Mr. Broadhurst was at the house awaiting their visitors.

The foreman stared at a spot beyond her shoulder, not following her order. She made a concession to the gods of production. "The sooner he is out, the sooner operations can resume."

The foreman scratched at his temple.

Summoning all the haughtiness of generations of aristocracy, she said with cool disdain, "Dissemble the machine now, sir, without further delay." She let her tone imply an *or else*.

Yet, her stomach twisted and a cold sweat started on her spine.

"Yes, ma'am." The foremen directed a worker to fetch tools.

A couple of the men pressed reddened cloths against the young man's arm. He would need a physician. All around, the men watched.

"Who can ride a horse well?" she asked.

"I can." An older man stepped forward.

"Take the horse tied by the office and fetch a doctor from Warrington. Get the one who was with the army in the Crimean. Tell him to hurry." Warrington was a decent sized town, but five miles away. Even at a gallop, it would take at least a quarter hour to get there. "Ride as fast as you can."

The man touched his forehead and bumped through the

growing crowd. Women and children from the upstairs weaving rooms filed into the room. "Oh my God, it's Jack!" one cried out.

The murmurs went back through the room, and the injured man coughed weakly. His skin was gray. Just minutes ago he had looked so alive, with the wind ruffling his hair.

"What happened?" cried someone.

"He's hurt bad," said one of the men pressing a cloth to Jack's arm. "The belt snapped on him and his ankle is crushed."

From other parts of the mill workers filed in, pushing and bumping closer. Had all of them come to watch him die? No, he couldn't die.

Reluctantly, Caroline tilted the child in her arms toward a group of women. "Take her out of here. Take all the children out of here. This is no sight for them."

A woman took the girl. Caroline gave the tiny girl a reassuring pat. Her stomach knotted, but she had to remain calm and keep in control.

She found the foreman in the crowd and met his eyes. "Clear the onlookers."

The foreman followed her instructions, ordering the idle workers out of the room. A mature woman stumbled forward, shouldering through the crowd. Caroline recognized her from injured man's home. Wanting to protect her from the sight of Jack on the floor, she stepped in front of the woman.

"What happened? Is it Jack?" The woman tilted, trying to see.

At Caroline's nod, the woman glared with icy eyes and skirted around her. If she was his mother, she would want to offer him comfort.

The woman drew to a halt and stared at the leg caught

in the machine. First in a whisper she said, "No." Then she screamed shrilly, "No, no!"

Hoping to calm her, Caroline put her hand on the woman's fleshy shoulder.

"How could you let this happen?" she shouted, while shoving back her lank colorless hair.

The short man working at freeing Jack said in a low voice, "He saved little Mattie when the belt snapped. She dropped her load of spindles and he rolled on one."

Mattie must be the little girl spattered with blood.

"Why would you do that? Have you no sense?" the woman screeched at Jack.

Caroline recoiled. How could she berate him for saving a little girl?

Jack glared up at the woman, his mouth flattening. His expression of concern over the little girl was gone. In its place a shuttered look appeared. He slowly turned his head away.

The animosity hung heavy in the air. Jack needed comforting not condemnation. Caroline tightened her grip on the woman and turned her shoulder.

The woman resisted and burst into noisy wails of "Why? Why?"

"He'll be all right. I've sent for the physician." More for Jack's sake than hers, Caroline kept her tone soothing. "We'll get him out."

"What good'll he be? He won't be able to work. I got another babe on the way. I can't take care of another cripple."

Appalled, Caroline gripped the woman firmly and shoved her toward one of the men. "Take her outside."

Another one of the millworkers, trying to pry the gear loose, kicked an empty spindle. It rolled across the floor and knocked into Caroline's foot. Wooden spindles littered the floor. Her chest tightened. How many had that little child been trying to carry?

Pressing her lips together, she moved closer and dropped to a knee beside the injured man. She found his hand and caught it, giving him a squeeze. He turned slowly, looking at her, and his hand tightened around hers. His grip was solid and reassured her that he was not on the verge of death. Odd that just holding his hand helped calm the skip of her heart. But his skin was too pale. The scarlet blood kept spreading out along the grooves of the floorboards and then filled in the surfaces.

Swallowing hard, she kept her features controlled and silently prayed Godspeed to the doctor.

"We'll get you out," she said softly. She should say something motherly and reassuring. Only she wasn't a mother, and up close she could see the beginnings of lines etched around his eyes. He must be older than she'd thought.

His breathing was steady if a little heavy. The gash on his arm was deep. But it was his caught foot that most disturbed Caroline, making her throat catch.

"Dammit, Caro, did you tell that man he could take my horse?" Robert stomped through the room. He drew to a halt when he saw the commotion. "Oh dear Lord."

"It's an emergency," said Caroline.

Her brother stopped beside her, pulled his snowy handkerchief from his pocket and patted his lips. She scowled at him. He should not allow his revulsion to show. Waving him away, she turned her attention back to the trapped man. Holding his gaze, she willed her strength to him.

The injured man's nostrils flared as he stared back at her.

The men around lapsed into an argument about how the machinery could be dismantled. Desperation clawed at her. Did no one know how to break down the spinning frame cogs?

Jack tugged on her hand. He struggled to rise to his elbows. She didn't want him looking at his mangled lower leg, and she put her hand to his chest to push him back down. In spite of the pressure she applied, he managed to achieve a half-reclined position.

"That bolt there." He pointed with his gashed arm. "Loosen that one and then those."

Caroline stared in amazement as the injured man directed the men how to disassemble the gears trapping him.

"You should come away," Robert said to her.

"I can't now, Robert." She shifted to prop up Jack as he directed men through the maze of bolts and fasteners holding the massive cogs together. Reaching up, she snatched Robert's handkerchief from him and folded it to press against Jack's injured arm. She wished she could wrap her arms around him and comfort him. She settled for holding his well-muscled arm still and pressing at the bleeding wound.

Jack seemed inclined to shake her off, but for a second his dark eyes met hers and he hesitated.

That she was the mill owner's wife probably stilled his protest.

"How often do these mishaps occur?" muttered Robert. "Good Lord above."

"Once is too often," said Caroline. There had been accidents before. There were deaths. The last had been a five-year-old boy who was knocked on the head by a loom. Mr. Broadhurst hadn't understood her tears for a child she didn't know. He never woke up, and passed a week later. She'd known then that she had to do whatever she could to get the children out of the mill, to make it safe for not only them, but everyone.

But as long as Mr. Broadhurst only paid lip service to

her decree, the tots continued to work alongside adults. And Granger's mills were worse.

After what seemed like hours, the men finally had the gear loosened and it fell down away from the mangled wreck of Jack's boot. He lifted his leg and reached to grab his foot, but it hung down at an unnatural angle. He missed, reaching in the place his foot should be.

The tall lanky man crashed to the floor in a dead faint.

Caroline buried her face against Jack's back. She inhaled his clean male scent while fighting the rise of bile in her throat. The cadence of his breathing changed to shallower and quicker. Of all the men for this horrid accident to befall, why did it have to be him?

He shifted, his shoulders tensing against her face. She needed to help, not hide away. Her weakness embarrassed her, and she struggled to regain command. No matter how hard it was for her to look, Jack shouldn't be trying to care for his own mangled limb. She crawled around, grasped his boot, and slowly lifted straightening the broken leg.

He groaned.

She scooted until she sat at his feet. As gingerly as she could she lowered his leg to her lap, trying to hold it in a normal position. Fighting the squeamishness that might show on her face and alarm him, she peeled Jack's bloody fingers away. "Lie down."

Most of the onlookers turned away.

"Would one of you men please go outside and see if the doctor has arrived?"

No longer laboring to free Jack, several of the men rushed toward the door. Jack threw his arm across his face. Caroline wished she could do more for him, but she was helpless. She plucked at his bloody laces, loosening them. She half feared his foot would come off when she removed his work boot. She gave up and circled her hands around his leg, trying to stem the flow of blood.

"Get back here and put this machine back together," shouted the foreman.

Dragging their heels the men traipsed back toward the dissembled gears. Two of the men lifted the largest of gears and reseated it on the shaft. One of the men put a wrench to a fastener.

"The other bolt . . . has to go on . . . first." Jack pointed. His arm dropped down as if it had grown too heavy and he labored to breathe.

"It's all right. They'll manage," Caroline soothed, and gestured for him to lie back.

He batted her hand away. "If they don't do it right . . . the gears will grind apart."

"We'll get it," muttered one of the men, but Jack kept an eye on them and directed them when they seemed uncertain.

"You don't have to hold my leg," he said at one point.

"Someone needs to keep it straight until the doctor gets here." She wished she could do more for him.

A couple of the women returned with cotton and strips of muslin and wrapped his gashed arm, put a pressure bandage around his calf above the break, and splinted the broken ankle. His hiss as she shifted his leg told her he was hurting.

Scooting back to his side, she took his hand in hers. His crushing grip conveyed the tight leash he was keeping on his pain. Not knowing what else to do, she murmured words of encouragement and stroked the skin on the back of his hand. Her heart pounding, she said, "You'll be fine."

He shot her a skeptical look, his brown eyes communicating a wealth of information. He wouldn't be fine, and he knew it. Fear and anger were dominate, but there was a yearning there she couldn't place. He turned his gaze away, leaving her feeling chastised for offering false hope.

"The doctor will know what to do," she said firmly, although she only hoped a man well versed in war injuries would be better skilled than others.

Not knowing what else to talk about, she said, "You have a big family, don't you?"

His lips tightened.

At long last the doctor arrived carrying his black bag. He shook his head as he bent over, assessing the broken leg. "I need to get him on a table to operate. We best get him to his home."

Caroline thought of the unusual interchange between Jack and his mother and made a decision she knew would upset her husband. "Take him up to the main house."

"Take me home," demanded Jack.

But the men carrying him ignored him. And it wasn't as if he could leap off the removed door they employed as a stretcher, not with the mangled mess of his lower leg. The pain sliced anew through him with each jog of the wood under his back. How could pushing little Mattie out of the way have led to this?

Jack grabbed the sleeve of his friend George. "Don't take me up there where that war surgeon will butcher me."

George looked down at him, and the pity in his expression made Jack want to punch him. But his hand slipped off George's arm as if he no longer had the strength to hold on. There could only be one reason that particular doctor had been summoned. A war surgeon got comfortable with slicing off legs and arms. A sick feeling invaded Jack's throat. He couldn't lose his leg. He'd never amount to anything as a cripple.

"Be grateful Mrs. Broadhurst is of a mind to look after

you," muttered George as he bore the stretcher toward the mansion.

That was part of the rub. "I don't want—" her to see him like this.

"Martha can't take care of you and your da."

Jack's head spun. He'd longed to speak with Mrs. Broadhurst, to hold her hand, but not as a helpless invalid, needing care, garnering her pity. And how was he going to make it to London in a fortnight? It was as if the Devil himself conspired to keep him in this wretched village. He groaned and gripped the sides of the door.

Partially denuded tree branches with their browned leaves clawed at the blue sky. His vision blurred, but he clung to the blue, hurtling prayers to a heaven that seemed to give him just a glimpse of hope before allowing his dreams to be crushed. For a second it was as if he floated along, before a body-wracking shiver made his teeth rattle.

Time seemed disjointed and he couldn't tell if he was hot or cold. The shivers must mean he was cold, only he felt more numb than cold. He seemed almost nothing, as if his life force had ebbed away in the red pools left on the mill floor.

"Hang on, Jack," urged George, his face crinkled in concern as he strained to bear the weight of hoisting Jack up the stairs.

"No," he moaned.

The view above him changed to ornate plasterwork in a recessed ceiling high above. Activity exploded around him as servants ran hither and thither. And Mrs. Broadhurst was in the center of it all, looking flushed and issuing commands in a calm voice.

"Quick, help me roll the carpet," she instructed a footman as she dragged two straight chairs to the wall.

Jack strained to watch her almost cursing at the men carrying him to move out of the way. Was he still bleeding? He couldn't find the energy to look as people swirled around him. Maids in their black dresses with white aprons and caps, footmen in their old-fashioned breeches and black coats, moved every which way, leaving him dizzy. Bobbing in between them was Mrs. Broadhurst.

She scooped off the tablecloth, thrust it into a startled maid's hands. "Take this away." She snapped her fingers and bent with the footman on the other side to roll back the rug. Another footman worked on rekindling the fire. A maid brought in a washbowl and water, another stood dumbstruck in the door with a stack of towels, and a third with an armful of linens plowed into the stopped girl.

"Coming through," shouted the man at his foot.

The men lifted and slid him onto the table like a haunch of meat. Pain shattered the numbness and he fought to contain screams. He couldn't appear so weak in front of her, but the pain bit and snarled like a demon tearing him to bits.

"What is this?" boomed Mr. Broadhurst from the doorway.

"There was an accident at the mill." Mrs. Broadhurst gestured toward his mangled leg.

"Good God, Mrs. Broadhurst go change at once. You cannot receive guests covered in blood. And get these men out of here."

Mrs. Broadhurst lowered her lashes and then put her shoulders back. She planted a hand on Jack's chest, keeping him pinned down. "Thank you, gentlemen," she told the men from the mill. "You may return to work now."

Was he to be without allies? He searched for George or one of his brothers or brother-in-laws, but the faces swam. All he could focus on was her pinched but determined face.

As the room emptied, Broadhurst glowered. "Get him out of here too."

"No. He stays." She stood defiantly in front of her husband.

Jack's breath caught.

"I don't think you heard me." Mr. Broadhurst glared at his wife, while the servants slunk about with their shoulders to their ears. "I want him out of here before more guests arrive."

Mrs. Broadhurst straightened. "I don't care for your tone, sir. If you entertain the slightest hope that I will acquiesce to your wishes, you will consider your actions carefully."

"You cannot bring millworkers into the house." Mr. Broadhurst's cold tone implied millworkers were lower than cockroaches and might infest the house if allowed to enter.

Jack shivered, wanting to get away, far, far away. He tried to roll to his side, but the doctor pushed him back.

Mrs. Broadhurst grimaced. "There was an infant in the mill. Because this man tried to stop her from getting hurt, he is now maimed. We owe him comfort and care. And if you cannot concede to that, I will attend him in his home—leaving your guests without a hostess at all."

Mr. Broadhurst stared at his wife. Jack wanted to tell her to do as her husband said. Didn't she know that he shouldn't be challenged? Her husband was not a good man, although he wasn't going to be the one to speak out against him. Not as long as his family needed their jobs at the mill. He didn't want Mr. Broadhurst noticing him, not in this way.

"It was my fault," said Jack. "I tripped."

Mrs. Broadhurst swiveled back toward him. Color stained her cheeks. "On a spindle dropped by a child too young to work in the mill. I have said again and again that these babes only cause accidents. She should have been in school."

Mattie had only dropped the spindles because he'd shoved her out of the way of the whipping belt, but it seemed a moot point. Jack pressed his lips together.

"You shouldn't have brought him here," growled Mr. Broadhurst.

The man was obviously not happy with the turn of events, but something Mrs. Broadhurst said had her husband struggling to contain his ire. It only made Jack's spine tighten. Mr. Broadhurst got rid of people who stood in his way, and Jack didn't want to be one of them.

"He needs surgery and doing it here is expedient," Mrs. Broadhurst said in a mildly reproving tone.

Bloody hell, he didn't want to be a bone they fought over. And he sure as hell didn't want surgery.

"He can't be here while we have guests," said Mr. Broadhurst.

"I'll leave." Jack tried to swing his legs to the side of the table. Waves of dizziness washed over him, spinning his head.

The surgeon shook his head as he pressed Jack back. "You'll lay still so I can look at your wounds."

"We can breakfast in the dining room," Mrs. Broadhurst said. "He won't be a bother if he recuperates here. Besides, there will be too many people to have only this small room available in the morning." Her voice was breezily dismissive.

Jack choked. This small room was bigger than all of the ground floor in his father's house.

Mr. Broadhurst's bushy gray eyebrows lowered over his beady eyes. More then ever Jack wanted out of here before he incurred the man's wrath. He didn't want to be like the union organizer a few years back. The man had disappeared one night, and no one was sure if he was just strongly encouraged to move on to greener pastures or if he'd been buried beneath one. Either way, Mr. Broadhurst was behind whatever happened, and no one dared talk of unions now.

"You cannot as a gentleman expel him when a young child working in the mill was the cause of his accident. You bear some responsibility for this tragedy," Mrs. Broadhurst said softly. "Besides, I will not entertain your guests in *any* way if you do not allow the boy to stay."

Jack wanted to object to being called a boy. He was likely of an age similar to Mrs. Broadhurst, but it hardly seemed important. And in this instance he agreed with Mr. Broadhurst. Leaving was far and away the best choice.

His beady eyes burning with impotent rage, Mr. Broadhurst turned toward Jack. The ireful look beat a path through him.

"I'm sorry, sir," he said. "I'll go home as soon as I am able." Home was his father's house. In spite of the fight this morning and Martha's reaction to his injury, he wanted to go there. She would calm down in time and his siblings could see to his care. Under no circumstances did he want that sawbones operating.

Nor could he miss the appointment in London.

What made him think he could get free of this miserable life? It seemed his every opportunity was thwarted, but he had savings. He could hire a cart to Manchester, take the train to London. He could still take his drawings to the appointment.

Broadhurst was staring at his wife intently. "You'll entertain them now, will you?" he growled.

All the color drained from Mrs. Broadhurst's face. Her hand tightened painfully on Jack's arm. "I will welcome them as any lady would. I should like your agreement that no child under the age of nine is allowed to work in the mill."

There was a tension between them as if a deeper negotiation was under way. Jack didn't understand. He didn't know if he cared. Whatever they were discussing wasn't about him. Strange, he'd thought Mrs. Broadhurst was always looking his way because she'd recognized the potential in him, but she seemed more interested in using his accident to implement changes. Maybe Martha had it right, and he wasn't any different than the rest of them.

Except now he was different.

If they took off his foot, he wouldn't be fit for work in the mill, nor would he be fit enough to work at the equipment manufactory. The only other course that was likely open to him was begging. God, he didn't want to be a beggar. No matter what, he needed to convince them to let his leg heal.

"See to it you do." Broadhurst pivoted away from the door, then Mrs. Broadhurst shut it.

"Ma'am, if you would, cut off his trousers." The doctor removed his coat and rolled back his sleeves.

Mrs. Broadhurst cast a lost look toward the doctor, then grimaced and began slicing at Jack's pants with scissors.

Jack reached out to stop her, but one of the footmen pushed his hands away.

After wiping his wet hands on a towel, the macabre doctor clipped away bandages and prodded at his ankle. Each poke shot agony through Jack. He bit his lip so hard he tasted blood, and a groan left his throat despite his efforts to hold it back.

The doctor pulled out a saw, and Jack's blood turned to ice.

"No!" He jerked up to a sitting position. The room spun and went dark around him. He reached blindly, determined to stop this madness.

Arms came around him and pulled him back.

His head thumped against a hand. Hers? "Don't cut off my leg."

"We may not have a choice, son," said the doctor in a calm voice. "The ankle is shattered."

Jack's strength deserted him and he heaved in gulps of air. "Try to save it." He grabbed the doctor's jacket. "I can pay. Whatever it costs to fix it. I have savings set by."

Shaking his head, the doctor said, "Hold him down, until I get him sedated."

Strong hands pushed him down. Two of the footmen held his arms.

Mrs. Broadhurst leaned over him. "Please, don't fight. We're trying to help."

"Don't make me a beggar," Jack rasped out.

She blinked and her expression went blank for a moment. "It'll be all right," she soothed.

He almost wanted to believe her. But what would he do without a foot? Certainly, he would no longer be able to work in the mill.

The doctor put a couple of drops of liquid on a handkerchief and held it above his mouth and nose. The sickly sweet smell thickened in his throat and the light faded.

Chapter 4

Caroline stared at the box on her bed. Her hands shook from the strain of the long surgery throughout the afternoon and the decision she'd reached. But the box was unexpected. She hadn't ordered anything.

She wanted to collapse and sleep the evening away, but there were guests she had to greet. As she'd handed the doctor tools, sopped up blood while blocking Jack's view, and checked to see if he still breathed, anger had built in her. She had tolerated Mr. Broadhurst for years with the understanding she would be independently wealthy with a mill to run one day, but he had yanked the firmament from underneath her. Returning home, destitute or not, was always an option, but not one she liked. No, she wanted control of her future.

She would seduce one of the men Robert had so thoughtfully supplied. She would do it because *she* wanted to control her destiny and that of the mill. Allowing anyone else to control her, to denigrate decisions she knew were right, was no longer acceptable. With a baby, she would be in charge of her future and his.

That the only acceptable avenues for a woman of her class were wife or poor relation was so unfair. She was as capable as any man. If she weren't so sick of her role as a model wife, she never would have decided to go along with Mr. Broadhurst's Machiavellian plan.

Had his plan included a new dress for her too? He seemed to have engineered the smallest details.

An envelope was tucked in the strings. Recognizing her sister's hand, she broke the seal and lifted out the single sheet of notepaper.

I thought these might come in handy. Amy

Frowning, Caroline untied the twine. Lifting the lid, she found a diaphanous nightgown and peignoir made of lace and chiffon.

Shoving the lid on the box, she drew back as if the thing might bite her. Never in a million years would she wear such a thing. Such garments weren't decent. She didn't even want the maid seeing them. Quickly she retied the twine.

Like Robert, Amy had probably thought she *wanted* to have an affair. How little her siblings knew her. But was that her fault? She saw them infrequently and couldn't fill letters with her desire to be anywhere but with Mr. Broadhurst. During her visits to their houses, Mr. Broadhurst never left her side, so she was never in a position to exchange confidences. Perhaps that was by his design.

The connecting door to her husband's room opened. Mr. Broadhurst stood in the opening. "Are you not dressed yet?"

Her stomach churned and tightened. He looked like the same man she'd spent the last fifteen years with, but she barely could stand the sight of him. "Really, Mr. Broadhurst. I cannot believe you would will everything to Mr. Granger."

She pitched the box into the bottom of her armoire. When she had more time, she'd cast them on the fire. She tried to close the armoire, but the box jutted out, preventing her. She slammed it harder, distorting the pasteboard, but the door still refused to close. She shoved the box on its end and forced the armoire shut.

"Figured that would stick in your craw." Mr. Broadhurst walked into the room and sat down in her reading chair. "But, I know he'll do whatever it takes to keep the mill profitable."

As if she would run it into the ground. Whatever improvements she made for workers' safety would all be for naught if the mill closed its doors. She would never let that happen. But, if she had been in charge, the accident today never would have occurred. "Leave me, so I might get ready."

"I'll wait. Did you have new dresses delivered?"

"Amelia sent some things." Would he just leave? Before she totally lost her temper and slapped him. The bloodthirsty urge surprised her. But violence never served.

"How unlike her," murmured Mr. Broadhurst as his eyes followed her.

Caroline yanked open the armoire again and took out an evening gown suitable for a London dinner party. Then she wrestled the peignoir box out of the way again to slam the door shut. She jerked on the bellpull. "I need my maid."

She could have dressed without her maid, but she didn't want to be alone with her husband, not with the way she felt about him at the moment. Because if he decided to lay a finger on her, she just might snap it off.

"Have her do your hair with hanging curls, and don't put a kerchief in your neckline." Broadhurst nodded toward the low-cut gown, which she often wore with a lace chemisette to fill in the décolletage, for warmth as much as modesty.

Was she to be outfitted like a whore in the best brothel? She closed her eyes. With all the effort she put into learning to run the mill, she was still seen as nothing more than a brood mare. She really hated him. *Hated* him.

All her prayers for tolerance and admiration were wasted effort. Knowing that he believed he could manipulate anyone to do what he wanted might make him a great businessman, but it made him an awful person and a worse husband. But she had implied an agreement to the bargain so Jack could stay, so there was no point in railing like a fishwife.

"We are understood, Caroline. If you are agreed to do as I've asked, your patient can stay. Otherwise I will have him thrown out."

Vibrating with anger, she clenched her jaw. "He was trying to save a child who should not have been in harm's way in the first place."

"Such a soft heart for the children. Don't you want one of your own?" he cajoled.

It wasn't fair. She'd wanted children. "Of course I do."

"Then you will do as you are bid."

"If you will have all the children under nine put out of the mill, I will . . . I shall . . . begin a flirtation tonight." Her spine tightened and she resisted the urge to draw her shoulders up to her ears. God, did she even know how? She'd never been particularly skilled in social intercourse. And how could she seduce one of the guests?

Mr. Broadhurst scowled at her. "This is why I cannot leave the mill to you. You are too concerned with the plight of children that don't matter."

He had been one of those children who didn't matter, but reminding him of that would only raise his ire. Instead she appealed to his greed. "Mr. Broadhurst, one of those little children caused the loss of a good worker. The only one who knew how to dismantle the machinery to get his leg out, I might add. The work completely stopped all because of one little girl who was too young to use good sense in where she walked."

"Very well, ma'am. I shall ban from the mill any child under the age of nine, henceforth. And you are agreed to lie with one of the guests tonight."

Her stomach cramped. "I cannot conduct every stage of an affair tonight. That isn't how it is done."

She didn't know that she could manage the final stage, but if she could gain a few days—long enough for him to decree all young children wouldn't be allowed to work—she could at least try to single out one of the men for an affair. *By having a baby, she gained the mill and independence.* A month of trying to get pregnant was better than another loveless marriage, or being a penniless dependent upon family members who neither understood her or she them.

Offering a rare concession, Mr. Broadhurst said, "Within the week, then, Mrs. Broadhurst, because these men cannot stay on forever."

She nodded jerkily. Her hands shook as she tried to undo a button. She couldn't have said if it was anger or fear or an odd mixture of both. "Really, sir. I need a few minutes to compose myself. And you should go down to offer our guests a cordial before dinner. You must spend time with them or their purpose for being here will be too obvious. I shall run the mill perfectly well while you are occupied with the guests."

One side of his mouth lifted in the nearest thing her husband ever managed resembling a smile. "It won't matter if you run the mill well for a month. Only a son will change the will's provisions."

Caroline blanched. Her heart thundered in her chest. "I need the practice for the day I will have to run it for our son."

"Agreed." Mr. Broadhurst pushed out of the chair. "I shall retire early to give you free hunting."

She nodded. At least that way if she made a hash of a flirtation, he would not be there to criticize. Stars above, had she really agreed to have an extramarital affair? Her stomach churning, she fought the bile rising in her throat.

Jack Applegate stared at the tinwork ceiling of the dim room. A fire blazed in the fireplace, apparently just for him. The doctor had given him morphine, but it just took the edge off enough so he could breathe in something other than a pant.

He had dozed, but woke thrashing as he dreamed of getting sucked deep into the cogs of the machine, it chewing him up and spitting him out in little chunks.

The bed creaked as he moved to his elbows. The room spun around him and his stomach roiled in protest.

He scooted back against the wooden headboard of the bed brought down and assembled for him. Pain seared through his body and made him gasp so hard his throat dried out. He coughed with a dry heave that only made his leg scream with each jar.

The door clicked open, and silhouetted in the doorway was a woman in a full gown. "Are you all right?"

Ahh, his savior, Mrs. Broadhurst, Caro—although he could never call her by her given name. He didn't know what she'd said to the doctor to convince him to save his leg, but he had no doubt she was the reason he remained in one piece.

Jack stifled the cough. He was far from all right. Even though the doctor told him the ankle had been repaired in a surgery that took hours, he also said it was unlikely he would ever walk again, and might still lose the leg if sepsis set in. And that he wouldn't be able to attempt walking for *two to three months.*

If he couldn't make it to London in two weeks, he'd never be *all* right again. But that wasn't the thing to say to the woman who opened her house to him, washed the blood from his leg and arm—all while directing her servants to make the breakfast room into a invalid's room for him. Curiously, she had taken care of him when she could have passed his care to her servants.

"I'll do," he managed, and then dissolved into a new spate of coughing.

He willed her to turn around and close the door. The last thing he wanted was her seeing him moaning or groaning in pain. She'd meant well. Weak as a mewling newborn kitten, he collapsed back against the head of the bed.

She crossed the room, bent to light a spill from the fire and then light the lamp on the table he'd been operated upon. The gore was gone. A slew of maids had cleaned the mess, while he watched the pile of red rags grow amazingly tall.

She leaned over him and put a cool hand to his forehead. But in doing so, she gave him a lovely glimpse of her bosom.

He gasped. He'd never seen Mrs. Broadhurst in anything that wasn't buttoned to her neck, but this frilled and flounced, robin's-egg-blue gown exposed her creamy white shoulders and the rounded tops of her breasts. A glittering blue-stone necklace fell away from her skin and dangled between them. Like a magpie, he wanted to grab it, to feel the heat from her in the gold, to let the back of his fingers graze her creamy skin underneath.

Jack closed his eyes. Never in a million years would she welcome his touch. Even if she had been sold into marriage with a rich old tradesman, she was as blue-blooded as they came. He was nothing better than a laborer. She'd never let him kiss her feet, let alone the things he wanted to do as he watched her from afar.

He'd thought if he could market his designs, he could one day have a chance at a woman like her.

"Where is the maid I left with you?" She pushed back hair that clung to his damp forehead.

Surprised at her touch, his eyes popped open. She pulled her hand back, and the loss was almost like losing a part of him.

"I asked her to leave me be," answered Jack. He hadn't wanted to restrain his cries any longer. As it was, he'd groaned into the pillow until the medicine cut the pain.

"You shouldn't be alone." Her voice was soothing, but her eyes were wide and her face pinched.

"I'd rather." He searched her expression, trying to understand the source of her anxiety.

"Were you trying to sit? Do you need more pillows?" Without waiting for his answer she exited to the hall. Shortly afterward she returned with two small cushions and stood with them as if waiting for him to lean forward.

He couldn't. Just getting up on his elbows made his arms shake with the effort. He should just lie back down, but he was afraid if he moved his leg, he wouldn't be able to restrain a groan.

Helpless, he stared and saw her as he never had before.

Instead of the tight bun she habitually wore, her hair was done in a loose knot with curls on her crown and one long curl caressing her neck. He would love to press his lips to every part the dark hair touched. "You look beautiful."

A flush spread over her chest and up her cheeks.

He winced. He should look away, but he couldn't deny himself the small pleasure of looking at her. The medicine had loosened his tongue, and it certainly wasn't his place to comment on her looks. "Beg pardon, ma'am."

"You've likely never seen me dressed for guests before."

Her voice trembled and her mouth tightened, as if the "guests" were distasteful to her. She pressed the two pillows against her chest as if they provided armor.

It wasn't the dress. He'd long ago noticed Mrs. Broadhurst. When he sat in church he stared at her dark hair swirled above her swanlike neck. Every chance he could he watched her enter or leave the mill office. He'd admired her efforts to educate the children of the millworkers, although he knew it was for the most part futile. Like him, most of them did what their parents before them had done and became millworkers.

He liked the way she would ponder a piece of machinery and ask, *Wouldn't the chain be less likely to catch a worker's clothes if a metal guard were here?*

She cared about their safety and education, unlike her husband who cared about his bottom line. She perhaps thought that some might want to rise above the circumstances of their birth. He took hope from that idea because it fit with what he wanted to believe about himself. But it was more than that with her. The way she occasionally tilted her chin down and looked up through her lashes sent shivers down his spine.

"I should get back. But do you need anything?"

Her. "No, ma'am."

She glanced over her shoulder at the door. Then her gaze returned to his face. "Do you want these pillows?"

He nodded and reached out for one, but feeling unable to move, he pulled it to his chest.

Her eyebrows briefly lowered. "Do you need help sitting up?"

How could she possibly see him as anything other than a weakling? Jack sighed. "Perhaps one of the men could help me."

She leaned over him again and slid her arm behind his back. "Here, I can assist you."

She helped him forward and stuffed the pillows behind his shoulders. He bit his lip at the wave of dizziness and grasped her shoulder. He wanted to enjoy the lovely sight in front of him, but pain blasted him. It was all he could do to not cry out.

She eased him back. "Oh, I'm hurting you."

"It's nothing," he managed to say as he uncurled his fingers from around her shoulder. He'd gripped her hard enough to blanch her fair skin. Bruising her would be a crime. "Beg pardon, ma'am."

"Think nothing of it." She looked over him for a long time, and he tried hard to erase any pain from his face, but he doubted he succeeded.

"Did you have any supper?"

"I don't believe I could eat, ma'am," he gritted out. Sweat beaded his forehead. Even though his mouth felt stuffed with cotton, he'd barely been able to drink half the glass of water the maid had poured for him.

Mrs. Broadhurst's eyes narrowed. "You need to eat to get your strength back. We had a lovely beef consommé for dinner. Would you like to try some?"

No. He'd like her to leave before he did something stupid like touch her creamy shoulder. "I don't know what that is."

She smiled, the corners of her blue eyes crinkling just a second before the edges of her mouth lifted. "A clear beef soup of a sort."

Even her language marked their differences. Perhaps she would leave him if he called for his supper, or perhaps she would smile more if he ate like a good invalid. "I could try it, ma'am."

She tugged on a loop of material near the door and then

pulled around the chair the maid had used, so she faced him. Arranging her wide skirts around her, she sat down.

A footman opened the door. "You rang, ma'am?"

"Yes, please ask Cook to send a bowl of the beef consommé and a bit of bread for our patient here, and please inform me when the gentlemen have left their port."

The footman nodded.

"Oh, and fetch the extra pillows from my room for Mister . . ." She swiveled toward Jack. "I'm sorry I don't know your last name."

"Applegate. John Applegate." He frowned, not knowing why he'd given his baptismal name. "But everyone calls me Jack."

"Mr. Applegate." The dip in her voice was like a lover's tone.

"Jack," he repeated. He shook his head. The medicine had made him befuddled. She wasn't interested in anything more than his health, and no more than any of the hundreds of other workers in her husband's mill. Or was she?

Caroline hated to leave Jack with the housekeeper, but the older woman would bully him into eating the consommé and drinking the sweetened orange water she had ordered for him. And perhaps Mrs. Burns was motherly enough that Jack would accept the comfort he refused from her.

His pain etched lines into his forehead and caused him to squint. The doctor had said there would be a lot of pain for the first two or three days.

Caroline tried to get her mind off Jack as she made a circuit of the drawing room. The gentlemen held cups of tea or snifters of brandy while discussing the upcoming days of hunting. She felt as out of place as a horse in a ballroom. Obviously she had dressed up for the occasion, while the gentlemen had settled into less formal country wear. However, if she was to attract one of them to her bed, she couldn't exactly wear her usual sober dresses. With more warning she could have ordered less flamboyant evening gowns instead of having to use her London wardrobe.

Lord Tremont moved beside her and said, "I hear there was a bit of excitement this afternoon."

"Yes, a bad accident. One of the workers had his ankle crushed in the machinery." She wished the words back as soon as she said them. She should have said something banal like, *I hope the noise did not disturb you.* Or *I'm sorry to not have greeted you in person when you arrived.*

"Poor blighter." Tremont lifted his brandy snifter and took a step away.

Caroline stiffened. She opened her mouth to defend Jack, but swallowed her words. Lord Tremont was supposed to be the man most likely to seduce her. With his curly golden hair and full brown mustache over an almost insolent grin, she imagined he had plenty of takers in the City.

"So tell me the latest news from London," she said.

"Do you not get the papers?"

Steeling herself, she put her hand on his arm. Her touch felt awkward, whereas touching Jack earlier had seemed natural. But he was too ill and weak to even consider as a possible candidate for fatherhood. No, one of the gentlemen, who were for the most part well-favored, would have to suffice. "Yes, but I know so little of the gossip. Tell me who is the most fawned upon actress and who is her protector."

He looked pointedly at her hand on his arm. "Oh that kind of gossip."

She pulled her hand back, hardly knowing if she had touched him too long or too obviously. It all felt hopelessly forced to her.

He took another drink of his brandy and moved away from her. "I'm not sure it is suitable for your ears."

Caroline could have screamed in frustration. "I am no innocent," she murmured, barely keeping her tone coy.

"Or that your husband should want you to hear it," he said under his breath. "He is looking daggers at me."

Across the room, Mr. Broadhurst stood and set his teacup on a table with a clatter. "I'm afraid this old man must bid you good-night. I am certain Mrs. Broadhurst would love to entertain all of you for the remainder of the evening."

Feeling the curious glances cast in her direction, Caroline studied the backs of her gloves as if they were stitched with great intricacy. All Mr. Broadhurst needed to do was add a wink and a nudge and his meaning couldn't have been clearer. Although it wasn't the first time he'd embarrassed her in polite company.

Tremont leaned toward her. "Does that mean you are not allowed to leave the room until we have all sought our beds?"

"Of course not." She couldn't bring herself to touch him again. Putting her arm around Jack to help him sit had seemed so easy. She had been testing herself a little, seeing if she could touch a man without picking up and running away. But Jack was safe. He was in no condition to molest her. Not that a man of his station would ever think of her that way. Unless, of course, he, like Mr. Broadhurst, rose above his birth and bought his way into society, bought a wife, and bought her bloodline as if she were a broodmare. Her jaw tightened.

"So I have heard tell of a certain young gentleman who frequents Lady Brennon's drawing rooms of late."

Caroline's mouth fell open. Good God, Lady Brennon was her sister. Was Amelia so bold with her affairs she was the subject of gossip?

Tremont smiled as if amused. "Perhaps you did not wish to know of tales so close to home."

"Is this gentleman an actor?" Amelia would never entertain an actor, but she was grasping for a titillating thing to say. Actresses and actors seemed so often involved in unseemly affairs.

Perhaps Amelia was trying to make her husband jealous or the caller wasn't receiving encouragement from her. Caroline couldn't fathom why her sister would willingly encourage the attentions of a man to whom she didn't have to submit.

"No, he's not," Tremont replied. "You have a fondness for those who tread the boards?"

Caroline shifted her shoulders. She tried for a casual shrug but failed to carry it any better than her attempt to start a ribald conversation.

"I'll admit to having tried my hand at a few amateur productions. I am told my voice is pleasing."

"I'm sure it must be." She winced. He'd offered a perfect opportunity to tell him she liked his voice and she'd missed it. He had a nice tenor, but Jack's rough voice was better suited to her distinctly unmusical ear.

Tremont leaned close enough his breath tickled. "I have it on good authority that the Prince of Wales frequents the stews in Whitechapel."

She gasped. The prince was hardly old enough, but then she rethought it. He must be in his late teens. Her face heated as she barely restrained herself from asking that he not gossip about the boy who would be king one day.

"Now I see I cannot find the right bit of gossip to please you," Tremont said. "Perhaps if we talked of other things."

Caroline drew a blank. She couldn't ask him how the hunting was going, because they hadn't been yet. The weather was too hackneyed a topic for her to throw out. She was absolutely certain Lord Tremont wouldn't give a fig about the possible impact of the growing conflict in the Americas and how it might affect the price of cotton. She had no idea how to talk nonsense, as flirting seemed to require. She'd never done it.

Silence stretched between them until she reached out and put her hand on his sleeve. Desperately she searched for something to say, but words caught in her throat.

"I hear tell you are allowing this millworker to convalesce in your house," said Tremont, putting his hand over hers.

She was trapped. "He really couldn't be moved so soon after the operation. Mr. Broadhurst is not happy that I had the boy brought here." Jack wasn't a boy, but calling him one made her feel less exposed.

"Why did you? Does he not have a home? The village seems closer to the mill than your house."

Caroline felt a twinge of uncertainty. "I do not know. In the moment, it seemed the right thing to do."

Perhaps Jack's concern over the little girl had slipped under her skin. Or the thought that he deserved better than to be left to a mother who seemed more upset about needing to care for him than she did about his injury. Or perhaps she'd been rebelling against her husband and his plan. If she were nursing an invalid and running the mill, she could hardly find the time to seduce one of the gentlemen. Except Jack's injury only clarified why she should do everything she could to take over the mill.

"You seem the capable sort one would want about in an emergency."

Caroline wondered if his observation was a veiled insult or a backhanded compliment. She pulled her hand back. "I'm not the swooning type."

"I suppose you are a suffragette."

Her chin went up. "I don't see any reason why a woman cannot run a business even if she is more compassionate toward the workers."

"Ah." Tremont took a step back. "I have touched a sore spot."

Caroline looked down at her clasped hands. "I apologize. I do believe a woman is happiest in the home." *Malarky!* "I just—" Her words halted. She could hint that she longed for babies, but it hardly seemed like the right course to seduce Lord Tremont. "I know Mr. Broadhurst considers me too softhearted, and I fear my actions today have only confirmed his suspicions."

Good heavens, if she meant to convince Mr. Broadhurst to allow her to run the mill after he passed, child or no child, her actions today had been all wrong. He'd said as much to her, but she hadn't thought it through.

Steeling herself to endure Lord Tremont's touch, she turned. Her skin crawled with the idea of allowing him the liberties Mr. Broadhurst had gained by right of marriage.

" . . . visit your patient."

"Yes." She hadn't been listening. "I plan to look in on him before I retire. My housekeeper is sitting with him now."

"It seems the others are engaged in cards. Now would be as good a time as any, would it not?"

She nodded. The last thing she wanted to do was take Lord Tremont to Jack's bedside.

Lord Tremont put his hand on the small of her back. She scuttled forward. Her throat tightened and she tried to tell herself she could endure a man's embrace and copulation with him. She had endured it for years with Mr. Broadhurst. Only with a lover she not only had to endure, but pretend she enjoyed him. Her insides flopped and she only hoped she wouldn't throw up.

They passed Robert. She stopped and turned toward him. "I'm taking Lord Tremont to see the young man who was hurt today."

Robert nodded. His eyebrows came together. "By all means, do sit with the poor chap awhile. I will make your excuses." He gave a slight negative shake of the head as if puzzled.

Caroline nodded as if a puppet master controlled her strings. She tried to smile, but it felt more like a grimace. Lord Tremont put his hand against her back and his touch jarred her forward.

Leading him out into the hallway, she kept trying to believe she could do this. She could let him grope her and slobber on her and do all the things that constituted the act that men loved and she hated, but a scream boiled inside her. Oh, God, she had to do this.

"He is downstairs in the breakfast room." She headed toward the staircase.

Before she reached the steps, Lord Tremont pulled her back. "We don't really need to go see the boy. I wouldn't want to disturb his rest."

"No, of course not." Caroline trembled. She was to have no reprieve.

Lord Tremont slid his hand around her waist and eased her around. No servants loitered about. The other guests remained in the drawing room. They were completely alone. His knotted necktie was not as fascinating as her attention to it would warrant, but she couldn't seem to look him in the eye. She swallowed hard.

He slid a finger under her chin. For a second she resisted letting him tilt her head. She silently prayed that in the dim light of the gaslights her repulsion would not show.

"Your brother informs me that you are lonely living out here in the middle of nowhere."

"Lancashire is hardly the end of the earth," she objected. *Foolish, foolish girl.* All she had to do was agree and supply him with a perfect excuse for her wanton behavior.

Lord Tremont searched her face, and his gaze dropped to her lips. Fighting to keep her mouth relaxed, she waited.

He pressed his lips to hers. Closing her eyes, she decided it was not so horrible. Unlike her husband, Lord Tremont's breath was not fetid with teeth that should be pulled. He was not invading her mouth as if she hid treasure inside. Maybe she could get through this.

Tilting back, he whispered, "Are you lonely, Caroline?"

Her head moved in more of a circle than in the up and down motion she strived for.

He ran his fingers along the edge of her bodice, and it was all she could do not to squirm away. She hated the groping, the pinching and the twisting that left her nipples sore. She dreaded the bruises a man could make with his mouth and the tenderness left in her woman's place.

His fingers insistent, he tilted up her head again. She hadn't even realized she had lowered her chin. He turned his head in an assessing way she didn't like. Suddenly nervous, she bounced up on her toes and pressed her lips to his. Their teeth clicked because of her clumsiness, but he adjusted and slid his tongue along her lips. She screwed her eyes shut and allowed him access.

Really, she would have much preferred to look in on Jack.

Chapter 5

"**W**hat are you doing, Mrs. Broadhurst?" Lord Tremont demanded. He stood in front of her with arms crossed and eyes narrowed.

"I should think it obvious," Caroline choked out. Heat flooded her face, and she couldn't resist wiping the back of her hand across her lips. Only after she had done it did she realize how insulting wiping away his kiss had been. And how base, as if she had taken on her husband's worst habits.

Lord Tremont's nostrils flared. "What is obvious is that you find this encounter distasteful. What game are you playing?"

Caroline stared at her would-be lover and swallowed hard. She shook her head. "I did want to be . . . alone with you."

"But you don't now. You find me distasteful."

Oh God, she would never get what she needed from him if she had botched it so badly. "No. I'm sorry. Truly, you are not distasteful . . . to me."

Even to her own ears, her warbling protest sounded full of deceit.

He took three steps down the hall, pivoted, strode back and halted in right in front of her. "Tell me what this is about. Your brother invites a dozen bachelors—not his closest friends, mind you—to a hunting party at *your* home. You are the only woman here. And"—his gaze raked over her—"you have been hanging on my sleeve—literally—half the evening. I am not an imbecile, Mrs. Broadhurst."

Her thoughts tripped over each other as she considered the ramifications of telling him the truth. But would he go along with her plan? His jaw ticked. She opened her mouth hardly knowing what was likely to come out. She almost hoped for a ceiling cave-in so she didn't have to say anything.

"What? Is your husband dying, Mrs. Broadhurst? Have you decided to *buy* a titled gentleman for your next husband with all the wealth you will inherit?"

Her eyebrows drew together. She tried to connect the dots to what Lord Tremont was saying. "My husband isn't dying. He is advanced in years, but still quite fit." He better be fit enough to claim a child as his own.

Lord Tremont continued as if she'd said nothing. "I suppose as an earl I must meet the qualifications to be your next husband. And Langley will one day be a marquis. Berkley is likely to inherit his uncle's Scottish earldom. Not a single man who will end as a commoner among us—could you not locate a prince to consider?"

She was still trying to consider his last point. Mr. Broadhurst was not the man he had been five years earlier. His robust frame had shrunk, his firm stride had withered to a shuffle, and the bedroom problems had followed. Had he pushed her into this unholy bargain because his health was failing? Was that why he wanted an heir now?

"Caroline, you are a passably pretty woman. I am sure if you are seeking a nobleman to enter into an agreement to marry you for your husband's wealth, you will find one. But not me."

"That was not my intent." She stared helplessly at Lord Tremont. Marriage to a titled man would mean moving to London every year while Parliament was in session. It would mean balls, dinners, salons, and the end to her quiet life. It would mean giving up control of the mill and giving a man the right to use her body at will. She shuddered.

How had he arrived at the conclusion that she wanted to marry him—after Mr. Broadhurst was dead and buried presumably? Stars above, she hoped she would be free of a husband and master then.

"When I marry, if I marry, I should imagine I want an heir, a son—"

"I want that too," she gushed. Perhaps all was not lost.

He touched her neck, and she flinched.

The corner of his moustache lifted. "And a woman who welcomes my touch."

Caroline dropped her eyes. "Forgive me. My nerves are a-jangle. I've never done anything like this before."

His voice softened. "I suppose an alliance with your family would be quite advantageous. Your brother is a viscount and may yet get that earldom he's petitioned the crown for. But I don't like to be tricked into anything."

"It was not a trick," mumbled Caroline. She wished the wall behind her would open up and she could escape. She should tell Lord Tremont she simply wanted an affair. "I just wanted to . . ." But the words were like lead in her mouth and too heavy to push out.

"To emulate your sisters?" He searched her face. "Why, when you find Amelia's behavior so shocking?"

It was not lost on her that he had used her sister's first name. Was he one of Amy's castoffs? Her cheeks burned with humiliation and not a little anger.

He answered himself. "No, I don't believe so. There is a deeper game afoot."

"I am not looking for my next husband."

His arched eyebrow said he doubted her words. The first time she had given him a truth, and he didn't believe it. She bit her lip. She should just blurt out she wanted a baby.

"Perhaps you should just have Robert approach your next choice with a proposal—after he makes sure that the man will not object to a barren wife."

She felt as though she'd been slapped. How had this exchange gone so horribly wrong? "I'm not . . ."

"No?" Again he lifted an eyebrow. "You have been married at least a dozen years without issue. I certainly would not gamble with those odds."

She should tell him the fault lay with her husband, but it felt so disloyal to speak of such a thing. Not knowing what to say, she said nothing, while heat rose in her face. Her tongue had never been nimble and it was wooden and mute now.

He took a step back. "Surely you realize I cannot help your brother with his petition."

"I don't know anything about that," she said.

He rolled his eyes. "I shall return to the drawing room and let it be known you have stayed with your patient. I wouldn't want to impede your chances with your next mark." He smoothed his jacket as if it had been disturbed in their exchange. "The next time I accept an invitation to a hunt, I shall make quite sure I am not the prey."

Her ears burned as she watched him walk away without a glance back. Her nose tickled and her eyes stung. To top that off, he had called her passably pretty.

Jack had done much better, although to be fair, it was likely her fine feathers. A lowly millworker wouldn't be familiar with fashionable evening gowns, while Lord Tremont saw the like on a regular basis in London. Still, he could have done better.

She'd picked Lord Tremont because Robert had insinuated he would be the easiest, but he had scorned her. She didn't have Amelia's coyness or Sarah's charm. Even the twins found it easy to tease men.

As Caroline marched to her room, determined to be free of the ridiculous gown, she thought of a dozen retorts, a half-dozen suggestive comments that might have smoothed the way. She could have told him that she longed to know what relations were like with a man her own age—or at least one not older than her father. She could have told him some nonsense about finding him manly or dashed handsome—he was probably used to such tripe.

But none of those rejoinders had occurred to her when they would have been useful. She yanked open her door, determined to shed her London gown and have done with seduction attempts this evening. Perhaps she shouldn't kiss a man in the hallway.

She kicked her train out of the way as she closed the door.

"You are not done so soon." Her husband's voice grated like machinery needing oil.

"What are you doing here?" she hissed.

Choosing a most ungentlemanly way of sitting, he crossed one ankle over his knee. "Making sure you don't leave the company early. I should hate to think you weren't putting your best effort into this."

"I was just chilled," she improvised. "I came to get a shawl."

Mr. Broadhurst lifted his bushy eyebrows. "Really? For you look quite flushed."

She bit her lip, rather than blurt out she was returning to the drawing room. It would have smacked of protesting too much.

She marched across the room to her wardrobe and threw open the doors. Mr. Broadhurst's eyes followed her. The stupid box containing the negligee fell out. Caroline shoved it back inside, searching for a wrap that wouldn't clash with her dress.

She grabbed a brown and green paisley shawl. Deuce take it. What difference would it make if she were unstylish?

"Need I remind you that you agreed to—"

"No." Caroline whirled. "You needn't. I have done as I said I would and have begun a flirtation." It was hardly her fault if the gentleman had ended it before it came to fruition. All right, it was a bit her fault for being so poor an actress, but pretending to want such a despicable thing was nearly impossible. Her hands shook, her whole body shook. "I will honor my word."

But she didn't know if she could. She had bargained for Mr. Applegate to remain in the house long enough to heal and to get the youngest of the children out of the mill. And she wanted to answer only to herself in the future—not a husband, not a brother, just herself with the power of the mill and the money it generated behind her. That was worth submitting to a man for a few weeks.

She had to conceive a child.

She lifted her chin and headed out the door. But as her steps took her down the stairs and closer to the drawing room, her heart thumped erratically. Her whole body trembled. Fearing she might be ill, she paused. She did not want to face Lord Tremont, but Mr. Broadhurst had followed her as if she couldn't be trusted to return on her own.

Who was she fooling? She had no desire to return to the drawing room tonight. He knew it. She knew it, but what else could she do?

Steeling herself, she reached for the door handle and twisted. She walked through the room, ignoring Tremont, while she ascertained if anyone needed anything—like a good hostess.

When sufficient time had passed for her husband to have gone back to his room, she made her excuses. After making a gracious exit, she headed down the servants' stairs to sit with Jack for a few hours. She would be safe there. Mr. Broadhurst would suspect she'd gone off with one of the gentlemen, and none of the guests would bother her.

Maybe when Jack was not in so much pain, she could seduce—

She missed a step. Was that the reason she'd had him brought to the house? Her heart hammered in her chest. He, at least, wouldn't think she wanted to marry him or was using him to form a political alliance.

But would he even be willing? Could he want *her*?

Jack woke to a cool hand on his forehead. For a second he wanted to believe that his mother was soothing him through a childhood illness. But his long gone mother had never made him feel like Mrs. Broadhurst did. Besides, he couldn't forget where he was or why he was here when his lower leg shrieked with pain.

He sluggishly reached to push her hand away or still the tremble—he wasn't certain—but her fingers pushed his hair back. She removed her hand, leaving him yearning for her touch. But why had her hand shook?

"He ate a bit of the soup and drank all the orange water," said the stout woman who'd been sitting with him. "Gave him his dose of laudanum at eight. Been sleeping in fits and starts, poor thing."

"Would you see to it one of the servants is assigned to take my place long about midnight?"

The stout woman agreed as her chair creaked.

After what he thought was a few seconds, he blinked his eyes open. In spite of the fire the room seemed dark, but he was only interested in seeing Mrs. Broadhurst. She stood at the foot of the bed and clutched a leather volume as if it were a lifeline.

Curiosity fought through the haze of the medicine. Had he taken a turn for the worse and wasn't aware yet?

She gathered a spotted shawl around her. It covered her creamy shoulders and breast, which he would have liked to see again. Her attention was over her shoulder on the door, as if she feared an intrusion. If she were freshly concerned over his condition, she would most likely be focused on him. Besides, the housekeeper's report hadn't sounded dire. Jack breathed deeply.

Mrs. Broadhurst turned and offered a half smile. "I hope I didn't wake you."

He shook his head and tried to ask what she was reading, but his words came out as a rusty croak. His mouth was drier than dirt.

"Are you thirsty?" she asked.

"Yes," he rasped out.

She rustled as she moved through the room. Her gown was not of the material made in her husband's mills. No, it was finer stuff probably imported from the Orient. His clothes, made of rejected cloth with dropped threads or knots in the weave, had been cut off and taken away. He supposed the cotton undergarments and nightshirt he now wore were made from mill cloth, but it was one of the higher grades of fabric and most likely belonged to Mr. Broadhurst.

She poured a glass of water, and the sound of liquid made Jack shiver. Earlier, he'd drunk an entire pitcher of the sweet drink she ordered for him. Perhaps drinking more was a mistake, but his mouth was so dry.

She paused beside the bed holding the glass. Her forehead furled.

He struggled to his elbows. The room spun and tilted. His head wobbled as if it were barely attached to his neck.

Mrs. Broadhurst sat on the bed beside him. God, how many times had he dreamed of having her in his bed, but not like this, never as his nurse. It was just plain wrong. And he had to get out of here before he slipped up and caressed her.

She pressed the glass to his lips.

He pulled his head back. "I can do it." Once he got himself propped up. His mewling weakness irritated him.

"You would like to sit, then?" she asked calmly.

"Yes." Risking jarring his leg, he pushed back. Pain flared like a rocket up and down his leg. He barely bit off an obscenity mid-word.

"Sorry." His apology hardly sounded contrite, but he couldn't call it back.

"No, it is all right. The surgeon said there would be a lot of pain for the first few days. I imagine it is hard to feel helpless." The look of pity in her eyes was the worst thing of all.

His arms shook and a thin layer of sweat broke out all over his body, as he managed to half prop his back against the curved headboard. Exhausted by the Herculean effort, he leaned back and breathed deeply.

She pushed the glass into his hand and moved off the bed. "You lost a lot of blood. You'll be very weak and likely light-headed for some time."

If he hadn't been such an ungrateful lout, perhaps she'd

still be seated beside him on the narrow mattress.

Once his heartbeat slowed to normal, Jack would lift the glass and just wet his mouth. At least the room had stopped spinning, but he was all too aware that he would need to relieve himself soon. How he'd manage that feat without help, he didn't know.

"But I have always heard impatience is sign of improvement in an invalid."

"Or just a bad-tempered patient," he offered. He needed to curb his frustration. Lifting the glass to take a sip, he ended up gulping the cool liquid down his parched throat.

She watched him silently, and he stopped to breathe. "Thank you for all that you are doing for me."

She picked up her book and sat in the chair. "Would you like me to read to you? I have here *A Tale of Two Cities* by Charles Dickens. But I could fetch another book, if you read it last year when it was released in serial form."

As if he could have read a novel released in serial form. Her earnest face suggested her question was sincere. "I have not read it. I would be glad to hear it."

She opened the volume and adjusted her chair so the light from the fire fell on the book. After flipping through several pages, she began, " 'It was the best of times, it was the worst of times, it was the age of wisdom, it was . . .' "

Jack let her voice flow over him. It was not so much melodic as even with understated inflections. He rather liked how she read, not as if he were a child, needing a narrator to create excitement. And the words were apropos. It was the best of dreams to be closeted in a room with her late in the evening, but a nightmare under the circumstances.

He watched her lips move and her hands as she turned the page. At times he closed his eyes and tried to ignore the pain. He would have fallen back asleep, except for the discomfort of his full bladder. Of all the ways he wanted to spend time alone with Mrs. Broadhurst, this was not it. Nor did he want to appear as an uncouth lout, but there was no hope for it.

He pushed himself up to sit and swung his legs over the side of the bed. One foot felt the cold floorboards, and as soon as the other touched down, pain exploded through his lower leg. He gasped. The warnings of the doctor echoed in his head. He couldn't put his right foot down at all.

His head spun and he had no idea how he would get about.

"What is wrong?" she asked. "You should be laying down."

Fighting the wave of nausea that accompanied being upright, he said, "I need to piss."

"Oh." Her chair screeched back as she stood. Red stained her cheeks. "Of course."

He should have considered his words. He could have made his need known in a less blunt way. "Is there a chamber pot?"

She leaned and looked under the bed and came up frowning as she glanced around the room. "I should have thought . . . we should have . . ." She moved over to the cord by the door and gave it a couple of good yanks. "The water closet . . ." Her voice kept trailing off.

"I can't wait." He gripped the sheets on either side of him, the dizziness fading away. The urge to relieve himself was making his legs cramp. He really had waited too long.

She gave another yank on the cord, then opened the door and looked out into a dimly lit hall. Her anxious frown was a pretty good indication none of the servants were standing about to help.

"Just one minute," she said, slipping out the door.

He didn't have a minute. The front door that Jack had

been carried through hours before was just across the tiled expanse. He could at least try to make it outside rather than making water on the floor. Using the chair she'd been sitting in, he pushed to stand on his good leg.

He winced, trying to figure out how he could make it to the front door. Picking up the chair, he plopped it down a foot in front of him and hopped closer.

The jolt shot pain through him. He paused trying to gather his strength, determined not to humiliate himself. Only he felt dangerously off balance and on the edge of losing control.

Mrs. Broadhurst swung back through the door. She had a walking stick with a carved handle in her hand. "I don't know why no one is coming, but the water closet is just under the stairs. With my support and this, we can get you there." She didn't meet his eyes as she handed the ivory-topped cane to him and moved to his side.

She pulled his arm over her shoulders, letting the shawl drop to the floor and slipping her hand around his waist.

He shivered at her embrace. His throbbing leg got lost in the folds of her skirt as he lurched forward. She staggered under his weight, but Jack was determined to make it to the necessary. Yet, he was aware of the woman at his side. This was not how or why he wanted to wrap an arm around her.

Her skin was silky and he thought in a few more minutes his urgency might be staved off by wanting to touch her more. The crown of her head was just a little above his shoulder, and she fit perfectly against him. Her fingers dug into his ribs as she steadied him.

He grunted. Each step or hop was like a mountain climb, and it was all he could do to keep moving forward. As if the air were thin, he panted heavily.

"Only a little farther," she encouraged.

Planting the cane, he leaned as much weight as he could on it rather than put the full burden of his weight on her. The ivory carved head bit into his hand and his arm shook.

An open door under the stairs led into a tiny room with a basin attached to the wall. A gaslight had been turned up inside, and with a few more lurches he was inside the door frame.

His head spun.

Mrs. Broadhurst let go of him, and he listed to the side, crashing into the wall.

Then from behind, her arms banded around his heaving chest. She pulled him upright. Planting his hand against the wall, he tried to stay balanced and not overset the both of them. Unable to use his injured leg, he was off-kilter, tilted in a way that couldn't be corrected. Now that he stood in front of the commode, he struggled to lift the nightshirt that suddenly seemed made of a thousand yards of material.

"Here, let me help you," she said. She shifted closer until he could feel her pressed against his back. Without loosening her arms from around him, she bunched the nightshirt in her crossed hands, drawing it upward.

He aimed and nothing happened. "Bloody hell."

She shifted against him and reached. A loud squeak was followed by the tinkle of running water in the basin by his side.

It was what he needed.

The relief was heavenly. He sighed as his stream hit the porcelain bowl.

Her forehead pressed in between his shoulder blades, but she didn't waver in holding him steady, even though he was weaving like a drunken man.

After he finished he hung his head and tried to catch his breath. He was humiliated, but what must helping a mere laborer to piss be like for the blue-blooded daughter of a lord?

Reaching around him, she batted about until she found the cord on the tank in front of him. She yanked. Water swirled around the bowl and down.

"If you turn a little, you can reach the soap." She let the nightshirt drop and then shifted, almost as if she would carry him back to the room.

Jack shuffled his foot around and hopped to face the basin with the water running down a hole in the center. He was far too aware of rubbing against her body as he jerked about. "I'm sorry. That had to be horrible for you."

"No," she said slowly. "It wasn't even the most unpleasant thing I've had to experience in the last hour."

He wanted to twist and see her, but he might topple like Humpty Dumpty. Instead he stuck his hands under the running water. "I had no idea reading out loud to me was so unpleasant."

She started against his back. "It wasn't. I en—"

"I know," he interrupted. "You were upset before you sat down beside me."

It wasn't his place to pry into her affairs, but anything was better than acknowledging he'd needed her help for the most basic of human functions. That she'd helped without the disdain he expected from a woman in her position surprised him. "If it is my presence causing problems between you and Mr. Broadhurst"—he couldn't bring himself to call Mr. Broadhurst her husband—"I will be gone as quickly as I can."

"I do not think you can control the rate of your healing, Mr. Applegate. Besides, I find being with my guests stressful, not the time I spend with you."

"In that case, I shall take my time." That was a lie. He needed to be out of here as soon as he could manage it. He had an appointment to keep in the city. And nothing was going to stop him from getting there, not even his futile hope of something happening between her and him.

Caroline wasn't expecting Jack to have a sense of humor, not on the day he'd suffered a terrible break in his leg. Nor had she expected to see to his personal needs, but it wasn't as if Mr. Broadhurst had ever spared her. After the water closets were installed, she'd banned chamber pots.

Mr. Broadhurst might grumble that he had to traipse down the hall at night, but at least she no longer had to witness him voiding.

She drew in a deep breath and looked over Jack's shoulder to meet his eyes in the small mirror. His chin dipped and his gaze slid away. Having to rely on a woman for help with a bodily need had undoubtedly upset him. The situation had the unreal feel of an impossible situation. Never in a thousand years would she have expected to be helping a man from the mill use the necessary, and not just any man, but Jack.

"Where does the water come from?" Jack turned the faucet off and then back on as if marveling at running water. He was probably just trying to distract them from the reason they were in the water closet.

"A cistern on the roof." She turned off the water and handed him the towel, all without meeting his eyes. Of course she still stood behind him, her arms against his sides just in case he pitched sideways again.

"Rainwater?" he questioned, but the words seemed a little forced, and he was panting hard.

"The servants pump the tank full with well water if the rain isn't enough."

He would not have experienced any of the modern conveniences either in the mill or in his home. Running water was hardly a new thing, and in places like London common. Not for the first time, she wondered how mean the laborers' lives were. They worked ten to twelve hour days, six days a week. They lived in two-room cottages at best. Luxuries like books, running water, or travel were out of their reach. He had cast her a skeptical look when she'd asked if he'd read *A Tale of Two Cities*.

Her mother made a point to visit all the tenants' homes, but it was different when the villagers were her husband's employees. She really didn't know much about how the mill-workers lived inside their small houses, and they reacted to her as if she were a spy or intruder when she'd made a few halfhearted efforts to look in on them.

If she had better social skills, she might have persisted, but she'd never been as outgoing as Sarah or Amelia. Even Robert had grown more sociable since inheriting the viscountcy and taking his seat in Parliament.

"Shall we get you back to bed?"

Jack leaned against the sink. "Yes."

She eased beside him, as much as the tiny space would allow. She pulled his arm across her shoulders. His warm fingers slid across her bare skin and a shudder traveled down her spine. But she wouldn't think too much about his touch because he needed her help right now.

She maneuvered Jack through the doorway and took a couple of small steps toward the breakfast room. He quivered as if the exertion was too much for him. She pulled him tighter against her side. If he collapsed, she might not be able to prevent a fall. His nightshirt was damp and the gaslight reflected off a sheen of perspiration on his face.

Mrs. Burns opened the baize-covered door leading to the bowels of the house. A voluminous wrapper enfolded her from head to toe, and a sleeping cap covered her gray curls. "I'm sorry, ma'am. I didn't hear the bell. It goes to the kitchen and the scullery maid heard it but wasn't sure if she should wake me."

"If you could help me get Mr. Applegate back to bed," Caroline said.

"Jack," he whispered into her ear.

A frisson ran down her spine. It was of course the response to the puff of air in such a sensitive organ. Not that she liked his breath in her ear.

"Yes, of course, ma'am," said the housekeeper, crossing the expanse of the hall.

Caroline hoped the older woman hadn't noted her shiver. She cast a glance toward Jack. He had. He was regarding her with pain-laced curiosity. Heat stole up her cheeks. He would most likely think her a complete ninny.

Her arm around him made her notice he was a fit man. Would relations be as unpleasant with a man like Jack?

Mrs. Burns took Jack's other arm, and between the two of them they got him back to the bed.

He collapsed against the sheets, his brow knit with pain. His hand slid across Caroline's shoulders, and she was left with the oddest sensation that he meant it as a tender sort of touch. Her heart hammered. Was he interested in her that way?

She wrapped her hands under his knee and gingerly lifted his injured leg onto the bed. Aware that Mrs. Burns was near, Caroline surreptitiously slid her palm from his knee to the inside of his thigh and deliberately brushed his flesh with her thumb before reaching to pull the covers over him. Her insides coiled and tightened, leaving her feeling not quite herself.

He screwed his eyes shut, his hands fisting in the covers.

Disappointment burned in her, and she turned to thank and dismiss the housekeeper.

Jack was probably in too much pain to even notice what she did, and her thoughts were running rampant on what kind of lovers the men in her house were. There must be men who made congress enjoyable enough for a woman to want to be with them. Was Jack that sort of man?

He would never think of so much as kissing her. He was just a millworker, and she was the owner's wife. Their stations were eons apart. Probably the only reason she could tolerate touching Jack Applegate was because she was completely safe from advances from him.

Chapter 6

"**B**egging your pardon, ma'am, but will Mr. Broadhurst be in today?" asked Mr. Smythe.

Caroline looked up from her husband's desk in the mill office. "He won't be in. What do you need?"

"He'll need to take a look at these contracts for next year's cotton."

"Bring them here. I'll look at them."

"Perhaps I should take them up to the house." Mr. Smythe shifted from one foot to another.

"My husband has guests and will not be working while they are here. I can take care of whatever needs done and I will inform him of the details."

The shipping clerk still looked uncertain. Caroline sighed. She pushed back from the desk and stood. "My husband is not a young man. Who do you think you will answer to when he is too infirm to work?"

"Why does he have guests? He never has entertained gents like this before." Mr. Smythe's face looked monkeyish in his confusion.

Caroline cast about for an explanation that would make sense. The only thing that popped into her head was Tremont suggesting that Robert might have wanted her to influence gentlemen to help in his petition to get an earldom—a petition she knew nothing about. "Mr. Broadhurst is hoping these gentlemen can influence the crown. He is hoping to be knighted."

The lie wasn't totally preposterous. Silently she begged forgiveness as she watched Mr. Smythe's face work through the information.

"Of course it won't happen right away, but one must court the right favor," said Caroline. Mr. Broadhurst would do better to build a hospital or college if he wanted a knighthood, but Mr. Smythe was unlikely to know that.

A commotion at the door brought her out of the office.

Mr. Whitton and Lord Tremont carried a groaning Lord Langley into the office. "Send for a carriage," shouted one of the men.

"Where is a doctor?"

A gamesman was trying to retrieve the guns from all the sportsmen.

"What happened?" asked Caroline.

"Stepped in a hole and turned his ankle."

She moved past the confused clerks to where Lord Langley sat on one of the chairs. One of the men was removing his boot.

"I need ice and a tot of whiskey," said Lord Langley. "I think I shall die."

When the boot and stocking were removed, Caroline could see no indication of a serious injury, just a bit of swelling. Nonetheless, she sent a clerk for the doctor and another to have the carriage brought around. The sooner she got them out of her office, the sooner work could resume.

"I have sent for the physician. In the meantime we should get Lord Langley to the house where he might be comfortable."

But lest she be thought a poor hostess, she accompanied

the group and made sure Langley was settled in his room with his leg iced and propped on pillows.

When the doctor arrived, he carefully manipulated Langley's ankle and pronounced it a sprain. But no one would have known it was such a minor injury, given the way Lord Langley moaned and demanded the servants fetch this and that.

What struck her was Jack's stoic reserve compared to the loud complaints of Lord Langley. But she seemed the only one perturbed as the gentlemen shook their heads over poor Langley's condition. Finally, she got the men back out the door to resume their hunting and convinced Lord Langley to take a bit of laudanum.

But the last thing she wanted to do was split her time between two sickrooms, especially when one of the patients wasn't really that injured. Although, splitting her time became a moot point, as Langley demanded all her attention until the laudanum and whiskey made him sleep.

The click of the door jarred Jack awake. It wasn't as if he slept well other than the first hour after the laudanum took effect. And he'd given up trying to lie down and doze propped against the pillows.

"Jack!" pipped Beth. Her little feet pattered across the floor. She raised a knee to scramble up onto the bed.

He closed his eyes and braced for the pain. After the doctor left, his leg had been on fire, but he was grateful to still have it.

A swift rustle and the absence of the mattress sinking down had him cracking an eye. Mrs. Broadhurst held Beth around the waist. Beth's legs dangled down. Both of them looked rather startled.

Beth twisted around to see who had grabbed her. "Who are you?"

Mrs. Broadhurst hesitated.

"This is Mrs. Broadhurst, Beth. This is her house." He switched his gaze to the woman he'd been waiting all day to spend time alone with. "This is my sister."

Mrs. Broadhurst bent over and set Beth on her feet. "You may sit in the chair, but you don't want to hurt your brother by climbing over him."

Beth wound her hands together and twisted back and forth. She cast a shy glance toward Mrs. Broadhurst and then turned toward Jack as if her curiosity would burst out of her if she contained it any longer. "Mama said you broke your leg."

Jack pulled back the covers and let her see the thick bandage and splint. Although he didn't want to pretend to be cheerful, he couldn't send Beth on her way after she'd walked all the way—he searched the doorway for another sibling—alone.

Beth's eyes grew round. "Can you walk?"

"Not really."

"He will in time," said Mrs. Broadhurst gently.

Beth climbed onto the chair. "Will he have a funny walk like that man at the dairy?"

"He limps," explained Jack.

"We'll have to see," said Mrs. Broadhurst with a smile.

Jack's heart thudded. If only her smile had been for him. He didn't known if the brush of her hand against his inner leg last night was an accident or deliberate, but he had been too exhausted to pursue it. If he touched her, would she welcome it? Or did he just want her so badly that he had put extra meaning on her assistance?

"School was crowded today," pronounced Beth. "There weren't enough seats for everyone. I had to sit on the floor."

Jack turned his gaze toward Mrs. Broadhurst.

"Children under the age of nine will no longer be allowed to work in the mill," she explained, "and children under twelve may work half hours only if they attend school for four hours."

Jack winced. So because of the accident, she had finally convinced her husband to banish the littlest ones from the mill. He only hoped he wouldn't be around to be blamed when the lost wages were felt. With luck he'd be in London and far removed from the troubles in this mill town.

"Mattie cried all day," Beth continued on, blithely unaware. "Her mother told her it was her fault they wouldn't have enough to eat."

"No one will starve," objected Mrs. Broadhurst.

"They might," said Jack. "Mattie's mother is a widow and they need all their wages to get by."

Mrs. Broadhurst paled and her lips pressed together.

He knew she meant well, but she didn't know what it was like for the families like his with lots of mouths to feed. "It would have helped if wages had gone up to compensate for the families who will lose money."

"Don't they want education for their children?"

"They want to eat first. Wages haven't changed in a decade, but the cost of food has."

Her throat worked. No doubt the situation was more complicated than she'd allowed. "I wouldn't let anyone starve. I can supply food to those in need."

"No one wants handouts. They want to earn their own way," Jack said softly. "They have their pride." Even his stepmother hated that she needed to rely on his wages to make ends meet.

"I see," Mrs. Broadhurst said stiffly.

He reached for her hand, but as soon as his fingers brushed hers, she jerked her hand away. He should have known better. She might place her hand on his forehead or assist him with his personal needs, but she wouldn't want to encourage him to think they were intimates. Obviously she didn't want *him* to touch *her.*

He must have misinterpreted her hand on his thigh. Likely she was only helping him and he'd magnified the brush of her hand into meaning more because he wanted it to mean more.

Beth squirmed on the chair, reminding him she was there.

Jack sighed. "Do you want to go over your lessons with me?"

Soon she would be beyond the lessons he could help with.

Beth ran over to the door where she'd dropped her lunch pail and slate.

Mrs. Broadhurst frowned. "Does your mother know she is here?"

"My mother is dead. But no, Beth's mother, Martha, my father's second wife, probably doesn't know where she is. Unless Beth is late for supper, she won't be missed."

Mrs. Broadhurst's cheeks pinked. "I'll make sure she is escorted back by then."

"If she found her way here, she can find her way home."

Mrs. Broadhurst stiffened. "Nevertheless, she is too young to be wandering about on her own. But I'll let you get on with your visit, then. I'll return when it is time for your medicine."

Jack wished he could call his curt words back. "Hold."

She turned and cast him such a disdainful expression he was reminded of his place. She wasn't his to command and he had overstepped. He should have known better. From the satin drapes to the thick carpets and paintings on the walls, the cost of the furnishings in this room alone would keep a mill family in cozy comfort for decades. He'd do best to remember that she had no interest in him as a person, only as a means to further her scheme of getting better conditions in the mill.

"Wanting to educate the children is a noble thing," he said.

"Noble, but not practical," she said with bitterness.

Caroline looked down at her hands. Her arm had sparked with raw energy that coiled and tightened in the pit of her stomach and lower when Jack touched her. The unexpected jolt had made her jerk away.

In a cruel twist of irony, he might be the only man who had ever made her feel anything like that. But his injury was too severe to think he could perform the sex act anytime soon. Dr. Hein had said he'd be far too weak for more than lying about for days, perhaps weeks.

"It is just the families need to feed their bellies before they can feed their children's minds," he said gently.

"But the children earn so very little."

Jack shrugged. "When the wages are so low, every ha'penny counts."

Her husband was often accusing her of letting her heart get in the way of her head. Jack must think that true too. No wonder Mr. Broadhurst thought her too softhearted to run the business. She'd thought Jack understood the value of education, supported it. But she hadn't realized the families were dependent on the piddling income of the children.

Even though she was nominally in control of the mill for the next month, to give the workers raises would only cement her husband's conviction that she could not be in charge.

She headed for her husband's study. She needed to give Mr. Broadhurst a report of the day's business. She only hoped she was early enough that he was still out and she could leave a note. The less contact she had with him the better. Her anger at him hadn't lessened. Since she learned of the provisions of the will, it had only grown like a monster inside her eating at her heart.

As she entered the room she drew up short. Mr. Broadhurst stared out the window. He turned toward her.

"Sir." Caroline bowed her head. It was too late to retreat. "You did not go hunting with the men?"

"I do not understand such idle pursuits," he said. "I returned early rather than spend all day traipsing through fields just to bring back more pheasants than can possibly be eaten before they spoil."

Her husband had never understood recreation or sport for pleasure's sake, and he deplored waste of any sort. "I believe the hunting is as much an excuse to experience the fresh air and company of men as anything.

"Did you need something?" he asked moving behind his desk.

Nervous that he would rail at her for her decision, she prevaricated, "I wanted to look at the books, and see how much the children were earning."

She'd dismissed the sums paid to children as negligible, which to her they were, but she should understand how much a family might be expected to earn and if the children's wages were vital to a family's existence. Knowing the wages they paid were on par with what other mills paid was important to running a business, but she needed to delve deeper and look at it from the mill families' perspective. She hoped Mr. Broadhurst didn't ask her about her sudden curiosity, because she couldn't admit she talked to a worker about such things.

"I have already calculated the savings. It won't be enough." Mr. Broadhurst stood and handed her a piece of paper with long columns of numbers.

"Enough?" She looked at the chicken scratches.

Mr. Broadhurst rubbed his forehead. "To make a profit if the price of cotton jumps as high as I think it might. The Americas . . ." He waved a hand toward the newspaper spread across his desk.

The news was a concern of hers too. What was happening in the United States was likely to affect the price of cotton. Swallowing against the dry spot in the back of her throat, she asked, "You read the disturbing news about several of the states threatening to secede if Lincoln is elected?"

She feared she was already late in acting, since the news would have been disseminated in London two days ago.

"Fools, the lot of them. It will be war."

That was the same conclusion she had arrived at. Sucking in a deep breath, she plunged in hoping Mr. Broadhurst would support her bold move. "I have sent contracts to buy cotton from both Egypt and our regular suppliers in the Americas at market price."

Mr. Broadhurst lowered his brow. "You cannot make promises you don't intend to keep."

She refused to address that he might be referring to her private bargain with him. "We will fulfill our commitments. The worst that can happen is we have too much cotton next year at a good price."

"There is no guarantee the price will be good."

"If there is a lot of cotton, the price will be good. If there isn't enough or not enough can make it to market, the price will be higher, but we won't pay for what we don't receive."

Mr. Broadhurst scratched his head. "So you would gamble on shortages."

"I already have." Caroline sucked in a deep breath, wondering if she had made a huge miscalculation. "If we have too much, we can store it or increase production. It shall not go to waste."

He shook his head. "Is this to show me you are capable of running the mill without me?"

Caroline's heart squeezed, not knowing what he would think of her plan. If she had guessed wrong, he might have even less faith in her ability to run the mill. "A decision had to be made and I made it. I too would wish for more certainty, but I thought long and hard about the consequences of every possible action. Not acting would be worse than if I miscalculated. I would rather have too much cotton than not enough."

He stared at her and then grudgingly nodded.

For a second she thought she might sink to the floor. It was not so much that she curried his approval, but his disapproval could be far worse.

She'd never seriously considered the ramifications of running the business without Mr. Broadhurst at the helm. She could handle the day-to-day things, but deciding where and how much cotton to buy in the future was not a task she'd handled before. But a decision had to be made and she'd made it. Even if Mr. Broadhurst disagreed, she was certain the choice was a good one.

"Your brother says you made progress last night."

Was Robert acting as a spy? Her face grew hot. "I have not decided which one will suit," she blurted.

To call what happened progress was laughable, but she wouldn't let Mr. Broadhurst know that. But Robert's betrayal sat like a hot poker under her breastbone. She couldn't ask him for guidance in how to seduce one of the men, for fear he would report directly back to Mr. Broadhurst.

"Decide quickly because I haven't patience for your games," said Mr. Broadhurst.

"My games? Would you have acceded to my demands to remove the children if you were not looking to cut costs? I think I sold my honor too cheaply."

Mr. Broadhurst folded his arms and breathed deeply. "What else do you want, Mrs. Broadhurst? Perhaps next time your brother can bring the bloody lot of Parliament."

Caroline hesitated only a second. She had nothing to lose, after all. "I want your assurance that you will continue to employ Mr. Applegate until he is fully healed."

"I'm not running a charity hospital. He won't be fit for his old job for months."

"He could work as a clerk. Writing won't require him to stand or walk about much."

"All the clerks have attended university. You know I don't hire villagers for those positions."

"I should think you could make an exception in this one case. He doesn't want to end up a beggar. Surely you can understand that. And if I am in the family way, I may not be able to do as much as in the past."

"Will there be a baby?"

"If God wills it," she whispered.

"God has nothing to do with whether or not you lie with one of the guests."

"I was not suggesting an immaculate conception." Caroline tucked her lips around her teeth.

Mr. Broadhurst had about as much use for sarcasm as he did for leisure pursuits.

"You ask too much. When he is healed, if he can do his old job, he can have that back." He gave a dismissive gesture. "It looks as if the men have returned. You should go to them."

The guarantee of Jack getting his old job back was better than nothing. She nodded. And now she had to face the men, one of whom she would have to pick for a lover.

The door opened and skirts swished through the breakfast room. Jack struggled to lift his weighted eyelids. God, how was he going to get to London in two weeks if he couldn't even stay awake?

"I'm to sit with 'im while you help with dinner," whispered a female voice. Not Mrs. Broadhurst.

Jack stopped trying to open his eyes. He'd been in and out of consciousness since the doctor's visit a few hours earlier. Mrs. Broadhurst had checked in on him in the morning and been present when the doctor was there, but other than that he'd been seen to by servants.

"Sleeping he is," said the redheaded maid who'd been sitting sewing in the corner since Beth left. "Not a peep out of him."

"Caw, least he's peaceable. My mistress was late getting dressed for dinner and I thought the master was like to kill her."

The new entrant to the room rattled on, "He stayed on while I dressed her, and tried to do her hair, but the way he kept looking at her—fair made my skin crawl."

"Hush, that be the master you're yapping about." The chair screeched back.

"Not him. I works for the missus. She goes, I go. It ain't right him leering after her. He's old enough to be her grandda."

"He's her husband. He has the right of her."

"'Fore I came in he was jawing on about getting a baby. As if that is going to happen after more'n a baker's dozen years of marriage."

Did Broadhurst blame his wife for her childlessness? Broadhurst had not had a single baby from his first two marriages. The fault probably lay with the old man.

"My aunt was married for fourteen years before my cousin was born. They had to go at it every night for nigh on a decade. He's her only. Fair dotes on him, she does."

"Pish," said the newcomer. "I think the master's so old his seed dried up."

"An old man in my village got him a new wife after his wife passed, and got five more babies on the new wife. He musta been ninety if he was a day."

"I suppose you'd have an answer for everything, but he ain't been to her bed for a month of Sundays. They won't get no babies like that."

"Shush, we shouldn't talk of such things, and I best get along before Cook is ready to roast me."

The conversation bothered Jack and wouldn't let him fall back into sleep. Was Mr. Broadhurst tired of his wife? Did he intend to be rid of her? Both of Broadhurst's wives were buried at the crossroads. Even if the deaths were more than three decades apart, it always seemed unlikely that both had taken their own lives.

But he had no room to judge.

He'd wanted to be like Broadhurst, just not in that respect. He'd put off marriage. He'd put off having children. All because he hadn't wanted to be held hostage to responsibilities to others. He'd hurt beyond measure the first girl he'd ever loved and forced her to a horrible choice. And it was probably all for naught.

With his injury, he would be lucky to live the life he'd been planning to rise above.

Jack shook off his gloomy foreboding. No, he would find a way to get to London, convince the owner of the machinery company he could still do the work. He could still design. He had money to live until he could prove he would be an asset to his company. He would figure out a way to get the machining done. He had to make it work, otherwise what point was there to his life?

Chapter 7

The interminable dinner was finally drawing to an end. Two hairpins jabbed Caroline's skull. After she walked Beth back to the village, her maid had worked a miracle getting her into fine London feathers and her hair coiffed in the space of a quarter hour. But the hasty twisting and pinning had led to a dull aching headache. Or perhaps Mr. Broadhurst's reminder that she was to fulfill her part of the bargain had been to blame.

If she could spend a few quiet minutes reading to Jack while the men lingered at the table, she could perhaps find her balance to begin a new attack on one of the men.

Before leaving, she surveyed the company. Mr. Whitton's thinning brown hair did nothing to move his looks out of the ordinary. He would be a baron one day, but he was not so well situated that she would be thought to be title chasing. Perhaps he would not be so full of himself as Lord Tremont. Hadn't Robert said he had several by-blows? As if he'd felt her watching him, Mr. Whitton looked up. Her gaze darted away. Trying to be obvious to her quarry without every other man in the room noticing was impossible.

She rose to leave. She reached the door just as Mr. Broadhurst barked out, "No reason to tarry over the table when we might be comfortable in the drawing room."

Caroline winced, but signaled to a footman to bring the glasses and the port.

Because Mr. Broadhurst must have decided the little break didn't fit with his master plan, she couldn't stop and look in on Jack while the men finished their port and cigars.

The footmen opened the doors for her, and she crossed the marble hall and put her hand on the balustrade. She dreaded each step.

Too loud and boisterous, the guests followed, gamely putting up with the quirks of their host. They needed their port to mellow them. Perhaps if she got one of them drunk, he'd be interested in lying with her. Maybe he wouldn't notice if she wasn't enthusiastic as long as she was willing. Or perhaps she needed to get drunk.

After the men all had a glass of port or brandy and broke into small conversations around the room, Caroline circled, chatting briefly with each man. Although they turned toward her and were polite, she couldn't help but feel out of place, unwanted. It was a man's gathering, after all, and she wasn't included in their politics, their hunting, or their horseflesh stories.

She took her place on the far sofa as the gentlemen settled into chairs and lit pipes and cigars. Mr. Broadhurst engaged the men in conversation and was doing his best to be a congenial host. She'd told him earlier it would be too obvious if he left the company early, and surprisingly, he agreed that he needed to maintain the facade of entertaining the guests during their sport.

Robert sat down beside her.

"Why didn't you tell me about petitioning for an earldom?" she asked.

"Oh that. The Earldom of Dunfer has reverted to the crown because the male line is extinct, but since our grandmother is of that line, I thought the crown might confer it on me. The income might help repair things."

Her neck tightened. Did Robert expect her to help with that too? "And did you bring men who might influence the crown's decision here?"

Robert frowned at her. "After I considered their marital state, their looks, and their fecundity, influence with the queen wasn't on my mind," he said in a low undertone. "Besides, the queen said if I could go five years without a scandal or weakness of character, she would reinstate the earldom to me. I think she wanted to make sure the apple fell far from the tree."

Every time she thought she was on firm ground, it turned to shifting sands. By helping her, Robert was risking the earldom. "Oh, you don't think this mess will be a scandal?"

"I hope not, Caro." He shrugged. "But if it is . . ."

"You should have brought our sisters and your wife," said Caroline. She wasn't quite ready to be mollified yet.

"I didn't want them to overshadow you."

"Thank you, Robert. I appreciate your faith in my feminine charms." She barely resisted rolling her eyes. But it wasn't as if she was deluded about her attractiveness.

"I didn't mean it that way," said Robert. "You're very quiet. People tend to forget you're there."

His explanation didn't make her feel better. "Yes, well it is impossible to be discreet when I'm the only woman in the room." Besides that, Amy and Sarah could have given her pointers on how exactly to go about indicating interest without making a complete cake of herself.

"Well why are you sitting all the way back here in the corner?"

"I always sit here." But it was because it was the farthest spot from Mr. Broadhurst's chair by the fire, and the one nearest the south window that occasionally allowed a little sun into the room. She could read or sew best here. But it was remote from the groups of men. Biting her lip, she couldn't decide if it made it easier or harder to engage a man. Perhaps if she could lure one—other than Robert—to her side.

Robert's voice dropped to barely above a whisper. "What happened? I thought you had him"—he jerked his head toward Tremont—"on your scent."

Her face heated. She plucked at the lace on her sleeves. She should stop before she caught a thread and unraveled the lot of it. "He thought I was looking for my next husband."

"Well, so did I when I got Broadhurst's first note." Robert put his hand over hers, stopping her fidgeting. "What can I do to help you?"

She drew in a deep breath and straightened. "Stop reporting my progress to Mr. Broadhurst."

"God, Caro, I only meant it to the good. He seemed convinced you had no intention of doing what he asked, but I assured him you had put forth considerable effort."

Caroline closed her eyes briefly. But the last thing she wanted to look like was a long-suffering saint. She had chosen to go along with Mr. Broadhurst's proposition. Returning home destitute, or a second marriage, might have been acceptable to many other women in her position, but those alternatives weren't acceptable to *her*. She needed control of her destiny.

She popped her eyes open and found Mr. Whitton in the room. She watched him bring a cigar to his lips and suck on it.

As if aware of her scrutiny, he turned toward her. This time instead of ducking away she gave him a slight smile and then deliberately turned toward her brother as if she knew her duty was to listen but thought Robert a bore.

"So have you decided Tremont won't do?" asked Robert. "Or do you want me to talk to him?"

"Tell me," Caroline said, trying to keep from narrowing her eyes. "How many sisters should one man have relations with?"

"He told you about Amelia?" said Robert, confirming her suspicions.

Her stomach plummeted. "Not in so many words, but the least you could have done was bring gentlemen who would not make unfavorable comparisons."

Robert looked chagrined.

"Perhaps my efforts wouldn't be so noticeable if Amelia were here and I wasn't the center of attention."

"I didn't think of that." Robert looked around the room. "I suppose it is obvious when you leave with one of the men. But couldn't you just flirt a bit and arrange to meet later?"

"Is that how it should be done?" Caroline asked through a forced smile. She looked at Mr. Whitton out of the corner of her eye.

At least he seemed to be watching her now. It vaguely reminded her of the way she had always noticed Jack in the mill, but without the strange flutters in her stomach. But she was playacting with Mr. Whitton.

Good gracious, had she found Jack attractive? Was that what made her always seek out his face among the myriad workers?

Mr. Whitton leaned forward in his chair as if to rise. The pleasant warmth she experienced when Jack was near was dismally absent. Her shock at her attraction to a man like him, perhaps a younger version of Mr. Broadhurst, was shoved away to a locked corner of her mind. She needed a baby, not a pleasant imagining of an encounter that would never happen.

And of course in all the times she watched Jack before his accident, she'd never imagined more than his assisting her over a walkway or around a mess in the mill. Perhaps holding her hand. A silly schoolgirl kind of daydream. Certainly she'd never thought of him intimately, not as she was trying to think of Mr. Whitton.

Mr. Whitton stood. Caroline glanced coyly at him.

Robert drew a deep breath and spoke. "If you want me to end this, I will—"

"Go," said Caroline under her breath.

"What?" Robert blinked.

"I have one on the line. Go, so I may reel him in."

Robert rose to his feet. In almost a theatrical voice, he said, "Looks like I need a refill."

He might need a refill, but she suspected she would need a whole bottle to relax.

Mrs. Broadhurst finally came at half eight. Jack had nearly given up hope of seeing her again today. But he kept his eyes glued to the page in front of him. He'd been trying to decipher it for the last hour. The small words were easy enough, but a word such as epoch baffled him. He could absolutely not think of a word that fit the letters that ended with a *ch* sound, as in *chain* or *child*. He read the word "incredulity" again and again, trying to hear Mrs. Broadhurst's voice as it flowed off her tongue. His mind churned with the effort to piece together parts until he recognized a word, but it continued to elude him, until he wondered if it was a nob word he never used.

The distinctive whisper of Mrs. Broadhurst's skirts neared, and stirred an excitement in him. The material sounded different than earlier in the day, but the same as last night. Now that he knew the sound, he'd never forget it.

Her husky voice murmuring instructions for a footman to return at nine curled through Jack. He wanted to protest at just having her for a half hour. He didn't, though. He waited until the maid engaged to mind him left the room. Mrs. Broadhurst might be used to the continual presence of servants, but he wasn't.

He shut the book lest she realize he had not made it past the first page. He wanted to just gaze on her creamy skin, but shut his eyes instead. He waited for her touch on his forehead, but it didn't come.

He opened his eyes.

With a shawl covering her shoulders, Mrs. Broadhurst stared into the fire grate. She raised a large glass of a dark liquid, took a sip, and then shuddered. It reminded him of the way the younger workers went at their gin after being paid. Not so much enjoyment of the drink, but because gulping it down was expedient to feeling the effects.

"Sugar helps," he said.

She swiveled so fast her burgundy skirts hesitated and then swirled past where she stopped. He watched fascinated as they moved back into position.

"I didn't want to disturb your reading." Her nose scrunched as if she were uncertain of his comment.

"You're not."

She glanced toward the door as if willing a maid to return.

"I don't need to be watched every minute," Jack protested.

"I prefer it," she said imperiously.

For a second they stared at each other. He didn't have the heart to fight her now. His leg throbbed, his head felt as if it wanted to explode, and even though he could easily fall into a stupor, he wanted to stay awake while she was with him. He began the slow process of shifting up on the pillows to a position that more closely resembled sitting. He'd never make it to London in time at the pace he was healing. What the hell was he to do if he couldn't get that job?

"How are you feeling?" Her voice was like the whisper of her dress. It curled around him and called to him.

"Like I broke a leg," he said slowly.

Her lips curled just slightly, enough to make him feel it wasn't a look of pity. He wanted to pretend he'd pull back the covers and his bones would be knitted once again and his toes would work. With her, he just wanted to try honesty. He had to grasp what this meant to his life, and where he went from here. Much as staying in her home was like heaven—or would have been if he weren't in pain—it wouldn't last once he was well enough to get by.

She moved to the chair. "They said you didn't eat much. Is there anything I could offer to tempt your appetite? Hot chocolate, plum pudding, steak and kidney pie?"

He shook his head. "Not hungry." Not for food anyway. He wished she didn't have that damn shawl blocking his view of her skin, not that he could manage more than interest.

"Really, I'm sure Cook has laid in good stores of everything for the guests." She leaned toward him and the shawl gaped a little. "I could send for most anything."

Ashamed of his lechery, he shook his head. She was nothing but good to him, and all he wanted was to look down her dress. He sighed and forced his gaze to a safe place.

She gripped the glass with both hands. Did she feel in need of Dutch courage? The conversation of the maids earlier entered his head. Did Mrs. Broadhurst know her husband would be joining her later? Was that why she would spend less time in the sickroom tonight?

Perhaps there was a bit of strain around her eyes. Her intimacies with her husband were certainly none of his business. But he had to wonder what it was like for her with a man old enough to be her father's father. Not pleasant, if the dark liquid in the glass was any indication.

"I'm feeling a bit better." At least he wasn't spending every waking moment gritting his teeth to keep from vomiting, although when the laudanum wore off he counted the seconds until his next dose. "Would you read to me again? I like listening."

She did smile then. "Reading has always been my sanctuary."

Her skirt rustled as she picked up the book from the bed beside him and settled back into her chair, her glass at her elbow. He took in her hair, twisted into a coronet, the curve of her neck and the pale rose on her cheeks. Damn, she was lovely.

"Did you read further? Would you like me to start where you left off?"

"No. I just reread the beginning. I thought I might have slept through parts." The words came out faint and mewling, as lies were wont to do. Would that he could read as much or as easily as she could.

She found the page where she'd left off and began reading.

"I've never needed sanctuary before now," he interrupted.

She closed the book over her index finger and took her time in looking at him. "You need not worry. I will see to it care is taken of you."

Didn't she understand? A charity case was no better than being a beggar, perhaps worse. He had no way to repay her for her generosity in bringing him into her house and having her servants wait on him. Just as becoming an invalid made him less than a man, depending on her kindness would make him lower than a worm. "I'd rather work," he muttered.

Her eyes flicked and she seemed to be considering his words.

He was better off being terrified of starvation or humbling himself. Charity robbed a man of self-respect and ambition. He had seen it too many times in the faces of the denizens of the workhouses. No, he wanted to make his own way in the world. If he accepted her charity, it would in the end emasculate him.

"When you are a little better we'll see what we can do about getting you back to work. But truly you are not well enough now." She put her hand over his. His heart thumped erratically.

He had to admit she was right, but he didn't know if she was patronizing him or not. He nodded.

Her soft smile stole his breath.

She read a few pages and then took a sip of the drink. He caught the whiff of alcohol. Glancing toward the clock, she grimaced.

The hands were spinning far too quickly for his liking, for hers too, if her anxious glances at the clock each time she turned a page were any indication.

She paused and took a heartier gulp from her glass and then a second. She scrunched her nose and shuddered, revealing her lack of familiarity with imbibing.

Why was she drinking? She hadn't the night before. Given the maids' conversation earlier, he was afraid he knew the answer. Broadhurst didn't want him here, and she had probably had to promise him reward. By God, if she needed strong spirits to face the rest of the night, he couldn't fail. His leg had to heal. And if he didn't get the job in London, he could try to set up his own business.

Jack sat up all the way. "Should you be drinking so much?"

For a second she looked vulnerable, before her features composed in a haughty mask.

"It is not as if I'll be able to catch you if you fall."

"I shan't fall," she said tightly.

He swung his legs over the edge of the bed. She scooted back as if afraid he might touch her. And he wanted nothing more.

"You will if you keep tippling like that. What is it? Whiskey?"

She thrust the glass out between them. He wasn't sure if she was using it to ward him off or offering it to him. He took the glass and raised it to his lips, watching her over the rim. The burn of the liquid ran down his throat. He blew out to counteract the heat. Definitely undiluted whiskey. A smoother, smokier blend than he ever tasted before, but he'd thought ladies abhorred strong spirits.

Her lips parted and her eyes darkened.

"Potent stuff." He wanted to turn the glass so her mouth would touch where his had been when she drank again. "If you are not used to it, you will make yourself ill, not to mention drunk."

"I only want to relax a little."

He should keep the glass away from her reach. Not that he could prevent her from tossing back the rest. "Do you not feel it?"

She shook her head and reached for the glass.

He pulled it back. "I'd rather go home now, if what you have to do for me to stay requires liquid fortification."

"Your staying costs me nothing."

"Are you very certain? Mr. Broadhurst doesn't want me here." He took another drink. Mixing liquor and the laudanum was a bad idea, but he was afraid she'd drink the entire amount if he handed it back to her. The glass was as large as any used for serving ale, but even with her regular sips, she hadn't downed a fourth of its contents yet. His fingers worked on the glass, twisting it.

She blinked slowly and her lips parted as she watched him drink. Then she suddenly seemed to snap to attention.

"Sir, if you please, I should like my drink back." Her voice dripped with icy formality. But he'd seen the cracks in the armor of her aristocratic pride.

"Have a care," he said, handing the glass back. "I want nothing bad to touch you."

Her slight tremble as she took the whiskey spoke volumes. Her eyes were like liquid pools in her face and her chest rose and fell with her every breath.

It was everything he could do to stop himself from reaching out to her. "Especially not on my account. You have done too much already, and I know of no way I can ever repay you."

She lowered her gaze. "I only want that you will be all right."

"I will be." One way or another he would find a way to get along in the world.

She swirled the contents of her glass and then raised it and gulped. She clapped her hand over her mouth as her eyes watered.

"Blow out," he told her gently as he put his hand to her back. But he knew as soon as he touched her it was a mistake.

She jerked away and spun out of her chair. She stared at him as if he'd suddenly turned into a monster. Ignoring her outraged stare, he reached for the back of the chair. "Are you all right?"

He prepared to stand rather than watch her offer false assurances. He could have begged her pardon for touching her, but he'd been intent on helping her.

"What are you doing?" She cast a troubled look toward the door. "The doctor doesn't want you out of bed unless necessary."

"I just need to stretch a minute." Tired of lying about, he

needed to move. Restlessness invaded his limbs like a pot ready to boil over. If she didn't move away from him, it was only a matter of time before he pulled her to him. Her spinning away suggested she wanted nothing to do with that. Her distaste couldn't have been more obvious. Except she moved around the chair, her hand out to steady him.

They were so close he could smell the liquor on her breath, and she tilted slightly toward him. Did she want him to touch her or not?

He wanted to climb the stairs and kill the man who'd brought her to drink like a Bedouin after forty days and nights without an oasis. But he needed a hell of a lot more strength before he could even contemplate stairs. Already his breath had shortened and the strain of just standing using only one leg seemed monumental.

He took the glass from her hand. He dashed the remaining liquid on the fire. Blue flames hissed.

"I could get more," she said.

"Don't. You will regret it." He handed her the empty glass. He searched her eyes, which were clear and focused. "And you should not be alone when the drink kicks in."

Her chin dropped. "Don't worry. I won't be."

He heard the tinge of bitterness in her tone, slight but there nonetheless, like a hint of castor oil in Davidson's Elixir.

Hell with it. He nudged her chin up with his fingertips. Her skin was soft as a whisper and she smelled sweet like springtime. He could almost feel her lips against his, taste her breath, feel her heat. He leaned closer, allowing her every chance to pull away. The blue of her eyes was just a rim around her pupils. Her lips parted. The wonder of it took his breath. She was going to allow him to kiss her, and he wanted it like nothing he'd ever wanted before.

Chapter 8

Jack's rough fingers slid ever so slightly along her chin, and the air seemed thin. Her head felt light and her pulse thrummed wildly. His striped nightshirt covered a body that was hard with muscles formed by labor. He was not of her class, not a man with soft hands or bound by the restrictions of propriety.

He was not a man anyone would think she should use to father a baby, but she didn't fear him the way she did most men. She wanted to know what his kiss was like. Perhaps she'd wanted to know him in that way for a long time.

The door rattled, and she sprang back as if bitten.

Her head spun and she gripped the back of the chair to keep from falling. What on earth was she doing?

"Sorry, I'm late, ma'am," said the footman swinging through the door. "One of the gentlemen required a bath."

"Would you be so good as to fetch my cloak?" she said to him, wanting a minute to let the furious flush in her cheeks cool.

"Certainly, ma'am," said the footman. She could hear the surprise in his voice, but the servants knew better than to question her, unlike Jack.

"He will be back shortly," she hissed.

"I didn't mean to scare you." Jack reached back for the headboard, putting a decorous amount of space between them.

"You didn't." But was that why she could hear each heartbeat in her own ears? He had been close enough that she could feel his heat, smell his scent. Her head swirled, and she shook it off.

She turned slowly to face Jack. He had intended a transgression all the more egregious for his being a worker employed by her husband, and she had been about to allow it, encourage it possibly. But to use him as she would use one of the gentlemen felt as if she would taint what was between them. As she met his gaze, he only watched her with concern.

Had she imagined that he meant to kiss her? Her head was muddled.

"I must be feeling the spirits." Surely her complete lapse of judgment could be blamed on that.

A flicker of unease crossed his features. He tilted his head sideways as if to question her.

She looked at his face—really looked. By any standards he was a handsome man, with his even features, lips neither too fat nor thin, a nose that was straight and regular, brown eyes that emitted warmth and sparkle when he was amused or seriousness like they did now, but it was more than the sum of the parts.

The air charged as they regarded each other. The tick of the mantel clock seemed to slow. He glanced toward the door, breaking the spell.

She sighed. Disappointment or relief, she wasn't sure. Perhaps both. He was neither suitable for an affair nor well enough. He was just a millworker. Did she want intimacy with a man she'd have to see all the time at the mill? Certainly it wasn't as if she could continue an affair with him afterward.

She liked the companionable comfort of reading to him as the night settled in around them.

Did she want to ruin that by encouraging him to have sex with her?

Jack sat down on the bed and gingerly swung up his legs. He was breathing hard and his forehead was glistening with perspiration. If what little energy he'd expended standing had drained him this much, he surely wouldn't be up to the exertion needed to copulate. No, she'd already made arrangements for tonight.

Glancing at the clock, she wished the hands had ceased to move.

It was time to meet Mr. Whitton outside.

The whiskey burned in her stomach, not giving her the desired ease to go forward with her plan. She'd meant to sip more as she went along, but left most of the strong drink till the last. And Jack had tossed the last quarter of the glass's contents.

She had told Mr. Whitton she liked to walk to clear her head before bed. The interest that flickered in his eyes was like letting loose a herd of spiders on her shoulders. "I have to go."

"Don't," Jack said simply.

But his future rested on her success too. Everything rested on her ability to conceive. She looked for a reason to stay. The fire didn't need tending, his pillows didn't need plumping, and it wasn't time for his medicine.

"I think I need a bit of air to clear my head," she said, not that she owed him an explanation.

"Stay. Read another chapter," he coaxed.

His low voice pulled her like a flicker of light in a window might beckon a weary traveler to a warm hearth.

Mr. Whitton was waiting.

Jack arranged the covers and leaned back with a sigh, but stars above, the idea of sliding in beside him was tempting. Except there weren't any locks on the door and a servant could interrupt them at any minute. No, it would have to be one of the gentlemen.

The footman returned with her cloak draped over his arm.

"Good night, Mr. Applegate," Caroline murmured, and turned toward the door. "Please make sure he gets his medicine at midnight."

The footman nodded, and Caroline moved out into the entry hall. Before she could turn lily-livered, she marched across the marble expanse and out the front door.

The cool night air pounded her and made her gasp. She should slip back inside, the temperature too frigid to encourage a late night stroll.

At the foot of the stairs a round red orb like a single dragon's eye glared at her. The steps seemed to stretch and tilt, even though she knew them to be shallow.

A form separated from the plinth where a stone lion perched. She held her breath, waiting for the dark beast with the single glowing eye to show its scales and pointed tail, but after a second she saw only a man. The eye become the tip of a cigar. Mr. Whitton.

He'd waited.

She'd hoped he had given up and returned inside to the warmth and sanity of the house. She couldn't do this, she wanted to return back inside, but she had to.

Needing support for her shaky legs, she moved to the stone balustrade nearest him and began her descent.

"I hope you don't mind that I came out to smoke a cigar," Mr. Whitton said.

"No, of course not. Won't you join me for a stroll down the lane? The canal is lovely when the moonlight hits it just so."

"I should like to see it, then."

Too straight to have been formed by nature, the canal was nothing more than a broad ditch dug out to power the mill. Picturesque it was not, although she supposed if one were to make the effort, it could have been made pretty. But Mr. Broadhurst had little patience for making things pleasing to the eye. He certainly didn't want to encourage millworkers to cavort along the canal.

"I would love to have your company." Her polite dissemblings were like sand in her mouth and nearly as hard to get out. "I dislike walking alone."

He sucked on the cigar. The tip flared red, taunting her with its insubstantial heat.

"Seems old man winter is on his way," she offered. She had descended into making banal observations about the weather.

He grunted rather than respond.

The macadam crunched under their feet as they walked down the drive. The silence hung over them like a heavy shroud.

"You were telling me of your travels about France. I should love to hear more." She'd been bored to tears earlier by his dry recitation of the places he'd been. He spoke of his travels as a crusty historian might speak of a battle date and location, without relaying any stories of the men who fought or fell there.

"I spent two days in Chartres."

"Ah, you must have seen the cathedral," she said. "Is it very beautiful?"

"Yes, quite."

Caroline laced her arm through his and pressed close. "Tell me what you shaw . . . saw." Surely that would prompt him beyond monosyllabic answers.

"Lots of spires, stained glass." He shrugged. "It was a cathedral. I saw what I'd expect to see."

"Did it move you?" she asked.

"Move me?" he muttered.

Caroline made an *mmm* sound rather than try to explain what she wasn't sure she meant.

"I can't say as I had a religious experience, if that is what you mean."

The dark had taken on a fuzziness Caroline wasn't sure was warranted. And she didn't remember the drive being so dashed uneven. She clung tighter to Mr. Whitton's arm. "That's good, I shuppose."

It wasn't as if she needed him being a zealot. After all, what true believer would commit adultery?

They walked along in silence. She felt less inclination to break it. She'd made the first effort and now her brain felt sluggish and worn-out.

Her tongue had swollen like a winter-ready caterpillar, while her toes grew wooden. Already she wished she'd stayed with Jack. He was so much easier to talk to.

The leaves crinkled with a chill wind, and those that had already fallen scuttled along the pavement like little furry creatures. Mr. Whitton's arm tensed.

"Are you certain it is safe for you to walk alone at night?"

Was he concerned about her safety or his?

"You'll protect me." She wished he'd warm her. The only part of her that felt warm was the boiling mass in her stomach. No wonder sailors called it rotgut, because that was exactly what it felt like—as if her innards were dissolving in a vat of acid.

He raised his cigar, and the glowing tip seemed to dance. Caroline closed her eyes against the jagged movements, but that was worse. Everything was spinning. She opened her eyes again determined to find her bearings.

He dropped the cigar and ground it out with his heel. "Perhaps we should start back."

She looked back to find the house wavering in the distance. The lamps burning by the doors seemed to hop about. "I'm sorry I'm not a good conversationalist."

She silently celebrated that she'd managed to get that word around the fuzzy caterpillar in her mouth.

He grunted.

"I jush . . . just get lonely."

"What of your husband?"

"He is a good . . . man." Caroline searched desperately for the right thing to say and came up blank.

"What would he say if he knew you were out here alone with me?"

He'd be shouting encouragement or asking why she hadn't met Mr. Whitton in his bedroom. "I . . . he is . . . too old. He can't anymore."

Mr. Whitton stopped walking.

Caroline stumbled and then looked at the ground for the rock or log that tripped her, but as she pulled her skirts back she saw nothing but the flat surface of the drive.

The man said nothing.

Her stomach continued to rot. The opportunity was slipping away. Did she have to spell it out for him letter by letter? "I have needs," she whispered.

"And you had your brother gather together men so you could pick one to service your 'needs'?"

"God no!" She stared at the man, but his features were too blurry for her to understand.

"I . . . no. Nothing to do with . . . arrangements. I thought, since you are here." Her head bobbed back and forth without her meaning it to. She struggled to gain control of her body, which felt as if it were ready to fall off her bones. Finally, the drink was hitting her. She had a moment of realizing the sensation of not caring must be what heavy drinkers sought. "I wished I'd given Mr. Broadhusht a baby and now he can't . . . can't . . ."

"Perform?"

"Yesh." Finally, Mr. Whitton seemed to understand.

"You want me to give you a baby?"

"Yesh."

"How much have you had to drink?"

Caroline rolled her eyes and then wished she hadn't, as the world kept right on rolling after she stopped moving her eyes. " 'Nough."

He tugged on her arm and moved her into the dark shadows of the trees.

The rough bark bit into her back and startled her out of a stupor. She knew she'd moved because they weren't on the paved drive anymore, but she could not remember how. He bent and pressed his mouth against hers. Her head lolled to the side. He repositioned her head. The smell of cigar smoke hung thickly on him.

His tongue thrust between her lips as his hand closed around one breast. He tasted sour and smoky, like a wet ashcan. She fought her revulsion and tried to pretend she liked his kiss, while a new hoard of spiders with cold clickety-clacking legs crawled over her. But it was too much. Her gorge rose in her throat. She futilely shoved him as she dropped to her knees and was sick all over his thighs.

Sometime in the night, her room had stopped spinning, but with the morning light her head pounded. She was afraid to move for fear her stomach would revolt again. And what in heaven's name had she told Mr. Whitton? She vaguely remembered asking him to give her a baby. How could she have been so stupid?

Her cheeks burned as she remembered the humiliating apologies, blaming the cigar and Mr. Whitton's calm questions about the canal, which he found and immersed himself in, while she fretted about him drowning—in four feet of water. But he emerged wet, cold, and uninterested. Oh he had been gentleman enough to drag her weaving, unresponsive-to-commands-body back inside. At her insistence, he'd left her slumped on a bench in the entry hall.

She wasn't entirely certain how she made it to her bedroom. She thought she might have crawled up the stairs and then slithered along the wall. For a person with two good legs, her inability to ambulate was shameful.

Groaning, Caroline rolled to her side. She would have pulled a pillow over her head to block the excruciating light, but she'd had all her extras taken down to Jack. Her stomach boiled like a witches' cauldron.

Jack. Would he be open to a brief affair with her? She'd thought he was about to kiss her when the footman interrupted them. She'd have to move Jack to a bedroom with locks on the door. All the guest bedrooms were occupied. Her pounding head protested solving a problem as if an engineer decided to install hydraulic looms and they were knocking back and forth against her skull.

"Ma'am, did you want woken?" her maid asked in a booming whisper.

Caroline jerked upright. "What o'clock is it?"

"It's gone seven, ma'am."

Heavens, she never slept past six, let alone seven. She would be late for the mill office. "I will be down directly."

Moving slowly, Caroline swung her feet to the floor. Her

head pounded, but at least her limbs functioned. Her maid had brought a large basin and towels, and Caroline reached to strip off what remained of her petticoats—apparently she hadn't made it into a nightgown.

But the moment she tried to stand up, her stomach rebelled. She swallowed hard, trying to control the revolt of her body. How on earth was she going to function today, feeling as if she'd been bowled over by a locomotive?

The visitors had started shortly after dawn. The footman dozing in the chair beside Jack jerked awake and then went out across the tiled floor to open the door. He returned with an uncertain look on his face and asked if Jack was "at home."

After a couple of minutes back and forth, Jack realized he could turn the visitors away. But of course he didn't.

He scooted up and leaned against the extra pillows. He appreciated the well-wishers, he really did, but his leg ached and he wanted Mrs. Broadhurst's quiet presence.

"You're a lucky fellow . . . but I guess you ain't out of the woods yet," muttered Abel while rolling his cap in his hand. "George stopped the doctor, and he told us to give you a couple of days of rest afore visiting."

Jack didn't feel so lucky, but he nodded.

"I'd say he landed on a mighty soft pillow," said another, whistling as he craned his head toward the tinwork on the ceiling.

"Thinks he deserves to live here and was bound to get here any way he could," said George, who'd been his closest friend before he married and his wife popped out three babies. Now, George had little time for him. Or they no longer had much in common. George concentrated on feeding his family, while Jack worked hard to avoid one.

"I didn't want to be brought here," he objected.

George patted his shoulder and gave a small mocking smile that took the sting out of his words. "I know, but you enjoy it while it lasts."

"Take care in what you wish for," muttered another man, evoking a chorus of murmured agreements.

Jack pushed his lips together. He had wished to *earn* a better life, not be pampered because he was injured. "I'd rather be working."

"We took a collection to help you out." George thrust a bundled handkerchief in Jack's direction.

"You shouldn't have." Jack eyed the clinking bundle with trepidation. He didn't want their charity, but he'd been the one to start such collections before. Just last year he'd gone around for Mattie's mother to help pay for her husband's burial. Taking the money was like admitting he would never be able to support himself again.

"You could pay the doctor."

To not take the collection would undoubtedly make the others think he thought so much of himself that he didn't need their money. In truth, he had a good-sized stash at home. He'd been saving for years.

George pulled back the handkerchief. "'Course, I could always give it to Martha. Wants a new stove, does she?"

It was too much to hope that the argument he'd had with his stepmother hadn't been repeated all around the village. He'd said things he shouldn't have, but so had Martha. The more he'd tried to stay calm, the more she shouted, while his father drank more gin.

Jack reached for the handkerchief. The bundle was slim, probably no more than a few shillings in total. Would his misfortune have been worth more if Martha hadn't been shouting that he thought he was too good to live like the rest of them? "Thank you."

Jack tucked the handkerchief under his pillows. A few of his family members hung back near the wall. He hadn't expected his father to manage the walk with his back, nor did he expect Martha with all the little ones, but an emptiness yawned inside him. Were the rest siding with Martha? His shoulders sagged with weariness.

The deep ache in his anklebone made him grit his teeth. He didn't think he was better than anyone. He just hated a life lived with nothing to show for it. He wanted to put a mark on the world, make something of himself, earn enough to live easily.

After a spell, Lucy shouldered her way through the throng. Her blue eyes were big and her heavy blond hair looked as if she'd pinned it up without a mirror. "Jack!"

He sighed. Once upon a time he'd liked that Lucy often looked like she'd just tumbled out of bed. Now he wondered whose bed besides his she'd tumbled out of. Not that Lucy would be stupid enough to get caught playing two men against each other. And lately she'd been laying claim to him in more and more obvious ways. As he always did when a girl started to think she owned him, he'd made excuses and stopped spending time alone with her. Or at least avoided intimacies that could lead to getting trapped.

She made a show of plumping his pillows and adjusting his covers.

"Leave it," he said.

Her eyes narrowed for just a second before she patted his hand as if he were just a grouchy boy. They both knew she was hanging onto him because she thought he might be the one to make a better life. He was already a lead mechanic, even though he was younger than the other mechanics by a decade. But the time had long since past when he would have proposed if he was going to. He should have made a clean break months ago.

Jack caught the glances at the bottom of his bed, but ignored the blatant curiosity.

A maid came in carrying an ash bucket, and a footman followed with a coal bucket. The two bent and made quick work of cleaning the remains of last night's fire and getting a new one flaring. The villagers watched and tried to stay out their way. The servants pretended they weren't there and left without fanfare once their duty was discharged. But it had dampened conversation.

"Best be getting on before the horn blows." One of the men ran his thumbs along the underside of his braces as if they had grown too tight. They needed to get to the mill before work started.

Jack didn't protest. Instead he thanked everyone for coming and wished for another dose of laudanum. The gray wall between his pain and him had been lowering for hours, until it was just a thin wisp of nothingness.

They all filtered out while the footman looked uncertain as to whether he should hold the door. He settled for standing near, probably to make sure the silver salver or the vases on the table near the entrance didn't exit with any of his visitors.

Lucy didn't leave. Instead she sat down in Mrs. Broadhurst's chair and reached for his hand.

"Would you be needing anything before I leave you, sir?" asked the footman.

"I'll take care of him," Lucy said before Jack got his mouth open.

The footman screwed up his face and then shut the door.

"Great. I need help to piss." Jack sat up. He'd bet his last ha'penny Lucy wouldn't help him.

She recoiled. "Jack!"

"Better call him back." Jack reclined against the pillows.

"But—"

"Don't you need to get to the mill?"

"I'm not working today. I'm here to take care of you."

Jack ground his teeth. The last thing he needed was more people taking care of him. And he'd rather she wasn't around when Mrs. Broadhurst checked in on him. Last night he was certain she would have allowed him to kiss her were it not for the interruption. He just hoped it wasn't only the haze of intoxication offering him encouragement. "Lucy, go to work."

Lucy reached to brush his hair away from his forehead, and he batted her hand away.

She scowled at him. "Why didn't you take me to London with you?"

Jack closed his eyes. He'd postponed marriage and a family of his own partly to help out his stepmother and his father, but mostly to not have his future held hostage by a wife and children. Once a man was responsible for more mouths than his own, he couldn't take risks. "Lucy, I don't need you weighing me down."

She patted his arm. "Looks to me like you'll need my help when you go back to London now. Your sister told me you have a job there."

He pushed her hand away. "Lucy—"

"I would go with you, Jack. I want to live in London."

Did she plan on supporting him until he was healed? "In that case, you really should go to the mill. You'll need the money for your fare, because I'm not taking you. You go to London on your own. We're done."

The whistle at the mill blew, announcing the workday had begun.

"You don't mean that," she said.

He did mean it, and he'd said it before. "Go to work, Lucy. I don't want you anymore."

She pouted and sulked, then stormed at him for leading her down the primrose path and not being willing to make an honest woman of her. He'd never lied to her or ever implied he'd marry her. Desperately, Jack tried to get her to leave. "I don't know that I'll ever be fit for work again. I'll probably be a beggar from here on out."

She looked around the room. "If this is the kind of charity you'll receive, it may not be so bad."

Hadn't she heard him? Jack rolled his eyes. "Don't count on it."

Lucy cast him a skeptical look. "Mrs. Broadhurst has never taken such a special interest in any other accident victim."

A flash of uneasy excitement raced through Jack. Last night, had she been hinting that he might have other benefits to recovering under her care? In the cold light of day it was too fantastic to believe she might stoop to a liaison with him. "She had her reasons. She wants the little ones out of the mill and in school."

Perhaps she wanted an excuse to get away from her guests. Her staff were as confused as he was about her motives, but it hadn't stopped them from speculating or grousing about the extra workload. "But I won't be taking any more charity from her as soon as I'm back on my feet."

Jack put his arm over his eyes. He had to stop thinking about Mrs. Broadhurst in that way. She was married, and he'd never consorted with married women. But if she were a widow . . . and he wasn't dependent on her care . . . and they were friends of a sort.

Lucy rubbed his arm. "Take me to London with you."

"No."

She leaned over, pressing her breasts into his chest and breathing against his chin. "Jack, you have a job there, don't you? It'll be lovely."

"It's not a certainty, especially not now." He was still going to London, but the last thing he wanted was Lucy following him. "I told you I wouldn't marry you."

She frowned. "I'll find work to help out. You'll need my help."

He wasn't in any shape to support a wife, and he'd be damned before he depended on a woman to support him.

The door opened and Lucy sat up rapidly.

"Oh, excuse me," Mrs. Broadhurst said.

Jack winced. He lowered his arm. Lucy belatedly jumped to her feet and bobbed an awkward curtsy.

But Mrs. Broadhurst was already pulling the door shut.

"Wait." He sat up and pushed the covers down.

Mrs. Broadhurst hesitated in the doorway, lit by the rosy streams of the rising sunlight. Her brownish-purple-colored gown this morning was buttoned to her neck. He regretted that he wouldn't get to see the morning sun on the skin of her shoulders.

And how was she doing after her bender last night?

Her lips pursed and her eyebrows were drawn together as if she were hurting.

"I need to use that room again." Damn was that the best he could think of to keep her from leaving? "It's not urgent. I'd just like to wash up." But damn Lucy for making it look as though they were still a couple.

Chapter 9

Her heart fluttering, Caroline sucked in a deep breath as she lingered in the doorway. She'd only meant to look in on Jack before heading to the mill office, but she was reluctant to leave him alone with the young woman who hadn't the sense to realize he was in pain.

Who was the girl? For a second she thought to march across the room and yank her off him. But with dawning dismay she realized the girl might be Jack's wife.

However, he'd expressed his needs to her, and she took that little piece and hung onto it. Of course it could be that he saw her as his benevolent benefactress, which made sense. It wasn't as if she were anything more. Her stomach ached, her chest ached, hell, her head especially ached.

She stepped out and beckoned to the footman standing at the dining room doors. After issuing instructions, she returned, pasted on a smile and said to Jack, "We'll have you fixed up in a trice."

He nodded with a grimace. His forehead was furrowed and his breathing was rapid.

Fearing that the putrid fever the doctor warned could kill him yet, Caroline crossed to Jack, leaned down and placed her palm against his forehead. His skin was clammy. No fever.

She breathed a sigh of relief, but the furrows under her hand hadn't smoothed out. Much as he tried to hide it, the pain was visible in the white brackets around his mouth. He, at least, had a better reason for his pain than she did. "Have you had any medicine since waking this morning?"

He shook his head.

Goodness, how long had he suffered in silence? She moved to the sideboard, poured the dose into a glass and added a little water. As he took the glass, his fingers brushed hers and a jolt ran up her arm.

"You should have told me to get your medicine," the blond woman said petulantly.

Jack drank the liquid quickly but gagged on the bitter laudanum. Nothing could mask the taste, but she could add sugar as he'd suggested might help with the whiskey. He turned his face away as if her scrutiny made him uncomfortable.

Caroline clasped her hands in front of her waist and turned to address the woman standing to one side. "The servants tell me there have been quite a few visitors already. I am glad so many are concerned for his welfare. Are you . . . family?"

"She's just a friend." Jack stared at the floor instead of looking at either of them.

"A particular friend," the young woman corrected.

Caroline's shoulders relaxed and she barely restrained her sigh of relief. Not a wife, then.

Jack sighed. "Mrs. Broadhurst, may I present Miss Dugan?"

Although Jack had managed the nicety of a proper introduction, he seemed reluctant. "Lucy, Mrs. Broadhurst."

"Nice to meet you, Miss Dugan," Caroline said perfunctorily.

Lucy nodded as if she were the queen. Caroline resisted making a comment. If the village children had more schooling, proper manners would have been part of their broader education. But she was inclined to dislike the young woman on sight because of the easy way she had been draped across Jack. A dawning realization stabbed at Caroline. Lucy must be his sweetheart.

Jack held out the empty glass. "Thank you."

Careful to avoid his fingers, Caroline took the glass from his hand. His gaze traveled up her arm and landed on her face. Her skin tingled almost as if he actually touched her. Her lips parted to speak, but her mind went blank and nothing came out. She couldn't seduce Jack if he were promised to another woman. A prettier, younger, *blond* woman.

If she had not been worrying so much about how and when she would seduce him, she might not have noticed the way Jack's touch made her quiver. Not that he was in any sort of condition for that sort of activity, and even if he had been, Lucy was probably the one he would want to do that with. Caroline's cheeks heated.

Lucy made a noise and then turned to Jack, her eyes narrowing.

The footman entered the room. "I have everything you asked for, ma'am." He turned to Jack. "The water closet is ready for you, sir."

Jack swiveled his legs to the side.

"Oh my God!" Lucy put her hands in front of her mouth. "You're still bleeding."

"The surgeon couldn't close the incision because of the swelling," said Caroline. "But he was able to return most of the pieces of bone to their proper alignment and fasten them together with silver wire."

Lucy clamped her hands tight against her lips and stared with horror at the bloody bandage.

Caroline swatted off a pesky fly of irritation. The young woman might be genuinely concerned for Jack, but if she was having trouble looking at his dressing, how would she have fared watching the surgeon work?

Jack met Caroline's eyes and his eyebrows dipped in question. "Feels like he took a sledgehammer to it."

"More like a gimlet."

"Still, that's much better than a saw." The ghost of a smile crossed his lips.

Lucy moaned.

Caroline was too irritated and too ill after last night's overindulgence to care if discussing Jack's surgery bothered the girl. He watched her, his expression curious. No doubt he wanted to know more about the surgery.

"It was a much more complex procedure than I anticipated." Caroline signaled the footman. "I believe Dr. Hein will better explain what he did, if you ask him."

She would have to send the doctor a note to collect her at the mill, so she could be here when he checked on Jack. As it was, she was already late.

The footman sat on the bed by Jack's good leg, while Caroline took her position to his right. They both pulled his arms across their shoulders.

"Ready?" she asked.

Jack nodded.

The three of them stood as a unit, while Lucy gaped in amazement.

They navigated him toward the open double doors. His steps were more normal than the hops he'd taken with just her yesterday. She hoped it was less jarring for him with the footman able to bear the bulk of Jack's weight.

"Steven has brought you a tall stool that you can use to balance. You will find all the toiletries and towels you should need." She tried to talk normally and not think about her arm around his waist, or his physique.

They reached the open door of the water closet. As she'd ordered, a fresh nightshirt and undergarments lay next to the basin. A comb, toothbrush, and tooth powder jar lay on a towel.

Jack tried to speak, but what came out was a weak cough, which he tried to catch in his shoulder, but not before she'd seen his eyes were watering. Did such a small kindness choke him up?

"Mr. Broadhurst's valet will come down and shave you, once he is done abovestairs." Resisting the urge to pat or rub Jack, she slid out from under his arm.

He had composed himself. "That's not necessary. I can—"

"Forgive me if picturing you with a razor in your hand with the difficulty you have maintaining your balance is unsettling."

"Gruesome image, is it?" Jack mocked.

"I fear I could lose the servants. They can tolerate only so much bloodletting."

Jack searched her eyes, his expression blank. She let her lips curl to let him know she was teasing. He tried a smile, but it faltered as she drew her supportive hand away. Really, she had hung on to him far longer than necessary to make sure he was steady.

"I will leave you to Steven's care now." She smiled brightly and wondered what was wrong with her that she wanted to hover and help him with his personal preparations for the day. Surely it was just an overabundance of concern for his welfare. It wasn't as if a man found a woman hovering at his elbow as he performed his ablutions attractive. He probably preferred privacy. If she were in his place, she would.

Caroline returned to the breakfast room, where Jack's bed had been set up, alarmed that she even wanted to hang onto him. "Will you be staying long, Miss Dugan?"

It was ungracious of her, but when she'd opened the door and seen Miss Dugan and Jack in an embrace, her breath had been snatched away. But why hadn't the young woman seen Jack's deeply furrowed brow and grimace of pain or done anything for him?

Miss Dugan lifted her chin. "I came to take care of him."

"I assure you, Mr. Applegate is getting the best care possible." *Nothing for you to do but go home.*

Without Jack in the room, Caroline took in the young woman's dewy skin, pink lips, and pert features. She turned to the sideboard hoping to compose her expression and blot out the resentment that threatened to swamp her. She supposed it could be that Miss Dugan had blond curls that had been made messy in whatever she was doing with Jack before the door opened. Or that her skin had the dewy softness that only young women retained, which reminded Caroline of how far past the first blush of youth she was. But really, seeing the pretty girl with Jack made her want to claw out Miss Dugan's eyes.

Caroline had no business feeling proprietary about him. And if this young woman offered him comfort, she should not interfere. She swallowed hard. "Although in a few weeks when he is well enough to go home, he will need friends to help care for him."

"He will hate that," said Miss Dugan.

Caroline's animosity drained out of her. She had no idea what Jack would or wouldn't like. "I imagine you know him better than I."

"I do," averred Miss Dugan. "I mean he doesn't even want to marry until he can support me and any children in comfort. Not that he couldn't now, but for he provides so much for his kinfolk."

Dismay sliced through Caroline, and she had to work hard to keep her hands relaxed in a ladylike manner. He was an engaged man and she'd nearly thrown herself at him. Thank God she'd found out before she made a complete fool of herself and asked him to bed her.

She couldn't interfere in Jack's happiness. It wasn't as if they could . . . as if there could be anything more than the attempts to get pregnant. He was planning a life with pretty, blond Miss Dugan, after all.

Fighting the burn of tears in her eyes, she moved along the sideboard straightening the pitcher and lining up the spoon next to the laudanum bottle. Although last night she'd thought Jack might be a potential candidate, she wouldn't touch him again—or at least no more than she needed to help him.

"Would you help Steven assist Jack back to bed when he is done, Miss Dugan?" Caroline thought her voice sounded fairly normal. The higher pitch was probably only noticeable to her. After Miss Dugan's nod, she added, "I will leave you to him, then."

Wanting to be alone, she couldn't exit the room fast enough, but as she entered the hall, Robert grabbed her arm. "I thought you had gone to the mill."

"I'm late," she rasped out. God, she would likely feel a thousand times better if she could just lop off her head.

Since Robert was here, the rest of the men must be too. Dread tightened her spine. She wasn't ready to face them, or to let Mr. Whitton know there would be no repeat of last night's drinking fiasco, but she was still willing to participate in the parts that could lead to a baby.

Robert tugged her back toward the stairs. "What the devil is going on, Caro?"

"You don't have to shout." Couldn't he just leave her alone?

"I'm not shouting!"

He most certainly was shouting. If he continued, her head would crack open. "Why aren't you out hunting or fishing or whatever entertainment was scheduled today?"

"We'll go out after things settle." He looked over his shoulder as if aware he shouldn't be overheard, and dropped his voice to a level that only mildly blasted her. "Besides, Langley is leaving this morning and Whitton decided to accompany him back to town. The men will wish to see them off."

Had her illness repulsed Mr. Whitton as much as that? The idea of starting anew with another of the guests was like a draught of bitter poison. She'd thought if she couldn't entice Jack, perhaps she could persuade Mr. Whitton to make the attempt again. He at least seemed willing before she botched it. She pressed the heel of her hand against her head. She was trying, but it seemed a hopeless cause. What else could possibly go wrong?

The butler strode through the hall and opened the front door as several footmen exited, carrying luggage to a carriage waiting at the bottom of the stairs.

The library door opened and Mr. Whitton emerged. Mr. Broadhurst stood behind him, making Mr. Whitton look almost juvenile. Or was it just that her husband's stooped shoulders, bushy gray eyebrows, and loose skin marked his age? Her thoughts flitted back to Tremont's accusation that her husband was ill and didn't have long for this world.

Mr. Broadhurst turned his cold gaze on her as he was

about to shut the door. His hands fisted and he stepped out into the hall. "Caroline!" She winced at his thundering anger. "Why aren't you at the mill?"

Robert moved protectively closer to her.

She fought the urge to turn tail and run. Taking a step forward, she extended her hand to Mr. Whitton. Her ears burned as her humiliation from last night was complete. "I'm sorry to hear you're leaving us. You will be missed."

"Ah well, duty calls." Mr. Whitton didn't even bat an eyelid at his polite fiction. Duty hadn't had a chance to call. He grasped her hand limply and stepped back quickly, his mouth tilted in a smirk. "I've already taken my leave of your husband."

Dear Lord, what had he said to Mr. Broadhurst?

The door to the gentleman's saloon opened and smoke wafted out. Her stomach roiled and bile rose in her throat, but she refused to get sick again. The gentlemen all watched her like pigeons waiting for crumbs.

Now would be the time that Amelia or Sarah would throw their hands against their foreheads and say they felt faint, or when they might gracefully swoon into Robert's arms, but she was not the swooning type.

"Mr. Broadhurst," she said, "a word with you in your study, if you please." She wanted to tell everyone to leave her alone, but she would have to deal with all of it. "Robert, check on Lord Langley and ascertain if he needs any assistance before he leaves."

Robert's jaw dropped.

Mr. Broadhurst folded his arms and glowered at her.

"Now," she added. Of course it wasn't her place to order the head of her family around, but she'd had more than she could take on the best of days—and this most certainly wasn't the best of days.

The doctor chose that moment to appear in the open doorway, his arm through a pair of wooden crutches and a paper sack in his hand. Why not? Surely another dozen witnesses to her anguish were about to appear, and she would have no time to compose herself.

"Ah, good, Dr. Hein, I will be with you shortly, and I have a favor to ask of you." First she had to deal with her husband.

With as much dignity as she could muster, she walked past a dumbstruck Mr. Whitton and her furious husband, through the library door, and into the inner sanctum of her husband's study.

She waited until Mr. Broadhurst joined her.

"You cannot order me about," he said. "I won't have it."

She simply shut the door behind him and with her dignity straining sat down in one of the chairs. "If you expect me to continue on the course I set, then you will allow the doctor to assure me that you will be around to welcome a child into this world."

"Did you—"

She swatted away his question like a pesky gnat. It didn't bear mentioning that the man she'd arranged to have a liaison with was now gone. "The doctor is here now. And I do not know that some illness or perception of illness on your part brought on this desire to insist upon children now."

"You turned nine and twenty on your last birth anniversary. Before you know it, you'll be too old to conceive."

Her age, not his. How like him to make this about her age, rather than his failings. She struggled to remain upright with her shoulders back. The demons of hell pulled on her and pressed on her and pounded the insides of her skull with instruments of torture. "And your health, sir?"

"My health is fine."

"No it isn't. You don't always walk to the mill anymore.

And I do not want to give birth with a husband on his death-bed. You must be around to protect my good name and reputation and that of the child." For at least a year or two.

"By all that is holy, you will play your part in this bargain with no further concessions or I will cut off my payments to your brother. I will send the little children back to work and I will petition Parliament for a divorce."

Icy liquid poured down her spine. She gasped. "You cannot do that."

"I can. Nesham can fight me in court if he wills it, but no judge will rule that you have upheld your end of the marriage contract. Your bloodline was what I bought and paid for. Now, did you meet with one of the gentlemen or not?"

Was that all she was to him, a broodmare with the right bloodline? Did he have no finer feeling toward her? Reeling, she swallowed hard, then forced herself to meet his eyes with disdain.

"Yes, I had a tryst with one of the gentlemen," she said with all the wintry coldness she felt. It wasn't a complete lie, although in her prayers she could pretend she was misleading Mr. Broadhurst into thinking the end had been rather different. Although, a little lie hardly compared to committing adultery, as far as her soul went.

Broadhurst scoffed. "Next time you arrange a tryst, you should not push your paramour into the canal." He stood and his voice knifed through her aching head.

Surely, Mr. Whitton hadn't informed her husband about last night's meeting.

"You are misinformed. He did go into the canal, but it was of his own volition. I am sure he assumed wet clothing would be easier to explain than stained."

Mr. Broadhurst jerked back.

Her face might turn to cinders; it could only flame so hot so long. "You will not divorce me, because I have not given you cause."

"Did you not have a tryst with Whitton last night?" Mr. Broadhurst asked with silky smoothness.

Feeling like a mouse caught under a cat's paw, Caroline kept her movements deliberately slow as she rose and leaned over his desk. He had even involved her entire family in setting her up to have an illicit affair. Had it all been so he had grounds to divorce her? Or did he only mean to hold all the cards in this game he played? More likely he wanted to keep all his options open. If she did not succeed in giving him a child, her adulterous behavior could be used as grounds for a divorce.

A cold rage poured through her, leaving empty channels behind. She would not be so used. She was done with being the perfect lady. If Broadhurst wanted war, he had seriously underestimated her strengths.

He'd destroyed any affection she might have ever had for him. She thoroughly despised him and his underhanded tactics, and she wouldn't be treated so cavalierly. If he thought all her years of obedience were indicative of her not having a spine, he was dead wrong. She had years of leaders in her blood, before a title was conferred on one of her forebearers, her ancestors had been knights and warriors. Their blood ran in her veins and she summoned it now.

"You will not even think of divorce, or I and my family will do whatever it takes to destroy you. Your contracts will dry up, your goods won't be shipped, and you'll be ruined."

She didn't know if her family retained enough clout to destroy him, but surely they could inflict damage to his reputation and standing in the business community. If he was willing to pay for their influence, he must think the lack would hurt him. And if they began campaigning against him, so much the better.

She shook with raw fury. She hadn't endured over fifteen years of marriage to be cast aside like a moldy crust of bread. She hadn't agreed to this unholy bargain to have it twisted into a means to destroy her.

Her husband regarded her speculatively. "You'd never do a thing that would hurt the millworkers."

"There are limits to what even I will take, Mr. Broadhurst. Do not think I am without any recourse." Her mouth felt odd, as if a demon had crawled inside her and was attempting to snarl and snap like a rabid dog. "My family retains enough influence to have you charged with a crime and sent to prison."

She had probably overstated the case, but Mr. Broadhurst hung his head down like a whipped dog.

"Very well, you have made your point," he said stiffly.

Her ire was feeding her like a shark in bloody waters. "And you will hire Mr. Applegate to work as a clerk until he can resume his old work."

"I will try him, but if he can't do the work, I will not keep him on."

"What is it you want? A baby or decimation?"

He glanced at her uncertainly. Dear Lord, he must be ill, to be cowing to her disingenuous argument. "A son bearing my name."

"Then you should bear in mind that shocks are bad for a pregnant woman and act accordingly."

Broadhurst stared at her, his skepticism shining through. "You had relations with Whitton, eh?"

She pushed her lips together. She would not give him any ammunition to use against her.

"Is this why you are already neglecting the mill?"

"I have every intention of going in shortly." Two days and he was already questioning her ability to run the place. Although, it was as much her fault for oversleeping. "I didn't feel well this morning." She'd drunk too much, but she'd let him draw his own conclusions.

Mr. Broadhurst leaned forward and tilted his head. "Perhaps you're already breeding."

Her face went hot. "I believe it would be impossible to know for certain." Caroline had no more cards to play without revealing how weak her hand was. Instead she reached for the door handle. "I will send in the doctor when he is done with Mr. Applegate."

"Tell him to be quick. I have an errand I need to discharge today."

"I will ask the doctor to be fast," she conceded. A man must have his little victories, she supposed.

Mr. Broadhurst assessed her coldly. "I will go in tomorrow to manage payroll and assess your work thus far."

She supposed it was a warning to make certain all the mill business was well in hand, but she was on top of everything.

Holding her spine stiff, she walked through the library and tried to keep from shattering into a million shards. Her husband was a ruthless man—he was hard-nosed and unfeeling in business dealings, but she hadn't thought such practices would extend to his wife. Regardless of how much she despised him, she needed him alive to shelter her reputation, especially if she had revealed too much to Mr. Whitton. But her victory felt too easily won, and she dreaded what Mr. Broadhurst's next move might be.

Chapter 10

J ack drifted on the morphine-induced haze, yet the knifing pain in his leg following the doctor stitching the surgical site, and then encasing most of his foot and leg to above the knee in a plaster of paris splint, wouldn't let him settle all the way into sleep. He stared at the gray behind his eyelids and waited for Mrs. Broadhurst to return.

Just as he was nodding off, the door clicked open.

The scratch of a chair told him the other occupant had stood.

"Mary, would you be so good as to fetch a spot of tea and a bun or bread and jam." Mrs. Broadhurst's voice flowed across the room and settled over him like a warm blanket pulling him deeper into the nothingness that proceeded sleep.

"Yes, ma'am," said his minder, and the door clicked again.

"I assume you wanted to talk. Is there somewhere we can be private?" asked the man in the room.

Interest perked Jack's senses. He wanted to learn everything he could about Mrs. Broadhurst.

"We're private enough here," she said. "I only have a few minutes before I have to go."

"But what about him?" the man objected.

"The doctor gives him an injection and he usually sleeps for a few hours afterward."

Jack's eyelids seemed fastened shut, and he sunk deeper into the mattress as if he no longer had any muscles.

Mrs. Broadhurst laid her hand on his forehead, and it seemed to release him. He had been waiting for her touch and now the world was right again.

When her hand crossed his brow, he strained to feel the silky softness of her palms. The smoothness came from the lack of labor. Her hands bore no calluses, or rather only a small one on her middle finger from holding a pen. Her nails were never broken and always buffed. She was too fine for the likes of him, but he had begun to need her touch.

"Did things go badly with Whitton? Is that why he left?" asked the man in a low whisper.

Mrs. Broadhurst leaned over and smoothed the blankets. Jack tried to open his eyes but succeeded in only a tiny crack where he could see little through the blur of his lashes. The drug had damn near made him insensible, but he supposed he welcomed the heavy curtain it made between him and the pain.

"Robert, how much money does Mr. Broadhurst send you annually?"

"Really, Caro—"

"I deserve to know what will be lost if Mr. Broadhurst divorces me."

Hope blossomed in Jack's chest. It was an odd thing, but with his rational mind muted by the morphine, he wanted to believe she would be available—not that she'd ever consider marriage to the likes of him, but perhaps a friendship.

"He's not going to divorce you, Caroline," exclaimed the man, Robert—he must be her brother or he would not be calling her by her given name.

She turned away. Jack could only see the purplish brown material of the gown she wore. It was the kind of thing she wore to the mill office, not the flashy, fussy kind of clothes she wore around her guests. Her everyday dresses were of Broadhurst-milled material, same as the women of the village, but she was always set apart by more than the better cut and trim. Her regal bearing and refinement were present in every movement she made. Even the first time he'd seen her, he noticed her quiet dignity. Yet, she'd been little more than a child with a husband more than thrice her age.

"He may," Mrs. Broadhurst replied.

"If you do as he wishes, he won't."

"How much? I know the original sum paid to Papa was around twenty thousand pounds."

Jack wondered if he had gasped. He felt as if he should have. It was an outrageous sum, more money than would pass through his family's hands in their entire lifetime. Probably two or three times as much as the entire eighteen members of his family and their current and future spouses would ever see even if they counted every penny ever made.

"Three thousand pounds per annum," answered the man.

Jack felt as if the hope had been crushed under the heel of a jackboot. He would never have so much to offer.

"Why do you think that is?" asked Caroline. "With the five-thousand-pound dowries paid for our sisters, Mr. Broadhurst has paid a king's ransom for me. What is that, seventy-five, eighty thousand to date?"

Eighty-two thousand, calculated Jack. Good God, how much money did Broadhurst have?

"Not a king's ransom. Richard the Lionhearted's ransom was one hundred and fifty marks, but of course a mark is less than a pound. So perhaps it is close to a king's—"

"Robert," Caroline cut through her brother's dithering. "Don't you find it odd he would pay so much for me? Mr. Broadhurst is a man who never makes a bad business decision."

"He has benefited immeasurably by his association with our family. The mill has prospered, we have all seen to it."

"Don't be silly. If he had invested that sum in another mill or two, or even on the Exchange, he would have made a great deal more." The chair creaked as Mrs. Broadhurst sat down beside the bed. "Other families such as ours had daughters they might have been willing to part with for far less, and it is not as if I am any great beauty—"

Jack raised his hand to protest. She was beautiful.

"—or our stature is so high within the realm. No, this is more like blackmail," she continued.

"Don't be absurd, Caro."

Why hadn't they noticed his hand?

"What did Papa share with you about my settlement?"

"There is a packet of papers in the safe at home that I am to consult if need be, but I am sure it is just a standard marriage contract. If I had known what was afoot, I would have consulted them before I came. But Papa could drive a shrewd bargain when he needed."

"Which is why Mr. Broadhurst got me instead of Sarah or Amelia," Caroline said bitterly. "But he looked . . . beaten when I suggested I'd find a way to send him to prison."

"Why would you do that?" Lord Nesham blurted.

Jack wanted to rise and stand between Caroline and her brother's ire, but they seemed oblivious to his presence—not so different than in the normal world. Nobs never recognized his sort in any kind of meaningful way.

"I was angry." Caroline's voice was calm and soothing.

"I just thought if he divorced me, after all this time, I would strike back. It was a thoughtless thing spoken in heat, but I think he believed me, which was odd."

Jack tried again to wave his hand. He knew why Broadhurst feared prison. Most of the villagers suspected. No one had any proof, and he was the man they depended on for their livelihoods. People just didn't speak out against a man with so much power over them. Not when the authorities could be tucked in his pocket. A man who could pay that kind of money for a wife could buy whatever justice he wanted.

Caroline should take the divorce and run.

The back of Jack's hand rubbed against the covers. No wonder Caroline and her brother weren't seeing his motion.

He tried harder, succeeded in opening his eyes for just a second and pushed his hand out against Caroline's knee. His voice feeling rusty as an old pump, he managed to croak out, "Killed his last wife."

But he was too drained to even register her response or if he was coherent. The drug and the effort to speak overpowered his will to stay awake against the sedating effect of the morphine. The gray nothingness sucked him down.

Caroline couldn't move for fear she would crack. Silence shuttered the room. It wasn't true. Couldn't be true. Jack had to be dreaming.

"What did he say?" demanded Robert.

"Jack," she whispered, hoping he would startle awake and look as if he'd been deep in a nightmare. His hand against her leg let her know he'd been awake, had intended for her to hear, but she refused to believe it. If Mr. Broadhurst had murdered his previous wife, if her father had known, if anyone had known, he'd be in prison or dead now. She wrapped her cold fingers around Jack's warm palm. He was very still, except for his deep breathing, and he didn't clasp her back.

Robert's brow furrowed and he leaned toward her. "He said—"

"He's under the influence of morphine," Caroline interrupted. The last thing she wanted was for the words to be repeated. She lifted Jack's limp hand. "Look, he is asleep."

Why would he have said such a thing? She pushed Jack's hand under the covers. She hadn't shattered, but only Jack's weakened state kept her from shaking him violently.

"Caro," whispered Robert. "It would make sense, wouldn't it?"

Like a knife running down her spine, Caroline wanted nothing to do with Jack's pronouncement. "No. Not for Papa to have allowed me to marry him, and not for what I know of my husband. He would never kill anyone."

But a tiny doubt niggled at her. Broadhurst could be ruthless.

"Caro, if there is even a chance it might be true, I cannot allow you to stay here."

"You can do without the three thousand pounds per annum?" she asked.

Robert put his hand over his face. "I'll break the entail to Nesham Hall and sell it. I'll find a way. I have a responsibility to you, even if Papa—"

"What of the scandal?"

"I don't need the earldom. Your safety is more important than that."

"It's not true, Robert. Just the ramblings of an injured man. Never think it is true." Even if it were possible, she'd spent fifteen years as Mr. Broadhurst's wife, and Robert had only been the head of the family for the last eighteen months.

She couldn't allow her brother to sell the family estate.

The fortified house with its many additions had been in their family since the sixteenth century. It was home in a way this house could never be. If Robert had to sell it, there was nowhere left for her to return if this marriage ended. And she had her pride. If her contribution had saved the family home, she didn't want to forgo that now. Besides it wasn't true. Mr. Broadhurst was a businessman, not a murderer.

"I'll just continue on as before. I would very much like a little one of my own." She tried to smile, but her face felt made of stone. Her heart was a stone too, heavy and painful in her chest. "I will be glad of it, really. I'm sorry I questioned anything."

The maid returned with Caroline's belated breakfast, effectively ending the conversation. But a woman made of stone couldn't eat.

At midday during the dinner break, several of his coworkers stopped by, along with his oldest sisters bringing apple tarts. He supposed they had been cooking when the earlier wave of visitors arrived. Still groggy from the injection of morphine the doctor had given him before unwrapping and frowning over his misshapen leg, Jack tried to choke down a few bites. At least the doctor's visit and his stitching the surgery scar together had chased away Lucy.

Mrs. Broadhurst had been there, but maddeningly far away. She hadn't made eye contact with him, and she left with the doctor.

The door swung open, and Jack hoped for Mrs. Broadhurst, but instead Mr. Broadhurst filled the doorway. "What is the meaning of this?"

The conversation died in mid-sentence.

Finally one of his sisters said, "Beg pardon, sir. We were visiting Jack."

"He doesn't need visitors." Mr. Broadhurst eyed the nightshirt Jack wore.

For once Jack agreed. "They were just leaving," he said. "Thank you all for coming."

One of the men cast an uncertain look toward Jack. He shook his head. It was one thing for him to incur Mr. Broadhurst's wrath, but the others were too dependent on their jobs at the mill. Still, Jack felt overmatched and puny compared to the old man.

No one moved. Broadhurst blocked the doorway.

"We'll just be leaving, then." One of the men shifted from one foot to the other as he eyed the doorway.

Jack's sister extended the plate. "Would you care for an apple tart, sir?"

It seemed to break Broadhurst free of his glare. He moved to the side. "Go on, then."

Everyone filed past, their chins tucked and their gazes down, as if to look at Broadhurst might invoke his wrath.

In a low, threatening voice, Broadhurst said, "No more visitors." He turned and yelled at a footman. "Do you hear me? No more millworkers are to be allowed in the house."

The only visitor Jack really wanted was Mrs. Broadhurst, but he couldn't resist saying, "Thank you, sir. They were keeping me from my rest."

Not that he could do much more than lie there and try not to think of the pain, but he was incredibly exhausted, and a catnap here and there was better than nothing.

Mr. Broadhurst crossed the room and stood above him. His silence didn't bode well, and the hairs on the back of Jack's neck lifted, but he resisted being the one to break the silence.

"Don't get used to this."

"I didn't want to come here in the first place." Jack clenched the covers. "Sir."

Broadhurst slowly turned his head, all the while keeping his eye on Jack, until it became a sideways look that sent chills down Jack's spine. "I expect a fair number of those who suffer an injury like yours don't live long."

"I'm told a few die of putrefaction," said Jack. "But I'm not showing signs of it."

"Yet," murmured Broadhurst.

"I plan to leave your house as soon as I'm able."

"See that you do," said Broadhurst as he exited the room.

Jack sucked in a deep breath. If the man had any idea of the way he thought of Mrs. Broadhurst, he'd be gone faster than he could shake a stick. And there'd be no telling if it was by fair means or foul.

Chapter 11

Caroline pushed back the wineglass. She was still too shaky to indulge in even just a glass with dinner.

The wind had blown in a rainstorm that put shadows into all the corners of the house. It suited her mood. But she smiled at the remaining men at the table and chatted lightly about the vagaries of October weather, how it could be crisp and clear one day, cold and rainy the next.

Caroline had long since given up the idea she could choose a man who even vaguely suited her. Mr. Berkley sat to her left. He was handsome enough, with a head of wavy russet hair and pale piercing eyes, but something about his thin lips put her off. Still, she sighed in resignation.

After spending most of dinner asking about him and listening with rapt attention as he droned on and on about his horses and his plans to improve his stables once he came into his inheritance, she needed to close the deal. And at least he was giving her increasingly longer looks as she let her gaze drift too often to his mouth.

"I do feel bad the weather is not cooperating. You will find us poor hosts and never return." She lowered her voice and purred, "I do hope I can make it up to you in some small way." She leaned toward him.

"I dare say we will not blame you for the weather." But he made it sound as if he would.

"I hope I could interest you in a few . . . indoor pursuits," she continued. She was trying to sound coquettish like Amelia. Caroline traced a fingertip along her neck and then dropped her hand to her lap, before anyone else noticed. But the flickering candelabra barely shed enough light to eat by.

His gaze dropped to her décolletage—pulled as low as she could make it without exposing her nipples—and then slowly back to her face.

"What do you like to do when it rains?" he asked.

"I like nothing better than to read in front of the fire in the library. If this keeps up, I imagine that is what I will do all day tomorrow while Mr. Broadhurst is engaged at the mill."

Mr. Berkley's eyes flicked to the head of the table and Mr. Broadhurst.

Her foot was nudged, and Caroline drew back.

Mr. Berkley flicked up an eyebrow.

Oh!

She toed off her slipper and reached for his leg with her stockinged foot. He trapped it between his, and seemed as if he would pull her off her chair. Was playing footsies supposed to be violent?

She squeaked in alarm and then grabbed her disdained wineglass and took a gulp to diffuse any attention, but the rest of the men hardly seemed to notice her, as Robert was doing his best to regale the company with tales of his first impassioned speech in Parliament. She'd heard the story before but Robert had added a few embellishments.

Mr. Berkley adjusted his chair and brought her foot into his lap. His thumb pressed into her arch and massaged. She barely kept from jerking her foot back. She stared at him and then remembered the role she was supposed to be playing.

Letting her lips part, she let her eyelids sink to half-mast. It seemed a rather silly expression, but he leaned closer.

After a minute he yanked her foot farther into his lap and pressed it against a bulge. Goodness, was that what she thought it was?

Then again, perhaps she had chosen the right man this time. He wasn't wasting time kissing her or perhaps even all that concerned with her response or lack of one.

He lifted his fork with his other hand as if he was no longer interested, but his fingers gripped her ankle firmly and rubbed her foot against his crotch.

"Is there anything you are reading now?" he asked, as if nothing were going on beneath the table.

"D-Dickens," she stuttered.

The corners of his eyes crinkled and he set down his fork. He reached under the table with his right hand and slid it up until he found her garter and liberated her stocking.

His hand against the bare flesh of her leg stunned her. But she smiled. This might be easier than she thought.

At the far end of the table, Mr. Broadhurst stood. "Mrs. Broadhurst, you seem to be done eating. Isn't it time you left us to our port?"

Caroline jerked her foot back, but Mr. Berkley didn't immediately let her go. Her heart caught in her throat, she hissed at her captor, "Sir."

An insolent sneer on his face, he released her. She searched with her bare toes for her slipper, but came up empty.

With as dignified a nod as she could manage, Caroline left the table. The footman opened the door and she scooted out, her bare sole protesting at the cold marble of the entry hall.

With a sigh of regret, she moved past the room housing Jack. Before she did anything more, she needed to put on a new stocking and shoes. Later, after the gentlemen joined her in the drawing room, she could return and retrieve her slipper, hopefully before the servants found it.

Jack groaned as he crutched around the room. Had he accused Mr. Broadhurst of murder earlier, or had it just been a bad dream? Bloody rot, he was staying in the man's house, eating the man's food, lusting after the man's wife. What kind of gratitude was that?

He had to get out of here before he started to believe this luxury was his due, or that Caroline might ever see him as a man worthy of her affection. He cursed at himself. Either he wanted to be near her or to avoid the fear that he wouldn't get the job in London. Neither reason was good. No, he had to go soon, before he made a fool of himself by revealing how much he wanted her.

The door clicked and he turned to see her enter. Her cheeks were faintly flushed and her dress dipped low on her chest, exposing her creamy skin. God, what he wouldn't do to have the right to put his mouth there. His breath whooshed out of him.

"I only have a minute, but I wanted to see if you needed anything," she said. Her hand remained on the doorknob.

"I'm fine." He'd been fed before his minder left for her own dinner. Unable to stop himself, he took a few lurching steps closer to her.

"I wanted to let you know, I've gotten Mr. Broadhurst's assurance that he will allow you to work as a clerk, until you are fully healed. Perhaps in a couple of weeks, you can come to the office."

Jack bit back a profanity. He barely could write his letters and he'd spent an inordinate amount of time trying to decipher one lousy paragraph of the book she'd left by his side. He put his hand over his face rather than let his dismay show.

It was a brilliant plan, really, a job a man with a broken leg could do. No walking, carrying, or lifting anything heavier than a pen. But unless that chance included schooling, he couldn't be a clerk.

He opened his mouth to outright refuse, but a bit of self-preservation reared its head. Jack seriously doubted he would be able to keep his appointment at the machine shop. If he couldn't convince them to hire him in London, he would need work. "I'm not a clerk."

"It's really not hard. Mostly recording orders and shipments, payments, a bit of correspondence." She frowned. "A lot of numbers. Adding and subtracting. It's more tedious than taxing. Clerks always start with the most mundane of tasks."

While his ciphering was better than most, he suspected what was done in the office was more than he could easily figure in his head. In a weird way, the opportunity was everything he'd hoped for, but he was so unprepared. He should have studied harder with his younger siblings. He should have spent more time learning what he could instead of sleeping—or spending time with Lucy. He couldn't be a clerk. The clerks were educated men. Not to mention working merc feet from Mr. and Mrs. Broadhurst would be a dream and a nightmare all rolled into one.

Yet, Mrs. Broadhurst had probably campaigned hard for this opportunity for him.

Like a loom clicking back and forth he was beginning to see a pattern emerge from the myriad threads coming together. The liquor, the maids' conversations. And he didn't like it. "What did Mr. Broadhurst's guarantee of a position cost you?"

Her expression of dismay flickered so fast he almost missed it. "Nothing."

Intent on every movement of her face, Jack knew it was a lie. "Mr. Broadhurst does nothing out of compassion unless he can profit from it."

"He is not so horrible as that." She nudged her chin up with a tiny head shake.

Her ready defense almost surprised him, but Jack disputed her denial. "Canny and shrewd he is. He profits from granting your wishes somehow."

He wasn't sure if he wanted to know if Mrs. Broadhurst had used the oldest bargaining chip a woman had with her husband, but he also was aware of how much he already owed her. Subjecting herself to any trial on his behalf had gone beyond proving her point that the little children should not work in the mill.

"I owe you too much already for you to put yourself out unnecessarily," he said. "I will get by with or without your assistance." Why would she even care?

Her mouth flattened. "I offered Mr. Broadhurst nothing I had not already agreed to. He wants a great deal from me right now, and I see no reason to not extract as much as possible in return."

"Spoken like a true tycoon."

She cast him an exasperated look, but he could see the hint of amusement in the crinkles at the corner of her eyes. Her hand came off the doorknob and she took a step toward him.

She wasn't close enough yet, but he held his breath, willing her to close the distance between them. He would do a lot to see her smile, but he feared his care was just another burden. "What does he want of you?"

She stiffened and the light mood was broken. He sensed her pulling away, and although she only moved back an inch or two, it was as if a great yawning river flowed into the breach between them, cutting off any hope he had of bridging to her side.

"I shall check on you later," she said.

At least she had not thwarted his question with a new lie. Most likely she had promised a bit of wifely duty to her husband in exchange for Mr. Broadhurst offering him a clerk's position.

Emptiness gaped in Jack. She was another man's wife. And much as he found the idea of her with that man disgusting, he could do nothing to stop it. Nor would she want him to.

Caroline served the after dinner tea, then moved to the window. She stood looking out at the rain streaming down and waited for Mr. Berkley to come to her side. He didn't. Instead he and several of the men played cards.

She glanced toward the table, and Mr. Berkley met her eyes. Well, at least he was aware of her.

She wished she were downstairs reading to Jack. His response to her offer of a clerking position surprised her. She'd thought he'd be grateful, but instead he asked her what the bargain cost her. The concern in his eyes almost undid her, and she'd needed to leave before her composure crumbled.

His opinion of Mr. Broadhurst was not high, and she was inclined to agree with him. Had her husband killed his last wife? She traced a pattern in the fog on the glass. If anyone were smart enough to outwit the authorities, he probably was.

What exactly she was to do with the information—assuming she could verify it—she didn't know. Her heart thumped erratically.

Finally, Mr. Broadhurst rose and wished the gentlemen good-night. He cast a narrow-eyed glance in Caroline's direction before exiting the room. She waited until fifteen interminable minutes clicked by and then carefully ducked out of the room.

By now the servants would have removed all of the dishes from the dining room. She would just creep down and retrieve her slipper, and then look in on Jack before seeking her own bed. After all, if Mr. Berkley wasn't going to pursue her further tonight, she wouldn't sit around waiting for him to notice her. After what happened at the dining room table, he could be in no doubt she was amenable to more.

The gas girandoles waged a futile battle against the darkness, barely providing enough light to see her way down the stairs and across the cold cavern of the entryway. Light peeped out from under the library doors. One of the gentlemen must have slipped out to read instead of joining in the card game.

Not wanting to be caught out, Caroline quickly slipped into the dark dining room. She left the door cracked to allow in a little light. *Please, please, let her slipper still be there.*

Pulling her chair back from her place at the foot of the table, she waited for her eyes to adjust to the nearly complete blackness.

She dropped to her knees and swept with her hands, looking for the missing shoe. Her fingers encountered nothing but the woolen strands of the carpet. Perhaps one of the servants had found it and returned it to her room. She crawled farther under the table, still searching.

"Looking for this, Cinderella?" said Mr. Berkley. "Or perhaps this?"

She twisted, looking behind her. One of the double doors to the hall stood wide open, allowing a spill of light to illuminate the white stocking he held. Her slipper dangled from the finger of his other hand.

"Yes," she muttered. "Both."

"What will you do to retrieve them?" he asked with an amused lilt to his voice.

Caroline pressed her lips together and then parted them. "Anything you desire."

"Oh but I am a man with great desires."

"I am but a woman who doesn't want the servants to discover my clothes where they don't belong." She backed out from under the table. Her stomach lurched. This was what she wanted, but she'd thought she would find her shoe, sit with Jack awhile, and then go to bed.

"Ah, it is a concern, when one leaves clothing in places one shouldn't."

Caroline rose to her feet. "I don't make a habit of it."

"Really? Tremont seemed to think you might."

Alarm knifed through her. Had they been discussing her?

"Now what I want to know is why Whitton thought it expedient to leave so soon."

"I'm sure I don't know."

"Don't you?" asked Mr. Berkley, setting the shoe and stocking in her chair.

She eyed them. Would he stop her if she grabbed them and dashed to her room? But she should take advantage of this opportunity. She stepped closer to Mr. Berkley, close enough that her skirts brushed his legs. "No, I don't. Do you?"

"I do find it curious that he was closeted with your husband before he left."

What on earth had been said? Had Mr. Broadhurst known nothing of consequence happened before he confronted her about her tryst? Her head whirled. "I can't imagine what they would have had to say to each other."

Mr. Berkley pulled the door shut behind him. The *snick* was as loud as a rifle shot in the blackened room. He stepped closer and it was everything Caroline could do to stand her ground.

His voice lowered. "I think a bored wife with too much time on her hands is a dangerous thing."

She screwed her eyes shut and searched for a response. "I adore my husband, but he is not the man he once was."

Mr. Berkley caught her elbows and pulled her against him. "Perhaps the physician can right whatever ails him."

"I am not terribly hopeful," she said. "Not much cures an advancement of years."

Mr. Berkley chuckled. "But perhaps we should be concerned with what ails you."

She puzzled a bit at that one, but could only make out a silhouette of his head and not his expression. But as the seconds ticked by, she finally managed a "Please."

She brought her hands up to cup his elbows. He kissed her on the cheek and then moved to her neck. "Yes, I'd like to please you. And might I say you are looking quite lovely tonight?"

"You might," she whispered. It was as close as she could come to thanking him for the insincere compliment. She should reply in kind, but her mind swirled with dread and sick anticipation.

His mouth slid down her neck and she was both relieved he wasn't kissing her on the mouth and appalled at the open wet trail left behind, as if he were slavering on her like a dog might. She closed her eyes and tilted her head back, giving him more access.

She couldn't stand like a statue or he would know how little she liked such things. Almost as if she stepped outside of herself, but could still issue commands, she slid her hands up his arms. They were not as firmly muscled as Jack's were. Disappointment registered, although she wondered at it. Had Jack become her physical ideal of a perfect man?

Because Mr. Berkley seemed to like it earlier, she toed off her slippers and tentatively slid her toes along his calf.

He whipped them around and she nearly fell. Then he pushed her against the closed door and his fingers dug into her derrière. He lifted her at the same time he ground his pelvis against her. A moan of protest left her mouth before she could stop it, but it only seemed to inflame him more.

He kissed her then, his mouth covering beyond her lips and his tongue plunging inside. He grabbed her breast and tugged the material of her dress down. Then he again moved to her neck, leaving her chin nearly dripping as he moved his head lower and suckled on her breast.

Another moan of protest left her mouth, but she fought her instinct to push him away and let him draw on her nipple. He pulled off and bared her other breast and repeated his nursing.

Breasts were for babies to suckle, grown men were too rough and it hurt. She whimpered. He pulled back and groped them. She tried not to think of the bruises she would likely have.

"I wish I could see you," he panted.

"Next time," she purred.

Biting her lip, she pushed at his coat jacket, trying to free him of his clothes. He seemed to be in that precoital frenzy she'd witnessed more often than she cared to with Mr. Broadhurst. Just to be certain, she reached down and checked Mr. Berkley's member.

He groaned and pushed her hand against his trousers. Yes, he was ready to perform, and while the dining room table was hardly ideal, it would have to do. She just had to free him of his clothes so he could impregnate her.

A pounding on the front door of the house made them spring apart.

"What the hell?" whispered Mr. Berkley.

Her heart jolted and her fingers on his buttons went still.

"Who in the hell calls at this time of night?"

"I don't know," she whispered. "I better go see."

He backed away, and she tugged at her neckline and wiped her face. As soon as she put herself back together, she opened the door.

The footman sitting with Jack had already moved across the hall. The door yawned open and a man stood there, his hat pulled low, his muffler wound high, and wearing a glistening-wet long greatcoat. "I got business with Broadhurst."

"I will just ascertain if he is home," said the confused servant.

"He's home," said the man in a gruff voice, pushing his way inside.

Across the expanse of the hall, the library door clicked open and Mr. Broadhurst emerged.

"Bloody hell," whispered Mr. Berkley behind her.

The man at the door stepped inside, a pool forming around the rim of his coat. Mr. Broadhurst flung open the library door. "Sir, if you will just step inside, we can conclude our business."

"Your coat, sir?" said the footman.

"I'll keep it," said the man, striding across the pristine marble, sullying it with dirty boots.

Mr. Broadhurst's gaze pinned her. His nostrils flared. "What the hell are you doing down here?"

Caroline held up her arm. "I lost my bracelet and I just found it under the table. The last time I saw it was at dinner.

I should take it to a jeweler to have the catch repaired."

"You are avoiding the guests," he growled.

"No. I had every intention of returning to the drawing room," she said. With Mr. Berkley so close he could hear every word, she dare not inform Mr. Broadhurst she was in the middle of carrying out his directive. An inappropriate bubble of a laugh threatened to burst from her. She'd finally almost succeeded and Mr. Broadhurst and his strange visitor had thwarted her.

As if Mr. Berkley wasn't standing just inside the dining room, fumbling with his clothes, she calmly closed the door.

"Who is that?" she asked.

"Go upstairs, Mrs. Broadhurst, his business doesn't concern you."

Not knowing what else to do, Caroline followed her husband's order.

But who was the man who came to their house at such a late hour?

Chapter 12

"**Y**ou may go to bed," Mrs. Broadhurst told the maid watching Jack. "I will stay until Steven comes on duty."

Once they were alone, he debated crutching toward her, finishing what he'd begun last night. But she'd been drinking then. He took a step toward her.

"Are you ready for your next dose of laudanum?" she asked softly as she skittered toward the sideboard.

He checked for the knifing pain that made him crave the oblivion of the medicine and found only a dull ache that was no longer setting his teeth on edge. He moved back to the bed and sat.

"Not yet. Doesn't hurt as bad." Even if she wasn't touching him, he didn't want to sleep while she was with him.

Her hair was different, loosely twisted—more as if to get it up rather than the elaborate kind of style that she wore in the evenings, and instead of a gown with a low dipping neckline, a tight waist with wide skirts, she wore a loose garment made of velvet.

"You don't want to go so long the pain gets out of control." She avoided his eyes.

Rather than continue to examine her, he nodded toward the sideboard. "I can fetch it myself, if need be." Moving gingerly, he scooted back on the bed. "Where are my clothes?"

"I'm afraid they were ruined when we removed them, but I will send for Mr. Broadhurst's tailor. You will need a suit or two to work in the office."

Jack winced. No, the sooner he returned home, the better chance he had of making it to London on time. "I don't need another suit. What I need are clothes so I can go home."

Her mouth tightened.

"I am grateful for all that you've done, I am, but I cannot afford a new suit." Especially not one made by Mr. Broadhurst's tailor.

"If you insist on paying, we'll deduct it from your wages."

He rubbed his hand over his face. Even if he didn't get the job in London, he needed to tell her he wouldn't be able to be a clerk. But admitting he could barely read and write would undoubtedly take him down another peg in her estimation. "I cannot afford Mr. Broadhurst's tailor."

She blinked. "There isn't one in the village. And I can assure you, Mr. Broadhurst would chose one in Manchester who offers the best value. Besides, you do not need clothing just yet. You must bear with being an invalid a bit longer."

"I should practice with the crutches. I should be clothed while I am out of this room." He'd have to manage stairs or suffer the indignity of being carried down them when he did leave. How he would ever manage the ladder to the loft where he slept in his father's home was another question. "Broken leg or no, I will have to get up and down stairs."

"Would you like to try now? It is gone one. No one is likely to be awake."

She'd avoided the issue of his getting dressed, but practice was probably more important than his dignity. He reached for his crutches again. "Why are you?"

Her cheeks bloomed and she tilted her head down. "With

all the guests, the servants are overtasked. If I sit with you a few hours, I can lessen their burden."

So was he to believe she wouldn't sit with him if not for the guests? Or was that what she wanted to believe? A wave of irritation passed through him. A man who could spend thousands upon thousands for a wife could afford the pittance of a few servants' salaries. "Hire more servants."

"Mr. Broadhurst cannot bear to see employees standing about, so they would be dismissed as soon as the guests leave."

He positioned his crutches. He could tell her he didn't need a minder, but he needed to learn to stand without assistance. As it was, his left leg shook like a palsy victim as he pushed up to a standing position. His arms shook too. He didn't know when he'd ever been this weak.

"Besides, Mr. Broadhurst would not approve the expenditure if I listed you as a cause. As it is, I am only granted this boon because I am in a position to bargain."

The reminder that she had anything to offer Mr. Broadhurst or what she was likely offering the miserly old man only made Jack clench his fists, but then he released them before she could notice.

She held out her hand. Taking her proffered assistance, he made it to his foot and positioned the crutches under his arms. He swung away from her.

"I need to learn to do for myself without help," he muttered by way of an apology. It sure as hell wasn't because he didn't want her to touch him, but then when he had her hand, he hadn't wanted to let go.

Her mouth tightened. "You're not exactly steady."

She followed him to the door. He leaned to open it and she put her hands at his waist. Knowing she only meant to stabilize him, he groaned. He wanted so much more.

Her hands slipped away as his crutches encountered the

marble floor. The marble was slick, so he concentrated on the placement. She glided across the floor and turned up the gaslights. Everywhere he looked there was a marker of how different her world was from his, yet he couldn't take his eyes off her. Everything about her made him want her more. If only she had been callous or cold, but she wasn't. The quietness about her, which others had taken as a superior attitude, was born of a calmness he admired.

As he planted the crutches on the bottom stair and prepared to swing up, she fisted her hands in the material at his sides.

"I shall stay right behind you in case the crutches slip," she said.

He couldn't even be aggravated at her lack of confidence in him. Truth was, he didn't know if he would have the ability to go up the risers or if there was a better way about it. "I don't want to hurt you if I fall."

"I won't let you fall," she said with such grim determination he believed her.

He went up the first stair. Her hands brushed his sides, but she let the effort be entirely his.

"How many people are in your family? Beth wasn't entirely certain. She started naming names and I lost count at eighteen."

"My father has sixteen children and one on the way," said Jack, taking another step.

"Is that typical for families in the village?"

"Having so many children, yes." He went up another riser. Ascending was not as tough as he feared. But without needing to concentrate on going up the stairs, he was even more aware of her hands brushing against his waist. "Most would say we have been lucky to only lose two children and my mother."

She sighed.

He looked over his shoulder.

Her eyes looked flat. "It seems to me that education is the only way to give those of the village hope to rise above their circumstances, but not only does Mr. Broadhurst fight me, you and the other villagers do as well. I want to understand. I want to help, but as long as Mr. Broadhurst is in charge there is only so much I can do."

Jack watched her face until she looked sideways up at him. Her blue gaze through the lace of her lashes hit him like a punch to the stomach. He sucked in a deep breath. "I know you do. I wish I was young enough to benefit from the schooling."

Her hands were still against him, touching his back and stomach, since he'd twisted. She stood a stair below, but she might as well be standing pressed against him, for what he felt. She cocked her head and studied him intently.

He had to stop thinking of her and that her husband might not be around much longer, as if she'd allow a millworker to comfort her when she was a widow.

"Did you not have schooling?"

"My mother taught me." Until he'd been too tired from working to even pay attention to the lessons. Now was a perfect time to tell her he was inadequate to be a clerk. But he couldn't force the words out. Instead he asked, "What will happen when Mr. Broadhurst is no longer in charge?"

Her chin and shoulders dropped, and she looked down at the marble of the entry hall. "It depends."

"On what?"

Her lips curled up, but the smile didn't touch her eyes. It might have been the saddest smile he'd ever witnessed, and it tugged at him. He would have reached out and touched her, cupped her arm, or pulled her into an embrace, but the crutches stopped him, which was a good thing.

"Should you like to continue up the stairs or shall we see about getting you down?" Her briskness returned as if the window she'd opened to her soul was best forgotten.

"Up." He could hardly fault her for keeping secrets when he wouldn't share his own. He twisted and swung up another stair.

After a couple of stairs she said, "Mr. Broadhurst does not like the idea of a woman being in charge. He believes we are too softhearted and too likely to make business decisions with our emotions."

Jack wasn't sure how to respond. He knew of no woman running so large an operation as the mill, but his knowledge was limited to Lancashire. There were women who seemed to run their own affairs well enough. Everyone knew the greengrocer's wife was the one who managed the store, and the midwife handled not only births but served as an apothecary.

"Perhaps he is right," she said on a sigh.

"Women are as capable of running a business as men are, but they do tend to get distracted by having children." Neither the midwife nor the grocer's wife had children, and perhaps that was what made it easy.

Mrs. Broadhurst made a sound somewhere between a gasp and a laugh.

Hell, it was a thoughtless thing to say. Most women wanted children. She was probably no different.

He swiveled and pitched toward his weighty cast.

Her arms circled his waist and she pulled him to her as he strained to find his balance.

As he regained his equilibrium, his harsh breathing echoed in the stillness of the night. The warmth of her body burned against his, and he wanted to stay pressed against her forever. Holding the crutches was the only thing that stopped him from wrapping his arms around her.

She stared up at him. Her lips parted, her chest rose and fell. She felt the pull between them too. He knew it just as sure as his name was John Applegate.

She backed away. "I don't know why I'm telling you these things." A shadow crossed her face. "Are you steady on your feet—foot?"

"Yes. Thanks." He turned back to take the rest of the stairs. "It hardly matters what you tell me. It's not as if I'm going to tell anyone. Even if I did, people would think I made up stories."

Her hands settled again at his waist, holding material but not touching him. "Why? Are you in the habit of telling false tales?"

"No, but no one would believe you picked me as a confidant. They'd probably believe that I dreamed it while on the laudanum."

Her voice dropped to whisper. "Did you dream what you said earlier about Mr. Broadhurst's previous wife?"

Jack winced. "I shouldn't have said that."

"You shouldn't have said it because it was true or because it was a dream?" Her hands tightened in the material of his nightshirt.

He'd given her the perfect opportunity to brush off what he'd said as the delusions of a drugged state, but with quiet determination she had plowed ahead. Did anything scare her?

"Her death was suspicious, supposedly by her own hand," Jack said in an undertone. "And he married you only a few weeks later."

"It wasn't a few weeks," she muttered.

"That's the way I remember it." He took another step and she nearly unbalanced him by tugging back. Leaning forward, he waited until she realized what she was doing.

She moved her hands forward. "How old were you?"

"Nearly four and ten. Old enough to remember." He wanted to turn and watch her face, but then perhaps she wouldn't like that.

He took the last few steps and leaned his weight on the crutches, glad to be on a flat level again. She had yet to move her hands away, but he doubted her continued clutching of his nightshirt was to assist him.

"Mr. Broadhurst has worked hard all his life," she said, but her voice wavered.

"That he has," agreed Jack. His admiration for the man's accomplishments hadn't set well with his coworkers. But it was a double-edged sword. He understood. When the demands one placed on oneself were high, one was often disappointed in the lackluster efforts of others. Yet, he hoped that were he in the same position, he would not be as harsh as Mr. Broadhurst. Twisting, Jack began the process of turning around.

Her hands dropped away. "He has been generous with me and my family."

"Very," agreed Jack. "Would that he was as generous with those who make him wealthy."

She stared at the floor. "Were he not concerned about how the difficulties in the Americas will affect the price of cotton, I could probably persuade him to raise wages. Although he would regard it as another mark of how I am too concerned for the welfare of the workers. Other mills employ more young women for they are cheaper labor."

Jack had to think beyond the needs of his family and see it from the perspective of the Broadhursts. Working in the office as a clerk would give him valuable knowledge—more than the mechanical workings of machines—how a business worked, how money was managed, how goods were ordered.

He wanted to learn, but he knew once he revealed his lack of education, the opportunity to clerk would be withdrawn. To delay his application for the job in London might destroy his chances there. But he was torn. She factored too much into his decision and had no idea of the way he thought about her.

But if Caroline were using feminine powers of persuasion to get him a chance, he wanted her to stop. That another man had the right of her body scorched him. "Then don't ask him," he said.

She lifted her gaze to his face. For a second they stared at each other.

"I don't understand what you want," she said. "I thought you could help me to know how I could best improve the lives of our workers—how to give them opportunities and prevent poverty amongst them, but—"

"I want this." Jack waved his arm around and then gripped his crutch.

"This?"

"To become wealthy like Mr. Broadhurst, to live well, to have a beautiful wife, like you." But he'd never conceived of paying a king's ransom for her or the mysterious woman who might eventually become his dream wife. A woman who looked like Caroline, had her poise and courage, and most of all had her generous heart. Hell, he wanted her. All along he'd wanted her, not some poor imitation of her.

Her cheeks colored and she looked away.

"But I am not the best example of a typical villager." He had postponed marriage to have a shot at a better life. "And even though I should relish the opportunity to learn, I won't do well as a clerk."

She blinked as she searched his face. "Why not?"

Looking down the staircase he had ascended, Jack

wanted back down in his bed and a new dose of laudanum to ease the increasing ache of his leg. He should just answer her question, but the words were gritty in his mouth.

"I suppose we should get you back downstairs," she said softly.

He leaned down to put his crutches on the stair below the landing, but the fall yawned before him. Caroline hurried around him and reached out to grip his nightgown.

He took the step, but felt as though one wrong move could pitch him headlong. Reversing the process of going up had seemed like a good idea in theory, but not so much in practice. The muscles in his good leg protested.

The next step, he tried to go leg first, but there was no way to lower the crutches. He brought his leg back to the second riser and stopped.

Caroline studied him and bit her lip.

"I would have thought going down would be easier than going up."

Her eyes narrowed and she looked at the railing. He did too.

"I could summon a footman. Or perhaps you could try scooting down like a child might."

"No. I'll figure it out." The last thing he wanted was to descend on his backside. He leaned one crutch against the banister and then gripped the bar as he went down the next step.

Her head nearly brushed his chest as she kept hold of the sides of his nightshirt. If he didn't fear toppling her and sending them both crashing down to the foot of the stairs, he might have used both crutches. This way took effort but was more in his control.

She looked up and caught him watching her. She flushed and looked away. "Are you sure you're strong enough for this now?"

"I'll manage," he gritted out. "If I have to I'll slide down like a child, I'll swallow my pride long enough to do it."

Her lips twitched. "I would probably find that less distressing."

"I would find it more." He took another step.

This time her head did brush his chest, and he couldn't resist letting go of the banister and touching her shoulder.

She jerked away as if he'd burned her.

"You could give me a little more room," he said. "So I don't topple you."

"Of course." She backed down two stairs and stared at his midsection.

He hated the gap between them. His breathing was labored with exertion and her proximity. But for his accident, he never would be this close to her. He had to stop thinking of this time with her as anything beyond an aberration. "I began working in the mill when I was five."

Her gaze shot up.

"Only little ones can get in and sweep under the looms, otherwise the lint builds up and catches fire."

"There has to be a better way."

"Perhaps. Using floor traps so an adult may clean underneath would be better. I've long wanted to try, but devices that eliminate labor are not welcomed by my people. If you want, I can draw some diagrams, so it might be done."

She shook her head. "You will be too busy in the office to worry about production."

Jack sighed. "I worked ten hours a day by my eighth year."

Her forehead crinkled.

He forced out the explanation. "I didn't get much schooling after that. I doubt I can clerk."

"But you insisted on helping Beth with her schoolwork."

"Because it is important, but my mother had many children after me, and she couldn't keep me awake long enough to learn. I can write my name, add and subtract, but I can't do much more."

Caroline's forehead only rippled more. She stared at him as if he had grown horns. "But you were reading Dickens."

"I was trying to read Dickens, but I did not make it beyond the first sentence." Now she knew his dreams were folly and his efforts to follow along with his youngest siblings' lessons had been halfhearted. He should have been trying harder. He knew his letters, he could read simple things, but words over five or six letters stumped him.

"Well it is a long sentence," she said with a soft smile that didn't erase the strain around her eyes.

"I have ideas to make the machinery more efficient." Jack bit his lip. "If I cannot convince some in London to implement my work, perhaps Mr. Broadhurst would let me rebuild a few pieces. I could save him money."

It wasn't how he wanted to share his inventions. He'd wanted to gain the backing of a company already engaged in making mill machinery, be given license to build his machinery, test it, patent it, and sell to any mill. Or he'd hoped to make enough from mill machinery to follow his true interest in building mechanized carriages one day. Horses were too expensive for villagers to keep, and in crowded towns like Manchester or even London, a horseless carriage would be so much more practical. But all that was nothing as he watched dismay spread over Caroline's face. "Say something," he said.

"I'm thinking." She turned her face toward his, her blue eyes serious. "Can you write at all?"

He hated that he'd disappointed her, but it was better now than later. "I know my letters. I just . . ." Would she help him? "If you teach me, I could learn."

Her forehead crinkled. Then her gaze slid down and away. "I'm sorry. I am no tutor, and between the mill and the guests, I couldn't spare the time."

Jack closed his eyes. She was doing so much for him already; he hadn't the right to expect more. "It doesn't matter."

She shook her head. "I will find easy books for you to read, and if you can master them, we will ask the vicar to give you lessons."

"He won't. I've asked him before."

Caroline's brow lowered and she bit her lip.

"It doesn't matter," he repeated. "I don't need to be a clerk. I can do other things. Do not put yourself out."

Her gaze tipped toward him.

"I'm good with machinery," he said when she didn't speak.

"I know." She still stood in front of him but had gone far away, as if he'd become too much trouble to her and she wanted out of his presence. His leg shook as he took the remaining few steps. His arms felt like noodles. She skipped up the stairs to fetch his other crutch, making his efforts to tackle the stairs seem puny in comparison. She handed him the crutch. "We will speak more of your future tomorrow, but you should rest now."

"Yes, ma'am," he answered as he wondered if he had lost her respect. He had to end this farce soon. For his sanity if nothing else, he needed to remember what it was like to live without servants, without his own room, fire, and bed. Without Caroline's soft hands touching him, without her concerned eyes following him, and her voice flowing over him as she read to him.

Chapter 13

Caroline pulled another book off the shelf in the library. She searched for one suitable for a beginning reader, but even as she opened a couple of her childhood favorites from home, she found them far too advanced. As she flipped through book after book, her head spun.

The door clicked open and she started. Mr. Berkley entered the room and swiftly shut the door—then locked it. A jolt hit her in the chest. She had almost forgotten that she'd hinted for him to meet her here.

"Can you not find a book to entertain?" he asked.

She looked at the stack of discarded books on the library table. "Nothing is catching my fancy today."

"Perhaps, I can be of assistance."

"Perhaps," said Caroline softly. A book for Jack would have to wait. "What did you have in mind?"

"Mr. Broadhurst is gone to the mill?"

"Yes, he always supervises the pay draws. He shan't return anytime soon." Apparently Mr. Broadhurst wouldn't trust her to do that correctly.

Mr. Berkley's lips disappeared into tiny lines as he smiled. She stared at his mouth as hers went dry.

He moved closer, and she returned the book in her hand to the shelf.

Her voice shook and she tried to gather herself before turning back around. She settled for what she hoped was a coy look over her shoulder. "Perhaps we could continue where we left off last night, before we were so rudely interrupted."

He laughed, wrapped his arms around her waist and pulled her back against him. "I thought if you wanted to continue, you would find your way to my room."

She'd intended to, but her courage had deserted her and she ended up in the breakfast room with Jack. But it hardly mattered now as Mr. Berkley kissed her neck. The library at least sported a sofa, and they could use that rather than the dining room table. Assuming things progressed that far. But they would. She ran her hands over the arms banding around her, and then with trembling fingers unbuttoned the neck of her gown.

"You are eager," he murmured, nuzzling her ear.

She jerked away from the tickle of his breath. He put his hand on the side of her head and held her steady as he lightly blew into the canal and then bit the lobe. Prickles traveled down her body and she couldn't decide if she loathed the sensation or merely despised it.

"I thought of you all night," she whispered.

A clap of thunder made her jerk as if God had intended to smite her down for lying. A sob broke from her lips.

She covered her mouth.

"Ahh, pet, don't be frightened of the storm. Think of me. I will make you forget all about it."

She'd never been frightened of storms, but she managed to bite back her protest. Pulling his hand to the open buttons, she tried not to tense as it dipped inside her bodice. "Yes, make me forget."

He cupped her breast and then tilted her head back so he could kiss her. She closed her eyes and fought to stay relaxed and pretend she enjoyed his touch—then thought of Jack and how he had almost kissed her. Her breath caught. His touch had been so gentle and not at all urgent.

Mr. Berkley took the hitch in her breath as encouragement. He roughly turned her in his arms and pressed the entire length of his body against hers. This time she would succeed in seducing a guest. She wrapped her arms around him and tried not to mind that his shoulders were bony and that he seemed to have his hands everywhere.

Then he dipped down and, as he had the night before, freed her breasts and mouthed them. She clenched her eyes shut and tried to let her mind go away, but her thoughts went back to Jack. She wished he were the one touching her, because surely he'd be more respectful.

Mr. Berkley backed away. She bit her lip and opened her eyes. He fumbled with the front of his pants, and she reached down to help him. It would all be over soon, she told herself.

She took a step toward the sofa, but Mr. Berkley had other ideas. He grabbed her hand and wrapped it around his exposed member. Never in all her years had she touched Mr. Broadhurst's male appendage with her bare hand.

"Stroke me," Mr. Berkley commanded.

Would Jack's member feel like this? Firm yet covered with skin with the texture of a rose petal. Hell's bells, why was she thinking of Jack?

She ran her fingers down the length of Mr. Berkley's rod. It was the giver of life, and if she brought him pleasure he might in return give her a baby. And she couldn't let any hint of repulsion show as she had with Lord Tremont.

"Harder," demanded Mr. Berkley. He squeezed her nipple.

She whimpered at the burst of sensation, part pain, part something else.

He fought with her skirts and pulled them up.

"The sof—"

His fingers pushed into the slit of her pantalets and touched her privates. She gasped. It wouldn't be long now.

He began to rub at the apex of her slit, and the roughness of his touch made her long to twist away, push his hand from her body. Closing her eyes, she focused her thoughts on Jack. Would his fingers be so cruel? The motion shifted to a less sensitive place, and her body responded in a way that frightened her. Her eyes popped open and reality intruded. It wasn't Jack.

She shoved away the thoughts of Jack. He was an affianced man.

Mr. Berkley clamped his hand around hers, circling his member, and pumped their hands up and down on his shaft. He returned his attention to her nipples, nipping and tugging hard, first one and then the other. The hint of pleasure died with a new wash of discomfort. He covered her mouth with his and she tried to match his movements and when her lips parted, his tongue probed inside. With his hand in her pantalets, he nudged her legs farther apart. Surely he didn't mean to perform standing.

His moans suggested he was nearing that frenzied convulsion she'd witnessed with Mr. Broadhurst. The flesh under her fingers and palm felt fuller, harder.

She wanted him to finish the deed.

He broke from the kiss, looked down at where their hands were wrapped around his member and stroked faster. She put her thumb against the tip and brushed over it. He groaned, "So close."

She tried to tug him toward the sofa, but he was having none of it. He yanked his hand out from under her skirts and pushed her shoulder so roughly she dropped to a knee.

"Use your mouth," he grunted.

His hand fisted in her hair, bringing her lips against the bobbing head. His hand was moving her hand so quickly she feared he would smack her mouth.

"Now."

She pursed her lips against the red flesh, wanting to pull away, not understanding if this was a game she didn't know.

His member jerked and began to throb. He groaned loudly and liquid spurted against her lips. She turned her face and her hair pulled. Another burst of the moisture went across her cheek. No, this wasn't what was supposed to happen. He was spilling his seed, but not inside her where she needed it.

When it was done she dropped the rest of the way to the floor. "Why would you do that?"

Mr. Berkley's harsh breathing filled the room. He sank down beside her and handed her a neatly folded handkerchief. Her hand shaking, she cleaned the mess from her face, but the moisture in her hair refused to wipe away.

"Couldn't wait." He took the handkerchief from her and wiped his fingers.

Caroline paused in buttoning her bodice. Had he just gotten carried away with lust?

"You're a handsome woman," he said.

"Thank you," she muttered. She bit her lip. But her objection burst forth. "That wasn't what I wanted to have happen."

Mr. Berkley paused in fastening his pants. "I won't risk getting you with child."

A pang stabbed at Caroline's breastbone. Had she done this awful thing for no reason? "Why not?"

"Your husband is a ruthless man, and I should not like to incur his wrath."

"Oh, please." His morality had more twists that a spool of thread. He'd commit adultery without a qualm—just wouldn't risk leaving proof of it.

But as she stared at the rain streaming down the library windows a hysterical laugh bubbled in her chest. Everything she'd done with Mr. Berkley was for naught. It seemed God was not fond of rewarding sinners. She couldn't do this degrading thing again. She just couldn't.

Jack leaned on his crutches and closed the door to the water closet behind him. He was getting around better today, even if his trips were restricted to the water closet and around his room. While no one was about, he planned to make a circuit of the entry hall.

Across the way a key rattled.

Not liking to be caught in a nightshirt, he thumped back behind the stairs. The last thing he wanted was to embarrass Mrs. Broadhurst.

The door opened and she emerged. Her face was flushed and her hair was mussed. He stared at her, taking in her disarray. The walls around them might have come down, but all he could do was stare as his chest ripped open. She hardly looked like his pure angel of mercy.

She glanced at the stairs and then back at him. "What are you doing out of bed?"

"Washing up before my minder returns with my midday meal." He was surprised he could find the words.

A man exited the door behind her, ducking his head, but not before Jack saw the smirk. "Thank you for your recommendation, Mrs. Broadhurst. A book *is* the best entertainment for a rainy day."

Neither of them had books in their hands. The man moved toward the stairs. And just moments earlier Jack had thought he heard a man's groan coming from the room. He'd put it down to mishearing a sound from the storm, but now he wasn't sure.

"Yes. You'll have to excuse me, Mr. Berkley. I must attend to our patient."

Jack fisted his hands around the crutch supports. He glared after the man, wanting to bean him with one of the crutches.

Mrs. Broadhurst didn't look as if she'd been forced into a locked room with him. She'd been intimate with that man. Icy water poured through Jack's veins. He leaned into the wall afraid he was about to fall.

Mrs. Broadhurst's expression faltered and then she hurried toward him. "You shouldn't be up unless someone is close, in case you lose your balance."

Jack pushed away and swung his crutches in front of him, blocking her from getting close.

She drew up short and stared, her eyes filled with hurt, as if he'd unexpectedly punched her, which he hadn't.

He'd practically leaned into her every chance he had. She was probably startled at his effort to keep the space between them. As he stared back at her, his insides twisted. "I have to get around on my own. I won't have an army of servants at home."

She didn't look like a woman who had been well loved. There was nothing of the sleepy satiety he aimed for when he seduced a woman, nothing in the way she stood looked relaxed. Her mouth and eyes were pinched. She raised a hand to her hair, and as if she just realized the messy state, her head jerked left and right.

Jack's gaze turned to the man ascending the stairs who was straightening his stock. No doubt about what had happened, but while he knew, he didn't want to believe more than a few stolen kisses had occurred. After waiting until the footfalls faded, he said, "You missed a button."

Her hand shot to her bodice and her gaze shot down.

He didn't wait until she discovered her buttons were all neatly in their holes. She had confirmed his worst misgivings. Pivoting, he went back in the room. His image of her was shattered and he no longer wanted to look at her. Bloody hell, what on earth was she doing?

He pushed the door to the breakfast room open and crossed to the bed.

"Jack." Her voice trembled.

He had no right to be angry or disappointed. She had not betrayed him. "What?" shot out of him.

He turned to sit on the bed. Her face creased with distress as she tried to moor her hair, but the task was hopeless.

"It's not what you think," she whispered.

Surely she didn't care what he thought. Or if she did, why would she? He was a millworker. Nothing to her. His kind didn't count in her world.

He pivoted and crutched back toward her. "What is it, then?"

Her blue eyes filmed over. Good God, she wasn't going to cry. Her mouth tightened and she put a hand over it as she turned away. She might as well have punched him in the stomach. Why would she care about his opinion of her? Or had what happened in the library distressed her?

Jack hesitated, wanting to offer comfort that at the same time warred with his keening disappointment.

Behind her the door opened and the maid who had been minding him earlier backed through with a tray in her hands.

Did Mrs. Broadhurst want the entire household gossiping about what she'd been doing in the library? She squeaked as she lifted her hair with both hands.

Jack pitched his crutches, leaned sideways to try to look as if he'd lost his balance and had to grab her to stay upright. But the two-stone plaster cast overbalanced him, thwarting the pretense. He tried to stop his fall by putting down his broken leg, but with the bent knee angle of the cast, getting his foot underneath him was impossible. He grabbed at Mrs. Broadhurst's shoulder and nearly brought her down with him.

She spun, trying to steady him, but his cast glanced on the floor. Pain burst up and down his leg. The maid dropped the tray she brought. The dishes clattered and crashed to the floor.

Mrs. Broadhurst circled her arms around him and tugged at him. "What happened?"

"Tried to turn too fast. Sorry I grabbed your hair," Jack said.

"You didn't—"

He quirked an eyebrow and moved his arm to her shoulder. Mrs. Broadhurst colored and her chin dipped.

The maid helped and in a few seconds they had him on the bed. Yet, the feel of Mrs. Broadhurst against him warred for primacy with the pain in his leg.

"Oh, I'm sorry, ma'am. Just went to fetch him nuncheon."

"It's quite all right. Would you be so kind as to send my maid to my room after you have cleaned the mess? It seems I need a bit of repair to my toilet."

"Yes, ma'am." The maid dropped to her knees by the door and used the napkin to sop up the liquid. She picked up the shards of plate and piled it with the food on the tray.

In his home, the food would have been sorted out from the broken dishes and put on the table, but this wasn't his home. "I'll take some medicine now," said Jack.

Mrs. Broadhurst hurried toward the sideboard and measured out the liquid. She returned with his glass. Biting her lip, she handed him the glass, but she wouldn't meet his gaze.

"Why would you toss aside your crutches like that?" she finally asked after the maid had left the room.

"You prefer the servants to gossip about why your hair was so mussed? They will, you know."

Her face reddened.

"I only meant to give you a credible explanation, but if you prefer the gossip, I won't trouble myself in the future."

"You won't need to in the future." She twisted her hands together and looked over her shoulder at the door. Her voice dropped to a barely audible whisper. "But thank you."

Did she mean no more impromptu encounters with one of her guests, or did she intend to be more careful of her appearance?

"The least I can do, after all you've done for me." He turned and looked at the well-tended fire. Then he drank his bitter medicine.

She fingered a bit of hair above her ear as if it annoyed her. "I must go fix . . . this . . ." She took a step backward and then whirled toward the door.

He wanted to stop her, to pin up her hair for her. She strode toward the door, her head tilted toward the strand she continued to worry.

"A gentleman would have repaired your appearance," he said. Many times he had stopped Lucy and tried to make sure her hair was at least pinned, not that she ever cared.

Who was he kidding? He wasn't a gentleman, and he was no longer certain that Caroline was a lady in any way beyond having blue blood. But either way, they were not on the same level. And her repeated rebuffs made it obvious she considered him too inconsequential to dally with, while the men of her class were encouraged. His chest hurt as if she had ripped out his heart, hopes, and dreams.

After midnight, Caroline slipped out of her room. Slowly, she traversed the hall ready to duck into a shadow if anyone was about. But if the weather cleared—and the storm had ended in the afternoon—the men were scheduled to hunt on the morrow, so all had taken to their beds at a reasonable hour.

Her thin soles made no sound on the carpet runner as she passed the guest rooms and neared Mr. Berkley's room. A tightness in her throat threatened to choke her. What Mr. Berkley had done was worse than anything she'd ever had to submit to with Mr. Broadhurst. Did any woman willingly do what he had forced her to do? Or was it that he thought her near enough a whore to do as he pleased?

She had debated with herself revealing to him that her husband wanted a child, a son, by any means possible, but she couldn't submit to any more of the unpleasantness.

She'd tried. Three times she'd tried. And failed. She would pretend she was leaving her room nightly for trysts and then when she failed to conceive, well, the men couldn't stay forever. Mr. Broadhurst couldn't hold it against her if he thought she was seriously making the attempt. Perpetrating a deception wasn't her nature, but neither was whoring. Surely her father had never envisioned this pretty pass when he sold her bloodline to Mr. Broadhurst.

Even though it felt underhanded to her, she'd sell off her jewelry, have Robert make investments for her, and she could buy cheaper wine—Mr. Broadhurst wouldn't know the difference—and economize in other ways to funnel money off the household accounts. With prudent investments, in a few years she might have a respectable nest egg—nothing that would allow her to live as she lived now, but enough that she could exercise some independence, even if she lived under her brother's roof. She forced away the niggling guilt at her plan.

She wasn't truly stealing. Her hand had been forced. Mr. Broadhurst should have never formed the intent to leave her destitute.

She tiptoed to the landing and looked down in the entry hall. The only person she was likely to run into was the night porter, whose business it was to walk the house and check for fire. So she had to go somewhere and not just skulk about the corridors.

Once she determined the coast was clear, she quickly descended the stairs. She would sit with Jack, because anything else would require too much explanation or leave her vulnerable to another encounter with Mr. Berkley if he sought her out.

Steeling herself, she opened the breakfast room door. With any luck Jack would be sleeping, and she wouldn't have to face the shock and accusation in his eyes.

The fire was low and the footman sat in the chair beside Jack's bed. The footman's chin was tucked against his chest and his mouth gaped open. He jerked back and then his head fell forward again.

Jack turned from where he lay on his side and watched her. Caroline sighed. Wrong man sleeping. Grimacing, she crossed the space and shook the shoulder of the footman.

When he blinked awake, she told him he might seek his bed. He mumbled an apology but didn't waste any time in leaving her alone with Jack.

She had planned to sit in a corner and perhaps read while Jack slept—except he was awake.

As long as he didn't mention his observations of this

morning, it would be all right. After all, she had sat with him most evenings. And if she had avoided him all day, he wouldn't know it was embarrassment keeping her away.

"Do you need more medicine?" she asked.

"No." He shifted to sit, but she didn't miss his wince. He turned his head away from her.

"Are you certain?" She would much prefer he take his medicine and be asleep in a half hour.

"I don't want to get dependent on it." He stared straight ahead, avoiding her eyes. His jaw ticked.

Was he disappointed in her? Angry? She felt a little like she'd been kicked, as she had earlier when he recoiled from her. He couldn't be more disappointed in her than she was in herself. She'd allowed Mr. Broadhurst to manipulate her into actions that were wrong.

Her eyes burned and she was frozen to the spot. Jack clearly didn't want her here, but she couldn't go back upstairs yet. Not if she wanted Mr. Broadhurst to believe she was engaging in an affair.

His voice flat, Jack said, "My father started drinking to ease his back."

It was an opening that had her knees buckling in relief. "He drinks too much, then?"

"Never stops." He closed his eyes.

He hadn't said much, but he'd conveyed a wealth of information. Her father had always imbibed rather liberally, but it had grown worse, until he spent more time in his cups than not. Sarah once said to Caroline that she was lucky to have missed the last few years, when their father was a complete sot. She opened her mouth to share her own father's failing, but snapped it shut. Speaking of it did no good. Certainly she shouldn't share a private family matter with Jack.

She choked and then said, "You're not like your father."

Jack flipped back the covers and stared at his foot. He was likely trying to make his toes move, a task that had been beyond him thus far. "How would you know? You've never met him."

The differences between herself and Jack seemed staggeringly monumental. Yet, they both had fathers who drank too much, they both were afraid of being dependent on others, and both of them didn't quite fit in their respective worlds. "Does you father wait for drink to be offered or does he call for it?"

Jack's gaze landed on her.

"Seems to me a man who has a problem with dependency would count the minutes until his next dose, would ask for more than is needed, and never would delay."

He slowly nodded, his gaze on her intense.

Unable to bear his scrutiny, she looked away until her gaze landed on the book on the sideboard. "Would you like me to read?"

"If this morning wasn't what I thought, what was it, then?" He steadily watched her as if he had taken in every moment of her struggle to keep family skeletons locked away.

Caroline cringed. She wanted to talk of her encounter in the library even less than she wanted to talk of her father.

She drew up and prepared to give him a haughty set-down and a lecture about knowing his place, but she couldn't force the words out. While she did not owe Jack an explanation, he didn't deserve to be treated so disparagingly after he'd preserved her reputation.

She turned toward the fire. "A mistake. I shouldn't like to repeat it, or talk about it."

He made a guttural sound, and it drew her toward him.

"What was the mistake? The man or the act?" He leaned forward on the bed.

Was it because she had chosen Berkley instead of Jack? It didn't matter. The act and all its variations were disgusting. If a man never touched her again, it would be too soon. She wouldn't try to get pregnant again. "All of it."

His eyes narrowed as he watched her. His obvious disappointment made her fixate on the horror of the encounter in the library. Her throat dry, Caroline walked across the room and gripped the door handle. But she couldn't return to her room. No doubt Mr. Broadhurst knew exactly when she left and likely would be waiting for her when she returned.

She hesitated.

"Don't go," Jack said in his burred voice.

Why his voice warmed her insides, she didn't understand. "Have I encouraged you to be so familiar?"

He took his time answering and his voice was reflective. "I thought you had, but perhaps you have changed your mind."

Caroline sagged. Perhaps she had been playing with fire, thinking when he was well enough he could make love to her . . . *Make love?* No, she only needed a man to father a baby. After all, she didn't *want* that disgusting sort of intimacy. On the other hand she'd had her arms around him many times in the last few days and not once had it made her squeamish. But then there hadn't been any real danger. He was far from well.

And was he interested in an affair with her, even though he was engaged to marry another woman? She couldn't bring herself to form the question, especially after she had just rebuked him for thinking she owed him explanations.

"Read," said Jack. "But let me watch the words as you do."

She retrieved the book from the sideboard and carried it to his bed. After lighting a lamp, she pulled the chair close.

His scent filled her nose, masculine and earthy. "Are you not tired?"

"I slept a good deal of the day." His brown eyes softened as he watched her. "But you didn't."

Heat crept up her face. She couldn't explain the trickery she meant to use on Mr. Broadhurst.

When she didn't provide an explanation, he sighed, leaned back against the headboard and folded his arms across his chest as if shutting her out. That bothered her far more than it should have.

She never should have touched him so much or so often, or caught his gaze at the mill. But she had, and in spite of their differences she felt a fragile intimacy with him. He knew more of her than perhaps anyone, and she didn't really want that bond to break. Perhaps she had to be willing to share more of herself it they were to be friends, but she didn't know how anymore. She was always so guarded with Mr. Broadhurst because he took her hopes and used them against her.

She opened the book and put her hand on the page to hold it open, but the words blurred before her eyes. "I believe my father drank himself into an early grave."

Jack stroked the back of her hand. His fingers were rough, callused, and the skin darker than hers, but she was mesmerized. Tingles raced up her arm and her breath hitched.

He pulled back. Barely a touch at all, but it left her shaken and uncertain.

Jack flipped the covers over his legs. "Why are you caring for me?"

Her body went rigid. Why indeed? Because of all the men in the world, *his* face popped into her head when she'd thought about picking a man to father a baby. Her cheeks heated. She could not give him *that* reason.

He tilted his head as if he could read her turmoil.

If it had been any other millworker, she wouldn't have been so adamant about taking him into her home or nursing him herself. Explanations tumbled out of her mouth in a hurried rush. "Because you saved that little girl. Your stepmother was angry with you. The doctor needed a place to operate. The accident was our fault for letting little children work." She pressed her lips together, halting the flow of half excuses. They were all true, but not important. One shoulder lifted. In a half whisper she said, "Because just before the accident you looked concerned about me when I was having a disagreement with my brother."

"Ah," he said softly, but his brown eyes were assessing.

The urge to pour out the contents of her disagreement with Robert hung in the back of her throat. But what was the point, since she'd decided not to go along with Mr. Broadhursts plan?

"I don't want to know if you weren't," she said with an attempt at levity.

The corner of his mouth turned up. "I was, but you shook me off."

The idea that he would have come to her if she beckoned rolled through her like a warm tide. As if she'd been encased in ice and the heat thawed her, the sensation was overpowering and unsettling. Her heart pounded. It was crazy and wrong to grow enamored of Jack, but that was what she was doing. Had been doing. Not knowing what to do or say next, she stared at the floor.

He put a finger on the title of the page. " 'Chapter Six. The Show—' "

"Ooh," she prompted. *Ah, reading, a sane occupation.* And he seemed determined to make her into his teacher, an occupation that at this moment might make more of a difference than running the mill if Broadhurst truly couldn't be persuaded to will it to her.

"Shoe . . . make . . . er. 'The Shoemaker.' "

She commenced reading, her voice fluttering at first but calming into a rhythm as she focused on the words and shut out the rest. But like a spark can turn to a conflagration, her thoughts kept circling back to her attraction to Jack. If only he weren't engaged.

Chapter 14

Caroline pushed the papers to the side and tried to keep her scratchy lids open. With her nightly excursions, she wasn't getting near enough sleep. Every night at midnight she crept down the stairs and read to Jack, her finger following the words, so he could trail along with his gaze.

On Saturday after work she'd taken the gig to the bookstore in Warrington and purchased a couple of children's books and a dictionary for him to study when she was working. Each night she questioned her sanity.

Just because he had been concerned about her didn't mean any great thing. He'd been "concerned" enough about Mattie to keep her from being hit by a broken belt.

For goodness sake he was an engaged man.

"Ma'am, the doctor's here," said Mr. Smythe. "Would you like for him to wait?"

"Yes." She popped out of the chair and reached for her cloak before she thought. Her eagerness gave her pause. It was as if seeing Jack was the best part of her day.

Hurrying outside, she tied her hat under her chin.

After they dispensed with pleasantries, Caroline felt that, outwardly at least, she had regained control of her emotions. Inside, she quivered like a pennant flapping in a gale.

Dr. Hein handed her up into his curricle. "How is our patient, today?"

"He was sleeping soundly when I last saw him this morning." Caroline settled on the seat. Jack was getting better and increasingly restless. He kept asking for clothes and she kept staving him off. Which was silly. If she didn't mean to use him to father a baby then there was no reason to keep him at the house, except he provided a safe haven when she was sneaking about pretending to conduct an affair. "But I can tell you, he is quite anxious to use his crutches more."

"As he should. He will need to rebuild his strength." The physician climbed into his gig and unwrapped the reins from the brake handle. "Has he been able to move his toes?"

Caroline shook her head. The inability to move his foot concerned Jack.

The doctor sighed. "I suppose he must have damaged a nerve in the accident."

"Will it heal?"

"It is in God's hands." The doctor shrugged. "He may never have full use of his foot. Or it might fully heal. Only time will tell. At least he seems to have escaped sepsis."

If his ankle didn't heal properly, Jack might need to work as a clerk permanently.

Dr. Hein slapped the reins, starting the horse forward. "And our other patient? He has been taking the foxglove a few days, long enough to see improvement."

Caroline frowned. His words didn't seem to make sense in her head.

"Is your husband feeling better?" asked the doctor anxiously. "Perhaps I should look in on him first."

Goodness, was she so concerned about Jack, she'd forgotten Mr. Broadhurst? "He has been well."

"Remember, your husband must not take too much of

ALL ABOUT SEDUCTION   195

the foxglove, but exactly as I prescribed it," the doctor was
saying. "Those who think the prescribed amount makes
them feel so well that more would make them feel better are
sadly disabused of the notion. Too much can make a heart
stop."

Caroline turned to the doctor. "You told Mr. Broadhurst
this, did you not?"

"Yes, of course, and I reiterated the dosing instructions
with your brother, as you had gone to the mill, but I find
with men it is often their wives that mind the details of their
lives."

"Perhaps he shouldn't take it at all if it is so dangerous,"
she said.

"I don't wish to alarm you, but his heart is weak. The foxglove will help, but his heart could give out at any time. All
this activity with his visitors might be too much for a man in
his condition. He is not hale."

Her fingers curled in until her nails bit her palms through
her gloves. She might not have years to build a nest egg
or work at persuading Mr. Broadhurst to change his mind
about leaving her with nothing. She had to go back to her
original plan of getting pregnant. Her heart thundered in her
chest. She couldn't tiptoe around anymore. Either she had to
solicit Jack or apply herself to seducing one of the remaining
gentlemen.

"Are you all right, Mrs. Broadhurst?" asked the doctor.

"I'm fine," she said in a wooden voice.

"I know it must be hard news—"

"Mrs. Broadhurst! Oh, Mrs. Broadhurst, Doctor, do stop."

Caroline swiveled to see Lucy running after them. Her
skirts were caught up in one hand and her black stockings
flashed beneath white petticoats as she chased them. In her
other hand she held a tied bundle.

The doctor stopped the horse.

Lucy caught the side of the vehicle and stood panting. A stray strand of blond hair curled over her rosy cheek and she pushed it back. "Would you give . . . these to Jack?" She held out the cloth bundle. "I baked him a batch of his favorite shortbread."

And then there was Lucy, bright-eyed, pretty blond Lucy, Jack's future wife. Caroline silently moaned. She couldn't make use of Jack when he was going to marry this girl, not do that with him and then work within feet of him in the mill office, knowing he would be going home to Lucy.

"You can have some too," the girl said cheekily to the doctor. "And give Jack my love. I have to get back before the foreman realizes I left." Her guileless eyes landed on Caroline. "Another girl's watching my spot, but you understand, don't you, Mrs. Broadhurst."

Not trusting her voice, Caroline nodded.

Oh God, she couldn't use Jack knowing this sweet girl was to be his wife.

Jack sat at the table writing on the sheaf of papers Mrs. Broadhurst had left him. Would she come to him tonight? She had for the last three nights and it was torture to have her so near, yet be unable to do anything more than listen as she read to him or talked about her idea to offer meals at the school so the families wouldn't feel the loss of wages so keenly.

He wanted her badly enough that if he didn't get out of here soon, he'd embarrass them both by pulling her into his bed. But he had no clothes and his boots had disappeared. He didn't want to brave the cold with just stockings and a nightshirt, although it might come to that.

The door clicked open behind him, and he tried to mask his stiff intake of breath.

She drew near and his senses swirled with her soft scent. His blood fired. But she hovered just out of reach.

He didn't know where he stood with her. She'd tolerated his probing questions, but had not always answered them. Occasionally it seemed as if she were baring her soul and glad to have him as a confidant. He didn't dare question why, for fear she wouldn't like the answer and would stop coming to him in the night.

Which would be a good thing, he told himself sternly. If their shoulders brushed as she read to him, she'd stiffen and move away. Not exactly the response that would lead him to believe she'd allow more contact. By the time she left in the early morning hours, he'd be randy as a goat, but trying to keep her from seeing how much being near her affected him.

And there was no telling what Broadhurst would do if he found her in a laborer's room. Broadhurst might have come from nothing, but to him the line between a mill owner and millworkers was demarcated in stone.

"What's this?" she asked, picking up his drawing of wheels connected to a mechanized shaft.

Jack tapped his pencil on the table. He should have·been working on his words. The dictionary she'd brought him was full of so many it seemed it would take him a lifetime to learn to spell them all. "I've been trying to figure out the right wheel configuration for horseless carriages."

She frowned. "These don't look like train wheels."

"They're not. It is just a matter of time before someone figures out how to make carriages that run on roads, not tracks, but the wheels are a problem." Needing to put some space between them so he could clear his head, he reached for his crutches and stood.

She blinked her crystal blue eyes. Eyes he wanted to drown in. "Regular wheels won't work?"

He dropped his gaze to her lips. Which was worse—or better. To touch his lips to hers would be heaven.

She lowered her gaze and put the paper down with jerky movements. Sidling to the chair beside his bed, she picked up the book and held it in front of her chest like a shield.

What would it take to get her to yield to him? At times it seemed like maybe she wanted him to touch her, but he was too uncertain to risk it. At first he wouldn't have placed that much importance on it, but now he didn't want to hurt her. Just two nights ago she had let him see her vulnerability, when she admitted that his willingness to intercede with her brother had affected her. Not that he could have done much more than interrupt their conversation. A conversation Caroline had waved off as a silly family matter when he asked what her brother had said to upset her.

She seemed skittish tonight. Uncertain. Instead of stepping closer, he held up the drawing. "With a carriage, you want as little friction with the road to make it easier for a horse to draw it, but with a mechanized carriage, you would need the wheels to transfer the power from the engine to the road. They would have to be wider for more friction and made out of a different material so as to not tear up the roads."

She stared at him, her lips parting. A jolt shot straight to his groin.

He took a few steps toward the bed. Would she allow him to hold her?

She skittered toward the fireplace, the book against her chest.

His crutching around left him tired, and he couldn't follow her as she darted around the room. He crutched to the bed and sat with a thump. "Will you read?"

"Jack . . ." She bit her lower lip and turned her head.

He waited, hoping there would be a word of encouragement that she was as aware of the sizzle in the air as he was.

Her gaze fastened on the tied bundle of treats resting on the sideboard. "You didn't eat the shortbread?"

He shrugged. "I had one. I'll send the rest home with Beth tomorrow. The children will enjoy them."

"It was very thoughtful of Miss Dugan to send them," she said.

No it wasn't. It was Lucy's effort to continue to claim him, when he'd told her that they were done. "She shouldn't have bothered."

Caroline's eyebrows knit.

Jack pushed the crutches to the side and lifted his heavy cast and leg onto the bed. His damn leg was starting its usual nightly burn.

"Do you need your medicine?" she asked.

The laudanum would ease the fire in his blood and the pain in his leg. He nodded, and she spent the next few minutes mixing it with water and sugar. He deliberately put his hand around hers as he took the glass. Her fingers were freezing. Perhaps she didn't feel the heat between them.

"Would you like me to warm your hands?"

She hesitated.

His heart thundered.

"I'll just stir up the fire a bit," she finally said.

His disappointment thick, he swallowed the bitter medicine and set the glass on the side table.

After she poked the fire a couple of times, she settled into the chair beside his bed and opened the book. His reading had improved but was a long way from her easy deciphering of the text. He tilted up to follow the words as she spoke them.

The door crashed open and they both jumped.

"What are you doing?" Mr. Broadhurst filled the door

frame. His glower transferred from Caroline to him and back to her.

Bloody hell.

"I am sitting with the patient." Caroline closed the book and stood.

Mr. Broadhurst glared at her. "This is where you are going every night? To sit and read to this . . . this bastard."

His blood running cold, Jack shot up to sit. Caroline held her hand out stopping him. "He is recovering. Nights are always the worst when one is in pain."

Mr. Broadhurst paced across the room. "This is where you have been sneaking off to," he muttered. "I have asked one thing of you in all our marriage and this is how you repay me?"

What had he asked of her?

"Sir—" Caroline tried to interrupt.

"After all I have done for you and your family, and your promises—need I remind you of your promises and all the bargains you struck?" He slashed at the air as if it impeded him, and paced faster and harder.

Jack frowned and tilted his head.

She stepped to block his view of Broadhurst or Broadhurst's view of him, he wasn't sure which.

Jack pushed at the covers. What could he do if Broadhurst was intent on hurting her? "Sir—"

"Stay out of this," said Broadhurst.

"Please, do not upset yourself, Mr. Broadhurst. It cannot be good for you," Caroline cajoled.

"I have had enough of your lies." He turned and made a chopping motion with his hand.

"Sir, she has only been a kind nurse," Jack said. For as much as he wanted more, nothing had ever happened between them.

"You, shut your mouth," said Broadhurst.

Jack reached for his crutches. He couldn't let the man abuse her.

"Sir, the patient is not well, please do not take out your wrath on him. I am the one with whom you are angry." Caroline's spine straightened and she moved toward the door. "And we should discuss this elsewhere."

Damn it, did she intend to throw herself to the lion?

The old man looked close to frothing at the lips. After a dark glare, Broadhurst stormed after her. Even though Caroline turned her palm toward him, Jack couldn't let her go off alone with Broadhurst. Not and live with himself. He might ruin everything for his family, because the man could be vengeful, but if Broadhurst hurt her, he could never forgive himself.

After closing the door on Jack's worried expression, Caroline crossed the hall, heading for the library, but Mr. Broadhurst grabbed her arm and yanked her back. "I have done everything I can to make this easy for you. I brought in all these men. Is it so much to ask that you—"

"Sir! We will discuss this in private."

"There is nothing to discuss." Mr. Broadhurst yanked her toward the stairs. "You will do as you're bid or I will toss you out on your ear."

She twisted her arm away and spun to face him. The hall wasn't the best place to discuss their bargain. "I have tried," she whispered.

"Are you with child?" he demanded.

Cringing, she tried to get him to lower his voice by patting his chest. "I don't know," but even as she said the words, her head moved back and forth in a negative motion. She had never been good at deception.

Jack's crutches thumping toward the door had her heart skittering in her throat. The last thing she needed was Jack interfering. She had made the bargain so he might stay, so he might work as a clerk, although mostly so she could be free of having a master one day. Her throat closing, she tried to soothe Mr. Broadhurst. "I will do as I promised. I have a plan."

"Dammit, Caroline, I thought . . ." He shook his head. "I find you reading. *Reading* to that . . . common son of bitch." Mr. Broadhurst shook her. "With all those men abovestairs of your class. You will not hide in his room anymore. If I catch you down here, I will have him horsewhipped."

The door opened.

Caroline leaned around Mr. Broadhurst. The last thing she needed was Jack coming to her defense. In his weakened state, he was not capable of helping her. Mr. Broadhurst would have him thrown out, wounded or not. She deliberately suppressed the nerves in her voice. "Please go back to bed, Mr. Applegate. This doesn't concern you."

He stared at her as if trying to discern the risk.

Mr. Broadhurst hissed, "Horsewhipped." He dropped his hands and folded his arms across his chest.

Caroline dipped her head and skirted around her husband. "Please, Mr. Applegate, you need to get back to bed before you fall again."

Jack shot her a dirty look as she held out her hand as if she would steer him. She didn't dare touch him, not while Mr. Broadhurst was watching. She mouthed the word *Please*.

She waited, her breath held until, Jack finally began to pivot around. "Thank you," she whispered.

Jack cast one look over his shoulder, but Caroline followed him into the room and bent to blow out the lamp as he settled on the bed.

"Are you sure you're all right?" he asked in a low voice.

"Of course I am all right."

"Would you call out for help you if you were not?" Jack asked in a low voice.

His concern filtered through her alarm, like a candle put in the window to welcome home a weary traveler, but she feared his interference could only make things much worse. "I assure you, with a house full of gentlemen including my brother, I am in no danger."

She hoped she wasn't in danger. Icy fingers tracked down her spine. If Mr. Broadhurst really had killed his last wife, what was to stop him from doing it again? No, she had to appease him, or neither of them were safe.

Jack searched her face with narrowed eyes.

Her shoulders stiff, she went to the door and murmured a good-night before closing the door.

Mr. Broadhurst grabbed her upper arm and propelled her toward the stairs.

"I can walk on my own."

"Walk faster." His hand bruised her as he forced her up the stairs.

When he got Caroline to her room, he shoved her through the doorway. Following her in, he shut the door, turned the key in the lock and removed it. "Strip."

"Wh-What?" whispered Caroline.

"I said, strip. Take off that dressing gown."

Caroline unfastened the buttons holding the heavy robe closed. She wouldn't need it for bed.

"The night is still young enough," Mr. Broadhurst muttered.

"I will arrange another tryst tomorrow." She draped the robe over the foot of her bed.

Mr. Broadhurst's eyes raked over her. They were cold and

hard. "Your family understands the importance of this."

"But—"

"I'll have that bastard sleeping in my house whipped, broken leg or not."

Jack hadn't done anything to deserve her husband's wrath. She reached for the covers of her bed, only to be jerked back.

"I've had enough of your games. I always thought you were an honorable woman, Caroline. That you would adhere to any bargain you made. It appears nobility of breeding is no indication of character."

Caroline's mouth worked. But the trouble was, she couldn't find the heart to object to what he said. She had welshed on her promise; not that she should have been asked to commit adultery in the pursuit of offspring. Nor could she claim failing to fulfill a bargain as the weakness of her sex—not when he would take it as another reason she could not run the mill. And seducing a gentleman and getting him to impregnate her wasn't as easy as he thought it was. It wasn't as if she were beautiful like her blond sisters. She was far from every man's ideal.

Mr. Broadhurst marched to her wardrobe, drew out the dressmaker's box and tossed it on the bed. "Take off that damn unsightly nightgown and put this on."

"No," she whispered, but her protest was barely audible.

"You knock on any one of our guest's doors wearing that and he'll know what to do."

A squeak of alarm left her, but icy fear ran in cold rivulets down her spine. She had determined that she would ask Jack when he was well enough, but she couldn't tell Mr. Broadhurst that.

Mr. Broadhurst pulled a penknife from his pocket and opened the blade. "If I have to cut that nightgown off of you, I'll send you out in nothing. Your choice, Caroline."

Her mind raced. How could she get out of this? But it would happen again and again until she played her part of this impure bargain. She straightened and reached for her buttons. "You will not horsewhip Jack. He is not a part of this."

He moved closer with the open blade. "You made him part when you bargained for a position for him." He sliced the twine around the box, but instead of closing the blade, he used it to emphasize his next words.

Shivers ran down her spine. If Mr. Broadhurst learned she planned to use Jack, he would not hesitate to hurt him. Doubly so if he thought it might hurt her too.

"And I swear, Caroline, I do not want you spending any more time with him. You will be spending the nights getting with child by one of the men your brother provided. All of your undergarments too."

"Sir," she protested. "That's indecent." She opened the box and was reminded of how very sheer the chiffon was.

"Your own sister sent you that. She understands. Now, I want results. Sleep with every man in this house, but do not—" He emphasized his point with the knife. "Do not tell any more of them you want a child because I cannot give you one."

Caroline went light-headed. He knew what she said to Mr. Whitton.

"Hurry up. You will not be allowed back in this room until you have fulfilled your nightly part of the bargain."

The servants were up before dawn, stirring fires to life, the valets carrying hot water to their gentlemen for shaving, the footmen preparing the dining room for breakfast. She couldn't be flitting around in the sheer negligee and lacy wrap. She should have burned them when she had a chance. "The men are hunting tomorrow, they will want their sleep."

"A man will give up sleep for a moment's pleasure." Mr.

Broadhurst stepped closer and grabbed the wrapper. "You won't need this."

"I'll freeze."

"If you don't find a warm bed."

"I have a plan. There is no need to send me out like a whore displaying her wares."

Mr. Broadhurst's gaze was reptilian. "You will do this tonight and the next and the next." He raised his arm as if to slap her, but it still contained the knife.

He was mad. Did he even remember he had the blade in his hand or was he in such a state of anger he would use it? Shaking, she shed the last of her undergarments and pulled the gossamer nightgown over her head. Even as the material whispered against her skin, it felt like nothing. She wanted to defy her husband, but standing in front of him nearly naked, her courage fled.

Mr. Broadhurst's nostrils flared. His voice softened, but it chilled her worse than his threats. "Come, darling, you want a child. I know you do. You used to say so."

She had wanted a child, desperately. Her mother had told her to think of that as she endured Mr. Broadhurst's visits. A woman had to submit in order to have a family. She had only to make herself available and think of conceiving, but that hadn't been true with Mr. Berkley, or Mr. Broadhurst. She no longer believed it could happen, not really.

She was tired of submitting, tired of the notion that the man was the head of the household and must be obeyed, tired of being nothing more than his servant. She wanted a child, but she'd be the one to decide when and how it was conceived. He might send her out like a harlot, but she would not go to one of the gentlemen.

"Now take down your hair, but use the ribbon to tie it back. No hiding like Lady Godiva for you."

She removed the pins that held up her night braid and un-plaited the strands. As good as naked, her fingers trembled while she followed his order, as her mind spun down useless tracks to avoid this travesty.

Mr. Broadhurst looked her up and down. "You've a fine figure. No man would turn you away."

Would Jack? Did she dare go back down the stairs to him?

In the moment of her hesitation, her husband grabbed her arm and pulled her to the door. He gave her a little shove as he followed, closed the door, pulled out the key and locked it.

She stumbled and caught herself. He stood by her door and folded his arms. "Go. I will return to your room and wait."

Caroline took a step down the hall, toward the rooms housing their guests. Her legs were weak and she fisted her hands in the material, trying to cover the darkness at the apex of her thighs. Her stomach clenched.

The unheated corridor terrified her. She couldn't tell if her skin was colder than her insides. Oh God, she couldn't do this again. But she had no choice. She couldn't go downstairs to Jack while Mr. Broadhurst watched her. Horsewhipping would be the least of it, if she were caught with him.

Her teeth chattered and her entire body shook as she neared the first doors. Her mind spun as she tried to remember which man was in the first room.

"Stop stalling," hissed Mr. Broadhurst.

She looked at the doors. First was Lord Edward's room. She passed Lord Tremont's door. Ahead was Mr. Berkley's room. He would at least not be shocked by her appearance at his door, although she had been careful to not be alone with him. However, without revealing her husband *wanted* to be cuckolded, she doubted she could convince him to do what was needed to impregnate her.

She cast a glance over her shoulder. Mr. Broadhurst

glared at her. She closed her eyes. Independence could be the reward for this. Her bravado disappeared in light of what Jack had said about the previous Mrs. Broadhurst, about her husband's threat to have Jack horsewhipped, and about her own shame at making a bargain and then failing.

Jack listened for sounds that Caroline needed help. If she were in trouble, would she scream or just suffer in silence with quiet dignity? Either way, he wanted to check on her, but she would find the intrusion into her personal life insolent and disrespectful. Lying in the bed, he felt useless. He was no more than her patient.

He pushed back the covers and sat. Dizziness assailed him. The laudanum was winding him down. He would have to go slowly, but he was determined to be certain she was not following in the path of Broadhurst's two previous wives.

He reached for his crutches and positioned them under his arms. Moving as quietly as he could, he moved out into the cavern of the entry hall and across the marble. His foot protested at the cold of the unheated stone, but he feared for Caroline.

The staircase loomed before him, but he'd taken the steps before. One flight up were the drawing rooms, music room, and unused ballroom. The bedrooms were two flights above him. He planted the crutches on the first stair and began the steady journey up into the parts of the house where his kind weren't allowed.

His heart thumping and his breathing harsh, he took each step until he reached the silent landing of the first floor. He heard a whisper and jerked his head trying to hear more. He took a couple of the risers. His chest heaved and beads of perspiration dotted his forehead. God, even if he could get to her, what could he do?

But he continued on. Just out of his line of vision a thin white thing went by. Now he was seeing ghosts. He shook his head and grabbed for the banister, barely hanging onto his crutch.

The form returned to the top of the stairs. "Do not follow me," she said in a low hiss. She wasn't looking down the stairs, but back down the hall from whence she came. What the hell was she wearing?

"Do not think of going down those stairs," was the answer in Broadhurst's creaky whisper, but the menace in his tone chilled Jack's blood.

Jack blinked and wondered if the laudanum was playing a trick on him, or if he'd gone to sleep and was dreaming, because it appeared that Mrs. Broadhurst wore a gown he could see through. The jut of her breast, the line of the thigh, dear God, the curve of her bum were all discernable. Behind her back, she made a shooing motion he almost missed because he was staring so hard at her sweet form.

He swallowed several times.

She turned on her heel and disappeared from sight. Jack stared into the darkness, wanting a chance to look longer and wondering if he had really seen her at all—and heard Broadhurst. But he was sure of it, none of the other men in the house would have raised his hackles the way Broadhurst did.

What on earth was going on? Just to think, Jack had to shake off the image that seemed forever locked in his brain. His thoughts moved as if through pudding and came out muddled. It couldn't be. The conclusion he reached was preposterous, but he ran through everything in his mind again and came to the same result.

Broadhurst wanted Caroline to have sex with the men staying in the house.

Chapter 15

Caroline couldn't believe Jack had followed her up from the ground floor. If he interfered, he would ruin everything. At least she was able to shoo him off before he climbed the next flight of stairs to the bedrooms. If Mr. Broadhurst threw Jack out of the house, she wouldn't be able to have him get her with child. Of course the point was probably moot, unless she happened on a gentleman who slept like the dead and didn't wake when she entered his room. She could go in without knocking and hope for the best.

Her heart threatening to pound out of her chest, she walked by another door. Mr. Broadhurst's eyes were burning holes in her back. His rage was a tangible thing that weighted the air. Nothing could have induced her to go back to him. But ahead was the horrible choice of one of the gentlemen.

Dear God, don't let one of them rise to use the water closet. Her thoughts refused to hold together as she worked to remember the room assignments. If she could barely remember, would Mr. Broadhurst have any inkling? There was Ivero's room on the left and Langley's on the right. She jerked to a halt.

Lord Langley had gone home. His room was vacant. Without another thought she burst into it, whirled around while closing the door. She turned the key. Her heart was beating so hard she thought it might be audible to anyone near.

She stumbled through the pitch-black room, stubbing her toe on a chair. Biting back her yelp, she formulated a plan. Langley's room connected to a dressing room, which lead out to the servant stairs. If she brought Jack from the first floor to the room . . .

At best it was a half-baked plan, but she didn't dare leave him to be caught by her husband. Only she could barely see. She headed for the empty hearth and scrabbled around on the mantel shelf until she found matches. She lit one and found a stubby night-light. She managed to touch the match to the wick just before the match singed her fingers.

Holding the candle aloft, the light only emphasized how very near to naked she was. Crossing the room, she grabbed the counterpane and wrapped the yards of material around her and over one shoulder like a Roman toga, leaving one arm free. At least if the night porter or one of the gentlemen stumbled on her, she could maintain some dignity. Biting her lip so hard she tasted the coppery flavor of blood, she slipped into the dressing room. Her feet protested as she left the carpet for the frigid bare wood.

Resisting the urge to walk only on the less sensitive sides of her feet, she scurried through the darkness to stairs. Nearly putting out the flame in her haste, she raced down the steps. She set the candle on a riser before opening the door to the first floor. She couldn't risk the candlelight being visible to Mr. Broadhurst.

Her heart thundering in the chest, she stepped out into the hallway.

Jack stood at the top of the main flight of stairs leading down to the ground floor.

"Jack," she whispered.

He swiveled so fast she feared he would overset himself. He drew his gaze over her as she walked toward him, the counterpane dragging behind her. His forehead crinkled and a half smile lifted the corner of his mouth.

"What—"

She pushed her icy finger against her lips and shook her head.

He tilted, looking up the stairs.

Damn, she did not need Mr. Broadhurst seeing him.

She caught his arm to pull him toward the servant stairs. His heat radiating through the nightshirt scorched her, but then her hands were cold. Running around nearly naked in cool late October was hardly conducive for a successful measure of skin temperature, but she hoped he wasn't developing a fever now.

He grunted softly as he planted his crutch to keep from being pulled off balance.

Realizing she couldn't tug him around, she winced.

He tilted his head down and slowly swiveled toward the open doorway. As soon as she had him in the steep narrow stairwell, she inched the door shut until it latched with a click that sounded like a gunshot. The steps went down to the kitchen, or she could take him back upstairs.

Looking down, Jack sagged against his crutches, breathing heavily. He was far from well and fit.

What if Mr. Broadhurst had followed her down the hall and listened at the door? He would expect to hear—Oh Lord—he would expect to hear the sounds of her with a man, and if he didn't . . .

She said sotto voce, "I need your help."

Jack turned and tilted his head, his expression shifting to wide-eyed speculation. "In what way?"

Oh God, how would she ask him to get a child upon her? Her chilled cheeks flashed with sudden heat. "I'll explain later. Can you make it up this flight of stairs?"

The flight was narrow, without a handrail, the steps twice as steep as the main stairs.

"Up will be easier than down," he whispered.

He searched her face, and she wondered how much he had seen earlier. And was Mr. Broadhurst right in that all she had to do was present herself in the sheer negligee and a man would know what to do? Would Jack? Was he well enough?

Unable to meet his eyes with her thoughts racing on such lurid paths, she ducked her head. "Hurry, please," she hissed.

He complied, his arms quivering under the strain. By the time she had him in the empty bedchamber, he breathed like a winded horse. He sagged against the crutches. "Need . . . rest," he heaved.

"Here, lie down on the bed," she whispered. Fearing he might collapse, she held onto his waist as he slowly rocked across the room.

He shook badly as he leaned against the edge of the stripped bare guest bed. Beads of perspiration dotted his forehead while he twisted and used the crutches to vault himself onto the high mattress. The bed creaked and he groaned.

She whimpered, fearing the exertion might make him develop an ague. And getting him back downstairs to his own bed before the night was over would strain him even more. Would he be capable of mating at all? She couldn't ask it of him tonight. Or would she even have to ask?

The doorknob to the main hall rattled and both of them jerked their heads to see the distinct double break in the spill of gaslight under the door. A jolt of alarm made her heart flip in her chest. Stars above, if Mr. Broadhurst caught her with Jack . . .

The events of the night seemed so peculiar that Jack wasn't sure if he was dreaming or riding the black mare. If this were his dream, Mrs. Broadhurst would be climbing into bed with him about now. Or if Mr. Broadhurst burst through the door, he would know it was a bad, bad nightmare.

He stared through the darkness at the door handle, seeing it twist just slightly but not enough to open. Mrs. Broadhurst must have had the foresight to turn the key.

Mrs. Broadhurst hid his crutches on the far side of the bed. While crawling over him, she unwound the bedcover. She jerked the spread to cover them and the bare mattress and unfortunately kept it over her.

He caught her arm, halting her frantic efforts. She jerked to pull away, but Jack had the advantage of seeing the terrorized way she stared at the shadows cast by two feet beyond the door. She feared what was on the other side worse than she feared anything he might do. He couldn't see much by the light of the single candle, but he could see that. And it wasn't any bogeyman standing at the door, but Broadhurst, who might be worse than any bogeyman.

"Hey," Jack whispered.

Mrs. Broadhurst twisted and covered his mouth. Her eyes begged him to be quiet. But he couldn't stop the grunt that left him as she bumped his broken leg in her haste to silence him. He wasn't sure if terror left her hand as cold as a corpse's or just the chill of an unheated room.

Her expression crumpled, but he shook his head and peeled her iciclelike fingers away. His breathing, still harsh from the rapid climb up the stairs, rasped in the quiet. He needed all the air he could suck into his lungs. He attempted to warm her hand by pressing it between his, but she snatched it away. After a second Jack twisted up to cup his hands around her closest ear.

"He wants one of the gentlemen to get you with child?"

She shuddered then pulled away, but her chin went down in a quick confirmatory nod. Then she wouldn't meet his gaze. Instead she leaned across and blew out the candle, plunging them into darkness before he had a chance to truly glimpse the treasures revealed by the gauzy garment she wore.

Jack's body pounded as he realized it was no dream, and he wanted her to reach across the expanse of the bed and touch him. He waited and waited. The darkness pressed him down.

She lay so still he wondered if she was breathing. He didn't know why he hoped she might turn to him. He wasn't a gentleman. He wasn't even a whole man. She had probably never even considered asking him to help her in that way.

Fighting the laudanum, the exhaustion, and his disappointment, he pushed up on an elbow to watch for the shadows to move. What was Broadhurst waiting for?

Jack tensed, waiting now too.

Caroline had been sneaking down to his bedside night after night. Was what he'd seen and heard in the library her attempt at seduction? The night before the library, she'd been drinking. Had she tried to seduce one of the gentlemen then too? Seducing men she barely knew was probably awful for her.

She probably hadn't been concerned about him at all. His room had been a safe place to go while pretending to follow her husband's bizarre request—order—whatever it was.

The man probably wanted proof that she was following his dictates this time. The space between the shadows darkened, as if Broadhurst had leaned his ear against the door.

Jack groaned and shifted on the bed. He twisted until he could brace his foot on the floor and rocked the bed until it responded with a rhythmic squeak and thump of the head-board against the wall.

Mrs. Broadhurst gasped. Ignoring her, Jack forced the bed to produce a steady beat. The solid bed took a lot of work to move. Doubtful that any man could trowel so hard into a woman, but he made the bed hit the wall, doing all he could to make it sound as if Mrs. Broadhurst was getting dipped.

He moaned louder and hoped he sounded more like a man in the throes of passion rather than in pain. He didn't dare murmur sweet nothings for fear Broadhurst might be able to identify his voice, but who could tell one man's moans from another?

"He's gone." Her whisper cut through the night.

Jack gave one final push and tried to catch his breath. He was thoroughly exhausted and disgusted with himself. If he were a whole man, he'd march down the hall and beat the living daylights out of Mr. Broadhurst for sending his wife out like a cock bawd sends out his whores.

Only the idea that if he stayed he could persuade her to let a lowly mill worker get her with child trumped any real desire to punish Mr. Broadhurst. And with that thought he'd sunk to a new low.

She slid out of the bed but left the cover over him. He cursed the darkness that prevented him from seeing her.

"You should stay under the covers." *You should let me hold you.*

She stopped moving.

Then, inexorably, the noises of her shuffling started again. Slowly, she rounded the bed. She patted the bedside table until she found the candle, and then crept away.

He had to stop thinking she saw him as anything more than a safe refuge. Even though she seemed like a woman who yearned for babies—the way she'd picked up Mattie in the mill, and her interaction with Beth, and her concerns about the young children working instead of being in school, all pointed to a woman who wanted a family—she'd never given any indication that she might consider *him* a possible candidate for fatherhood. Every time *he* tried to touch *her,* she'd jerked away as if he were scalding her.

She scrabbled on the mantel and then was back by his side. He stared into the darkness, wishing to see more than the thin white outline against the overcast midnight darkness. Where was the moon when it was needed?

The clicking next to him must be her teeth chattering.

The rasp of a match and the sudden flare had him throwing his hand over his eyes. He wanted to see her, not have his eyeballs burned. He squinted and shaded his eyes, but the flash of the match was imprinted in the center of his vision.

From what he could see, Mrs. Broadhurst was shaking like the last autumn leaf in a stiff breeze. He desperately wanted to make out her form under the nightgown, and in the corners of his vision the dark shadow at the juncture of her legs drew him, just before she wadded the material in front of her. Damn, if she didn't want him to look, why had she lit the candle?

He closed his eyes briefly, trying to blot out the stain from the fire.

He didn't dare reach for her again.

She shook so much the flame wavered. Then just as his eyes were beginning to function properly again, she twisted away. It wasn't soon enough. Her nipples showed as rosy shadows. Her curves were outlined. Even the slight darkening that marked her navel drew him to want to dip his tongue there. Pings of excitement bounced through him and his mouth watered.

But she was chilled. He lifted the coverlet. "Take this," he rasped.

"Keep under the covers, I don't want you getting a fever now. I'll light the fire." Her voice was high and wavering, not the low tones of a seductress.

Damn. He didn't need the covers. He was burning. The room was chill around him, but only seemed to magnify the heat of his skin. A low energy thrummed in him as she knelt in front of the fireplace with the candle in front of her.

She was the one who needed warmth, and it would take a bit of time to get the coal burning in the grate. Had she ever lit a fire before?

He swung to slide off the bed. "I'll do it."

She cast a tense look over her shoulder. "Stay there. You should rest before we have to get you back downstairs."

What in the world was going on with her? Her husband wanted her to sleep with other men, she was cold and she wouldn't stay under the covers next to him. Did she find him that repulsive? And was it because he was a laborer—a next to illiterate millworker?

Jack sighed, as if he could sort anything out when she was across the room from him, nearly naked. He couldn't think about anything more than the glimpse of flesh he'd already had and wanting to see more. It wasn't terribly gentlemanly of him, but there you had it. He'd never been delusional about what he wanted from her.

He lay back on the bed and stared at the underside of the bed canopy. The blood rushed in his ears, but he also felt the languor brought on by the dose of laudanum pulling him down.

So cold Caroline wondered if ice were forming in her

organs, she could barely control her shaking long enough to hold the candle under the grate. Her eyes stung as she lit the crumpled newspaper beneath the coal that had been laid for Langley's fire, obviously before the servants grew aware that he was leaving. She supposed she should be grateful for that.

But she wanted to crawl away to a dark hole and curl in a ball. All she'd had to do was show herself in the transparent gown—right. That worked so well. Jack had covered his eyes as if the sight of her might turn him into a salt pillar like Lot's wife.

If Jack wasn't interested, she didn't know what she would do. The idea of going back to pursuing one of the gentlemen made her skin crawl. But she did want a baby, and Jack had rocked the bed in an imitation of the act she needed. A sob caught in her throat. She needed him to do the real thing, but he hadn't given her any indication he was inclined to do more than fake it.

Now, if the medicine would just take effect, she could find a way to regain her equilibrium. She should have taken the coverlet when he offered.

The newspaper burnt out, the edges going orange then gray, and the coal just lay there not burning or glowing. She couldn't light any kind of fire tonight. She shoved the candle under the grate and shifted away.

She should just complete her humiliation and ask Jack outright, but her voice was a disturbing three octaves higher than normal and she had no idea how to ask such a thing. She wasn't pretty or blond or young like his Lucy.

The candle flame licked the coal. She watched it thinking it would never reach the coldness inside of her, which was like a black void of nothingness.

She would go back to her room and pretend to Mr. Broadhurst that she had done it, but before dawn she would have to get Jack back down to the breakfast room or there would be hell to pay.

An uncontrollable shudder rippled through her.

The bed creaked and she tensed. Something soft landed against her back.

"At least put that on if you won't take the spread."

He'd thrown his nightshirt at her. He wanted her to cover up. He didn't even want to look at her in the negligee. She made a sound through her nose, almost like a laugh, certainly unladylike. Oh God, she was a miserable failure. Even a millworker didn't want plain quiet Caroline.

Her hands shook as she opened the nightshirt and pulled it over her head. If she could run away, she would run until she couldn't run anymore. But this was her life and she couldn't get away from it, and damn Mr. Broadhurst for making her have to explain to Jack now, instead of in her own time, when he was further on the path to recovery.

She climbed onto the chair she'd stubbed her toe on earlier and pulled her legs up to her chest, the skin of her thighs cold and strange against her belly. Tucking as much of the material as she could get under her feet, she risked looking at Jack.

He was on his elbows, his undershirt baring his muscled arms. Her stomach tickled with apprehension at what she was about to ask him to do. She opened her mouth. The words wouldn't come out.

She tucked her chin down. The nightshirt smelled of him. She closed her eyes and breathed in deeply as she tried to rub warmth into her arms.

He continued to regard her silently, as if waiting for the explanation she'd promised him.

"I'm so sorry for all this," she said, and was pleased her voice wasn't nearly as squeaky as before. "And that there aren't any linens on the bed—or a fire in the grate—or just everything."

Jack's heart thumped irregularly as he watched her. Even in the minimal light of the room, the dusky color across her cheeks was apparent. And he regretted that he'd given her the nightshirt to cover up with, but he couldn't think straight when she was nearly naked in front of him. But with the striped material tented around her, the ache in his groin hadn't eased. Yet, she couldn't have been any more clear about where he stood in regards to that.

"Do you want a child too, or is it only your husband who wants you pregnant?" he said conversationally. There was no other way to approach this.

Caroline's arm rubbing jerked to a halt. She looked up, her eyes filled with hurt. She was desperately cold, but still wouldn't turn to him for a basic need like warmth. He swallowed down his disappointment.

Her voice started barely audible but rose as she spoke. "I've *always* wanted a baby. But this unholy plan was not of my making." She pushed her hand against her mouth as if she regretted what she had said.

Jack watched her struggle. Wondering if he dared offer to help and how she would take it. His crutches were out of reach, as if she wanted to keep as much distance between them as possible. She lowered her hand and lowered her legs, pulling them back and to the side and folding her hands in her lap. She straightened her spine and lifted her chin with the slightest toss of her head.

"It takes a strange man to loan out his wife to other men to get her with child."

She closed her eyes and pressed her lips together. "He just wants a son to pass the mill on to. I know it seems odd . . ."

"Broadhurst can't father children," Jack offered.

She fisted the material at her neck. "How do you know that?"

Curious that she didn't offer a denial.

"You are his third childless wife. It has to be him." And his last wife had died by her own hand or his when she passed the age of childbearing.

Caroline looked down at the floor and spoke in a flat voice. "I always thought that it was my fault, and it is not as if I would have ever known different if he had not presented this plan. I almost hate him for making me hope again."

"You want children."

Caroline shook her head, but it wasn't in disagreement, but as if the knowledge surprised her. "I suggested an adoption, but he is set on it being a child with blue blood and legitimate connections."

"Your child."

She nodded. Her eyes begged him to understand. "Broadhurst wants a child who has no doors closed to him due to the circumstances of his birth. One that will have a better life than he had."

Perhaps the old man possessed a few human traits. Jack still wanted to kill him, but he understood better than he wanted. Perhaps his fascination with her or a woman like her was to help give his offspring—assuming he ever had any—advantages he hadn't had. He ticked off things in his head: education, not needing to work at the age of five, plenty of food, a warm bed all his own. Her child would have everything.

"And you agreed to do this?" he asked.

She laughed, but sounded anything but amused. "I did. It's wrong, I know." Her mouth pursed but her eyes flashed.

Which still left him uncertain of what she wanted. "And what will he do to you when he discovers you are not in a gentleman's bed?" Jack scooted back so his head did not loll as he tried to carry on a conversation with her. God help him, but he'd take being horsewhipped if it meant he could have her.

Her chin lowered and she turned away.

"And you have not found one of the men to your liking?"

"I find I am not cut out to be an adulteress." Caroline's hands fisted in the nightshirt. "If there were any other way . . ."

"There is only one way to conceive a child. What of the man from the library?" Jack shook his head, but couldn't seem to stop himself. He wanted to solve the problem for her.

Spots of red appeared in her cheeks. "He assured me he will not do anything that might result in a pregnancy, and I am forbidden to suggest to him that Mr. Broadhurst is incapable of fathering a child. It wouldn't do for all of society to know that he is not the father of any child I might bear."

A twinge of regret passed through Jack as he thought of all the times he too had refused to commit the act that could lead to a pregnancy. Avoiding marriage hardly seemed a worthwhile goal, but then he'd hoped to better himself before choosing to marry. He squeezed his eyes shut. "You could tell him you are in an infertile time."

She gaped at him. Then sputtered, "And how would any woman know when she is fertile? We don't go into heat like cats and dogs."

He didn't want to help her lay with another man, but if she didn't fulfill her husband's demand, he feared she would end up like the second Mrs. Broadhurst. "If you are regular, two weeks before your flow and the days around that time."

She gaped at him as her skin fired. "You would know this how?"

Jack struggled to sit up straighter, but his limbs were

loose and not responding. "The midwife." He shrugged, then added, "And it has worked for me. Avoiding that time, anyway."

She continued to stare at him, but closed her mouth tightly.

"The days of a woman's flow, the week before and only a day or two after are the safest if one means to avoid conception." Not that he entirely relied on avoiding fertile periods; he also withdrew. But that method alone could fail.

He could see Caroline calculating in her head and her eyes widened. Was she even now in a fertile period?

"Do you want a child?" Jack asked softly.

"I thought I did." She stood and picked up the poker, but there weren't any coals to stir and she shoved the poker at the stand and ignored it when it clattered to the hearth. She paced away, her steps long and kicking the nightshirt that dragged on the floor as she walked. "But I cannot abide the pawing and . . . pinching." She put a hand across her breasts as if to shield them. "I tried to get drunk—"

"I saw."

She continued as if she hadn't heard his interruption. "—but that just made me sick."

He watched her agitated pacing.

"Apparently I am too plain to draw men to me. And I hate pretending to enjoy an act I despise." Her passion made her nostrils flare as the long tail of her hair whipped behind her.

"You're beautiful." In spite of her rant, he couldn't feel the same. He wanted her, even if she took gentle handling to awaken her desires.

She stopped. "You are kind to say so, but you do not have to lie to me. We are better . . . friends than that, aren't we?"

Nothing would ever erase the image of her in that sheer

material, but that probably wasn't the reassurance of her beauty that she wanted or would understand. He only hated that she disliked an act that could be so enjoyable. But she'd been little more than a child when Broadhurst married her. Had the man ever tried to see to her pleasure? "We are friends."

"When my husband stopped coming to my room, I thought I'd never have to endure a man's touch again." She halted and gripped the back of the chair as if she might break it. Her chest heaved and her eyes looked wild. "But to get a child . . ."

Bloody hell, he did not want to see her go to another man and fuck him. "Did you ever think of asking me?"

Caroline's mouth worked but no sound came out. She stared at him. Her head dropped.

She likely thought of him as less than a whole man. Or an encroaching toady to think he could be her stud. He was not of her class, her wealth, or even a gentleman, but he could offer one thing none of the guests could. He knew what she wanted, and she did not fear him.

"I could promise not to pinch or paw." He lowered his voice. "You wouldn't have to pretend."

Caroline circled the chair and sat down hard. She still hadn't said anything.

"I could repay you for all your care, in a way." He plucked at the coverlet, waiting for a response beyond her astonishment.

"What about your engagement to Miss Dugan?"

"I'm not engaged to Lucy, and I never have been. Did she . . . ?" He didn't need to finish the question. Of course Lucy had claimed an engagement. He sucked in a deep breath. Anger in the face of Caroline's fear could only make matters worse. And God forgive him, he wanted Caroline bad enough to keep a leash on his temper. "I told her we were finished."

Silence echoed in the room and her eyes seemed to widen as her mouth rounded.

He waited, the air thickening with each passing second. To push or attempt to persuade would be the wrong tack. Or would it?

"Are you certain you could?" she asked in a quavering voice.

Of course he could perform the act that brought children. "I broke my leg, not my—"

Her hand shot out, stopping him. "Have you any natural children?"

Her question was reasonable, but it took him to a place he didn't want to examine.

She tilted her chin down and then looked through her lashes at him. A surge of wanting thrummed low in him, but he needed to reassure her the effort would not be wasted with him. "I would have a child, if its mother had not . . ."

Her gaze turned more direct and her brow furrowed.

Jack settled for a half-truth, " . . . passed before the babe was due. I have been careful since."

Her mouth tightened. She hadn't repulsed him, but she hadn't consented either. He tried not to press.

"How did she pass?"

Jack turned to look into the fireplace, where the coal was just starting to glow a little. "By her own hand, trying to rid herself of the baby."

"I am sorry," said Caroline.

Hoping to stave off more questions, he said, "We were young. I made mistakes. It was a long time ago." He should have married her straight off, instead of refusing to believe the baby was his because he had withdrawn. It hadn't taken more than a couple of days to realize he was being an idiot, but she had already drunk the entire concoction of pennyroyal and mugwort meant to be taken over several days.

Caroline folded her arms across her chest and made a sound. "Yes, I thought of you."

His heart leapt and he thought he might float off the bed with happiness.

"I wanted to wait until you were more healed, before asking." Under her haughty almost disdain he heard a vulnerability, as if she thought he might refuse.

"I'm healed enough." Satisfied he sounded as business-like about it as she did, it took a huge amount of willpower to keep from grinning like a fool.

"If you do this—" She turned her head as if she couldn't bear to look at him. "—I don't want you to touch me or kiss me or anything other than what is absolutely necessary."

His spine knotted. "You don't want me to hold you?"

She shook her head.

His stomach dropped. What she was describing was like most men's fantasies: not having to worry about the woman's pleasure, not having to spend a lot of time getting her ready, and just focusing on his release. Instead it sounded coldly mechanical—not what he'd envisioned. Not what he hoped. And not at all what he wanted.

Chapter 16

Caroline watched Jack's face twist as if her conditions pained him. Or more likely his leg hurt. He might think he was physically capable, but she wasn't so sure. On the other hand it was now or never.

His arm muscles flexed as he struggled to sit up all the way. She gasped. His undershirt only concealed his torso, leaving no doubt he was a man, and available.

"All right. I will agree to not pinch or grope."

"No touching or kissing."

His eyes narrowed. "Agreed. No touching beyond the necessary, or anything tender during the act."

She gave a short nod. "You must never tell anyone."

"No one would believe me if I did, but I won't." His lip curled as if disgusted. "In exchange, you should help me to read and write better."

Her dry mouth worked, but she had a hard time forcing her agreement. She'd refused to do more than read to him and supply him with materials before, thinking she couldn't spare the time away from her seduction attempts or the mill, but she was desperate. Mr. Broadhurst wouldn't allow her any more leeway. Then again, she wouldn't have to dedicate so much time to the guests if Jack would get a child on her.

A jittering demon's energy shook her with cold clammy

claws. Finally, she gave one short nod, her head refusing to give more compliance than that.

"You might have to come over here, because I don't think any man can manage across a room."

Tension screamed through her body. According to Jack, she was in or near a fertile time. She didn't know how to measure his veracity or knowledge, but she had no reason to doubt he knew what he was talking about. Besides, he'd come from a prolific clan, unlike Mr. Broadhurst, who had no living relatives.

A horrible thought occurred to her. "You don't *need* to grope me or anything to be successful, do you?"

His lips twitched. "I am tempted to lie and say yes, but no. I don't need to caress you, or kiss you or cradle you to me, but I imagine there will be some inevitable contact . . . uh, beyond what is required."

His weight would press her into the bed, and even if he kept his hands to the sides, she would feel his breathing near her ear. She would smell him and hear him as his instrument scraped in and out, but she tried not to think of that. Her legs shook and a cold dread pooled in her stomach.

"If I do anything too outrageous, I'm certain you could get away from me. It isn't as if I could run after you."

But she wouldn't be able to get away once they were engaged. She wouldn't be able to shift his weight off her without his cooperation, not unless she kicked his broken leg. The last thing she wanted was to cause him more pain. "How is your leg feeling?"

He held out his hand, but she ignored it and continued sitting in the chair by the fireplace. He might be willing, but she wasn't sure he was fit enough for such vigorous activity.

His eyes narrowed. "I don't feel it much after the laudanum."

She twisted the material of his nightshirt against her throat. His scent wafted off it, which was both comforting and frightening. They were friends. Friends helped each other. He would help her—she would help him.

"So, when is a good time for you to conceive?" His voice was coaxing, encouraging. But his eyelids were drooping and he looked tired.

"This week." She bit her lip hard enough to taste the coppery flavor of blood.

"Good." He unbuttoned his undershirt and stripped it off.

"You don't have to undress . . ." Her voice trailed off as he shot her a skeptical look.

"I suppose that means you don't intend to do more than lift your nightgown," he said, sounding regretful.

His nightshirt. The insubstantial thing she had on underneath didn't count. She twisted more material in her fingers and avoided looking at the indecent expanse of his chest and stomach. "I don't see any reason it would be necessary."

He shifted, removing his drawers under the coverlet, and cast her a half smile. "It doesn't occur to you that I would like to look upon you, even if I cannot touch."

As he worked his drawers over his cast, his naked hip peeked from below the coverlet, the flesh pale and smooth.

Caroline sprang out of the chair, went to the dressing room door, clicked it closed and turned the key. Not that she expected anyone to interrupt them here. Her chest squeezed and she knew she was near achieving her part of the bargain, or at least knowing a man, even if he wasn't one of the designated gentlemen. Her shoulders knotted. She would have to relax to even allow the event to take place.

Wanting to escape, she returned to the chair by the fireplace and sat down gingerly. "Are you certain you're strong enough? You are not completely healed."

He twisted to reposition the pillows behind him, exposing one pale flank. Fighting an inexplicable need to stare at him, Caroline clenched her eyes shut, uncertain why she wanted to look upon his form.

"Then you should do the work," he said.

Her eyes popped open. "Excuse me?"

She didn't know how *she* could do the work. That was the man's role. Her mind reeled through possibilities and rejected them all. A tremor passed down her spine and knotted her neck.

He slid down on the bed to his elbows, and the coverlet reached his waist, allowing her to draw a breath. His look turned questing. Jack seemed to be waiting, as if he thought she'd know how to manage to provide the motion.

Caroline found her nail in her teeth, a habit her governess had cured two decades ago. She deliberately dropped her hand. "I'm not certain I know how."

"You should mount me, sweetheart." His mouth flattened. "It will give you control of how much we do touch."

She thought about protesting his term of endearment, but she supposed it was just something to call her rather than ma'am or Mrs. Broadhurst. "Are you certain that would work?"

Never had she considered that she could be on top. And the idea of being in control of their encounter made her shake. She had never been more than a passive participant. Always when Mr. Broadhurst mounted her, she'd lay there as still as a church mouse, afraid to make a peep for fear he could actually rend her in two, as it always felt he was doing.

Yet, this with Jack was sounding all very clinical, like a doctor's examination. But that was how she wanted it. Wasn't it?

His mouth worked as if he were restraining a laugh. "Yes, it will work."

She almost wanted to hit him. "I mean to get me with . . . child?"

"That's what I meant." Jack held out his hand and beckoned her. "My da's been on his back for years and it hasn't stopped Martha from conceiving."

Shock that he knew such details of his father's private life made her back feel as if a metal rod had landed against her spine.

"He injured his back some time ago," said Jack, no doubt feeling she needed an explanation.

And his explanation didn't mean he *knew* how his father and stepmother interacted, just that he could surmise it. Although, the workers' houses were small and without much privacy.

"Are you ready?" he asked.

"As ready as I'll ever be. " Her voice sounded too shrill in the room.

"Ah, I've been ready since I saw you at the top of the stairs. You're very tempting to look upon."

He seemed comfortable with his words in the night. The low rasp of his voice curled around and touched a part of her that wanted more than this business arrangement. On shaking legs she stood and stepped closer to the bed. She no longer trusted her voice to sound normal.

Jack's dark eyes watched her as he sat, bunching the muscles in his stomach, showing their form as they moved under his tight skin. He pushed the covers down to his thighs and exposed his instrument.

Caroline gasped. His thick shaft seemed much too large. The back of her legs cramped as he lay back down, moved his hands away from his sides and gripped the mattress ticking beneath him.

Jack waited for Caroline to do more than stare with widened eyes. His body was eager, even as he wondered how pleasurable the sex could be for her when she treated it as only a means to the end of getting pregnant.

Caroline averted her face and stood still as a statue.

He sensed that patience would be of paramount importance. She seemed a woman who would need to be awakened slowly. To move too fast would be to risk losing her. And he could be patient, but this was all backward. Yet, he hoped he could turn it around, but he only had a day or so to get her to stop dreading their encounters. Whatever had gone on between her and Broadhurst, she was still naive and uncertain.

But as time stretched thin, he could see the war within her. That she wanted to flee was obvious.

The long case clock in the entry hall began to chime, its sound faint this far away. He silently counted, one, two, three. But the tolling of the bell jerked Caroline out of her stupor.

She gathered up the nightshirt to mid-thigh and put one knee on the mattress. Jack clutched the mattress under him tighter, resisting the urge to guide her as she swung over to straddle him.

The coolness of her inner leg against the searing heat of his skin startled him. She was poised above him as if afraid to bring their privates together.

He tilted up and brought the covers over her legs. "You're cold."

She made a small squeak and nodded. Then she brought her warm woman's core against his pelvis. Gasping, he grasped the covers, wanting to touch her but honoring her demands.

The moment he had dreamed about and fantasized about

was here, except as she moved it became an awkward farce as he fought to keep his hands to himself. Had he ever attempted this position without using his hand to guide his cock into a woman?

He tilted his hips back to give her a better angle, and then she was pushing onto him, her face a mask of concentration. His foreskin pulled back and back. If he hadn't been so keyed up, it would have hurt. Instead it was a grating raw sensation. But if he was feeling discomfort, she had to be in pain. She was no more ready for him than he was ready to run a mile.

Disappointment and alarm cooled his blood. "Stop."

She twisted her eyes wide, but pain etched her forehead. "Am I hurting you?"

"I'm hurting you. You aren't ready for me." No, she was dry as a desert. His hands hovered at her hips, ready to hold her pelvis against his until she had time to adjust.

She shook her head and shifted apart a little. "It always hurts."

"It shouldn't." A rush of concern and anger burned through him. Had her husband never seen to her comfort?

She cast him a skeptical glance and then turned her head to the side. "We don't have much time. The servants start stirring by four."

She raised her bottom to begin the in and out. Excitement warred with his image of himself. He didn't hurt women—at least not physically.

He lifted his hips to stay joined with her. "A minute won't make a difference."

But she was concentrating on moving, and damn, he'd looked forward to joining with her too long to be oblivious to the sensations. He groaned.

Only, as she moved in a jerky fashion, he was far too

aware that she was trying to hide her pain. Her choice to not lean down on him made it possible to view her expression no matter how much she looked away. In the past he'd had his share of awkward moments, but this was beyond them.

She not only didn't like it, she hated it. But she wanted a baby, and he'd offered to provide one for her. His breastbone ached as he tried to concentrate on the sensations, but he couldn't entirely block her distress. Yet, he'd promised her she didn't have to pretend.

She lifted again and again, at first uncertain, but then gaining a momentum that should have pushed him over the edge. But the laudanum, which blocked his pain, combined with his concern for her, blocked his pleasure too. Although if she kept increasing the speed and vigor with which she bounced on him, spilling his seed would be inevitable.

Then she lifted up too far and he came out all the way. She tried to reseat herself, bending his cock.

He twisted away and pushed her hips back. *"Ow!"*

He removed his hands from her, grabbed the covers and tried to ignore the blast of pain, ignore her clumsy efforts, ignore that she hated intimacy with him.

"I'm sorry," she whispered, but there was a catch in her voice. "What am I doing wrong?"

"You're doing fine." He sucked in a few deep breaths.

"I'm not." She bit her lip. "I'm not certain how long I can do this."

"I was close," he bit out through clenched teeth. God, if he ever understood why a woman would fake a climax, this time was it. He wanted it done and over with.

How could an act he dreamed about, longed for, have turned out so wrong? How could their bodies be joined so intimately, but he felt so disjointed? He was embarrassed by the time it was taking—a feat that would ordinarily be boastworthy was in this instance a curse. A minute or ten might make a difference as he struggled to find his release.

She tried to rejoin them, but the earlier painful miss had made him soften.

"Are you certain you can do this?" she asked.

"It would help if I didn't feel like I was raping you," he blurted.

Her gaze jerked to his and she seemed genuinely puzzled. Did she not have any idea what congress between a man and a woman was supposed to be like? All he wanted to do was cradle her in his arms and fall asleep, but that of course would not get her pregnant. His anger softened. This couldn't be any easier for her. Actually, as he thought about it, she must find it far worse. He at least anticipated pleasure.

"This isn't how it should be," he said softly.

Her mouth tightened. "I'm sorry to disappointment you. I don't enjoy this. I can't imagine that I ever should. Now could you finish, please?"

"You aren't made any different than any other woman. You can feel pleasure too." His angry tone was hardly seductive and he silently cursed himself. What had he thought— she'd take a ride on his magic pole and find incredible pleasure? Or worse, had he believed she cared about him? Clearly she didn't. "Let me show you."

She jerked. "No. I'm different. I don't—"

Fearing she might change her mind about continuing, he sighed. "All right."

Silence settled back between them as she lifted upward and shifted, trying to rejoin them. Clumsy was the last thing he'd expected from an otherwise graceful woman. Even if she wouldn't let him show her pleasure, he could at least teach her to move.

"Caro, I'm just going to put my hands on your hips."

An objection flashed across her face, but he wasn't sure if it was to his use of her name or that he was insisting on touching her.

"Nowhere else, and just to help guide your motion." The last thing he needed was her unseating herself and causing more delay.

"Do you . . . do you want to be on top?" Her face was bright red.

"Not unless you feel unable to continue." Jack wasn't sure he wanted to test how well his leg could handle the exertion. And the likely adjustments he might have to try, to compensate for the heavy cast, would only lead to more embarrassing awkwardness. As it was now, he felt near exhausted, although his desire was returning. He couldn't feel Caroline's naked bottom on his lap without interest stirring in him.

He wanted to do this for her—and for himself. He wanted to feel like he was a whole man. Hell, he just wanted to come inside a woman, as he'd never done. Although his first thought had been that it would bind her to him, in a way she couldn't escape. But she saw this as a business arrangement. A necessary evil.

He settled his hands on her hips and helped her squirm back onto him. He tried to direct his thoughts. This was Caroline, the woman he'd craved for years now. A rush of sensation spilled down his spine. "It's good. Just rock a little."

She winced. The pleasurable sensation all but withered.

"Bloody hell, are you still hurting?" He pushed her hips down and held her still.

"Sir, your language."

"Caro?" How could it still be hurting? Other than she probably had a crick in her neck from averting her face. "You have to help me."

Alarm skittered across her features. Much as he wanted to change the parameters of their encounter, he couldn't risk it. Not until she believed he didn't want to hurt her.

"Only my family calls me Caro."

"If I give you a child, we'll be kin." They would always be connected to each other. If only she wanted him the way he wanted her. "But I'll only call you that in private."

She appeared to consider his promise, then nodded. "What can I do to help you finish?"

Back to the business at hand. "Look at me."

She scrunched her face and then turned. Her color was high as he slowly guided her hips up and back down. Bright red crept from her neck up over her face. He was done letting her pretend this wasn't happening, and it wasn't working to let her have all the control.

"Just because you don't want to be touched doesn't mean I don't want you . . . to touch me."

Her face twisted. But she'd set the conditions too stringently. If his leg didn't hurt or he hadn't taken the laudanum, or if she weren't disgusted by the act, he might have managed with just the genital stimulation, but he needed more from her.

Tentatively she touched his shoulder.

"That's it," he murmured as he helped her rock a little faster and tilted his hips to meet her.

"Oh," Caroline squeaked.

"I've wanted you for a long time," he coaxed.

Sensation began to build in him as he tried to ignore that she might be uncomfortable. Making eye contact as he focused on reaching release was oddly intimate and he liked it, even as she shook her head. He silently dared her to stop pretending he was one of the gentlemen, or that this wasn't happening. She was here, riding him, and he wanted her to remember that. And when he came back a success, she wouldn't have to be ashamed that she'd known him intimately.

"I've always thought you beautiful."

She shook her head.

He nodded. "The way you move, the way you hold yourself, the way you see every detail when you look around. Even when you first came here and you were all big eyes and elbows, I noticed you."

She shifted her hand along his shoulder. The buzz of his excitement magnified.

"Lower," he murmured. "I know you saw me watching you."

Her chin dipped and her cheeks bloomed. She was damn lovely, even if she didn't know it. And he knew he was revealing too much, but the only thing he had to seduce her with was words.

Her trembling fingertips were cool. His skin was hot. All he needed was one little sign that she was feeling a twinge or two of pleasure.

He pushed her hips down and rolled his. Her eyebrows drew together and her insides tightened around him. Then she struggled to pull away from him, planting her hand in the center of his chest.

"That's it, Caro. That feels good," he purred.

He could see she was torn, but he kept her moving, kept his hips sliding opposite hers. The last thing he wanted was her realizing that he was after her pleasure as much as his own. She made a strangled sound and then tried to match his movements. He murmured encouragement and praise. He bit his lip before telling her to just feel, not think.

Her eyes closed, and he insisted she open them. She lifted her lashes to half-mast over her darkened eyes. Even if she didn't realize it, her deepened breathing, her dewy eyes, the clenching of her nether muscles, revealed she was not as adverse to the act as she wanted to believe. She was meant for pleasure, and her body was built for it, even if she didn't understand.

His breathing grew harsh. She moved her warming fingers across his chest, over his nipple. Spikes of sensation rocketed to his groin. It wouldn't take much more. The next time he might stop and concentrate on her—with what little he could do without kissing or caressing her—but time was hurtling by and he needed to prove he could, at least, do what was needed to provide her with a babe, or she wouldn't allow for a next time.

He watched her face, looked deep into her eyes until her lips parted and her legs trembled. Then he was there, pushing her hips tight against him and letting the sensation roll down his spine as he groaned through his release.

Caroline almost sobbed as she moved off Jack. She felt strange; almost as if once the pain had passed it had been almost—nice—or at least not as unpleasant as she expected, which confused her.

Jack caught her hand, and a jolt of energy ran through her.

"Are you all right?" He blinked at her, although his heavy breathing still echoed in the room.

Not trusting her voice, she nodded and pulled her hand away. She needed to get him back before an early servant discovered them. She picked up his underclothes and held them out to him.

He grunted and let his hand drop to the bed, fisted around his smalls. He turned to his side and closed his eyes.

She shook his shoulder.

His eyes were glassy and unfocused when he opened them, then his lashes shuttered down.

"Jack."

"Mmm."

"You have to get dressed." She tugged on his arm trying to get him to sit.

"Prefer wearin' you," he mumbled. He broke her hold and grabbed her arm in an effortless maneuver. He dragged her down beside him and curled his arm around her. "I can hold you now."

"That doesn't even make any sense." The softening and tensing reaction she experienced didn't make sense either. She pushed his heavy arm away and slid off the bed. Leaning over him, she begged him to see reason, "Please. You cannot be caught upstairs, naked."

He put his hand on her cheek. "All right, two minutes."

Startled by how much she wanted to linger and feel his caresses, Caroline backed away from him. His arm fell heavily to the bed. She stood to see the mantel clock.

It was nearly a quarter till. Panic threatened to choke her. They still had to make it through the darkened service stairs before anyone else thought to use them.

"We don't have two minutes, John Applegate," she whispered as sternly as she could.

Pulling down the covers, she lifted his good leg and pulled his drawers over it. When she made it to the cast on his other leg, she gingerly worked the material over it. He rolled to his back and lifted his leg to make it easy on her.

She looked up to find him regarding her intensely. Had the sleep been a pretense? But then Mr. Broadhurst had often rolled over after intercourse and almost immediately begun snoring.

She averted her head and pulled the material up. She refused to think of how less threatening his manhood looked now, less full and glistening with moisture. He dug his foot into the bed and lifted his hips. She opened his undershirt and held it out.

Jack groaned and sat up. Her gaze was drawn to the ripple of muscle under his skin.

Hesitating, she reached for the hem of his nightshirt.

"You would take that off now." He sounded mildly aggrieved.

Had he wanted her to take it off earlier? Would it have been faster if she had? Jack tugged on the nightshirt, pulling it down where she had lifted it up to her thighs.

"Much as I would like you to take it off, you should keep it on until you get back to your room. I can guarantee no man would want to let you get away wearing that *negligee*."

He buttoned the undershirt. The coals provided little more than a faint orange glow in the predawn darkness, and his breath formed mist in the air. "You'll need it," she protested. "I'll just wrap up in the bedspread again."

"I need your help getting down the stairs, and if I trip on that damn thing . . ." He watched her intently. "If I had regular clothes, I could dress and tell my morning minder I was up early."

Caroline closed her eyes. She'd refused to let him have clothes for fear he'd leave before he was adequately healed.

Jack reached for his crutches. "Go. If you can't return the nightshirt to me, then I'll tell whoever comes I spilled upon it and you took it to be laundered—or better yet, I was sick upon it."

"Do lies come so easy to you?"

He stood. "Only when I need to protect a lady's reputation. Let's go, Mrs. Broadhurst, before the servants catch you consorting with a millworker."

Chapter 17

Caroline sneaked back up the servants' stair, into the dressing room attached to Lord Langley's former room. She shed Jack's nightshirt and stuffed it in a dresser drawer before checking the main hallway. When she saw no one, she slipped out of the empty bedchamber. Breathing a sigh of relief, she scurried down the hall to her room.

The door was locked. She rattled it. Fearing she might be trapped in the hallway, apprehension scuttled down her spine. No response. On her toes, she skittered down the hall to Mr. Broadhurst's room. Her husband's door was locked too.

Her mouth dry, she tapped and called out softly.

Mr. Broadhurst was usually not a heavy sleeper. When he didn't answer, panic rose in her throat. She just couldn't be caught standing here in a transparent gown.

Above her on the attic floor, soft thumps and rattles signified the servants' first stirrings. Her elbows pressed into her ribs. The housemaids were getting ready for their day and would be descending any minute.

Caroline knocked louder.

Still no response.

She twisted. Could she try to find a key before she was

caught? Or would one of the other keys even work in her door?

Heavy footfalls ascended from the floor below. Dear God, the gentlemen's gentlemen were probably about to come upon her. She pounded the flat of her hand on the wood.

Down the hall her door jerked open.

Caroline heaved a sigh of relief and darted back toward her room, but when she got there, Mr. Broadhurst filled the frame.

"Sir, let me in." Rather than shove him out of the way, she recoiled from touching him. He was a loathsome creature and she would feel slimy.

He didn't step to the side. "Have you done what you were supposed to do?"

"Yes, I have." Her skin fired and she couldn't look at the man she'd spent the last fifteen years of her life with. A man she had thought she knew. Jerking her head to look over her shoulder, she swallowed hard.

"Which man?"

Caroline gasped. Did he know she ducked into an empty room? Surely Mr. Broadhurst hadn't concerned himself with the sleeping arrangements. She couldn't tell him she'd been with Jack. Besides, he'd heard Jack's staged exercise. Her legs—already feeling weak from the unfamiliar activity—threatened to give out on her. "Sir, that is none of your affair."

He folded his arms over his striped nightshirt—so like the one Jack had given her to wear.

"I cannot stay out here in the hall, the servants are about." She would have to push him out of the way, but her strength had never been any match for her husband.

Mr. Broadhurst reached out and tilted up her chin. "You do not have the look of a woman who has just left a man's bed. Your hair is not mussed. Your lips are not swollen. You look untouched. You're lying. Again."

Panic threatened to choke her. Gathering strength to confront her husband, she spit out, "I did not need to be *kissed* to accomplish what was necessary."

"Caroline." His look was doubtful.

Her face hot, she hissed, "I hardly think my mission will be successful if his seed all runs down my legs."

Mr. Broadhurst's eyes narrowed, then he yanked her into the room.

She jerked away.

"Get in bed," he commanded.

Caroline gathered the nightgown she'd left on the covers.

Mr. Broadhurst yanked it away. She turned and found he was standing naked behind her. Had he been wearing nothing under his nightshirt?

His body was old, the skin wrinkled and sagging over flabby spotted flesh. She shuddered. "What are you doing?"

"You want everyone to think the child is mine. The staff will expect us to have relations."

Caroline shrunk back. He hadn't been able to carry out his part for months, but now his member jutted out. Cold dread poured down her spine.

"It seems the medicine the doctor has given me makes me feel like a new man."

"I cannot have relations with you and another man. I am sore enough as it is." She had little hope that he would care. Jack had at least minded that she was in pain. Nothing had ever mattered to Mr. Broadhurst, not tears, not cries of pain, not pretending to be asleep when he joined her. It was his right as her husband, and he often reminded her he'd paid dearly for the privilege. But so had she.

Feeling cold all through her, Caroline climbed into the bed.

Mr. Broadhurst followed, and her skin crawled. He lifted her sheer nightgown and rubbed his hand over her thigh.

"Did you not enjoy it?" he questioned.

"No!"

She scooted across the expanse of the mattress to the far side.

"I despise the act," she hissed. "With you, with him, with any man. Now leave me be."

"You are still *my* wife."

Caroline stared into the darkness of her room and waited for Mr. Broadhurst to claim his marital rights. She shut down her thoughts and reactions, as she had learned to do to tolerate his touch.

Yet, she hadn't shut out everything with Jack. She hadn't needed to go numb. Perhaps she hadn't despised it entirely with him. Toward the end, she thought she might have not have minded the unsettled way it made her feel. If the act weren't a sin, weren't a betrayal, it almost would have been easy with Jack.

Her stomach turned as Mr. Broadhurst stroked her skin.

At no time with Jack had she felt nauseous the way she felt now.

Before Jack opened his eyes he knew he wasn't alone in the breakfast room. Having another person in the room when he woke wasn't unusual, but the menace he felt wasn't present when one of the servants entered. He slowly opened his eyes. The predawn murkiness barely illuminated Mr. Broadhurst standing at the sideboard where his bottle of laudanum rested.

"Dr. Hein says you are not out of the woods yet." Broad-hurst said without turning around.

A shudder rippled down Jack's spine. "Sir."

Did the man know Caroline had been with him last night? Had Broadhurst seen her wearing the nightshirt he insisted she wear as she went through the house? A night-shirt Broadhurst might have recognized as his own. Jack eased the covers around his chin to conceal his undershirt and bare arms.

"A man with such a serious injury could die at any time." The laudanum bottle clinked and Broadhurst turned around, his expression thoughtful.

"I'd rather not." Jack didn't lift his eyes from the man as every muscle in his body tightened.

Broadhurst moved across the floor and towered above the bed. "I'd rather my wife didn't spend time with you."

Jack wanted to stand to face Broadhurst, but he couldn't risk exposing his lack of a nightshirt. Instead he lay flat on his back, clenching his fists under the covers. He hated the way the submissive posture left him feeling emasculated and impotent. But he couldn't risk behaving differently than any other millworker would. To act as if they were equals or rivals might confirm Broadhurst's suspicions and put Caro-line at risk. The idea of Broadhurst knowing she had turned to him chilled Jack's blood.

Broadhurst's eyes flattened like those of a dead man. "She shouldn't concern herself with you."

"I am just an outlet for her feminine urges to comfort and care for a weaker being." Jack held his breath as he hoped his words weren't misinterpreted. The woman would be an excellent mother if he had succeeded last night.

"Don't think *my wife* will protect you forever."

"No, sir. I don't, sir." Jack pressed his lips together. He sounded servile, but then again, any trouble he created could spill over to Caroline. The last thing he wanted was for her to become the third Mrs. Broadhurst to rest underground. "I'd rather not rely on anyone's protection, least of all a woman's."

Then again, he wasn't particularly keen to find out exactly what Broadhurst had in mind in regards to him. If it wasn't for Caroline's interest, he would have been booted out the first day.

The door clicked open and a maid carrying a coal bucket stepped inside.

Jack couldn't hold back his relief. It escaped him in a hiss.

"I expect clerks to work hard, have a legible hand, and to not make mistakes with their math," said Broadhurst in a mild tone.

Jack blinked, startled by the change in the old man's voice.

"Reasonable expectations, I'd say," added Broadhurst with a curling of his lips that on another man might have looked like an indulgent smile.

"Absolutely, sir," answered Jack. "I would expect nothing less, were I in your position."

Broadhurst's eyes flashed, but the genial expression stayed on his face. "We are understood, then."

"Yes, sir." Jack nodded, wondering if he'd been threatened or simply warned that the clerk job would vanish at his first mistake. If he made it to London, got the job as a machinist, the clerk job would be a moot point. But he didn't dare refuse the place at the mill until he knew.

Broadhurst left the room without acknowledging the maid working to clean out last night's ashes.

If he stayed and became a clerk—assuming Mrs. Broadhurst could help him learn enough so he could do it—he would see her daily. Leaving would likely mean he would never see her again, and that left him feeling strangely lost.

Then again, last night had been one of the most awkward and frustrating of his life. He'd wanted to make it at least pleasant for her, but she'd been so . . . distant, resistant to letting go. He'd always admired her reserve, but in bed it was a barrier. Her helping him down the back stairs was far more intimate then their sexual encounter. Her arm had been around his waist, his over her shoulders, their sides pressed together as he navigated the narrow flight. A frisson of interest rolled through him. How could he want *that* again?

Jack groaned and flipped to his side, facing the empty fireplace, but taking care not to let the blanket slide off his shoulder.

"Would you like your medicine, sir?" The girl rose to a knee.

"No!" He wasn't taking the laudanum after Broadhurst had been near it. Not even if his leg was screaming and he was in agony.

The maid stared back at him, no doubt confused by his vehemence.

Jack let his lips curl up as if nothing were wrong. He gave her a warm sleepy look that worked on most women. Except of course Caroline. Nothing seemed to work on her. Damn, he wanted so much more than the coldly functional encounter they'd had. "I'd much prefer the fire lit, miss."

"Oh, of course," the girl fluttered, and then went back to work.

The whistle at the mill blasted. Jack tried to sort in his mind if he'd heard it the day before. "What day is it?"

"Tuesday, sir."

He had to be in London Friday morning, and it was a full day of train travel to get there from Manchester, which meant he had to be in Manchester by Thursday morning.

Getting to Manchester might not be as easy as it once was when he had two good legs. Damn, he hadn't been thinking of getting to London last night. He hadn't been thinking the appointment would interfere in his offer to get Caroline with child. He'd been so eager to have her, he never considered having to abandon his dream to help her. How could he have been so stupid? He groaned again.

"Are you certain you wouldn't like your medicine?" asked the maid.

Not only was he concerned that Broadhurst had added something to it, but the laudanum had been clouding his thinking, making the passage of time seem unimportant. He had to get home, retrieve his money, and make arrangements to get to London. He couldn't risk taking the laudanum anymore.

"I'm all right," he said softly.

The maid looked young and uncertain. Perhaps easily manipulated. He'd need her to do his bidding to get out of here. He hated that he would be abandoning his deal with Caroline, but if he didn't get to London on Friday, he'd never be worthy of her. And he wanted more than the cold impersonal business of getting her pregnant, which might have been accomplished last night. "Could you find me clothes? If I have to spend another day in bed, I will go mad. Surely there is a footman or groom close to my size."

Her mouth twisted. "I don't know as I should."

Jack gave her his best smile. "Please. I know your mistress thinks I should remain abed, but I only want a little exercise."

She looked uncertain. "You should ask her."

Cursing in his head, Jack tried to keep his expression pleasant. "Would you see if I could speak with her, then?"

How would he explain this to her? The words twisted in his head and felt ineffectual and wrong, but dammit, he'd sworn nothing would keep him from London this time.

The maid twisted her hands in her apron. "She's gone to the mill for the day."

When did Caroline sleep? Jack pressed harder, "The doctor said yesterday it is time I walk farther than I can manage in this room. It would mean a lot to me if I could show Mrs. Broadhurst I am getting well, thanks to her kind hospitality and care."

The girl chewed her lip and Jack added a silent entreaty.

She dipped her head as she picked up the empty coal bucket. "I'll see what I can do, sir."

With luck he would be dressed and out of the house before any of the servants had any inkling of his intentions. He could get home, retrieve his money, and see if he could hitch a ride or hire conveyance to Manchester. He swiped his hand over his face.

He would have to go to the mill and ask to speak to Caroline and hope he could make her understand. But then again, it wasn't as if she'd exhibited any softer feelings toward him. He was a convenience to her. The yearning for a deeper connection between them was all on his side.

Less than a half hour later Jack stood at the top of the wide stone staircase at the front of the Broadhurst house. His heart pounding and his mouth dry, he considered how best to get down without tumbling to the ground.

Caroline wasn't here to hold onto him if he stumbled or lost his balance. The stone walls, to each side, didn't give him anything to hold like the railing on the inside staircase. The stairs might thwart him yet.

Sucking in a deep breath, he lowered his crutches to the next elongated step and inched his foot forward to the edge, took a little hop and landed on the step below.

Halfway down he was sweating and cursing. His good leg

shook with the unfamiliar use. All his life he'd been working toward this opportunity in London, but his thoughts wouldn't leave the encounter last night. He didn't know what he would tell Caroline, but he couldn't bear a whole lot of nights like last night, with her in pain as he tried to impregnate her.

His fantasy had been more like a nightmare. He'd been reduced to being a stud for a very unwilling and uncomfortable woman. And how, if he too ignored Caroline's pain, was he a better man than Broadhurst?

Even if he made a success of his life and returned home when the old man finally kicked the bucket, Caroline would likely have none of him. But he couldn't help but envision a warm welcome upon a return as a man with accomplishments and wealth.

Feeling a bit like he was breaking out of a jail, he cast a backward glance over his shoulder to make certain he wasn't being followed. But the servants were engaged in the flurry of morning activities, cleaning grates, toting coal and ash buckets up and down, hauling wash water and linens. He'd picked a moment when the hall cleared and made his escape.

At this rate he would never get to the village, let alone London. Swallowing his bitter pride, he plunked to his backside and thumped down the rest of the way. The jarring made his leg throb, but he gritted his teeth and continued.

By the time he arrived home, his arms were shaking, his good leg was on fire, and his head seemed likely to detach from his head and float away. The walk had taken him thrice the normal time, and he'd had to rest several times, leaning against a tree or on his crutches. He didn't remember ever being this weak and mewling. Fine stud animal he made. If he were part of a herd, he'd be culled from the breeding stock for lack of fitness.

He opened the door to the familiar smell of cabbage and

too many children crammed in a small house. Beth was in school, so three-year-old Daphne, her face full of grim concentration, rocked the baby in his cradle. Their father yelled from the bedroom, "Who's there?"

Daphne popped up from her chair and shot across the room. "Jack!"

Her little face transformed into a smile and then melted into shock as she realized his leg was twice as thick as it should have been. She backed toward the soot-grayed wall. The wavy glass let in little light, but what did landed on her mouth rounded in an O.

"It's still me," he said with as much of a smile as he could manage. He suspected it was more of a grimace.

He crutched toward the vacated chair and sat, heedless of the cries emerging from the cradle. Years of practice making the movement automatic, he set his foot on the runner and restarted the rocking motion. He willed his youngest brother to sleep before his leg could no longer work.

Daphne stared at him. He suspected she would come around if he acted normal, but he no longer felt normal.

His father emerged from the single bedroom, stooped and shuffling across the scuffed wood floors in a way that made him look older than Mr. Broadhurst although he was decades younger. His eyes glistened with uncharacteristic moisture. "Martha isn't going to want you here. Said you kept too much of what you made anyhow."

Jack understood Martha wanting more of his wages—there was never enough. But that his father wouldn't fight for his oldest son to stay left Jack feeling as if a rope had tightened around his chest. He had to get out of here. "I just came to get my things."

His father heaved a sigh of relief. "How long you going to live up in the fancy house?"

"I was only staying until I can go to London," Jack said.

Daphne patted his leg. He tilted his crutches against his side and curled his arm around her shoulder, moving her hand away from the throbbing ache in his leg.

"You always was lucky," muttered his father. "Getting to stay up there."

"I'd rather have not had my leg crushed," said Jack.

"Mama got a new stove," piped Daphne into the awkward silence.

Jack twisted toward the cooking area behind the main room. A big cast-iron affair had replaced the old rusted stove that had been in the house since he was little. How had Martha managed to . . . His stomach churned. He turned back toward his father and the evasive eyes, the dusky wash of red on his father's sallow cheeks screaming shame told him everything.

Trying to hold back the wall of angry despair, he said, "Do I have anything left?"

Her brother stood in the entrance hall, and several of the gentlemen came down from the first floor. The butler had the silver salver with several letters on it and was holding it out to the men, but mostly Caroline noticed the closed breakfast room doors across from her. Her heart thumped erratically in her chest as she anticipated seeing Jack again, as if she hadn't seen him just hours before.

Her eagerness to see him heated her like a hot fire after a day outside in the winter. Would he be glad to see her? Anticipating her visit in the night? She pressed hands to her hot cheeks, trying to cool them.

She had to calm down. No one could know of what transpired last night. She must act as she always did. Not think about Jack's dark eyes holding her gaze, his hands on her hips guiding her and his member inside her, filling her.

As she reached for the handle, the butler stopped beside them.

"Uh, ma'am . . . Mr. Applegate isn't here."

Caroline's chest squeezed. "Where is he?"

"I don't rightly know," answered the butler.

Like a stuck plaster had been ripped off her entire being, Caroline felt raw.

The butler turned away.

"Stop." Her mind was spinning with the idea that Jack wasn't where she left him. "When was Mr. Applegate last seen?"

"He had the tweeny bring him clothes early this morning, but no one saw him leave. We were all busy."

Why had he left? Had he hated their encounter so much? Caroline wanted to dissolve on the ground into a puddle, but she couldn't let the butler—or for that matter the gentlemen standing about reading their correspondence—know how much Jack's leaving upset her.

Caroline's knees buckled. Jack was gone. What of their bargain?

And what was she to do? If she sent servants after him, everyone would question why she was so concerned with the welfare of one injured worker.

Her hands shook so badly she could scarcely untie her cloak. Jack had left.

She'd known the minute he had clothes he would leave. But after last night, she would have thought . . .

What? That he truly thought she was pretty and desirable? She'd always known she wasn't the kind of woman who inspired passion.

As if a demon had ripped out all her entrails and left a big gaping hole inside, she clutched her stomach. She wanted to curl into a ball on the floor. She had to regain her composure. Thankfully, none of the gentlemen seemed interested in her. With Jack gone, she would have to try again with one of them. Dread knotted her spine.

She couldn't help but look in the breakfast room, as if she might find Jack lurking behind the sideboard.

But he wasn't here. She felt brittle, as if she might break into a thousand pieces. She touched the headboard as though it would give her some assurance that Jack would return, but the bedstead was cold and sucked all the warmth from her.

"Caro."

She swiveled hoping to find Jack behind her, even as she recognized the voice as her brother's.

"In here," she called, and was alarmed at how foreign her voice sounded to her ears.

"Caro," her brother repeated. He hesitated in the doorway.

She whirled, staring at the empty bed so out of place in the breakfast room. Her heart thumped hard in her chest and a tingling sensation ran down her arms.

She drew in a deep breath and tried to gather all the pieces of her into one whole that could act as she should. Robert's face was as white as the letter he clutched in his fist. He vibrated with agitation.

Bad news from home? Her breath ripped out of her. She couldn't bear more bad news.

"What is it?" She rushed toward him. "Are the children . . . ?"

Robert shook his head and held out his palm. "Whitton has been slain."

For a minute Caroline searched her brain for which of her brother's children might be called Whitton before it dawned on her that Mr. Whitton—the man she had tried to seduce while drunk—was whom Robert was talking about.

"What?"

"Whitton was murdered by a highwayman." Robert thrust the letter at her.

Caroline crushed the page to her chest, trying to still the mad racing of her heart. Mr. Whitton was dead? Murdered?

"We returned for the day and this letter was awaiting me," Robert explained. "Actually there were several letters. Langley said they were stopped by a ruffian in a greatcoat, low hat, and high muffler who demanded to know which was Whitton, and then he shot him."

Beyond Robert, the men milled about the hall. Their mutterings drifted in to her.

"Who would kill Whitton?"

"Too much like the revenge of a cuckolded man," said one man.

Lord Tremont narrowed his eyes and stared at Caroline.

What was a lady to do when her legs might give out on her and her heart was beating faster than any drum could be beaten?

A couple more men turned to her and regarded her speculatively.

"Don't think I'd want to tamper with a man's wife about now," said another.

Had her encounter with Whitton had anything to do with his death? Her thoughts swirled. Before he left, Whitton had been sequestered with Mr. Broadhurst. Then that same night, there was that stranger who refused to let a servant take his dripping greatcoat or remove his pulled low hat. He'd said he had business with her husband. What sort of business was conducted so late in the evening? Her hand went to her mouth.

Dear God, had Mr. Broadhurst had anything to do with Mr. Whitton's murder?

Worse yet, had Jack left of his own free will?

Chapter 18

Jack made his way to the midwife's apothecary shop. He struggled to open the door without toppling over. The pack on his back containing all his worldly goods exacerbated the precariousness of his balance. The bell jangled and clanked as the door swung closed on him. A shooting pain radiated down to the bone of his broken leg. Gritting his teeth, he held back a cry. Shoving the door off his leg and crutch took almost more strength than he possessed. To make everything worse, except for the change tied in the handkerchief, he was flat broke.

Years of savings—gone in a week. He wouldn't make it to London in time for his appointment. Hell, without wages he might never make it, might never get out of this mill town, might never be his own man. His only choice now was to go back to the Broadhurst house and hope that Mr. Broadhurst had no immediate plans to rid the world of one useless cripple. Jack had poured out the laudanum just in case.

The midwife arranged bottles on a shelf behind a counter. Brushing back a strand of salt and pepper hair, she turned. Her eyes widened, "Jack Applegate."

"Mrs. Goode," he acknowledged. He didn't know if she'd ever been married, but a woman of her age and stature in the community was accorded respect.

"Can't say I expected to see you so soon." She pulled a small dark bottle from a crate packed with straw and stood on her toes to put the glass jar on a high shelf.

Jack crutched over to the stool in the corner and jogged around until he could sit. Maneuvering on crutches was still a learning experience. He expected at any time to pitch onto his face. More than once he'd had to grab whatever was near to stay upright.

"What can I do for you?" She scraped a bit of straw back into the crate and moved it to the floor.

He opened his mouth to ask for laudanum, but the image in his head of his father, bleary-eyed and unrepentant, tipping up the bottle of gin, stopped the request on his lips. "I need a crock of honeymoon ointment."

Mrs. Goode swung around, her lips pressed into a disapproving line. "For heaven's sake, Jack, are you already at one of the housemaids?"

"No. Don't think any of the housemaids would be interested in a cripple." Mrs. Broadhurst wasn't interested in him as a lover either, just for his potential to sire a baby. He tilted his head down and sighed.

Mrs. Goode eyed him sharply. He could have told her that when he was bent on seduction, he didn't need help from ointments. But that wasn't true with Mrs. Broadhurst. Nor was it the sort of thing one said to a woman—even if she was a midwife who knew things about him no one else knew.

He met Mrs. Goode's gaze doing his best to look guileless. "I need it for . . . my scars. Dr. Hein says I have to make sure the skin doesn't dry out and crack."

"I can just give you the lanolin that would go in it. That's all you'll need to keep the skin supple."

"I want the ointment. Need help with soothing the soreness too."

Watching him speculatively, Mrs. Goode tilted her head.

Jack twisted putting his crutches together and leaning them against the wall. He might not have known about the honeymoon ointment—good for dryness after childbirth too—if not for his five married sisters' low conversations to each other. Unlike in the Broadhurst house, where everyone was separated, few secrets were possible in the Applegate home. He pulled out the handkerchief, untied it and pulled out a shilling. "How much?"

She startled and rubbed her back. "It will take me a few minutes to mix it. And I might be called away. Parson's wife was having pains this morning."

"I could use the rest while I wait." Jack wondered if he could even make it back to the Broadhursts'.

She gave him another sideways look and then reached around to pull a few jars and crocks off the shelf. Hell, would she remember this conversation if Caroline eventually delivered his child? Jack squeezed his eyes shut and hoped he hadn't let the cat out of the bag.

"Do you have something for pain besides laudanum? I don't want to keep taking that. I need to be more aware." He would be going back into a situation where he didn't trust his host; not at all.

She turned, pulled a bottle from a shelf and poured a small amount in a metal cup and brought it to him. "You look exhausted."

Jack was more than exhausted; he was bone-tired and world-weary. Everything he had worked to achieve had gone up in smoke. He'd saved for a decade to have enough funds to move to London and see his ideas into fruition. His family had stolen his life savings. Caroline had offered him the one thing he might have stayed here for and turned it into a nightmare, and the mill machinery had crushed his leg.

It was as if the entire world and all the stars in the heavens were lining up against him.

After downing the bitter liquid, he loosened the pack he had made from a burlap bag. Setting the sack on the floor at his feet, he scooted the stool closer to the wall and leaned against it. Crossing his arms, he closed his eyes. He would damn near give his right arm to lie down and rest.

Mrs. Goode hadn't moved.

He opened his eyes. Her faded eyes bored into his.

"Do you know what you're doing, Jack?"

He blinked at her. "It's for my leg, really."

The corners of her lips pulled back—not a smile—but more a rueful acceptance. "Come, there is a cot in my workroom. You can rest there while I get the ointment made up for you."

"That sounds heavenly," he said, reaching for his crutches. Much as Mrs. Goode might disapprove of him, he wouldn't have to sleep with one eye open.

One of the footmen leaned close and whispered in Caroline's ear. "You said to tell you if Mr. Applegate returns. He is coming up the drive."

Knowing Jack was safe sent a rush of relief through her.

Where had he been? Caroline fisted her napkin in her lap. She needed to see him to ease her mind. "Thank you. Please tell Mrs. Burns to see me in my sitting room."

Dinner was only half served, but she had no appetite. She looked around the glum faces of the gentlemen at the table and pushed back her chair. "If you will excuse me, gentlemen. There is a matter I must see to."

They stood and half of them refused to meet her eyes. The other half glared in her direction as if she had ordered Whitton murdered. She was numb. Her heart refused to believe that Whitton's death had anything to do with her or the hunting party, but doubts kept niggling at her. And she'd been so afraid that a similar fate had befallen Jack.

"A problem, my dear?" Mr. Broadhurst's eyes narrowed.

"Just a domestic issue I must address. Nothing of concern."

He watched her as she made her way into the hall. She couldn't linger or she would raise his suspicions. But until she saw Jack with her own eyes, she couldn't be easy.

Once in her sitting room she peeked out through the drapes and saw the figure on crutches at the far end of the drive. He seemed to be moving ever so slowly, but there was no doubt, even at this distance, the figure was Jack. Her stomach danced and it was all she could do not to run out to him.

The housekeeper entered the room. "You wished to see me, ma'am?"

Caroline reluctantly turned around. "It seems our patient has returned after all."

Mrs. Burns pressed her lips into a thin line, but she didn't bat an eye as she asked, "Would you like the bed returned to the breakfast room?"

The breakfast room, while segregated from the rest of the sleeping area, had no locks on the doors. "No, he is capable of managing stairs, so I think it best we put him in one of the far bedchambers. Out of the way of the guests." One of the rooms had an escritoire where Jack could practice his writing and arithmetic. "Perhaps the northernmost chamber of the east el. The one attached to the nursery." It was a room designated for a tutor, should there ever be a need for one.

The housekeeper sniffed.

"I would put him in one of the servant rooms, but I think

it is best he has a fire for now." Caroline felt her face heating and turned to look out the window, lest her expression betray her. She didn't know why she was explaining to the housekeeper, except the woman seemed to disapprove. "In spite of his jaunt today, Mr. Applegate still has a long journey to recovery."

"Very good, ma'am."

Where in heaven's name had Jack gone today? And why? After last night, she would have thought he would stay put. Her stomach turned.

When the housekeeper didn't leave, Caroline turned to face her. "Is there something you wish to say, Mrs. Burns?"

Caroline dreaded dealing with an objection. The woman had been here almost as long as she had, and they had a good understanding. But housing a millworker on the same floor as people of quality had to seem odd, even if he was tucked in the remotest corner.

"I need to tell you, ma'am, that one of the empty guest rooms was disturbed last night. It looks as though there may have been a bit of havey-cavey business going on."

Caroline drew in a sharp breath as her muscles tensed. For once she wished her housekeeper were less efficient. She'd left the ashes in the grate and the bed disturbed, but hadn't expected anyone to have any reason to go into the room, at least not for a few days. Fearing she was on the verge of being discovered, her hands shook. "I'm certain things will settle down when the guests leave."

"If I determine which of the servants might have been in there, I will dismiss them."

"I would hope that if one of the gentlemen persuaded one of the maids to misbehave, he at least compensated her well." The last thing she wanted was the servants speculating about who had been in the room.

"I can't think it was one of the gentlemen, ma'am. If it were, why wouldn't it be in his own room?"

Her deception coiled tighter around Caroline and wouldn't let her breathe. "I'm certain I don't wish to know the machinations of the guests." And the last thing she wanted was the housekeeper investigating. "Let it go for now, Mrs. Burns. With all the needs of the guests, you don't have time to waste. If it becomes an ongoing problem, we'll deal with it."

The sour expression on Mrs. Burns face showed she didn't agree, but she didn't argue as she left the sitting room to prepare for Jack's arrival.

Caroline took one last look out the window. Jack had only progressed a few yards. He leaned against his crutches, not moving at all. He was returning, wasn't he? Winged creatures in her stomach took flight.

As if aware of her gaze on him, he raised his face toward the house. Perhaps he needed help. She hurried downstairs to the entry hall.

Caution slowed her headlong progress. She should send a footman out to help him.

The hall was empty and no amount of pacing around it made it less so. The footmen were engaged in serving dinner, and the wait wound her tighter than a coiled spring. She finally opened the front door and looked out. Jack remained slumped over his crutches.

Slowly, he raised his face and started toward her. In the dusky evening, she couldn't make out his expression, but she could no longer bear to remain standing, waiting. Without thinking, she was down the stairs and striding toward him, the train of her evening gown dragging in the pressed gravel.

"Where have you been?" she spit in an undertone as she neared him. The words were like a fishwife's or a jilted lover. She was neither, and she wished she could call the words back.

Jack stopped and looked wearily at her. His chest heaved and, in spite of the chilly air, beads of perspiration dotted his forehead. "I went to my father's house."

She couldn't seem to stop herself as a wave of anger rose in her. Her nails bit into her palms and her stomach burned. "What were you thinking? I have been worried sick. I thought we had a bargain."

His eyes tightened and his mouth flattened. "I'm here, aren't I?"

A flatness in his tone told her that he wasn't happy about being here. It stung and drained the anger from her, leaving her raw and exposed. Why not? She was sore on the inside, might as well be aching all over. She turned her head toward the horizon, fighting the burn in her eyes and the dryness at the back of her throat.

She couldn't fall apart now. And Jack shouldn't have the power to hurt her. He was just . . . just a man she was using to get pregnant. Certainly no lady ever raised her voice at a . . . laborer or a friend—whatever he was.

It didn't matter what he was, beyond that he was the man she needed to father her child. More than that, *he* was the man she *wanted* to father her child.

God, last night had changed everything. She couldn't think of him as simply a friend. They'd been intimate—in a manner of speaking—and as much as she'd tried to keep it on a practical level, her feelings were in a knot. Suddenly she was very aware of the chaffing in her female core. She'd almost convinced herself a night's reprieve was what she needed, but it wasn't what she wanted. She'd wanted to see Jack, to share the quiet hours of the night alone with him.

Perhaps tonight they could work on his reading, but she

needed the other to get a baby. A shiver of anticipation ran down her spine. Part of her wanted to engage in intimacy, though she'd always found it repulsive before. It was different with Jack. He seemed to want more than the physical, and didn't want his pleasure to come at her expense. She had disappointed him, but she didn't know if she could ever fully desire a man. A part of her wanted to try. For him she wanted to try.

She swiveled toward him. Lines of weariness and pain were etched into his face. He swung the crutches forward and took a careful step. His arms quivered as they bore his weight. He must be exhausted and had likely overtaxed his weakened body.

Chagrin made her shoulders drop. He didn't need anger from her. He couldn't know the news of Whitton's murder and her suspicions, fears, downright terror that he'd fallen victim to Mr. Broadhurst's ire. The burlap sack anchored to his back told of a man getting his things, not a man running away. She drew in a deep breath and straightened her fingers.

"We need to get you to bed," she said softly. Only his bed likely wasn't ready yet.

"Yes." He planted the crutches and leaned forward onto them. Slowly, he twisted to look at her.

For a reason beyond her ken, his look called to mind the night before, and her cheeks fired and her body tingled. All her thoughts scattered. For the first time in her life she was looking forward to the night's activities.

She was turning into a wicked adulteress. She tried to tell herself it was just that she was eager to have a family, a baby, but even she didn't believe that. She wanted to be with Jack and be done with all the gentlemen in her house. And she sure didn't want to be anywhere near Mr. Broadhurst during the night.

Jack thought he might fall over at any minute. His good leg protested the exertion. A week ago he'd walked over fifteen miles in a day with little ill effect, and today he couldn't manage a couple of miles. But there it was.

His underarms stung where the crutches rubbed. His shoulders and arms were rubbery with fatigue. Worst of all it felt as if a knife had lodged in his lower back and twisted with each step he took. And the heavy cast chafed his foot. He was fairly certain every movement would be the last he could manage.

Caroline stood beside him, looking angry and hurt and all kinds of things that didn't make sense coupled with her efforts to keep him at arm's length. But women never made a lot of sense when they had their dander up.

She also looked refined, elegant, and so beautiful his breath caught. The way her hair gleamed, clean and shiny, the long curl caressing parts of her neck and cleavage he was forbidden to touch, made his heart beat a little faster. Her skin was so pale he could see a tracing of blue veins under it. Blue blood ran in those veins. Yet, he, a red-blooded worker, was being given the opportunity to create a child with her. He wanted the tie to her, a blood connection that could never be broken.

He could tell himself it was for all the advantages that could be wrought by having a member of a noble family willing to patronize him. He doubted she would let him starve, if it ever came to that. And she might open doors for him. That alone might be worth having a child he could never claim.

But it wasn't that. Besides, the tie might forever be secret.

No, he wanted her bound to him forever, and he didn't even understand why. Something deep in his soul was drawn to the way she bore up under the strain of being married to a man who didn't deserve her. Yet, she wanted to provide the opportunity for anyone who wanted to be successful like her husband.

God, if she only wanted him a tenth as much as he wanted her, he could . . . Nothing. He could give her nothing that a man wants to give a woman he cares about. He couldn't give her the world or provide for her in any meaningful way. The best he could do was give her a child.

Jack took another step, because he didn't want her to witness him failing. He didn't want to fail at one more thing today, but he didn't know if he had the strength to make it up the stairs that loomed in front of him.

"Let me take your sack."

He was too tired to protest. He let her untuck it from his braces. Each time her hands brushed him, he wanted to beg her to just hold onto him, but he held back the words. She already saw him as inferior; he didn't want her to think of him as weak too.

"Would you like me to fetch the footmen to assist you up the stairs?"

"No. I can do it." He would make it up the stairs, inside, and collapse in his bed until midnight. By then he hoped he would feel well enough to provide stud service to Caroline.

"Jack," she said on a sigh.

He pivoted toward her, angry that she would question his determination and ability, and more angry that she was right to think he couldn't make it on his own. A bitter taste lingered in his mouth when she hadn't reached for his waist or moved in to put her arm around him as she had before. "What? Are you worried I won't be able manage tonight?"

She recoiled, but her words came out clipped and haughty. "Should I be?"

Honestly, maybe she should be, because he was worried. If it was a repeat of last night, he might have trouble. Or surely that had been the laudanum, the ache in his unhealed leg and knowing she was hurting. He wouldn't take the laudanum, the honeymoon cream should ease her discomfort— and his pain he'd ignore.

Her forehead crinkled. "If you need to rest tonight . . ." She looked down.

His heart thumped erratically. He didn't want her to stay away from him. Certainly, he didn't want her finding her way into one of the gentlemen's beds, pretending to enjoy something she hated. She needed a man who could coax her through and didn't ignore her discomfort. Years of Mr. Broadhurst's abuse wouldn't be undone in a day. He sighed. Patience would win her if he'd let it. Surely he could get her to not hate the act, perhaps learn to like it.

Had she hated every minute with him? He was certain the tenor of their encounter had changed toward the end— or he'd needed to believe he was getting under her skin to complete the act.

But she was a passionate woman underneath. He knew that, had seen glimpses of it, watched her struggle to hide it. If he could just get through to the passion inside her, he could tempt her into letting loose. She hid her emotions with manners and correctness and a mild voice, except a minute ago she'd exposed her anger at his being gone. Now, while her passions were near the surface, was the time to seduce her.

He glanced up toward the closed doors. The sides of the staircase would block the view from most of the windows, except the ones directly above the entry. If Broadhurst saw him, he would be dead before morning, but he had to risk being seen to break through her resistance.

Jack reached out and traced his finger along the edge of the long curl. She drew in a deep breath through her nose. Her eyes widened. Slowly, he pushed the pads of his fingers against her skin and ran them along the edge of her low neckline, feeling the softness of the upper curve of her breast, the hard bone under her sternum, and then up to the hollow at the base of her throat where her pulse fluttered wildly. "I don't want to rest. I want you."

Her blue eyes darkened and her nostrils flared as her lips parted. Under his fingers her chest rose and fell with her rapid breathing. Pink spread from under her bodice, coloring her chest and then her face. Belatedly, she grabbed his fingers, crushing them with a desperate grip. "You promised not to touch me."

"Only during the act, Caro." His voice was rough as he added, "Which we are not at present engaged in."

He moved in close enough he could feel her breath whisper across his lips. Their hands were trapped between them, her knuckles brushing his chest. His pain receded and his interest rose. She was so damn beautiful, and skittish as a doe with fawns.

Just as she tilted toward him, he eased back. Always better to leave a woman hungry for more.

She dropped his hand and stared at him as if he'd grown a horn in the center of his head. But she'd already betrayed her desire for him. She might not like it, or might think she was incapable, but clearly she wasn't.

If she responded tonight with half the interest she'd just shown, he would more than manage. "So you will come to me tonight?"

She nodded and swallowed. Her eyes darted to the each side as if she'd stolen something.

He rather preferred that she was unpracticed in the ways of adultery. Now, all he had to do was make it up the entry stairs across the hall and into bed and then rest up so he would be fit enough.

He was halfway up, arms quivering, back and good leg aching, when she said, "I've put you in a room on the second floor at the far end."

Not only the rest of these stairs, but two more flights and a passageway to negotiate. "Are you trying to be the death of me?"

She raised her chin. "*You* are the one who thought you could traipse all over. *I* am the one who thought you should remain in the house close to bed for at least another week."

He closed his eyes. She was right. He was weak, and frustrated with his weakness. "It didn't seem like a great distance when I left."

"There is no shame in needing time to heal, Jack. I cannot see it as a fault, but I fear your determination to get better may make you overextend yourself," she said softly. "I do not know of another man who would push himself so hard."

"I hate being a cripple."

"If you had insisted upon visiting your family, I could have arranged for a carriage, or a pony cart if you would have found that less ostentatious, so you didn't have to walk the entire way."

Would she feel so generous about offering him conveyance to Manchester? Was there a way he could still make it to London? But then he'd need to walk miles to get from the station to the manufacturing district and to the inn where he would stay. Even if he could make it to London on time—

assuming he could find the money for the train—he didn't know if he could get to his appointment.

She went up the last of the stairs and turned to look over her shoulder. "I will send servants to help you the rest of the way. I wouldn't want you to be too drained. You need your strength for later. Besides, the bedchamber abovestairs has doors that lock. The breakfast room does not."

Her face colored red, and she darted through the door, leaving it open above him. He wanted to call her back, but her reference to his stamina had him feeling lighter and more determined than ever to make it to his new room with locks on the door. Because if he achieved nothing else, he was going to make sure Caroline was well pleasured. In that way if in no other, he could assure himself he was worthy of her in a way no other man was.

Chapter 19

"What was the domestic matter you had to see to?" asked Mr. Broadhurst, making Caroline jump an inch off her dressing stool.

Her maid mumbled an apology as if she had caused her mistress to startle.

"A bit of spilled pomade necessitated a room change," lied Caroline.

Her maid's eyebrows dipped in a vee above her nose.

All these lies that kept rolling off her tongue shamed Caroline. But she saw no reason to point out to Mr. Broadhurst that Jack had returned. She wouldn't hide the truth if her husband asked, but this was a time when discretion seemed the better part of valor.

In the looking glass reflection, Mr. Broadhurst's expression turned dark, but he could not pursue the matter with the maid in her room.

"My dressing gown, if you please," Caroline stood and held out her arms.

Her maid complied, pulling the heavy velvet robe around her, and Caroline fastened the frogged buttons up the front.

Mr. Broadhurst stepped into the room, his hand at the belt of his paisley robe. Surely he didn't mean to sleep in her bed again tonight. Even the servants would wonder at that.

Her skin crawling, Caroline dismissed her maid.

As soon as they were alone, Mr. Broadhurst turned to her and said, "Are you deliberately trying to obscure which gentleman you are sleeping with?"

"Yes." She fiddled with the button and its braided loop at her neck. "I cannot see that you need to know which man I use. Once I am pregnant I will never want his attention again." As the words came out, they felt false.

She didn't like intercourse. The act always hurt and made her feel invaded, almost as if she were being cleaved in two. She couldn't have imagined ever wanting it, but the way Jack touched her exposed skin had shifted something inside her. He'd left her breathing fast, faintly tingly and yearning for more of the same—perhaps even a gentle kiss. Of course what she needed from him was a baby.

But there likely would be too little of the noninvasive sort of touch if she allowed him more liberty to grope her or kiss her. Men seemed intent on fondling and kissing in a way that disgusted her. But to send Jack out of her life in totality, that was more than she could bear to contemplate. As long as Mr. Broadhurst never knew, she would still be able to see Jack. Daily, if he worked in the mill office.

Mr. Broadhurst grabbed the neck of her dressing gown, crushing her hand in his. He pulled her until she was on her toes and growled, "Do not forget you are my wife. When we are certain what is needed is done, you will never see him again."

Her heart thumped madly and cold rivulets of fear ran down her back, but she was able to keep her voice even. "As I would wish it. Unhand me, Mr. Broadhurst. There is no call to act uncivilized."

"Don't you dare get used to this." He shook her, his eyes burning with a manic intensity.

"Let me go," she said firmly, but every part of her was filled with terror. It was as if she saw the pits of hell in his eyes.

A cold miasma of dread shrouded her, and she couldn't move, couldn't breathe, couldn't break the spell.

He shoved her back.

Gasping, she stumbled and then caught her balance. Keeping her eyes down, she slowly backed to the door. "I am going now."

Had she betrayed her affection for Jack in her expression? She didn't know. But she didn't dare allow herself to feel any tenderness toward him. If Mr. Broadhurst had ordered Mr. Whitton killed, she was playing too dangerous a game with Jack. Mr. Whitton had friends and connections, and his murder would be investigated, but Jack had nothing to protect him. His family hadn't the resources to fund an inquiry. No one would look deeply into his death.

Her heart skittering, Caroline hurried down the hall and swung into the room where she and Jack had been last night. She twisted the key in the lock and then went out through the dressing room, down the servant stairs, and then to the first floor.

Repeatedly checking over her shoulder didn't reassure her she wasn't being followed or watched. She darted around a corner and raced to a spiral staircase that reached the northern el of the house. All this cloak and dagger slipping around might be overkill, but she couldn't risk Mr. Broadhurst learning that she was going to Jack.

When she first came to live here, she'd spent hours learning the layout of the house, always imagining which way she could go if she needed to escape. She'd told herself it was wise to know all exits in case of a fire, but in her mind she always envisioned running away from Mr. Broadhurst.

Until now that had never made sense. Her fear always seemed misplaced. Except for doing her duty, marriage to Mr. Broadhurst had not been onerous. Now, however, she didn't know if he was the sometimes brusque older man she knew or a man who thought anything he wanted should be his because he could pay for it. Worse yet, he seemed to believe that anyone who stood in the way of what he wanted could be destroyed because he willed it.

Her breath held, she twisted the knob to Jack's room and then slipped inside, pulling the door shut and twisting the key. She eased out her breath, half expecting Mr. Broadhurst to thwart her. The escritoire stood next to the window. A wardrobe occupied the far corner. Everything seemed normal and ordinary. As she stared into the darkened room, no shadow took a form it shouldn't. All was as it should be.

The old-fashioned washstand with pitcher and bowl had been shifted close to the fire. The chair from the desk was beside it. She imagined Jack stripping down and washing while sitting there, and she shuddered. Not only was such a thought unseemly, but after Mr. Broadhurst's unspoken threat she couldn't allow herself to think that way.

A low fire burned in the fireplace behind a heavy screen. She turned toward the bed dominating the center of the room. Her pulse raced, fear still leaving a bitter copper tang in her mouth.

The lump in the middle was Jack. As her ragged breathing stopped clouding her ears, she heard the deep regular sound of him sleeping. Her shoulders dropped and she sighed.

Poor Jack had to be exhausted. The doctor had warned that he should not exercise for more than a few minutes at a time. She should let him sleep. She tiptoed toward the wing chair on the far side of the fire. The floor creaked and she froze.

"Caro, come to bed." Jack's voice was sleep roughened and moved through her like warm honey. Shifting to the far side, he pushed the covers back, exposing a plain unbleached nightshirt. His own sleeping garment, not Mr. Broadhurst's.

She caught the post at the bottom of the bed, suddenly far too aware that she was very sore and her female flesh felt swollen and abused. "If you are very tired . . ."

"I'm not so tired I don't want you."

The words made her shiver. She brushed her dampening palms against her dressing gown and swallowed several times. Her heart was still fluttering and she took one last look over her shoulder at the door.

Jack leaned up on an elbow and watched her.

Caroline dropped her eyes. "I suppose we should get this over with."

He sighed loudly and rolled to his back. "If that is what you want."

The sooner it was done, the sooner she could relax. He would fall asleep, she could rest on the far side of the bed until dawn. She wasn't going back to her room until she absolutely had to. As much as Mr. Broadhurst thought the servants needed to believe the pregnancy was his doing, she didn't want to spend any more time alone with him than was necessary.

"It is what I want," she said. But it wasn't. The way Jack had touched her on the stairs awoke a need in her she didn't know she had, but she couldn't allow herself to feel affection for him. She was putting him in too much danger as it was.

He looked at the canopy and sighed. "Fine."

She closed her eyes. This was so wrong.

Besides, she knew copulation would hurt, and hurt worse than it had the night before. Mr. Broadhurst had ensured that, which perhaps was his plan.

In the first month of her marriage, she had to beg Mr. Broadhurst for time to heal between his visits. Coldness swept through her. Perhaps he derived satisfaction from knowing the act of conception would be uncomfortable for her.

The bed rustled as Jack removed his nightclothes.

She reached for the frogged buttons of her dressing gown, but her fingers felt wooden.

"Caro," he whispered.

She jerked her eyes open. He sat, his bare chest gleaming in the firelight, the covers thankfully around his waist. Her body went hot and then cold.

He held his hand out. "Come here and let me help you."

She hesitated, not knowing if she wanted this done faster or slower, but her fingers were clumsy. The loops seemed too small to fit around the covered buttons. She stepped up to the side of the bed and Jack slid toward her. His hip peeked out and she tried to avert her eyes, but the smooth flesh drew her gaze.

He wrapped his warm fingers around her hands, stilling her shaking. "It will be better tonight, I promise," he said softly, his brown eyes holding hers.

She shook her head and pressed her lips together. After Mr. Broadhurst, it couldn't be better. She would have to try harder to keep Jack from seeing her pain, since it bothered him.

He pulled her hands toward him and put them on his shoulders. His skin seemed to leap under her fingers. Her breath snagged as fresh tingles traveled up her arm, almost as if touching him electrified her. He slid his hands along her forearms and then reached for the button at her throat. "I'm just going to undo these, sweetheart."

She nodded, thinking he would make short work of them. But he didn't.

The one at the top of her neck was first, and then he scooted closer and reached for the lowest button. He didn't have trouble with them, the fastenings almost seemed to melt open, but he took a painstakingly long time between each button, until she was mentally urging him to hurry. Then the heels of his hands rested against her breasts as he unbuttoned the center. Her chest rose and fell rapidly, and with each breath his hands were there, not groping or pinching, just there, making her want . . . more.

When he finally undid the last one, she stepped back, jerked the dressing gown from her shoulders and tossed it across the bottom of the bed. She turned her back to him as she lifted her nightgown, untied her pantalets, and let them fall to the floor.

She turned around to find Jack leaning on one palm and frowning.

"I'm ready," she squeaked.

He shook his head. "No you're not."

"Jack," she protested.

His eyes narrowed. "If you'd let me undo the top of your nightgown, I could touch you as I did on the stairs." His voice was low and coaxing. "Nothing more, unless—"

She shook her head.

"You liked it," he whispered.

She couldn't allow herself to savor his touch, but she didn't know what explanation to give him. She drew on the otherwise useless hauteur bred in her. "You surprised me is all. I don't—"

"I just want to make this less unpleasant for you," he interrupted, sliding closer to her and tilting his head toward hers until his breath whispered across her lips.

It would take so little to close the distance, to feel his lips on hers. She couldn't allow this, but oh she wanted to, and she tilted closer. His gaze alternated between her eyes and her lips. Her pulse raced, her lips tingled, and her mouth watered. He drew her like a flame draws a moth.

"Kiss me," he rasped.

His words broke the spell. What was she doing? She had nearly . . . Twisting her head to the side, she fought to pull back. Panic rolled through her in waves. "I only need you to get me—"

"I know why I'm here." His voice was flat and his mouth tightened. He moved back toward the center of the bed and then lowered himself to his back.

Her throat tightened and a wave of sadness rolled through her. She cared for him too much as it was. Hell, she more than cared for him, she feared she already loved him. But she couldn't, Mr. Broadhurst would punish him. And there was no future for them. Her chest grew tight, as if her heart were being squeezed. Her whisper was scratchy as she said, "This is all it can be."

"It doesn't matter."

But clearly it did. She could hear it in his resigned tone and it hurt deep inside her. Her throat closed and her eyes burned with unshed tears. She had looked forward to this moment, had wanted to feel Jack underneath her, inside her, maybe release him from the promise he made to keep his hands off of her, but she feared what Mr. Broadhurst would do if she let herself get drawn into loving Jack. "I'm sorry to disappoint you."

"You're not disappointing me." The edges of his lips

turned up, but his eyes looked sad. "We can get this done whenever you're ready."

He twisted, reaching under the pillow beside him. She feasted on his long lean form and the way the muscles bunched under his skin as he moved. He rolled back, then pushed the covers down, exposing his thick male instrument surrounded by a nest of dark hair. Her fingers itched to explore him.

Jack cursed silently to himself as he drew out the ointment he'd stashed under the pillow. He'd blown it. She had been a hairbreadth away from touching her lips to his and he couldn't resist telling her to kiss him. If he'd just been a second or two more patient, she would have closed the distance. But his blood thrummed in his veins and throbbed in his cock. The wait for any response from her was driving him mad. She was so close to giving in, but stubbornly resisting.

She couldn't know it, but that near kiss had been what pushed him to readiness. And if all it was to be was stud service, he needed her to get on now, before the deep aches in his body made his desire recede. Maybe in the aftermath he could tempt her further.

She pulled her nightgown up around her thighs. He watched, hoping for a glimpse of heaven, but she seemed oddly determined to retain whatever modesty she still possessed. He hadn't kissed her, hadn't ever seen her totally naked, hadn't so much as caressed her breast, but he had slid his cock in her and come. Modesty at this point seemed oddly endearing, and hugely frustrating.

She clutched the hem of her nightgown tighter and put one knee on the bed and then the other, and then she swung her leg over him like she was mounting a horse. On her knees, she hovered above him as if gathering courage to bring their bodies together.

"Before we begin, I got this for you." He removed the lid from the earthenware crock and held it out.

She looked at the creamy contents and then back at him, her forehead furled.

"It's honeymoon ointment. It should ease you."

She blinked rapidly several times and then averted her face. She tilted forward and planted her hands on the mattress to his sides. She was so close, but so far away.

"Down there," he added, because she seemed confused. "I don't want to keep hurting you."

She made a peeping sound of protest.

He waited for her to move or say something, but she hung over him, the soft insides of her thighs against his hips, her nightgown brushing his cock, her hands planted on either side of his chest. Her head dipped down, her hair dragging across his chest, preventing him from reading her expression.

He put his free hand on her hip and she startled.

"Caro?"

She squeaked again.

"Do you want me to put it on you?" He held his breath, knowing she would refuse to let him touch her there.

Then she moved her head up and down.

Excitement pulsed through his body. Before she changed her mind, he dipped his fingers into the crock and came out with a generous dollop. With his other hand he lifted her nightgown—not that he could see anything with her head nearly on his shoulder—and reached down to press the thick glob between her inner folds.

She tensed.

Resisting the urge to spread the ointment around, to explore her secret garden, he held his fingers motionless. "It will take a minute to soften."

But he could already feel the consistency changing from lardlike to greasy with her heat. She tensed, clutched the sheet and held very still.

"Am I hurting you?" Slowly, he smeared the ointment around.

She shook her head, her hair dragging his chest and sending spikes of wanting to his groin.

But her female flesh felt puffy, as if inflamed and sore. God, had he done this? His heart flopped oddly in his chest. He swallowed hard trying to rid himself of the tightness in his throat. How could he ever convince her sex could be enjoyable if she were suffering?

She whimpered. With her face averted, he couldn't tell if it was pain or pleasure.

"You feel swollen," he whispered. "I must have hurt you a lot last night. I'm so sorry."

"Not your fault," she warbled, and then cleared her throat. "It's s-soothing . . . feels almost c-c-cool."

That didn't relieve his guilt. Concentrating on coating the opening of her body, he dipped one finger inside her and then a second. No wonder she was more reluctant tonight. He wanted to look and see if his fingers were reading her correctly, but she would never allow it.

"Caro, sweetheart, you don't have to like this, but don't pretend it doesn't hurt if it does."

She made a sound of protest.

Touching her in her private place was raising his need for her. But for her desire for a pregnancy, he would have begged her to wrap her fingers around him and let him find satisfaction that way instead of risking making her sorer.

But that wasn't why she was in bed with him. She wanted his release only to get her pregnant, not because she wanted sex with him. If only he could convince her to fool around awhile first, he could wait until he was close to coming and then finish quickly inside her.

"Sweet, let me see your face," he whispered near her ear.

He slipped his fingers higher, looking for that elusive little nubbin where a woman's pleasure was centered.

She lifted her head, and he thought she might turn toward him. He found what he was looking for and caught it. Careful to use only a little pressure, he tightened his fingers and rubbed the nubbin between them.

She gasped and jerked toward the head of the bed and away from his hand. "Jack!"

Ah, he'd found her sweet spot, and had just as quickly lost it when she shot away from him. But she hadn't yelped in pain. No, her reaction was surprise. Her neck was near his face and it was all he could do to stop himself from pressing his lips there. He turned into her, burying his nose in the fold between her shoulder and neck, breathing in the sweet scent of her skin. "You liked that," he murmured.

She shuddered and then tensed, but didn't protest.

Yes, he thought. He could yet show her pleasure, if only she would let him touch her, kiss her, hold her.

She tilted her head farther away then lowered herself back down. She kept a space between their bodies, as if she could keep this all business and no pleasure. He reached again to slide his fingers in her feminine folds.

She caught his wrist and pulled it away. "I'm sure that is enough."

She drew in a deep breath and lowered her bottom onto him. He didn't help her to join their bodies, although the heat of her flesh against him caused rush after rush to slide down his spine and throb in his cock. Wanting to slow everything down, he reached for her hips.

"Caro, if we touch—if *you* touch me awhile before we

are joined—I can be fast." Why wouldn't she look at him?

"Please, could we finish this?" Her voice quivered.

"Just be a part of it with me," he begged. He needed to watch her expression for signs of pain. He needed to know she was all right. He needed her to connect with him.

"I can't. I can't like this. I can't like *you*," she quavered.

Her words stunned him. She couldn't like him? Or didn't want to?

She reached down and positioned his cock against her. A burst of physical pleasure spiraled through him. He wanted her so badly. Then she was pushing down, joining them. He grunted, as his cock slid inside her. A soft moan left her, even though he could tell she'd tried to hold it back.

His head spun while she rocked on him. Her body felt so right, warm and slick this time.

Part of him wanted to shove her off, but another part wanted to be like this, forever buried deep inside of her. But he wanted this and so much more. He didn't know that he'd ever thought too much about connecting with a woman on more than the physical level, but this purely mechanical act left him hungry and angry, as if she'd taken his heart, soul, and body and given him nothing in return.

He'd had enough things taken from him today. If it killed him, he was going to get her to be part of this. Her face had gone soft with desire on the stairs. A minute ago she'd looked like a woman who wanted to be kissed. She wanted this for more than getting pregnant. The exchange of looks at the mill hadn't been one-sided. She'd been attracted to him for a long time. She might lie to herself, but he'd be damned if he would allow her to lie to him. Not now, not in bed, not while their bodies were locked together. Grasping her hips tightly, he held her down, stopping her rocking.

"Why are you determined to not enjoy this?" he demanded.

"Jack," she protested. Her voice was thready and high, and her body tensed. Everywhere.

He groaned, but had to ignore the throbbing heat and the urge to continue.

"Why?" he repeated. Was she determined to keep him at arm's length because he was a laborer, because he was poorly educated, or because he was a sad specimen of a man unable to support himself, let alone a wife? His heart pounded as he waited for her answer.

"It's . . . it's a sin," she hissed.

He rolled his eyes and let out a loud impatient sigh. "So it is all right to sin, but not to enjoy it? I think even God would find such logic twisted."

She put her fingers over his mouth.

He supposed that was a signal to stop talking and get on with the action. He pushed down harder on her hips and kissed her fingers. Tilting his head back, he caught the tips between his lips and flicked his tongue against them.

She jerked her hand away with such violence, the inch of space she tried to keep between them disappeared. He breathed deeply, loving the feeling of her breasts against his chest. She slapped her palms against the mattress.

"Stay there," he whispered. "Stay against me, Caro. I just want you close to me."

He wanted to shake her, but mostly he wanted to love her.

She sobbed and everything in him went cold. She was so tender, he knew they should have done more to get him close before he dipped his wick.

"Dammit, Caro, I'm hurting you."

"No-o," she whimpered. But a huge sob followed and then another.

With every shudder of her body, every time her stomach quivered, a stab of dismay went into his chest. His lungs grew tight, as if he were being suffocated. All he wanted was this to be pleasant for her, and she was crying as if her heart was broken.

"Then why are you crying?" He tried to not sound impatient, but his success was doubtful.

She sniffed as if she'd been trying to hold it back for a long time. Her body shook as sobs rattled through her. "Because it *doesn't* hurt."

Chapter 20

He pushed her off him. She tried to hang on, but he was stronger than she was. He scooted across the bed, taking a part of her heart with him. Sobs wrenched out of a deep place inside her as if powered by volcanic fury.

"I'm sorry. I'll stop. I don't know what's wrong with me-e-e." She sniffed again, which was completely unlady-like, but so was a runny nose.

He sat on the edge of the bed, the firelight casting a golden glow over his skin. He leaned and grabbed his crutches. The muscles in his broad shoulders shifted, stealing her breath away.

"I'm s-sorry. We can con . . . tin . . . ue." Did he even want to or had she repulsed him with her outburst? She didn't know what was wrong with her that she couldn't stop herself. Well-bred ladies weren't supposed to carry on like spoiled children deprived of their toys.

He leaned the crutches back against the bed as he pulled on the smalls he'd retrieved from the floor. His voice low and tight, he said, "You're killing me, Caro. I'm a man, not an animal that can ignore your bawling."

Bawling sounded so crass, but she supposed that was

as good a descriptor as having the vapors. She brushed his shoulder with her fingertips. He shrugged away as if her touch scorched him.

A fresh sob erupted, and she tried to will it away. She couldn't even form the words to beg him not to be angry. She curled on the bed feeling as if she was broken into a hundred pieces.

She'd ruined everything. She didn't even care if he got her with child. She wanted Jack inside her, staring up at her as if she were the most wonderful woman in the world. She wanted this man who had exhausted himself getting her an ointment she didn't even know existed, so *she* wouldn't feel pain. She wanted more than this stolen illicit affair, yet she knew it could never be anything more than a brief fling to get her pregnant.

Even if she weren't married, their stations were too far apart.

"Go ahead and cry. Lord knows you probably need the release," he muttered. "Just give me a minute."

"I don't normally do this," she whispered. "It has been the most horrid day."

"Yes, it has," he said tightly.

More tears flowed, and she swallowed hard trying to regain control.

The bed rocked as he stood. He must want to get as far away from her as possible. His crutches thumped across the room. If he had two sound legs, he'd probably be in the next county by now.

Then the thumps grew louder. Her breath quivered. He was returning to her. She risked peeking at him. His smalls rode low on his hips, the tie loosely looped in front. A line of dark hair ran down from his navel. Her breath hitched. The material hid little, but clearly he was no longer in a state to finish. She should have felt relief, but instead a hole gaped inside her.

He flapped a worn white handkerchief in front of her face. "I hope it doesn't reek too badly of coins."

Even when he was impatient with her, he was still concerned about whether a handkerchief might offend her over-weening sensibilities. She held out her hand. He pressed the handkerchief in her palm, then pulled back to grip his crutch. She came undone all over again.

He seemed as if he were a thousand miles away, and she didn't dare reach out to him again.

Her shoulders shook as she mopped at her eyes and wiped her nose. Pressing her lips together, she tried to hold back the words bubbling up and frothing out. "I didn't know what happened to you this morning. You were gone, and I thought something *horrible* had befallen you. I was so worried. I thought Mr. Broadhurst found out about us. Oh God, Mr. Whitton is dead, and I think my husband is a murderer."

Saying it out loud meant her suspicions were no long nebulous things to be dismissed to the back of her mind. She'd seen the man in the overcoat. The man Mr. Broadhurst had hired and spoken to secretively the night of Mr. Whitton's departure. "It is all my fault Mr. Whitton was shot. And I thought you . . ."

The thought was so awful she couldn't finish it, and now Jack would know how dangerous it was for him to be with her. Surely, he would want to get out now, while he still could.

If she could only be with Jack. Run away with him and live with him. Except, she'd make him a horrible companion. She couldn't cook. She had no idea how to clean a house, wash clothes, or grow vegetables in a garden. What she could do—plan a menu, summon the correct servant, and lay out ordered flower beds—were useless skills. She couldn't do half the things she would need to do if they didn't have money. Assuming Jack would even *want her* with him.

God, why did money have to matter at all? He was the epitome of a gentle man, and wasn't that where being a gentleman started? With a better start in life, he would have achieved a great deal. He was smart, he was ambitious and willing to learn. And because of the stupid mill, he was a cripple.

He slid her dressing gown from the bottom of the bed and tossed it over his shoulder. Tilting his head, he said, "Come with me."

"Where?" she hiccupped. They were in a small bedchamber and he wasn't decent.

He turned his head and sighed. "We're going to sit in front of the fire. We won't be in bed. We won't be engaged in the act, I don't have to adhere to the rules of our bargain, and I'm going to hold you." A dark stain spread across his cheek as he stared at the solitary wing chair in front of the fireplace. "I'd carry you, but I don't think I'm ever going to carry anyone again."

He crutched across the carpet. Gingerly, he lowered himself, wincing as he sat. And he was worried about her pain. Her eyes dropped to his cast. The material below it was dark.

Her chest squeezing, she slid off the bed, pulling her nightgown down. "You're bleeding, Jack."

"It's not fresh, and you can't do a thing for it anyway." The crutches clicked together as he leaned them against the wall. His face was haggard.

"You should let me look at your leg." She should leave and let him sleep.

"Not now, Caro." He turned toward her and patted his good thigh. "Come here."

She bit her lip. He shouldn't have missed the doctor today, but the reason he had sent a warm wave of affection through her. She wanted to fly to him, but forced herself to take mincing ladylike steps. "I cannot sit on you."

He caught her arm and yanked her down so fast her breath whooshed out of her. Then he tucked his arm under her legs, pulling her onto his lap the way one would seat a small child.

Pushing against the chair arms, she lifted her weight. "I will hurt your leg."

"I'll make a bargain with you." Jack shifted her dressing gown off his shoulder and wrapped it around her, tugging her down in the process. "I will let you know if anything you do causes me pain, if you will promise the same."

"It didn't hurt. I didn't know I could ever be free of pain." Her lower lip quivered and she tried to stop it, and ended up tucking her face into his shoulder. "I didn't think men cared if a woman was hurting."

Jack snorted.

For a minute Caroline didn't know what to do with her hands, but holding them clasped in front of her felt ridiculous. She tentatively put one hand on Jack's shoulder. His skin was warm and seemed charged.

He splayed his hand against her back and shifted his arm under her knees until it rested along her thigh. "Most men prefer a woman to be comfortable if not downright enjoying things."

Her cheeks heated. She didn't know the first thing about enjoying. Tolerating, sending her mind away so she could endure, that was what she knew.

"Is Whitton the man from the library?"

Caroline squeezed her eyes shut. "No, I was with Mr. Whitton the night I was drunk."

"Did he hurt you?" Jack stiffened.

"No." She grimaced, remembering the cool night and her disgraceful behavior. "I got sick."

The corner of Jack's mouth lifted. "The man from the library?"

Caroline lifted a shoulder. Mr. Berkley had been rough and disgusting, but she couldn't say he'd truly hurt her. "Not really."

Jack's hand slid on her leg a little, leaving a wake of tingles. "Any others?"

Lord Tremont had only kissed her, so he didn't really count. Caroline's face burned. "Only you."

"In the library man's defense, he probably thought you were eager and would tell him if anything bothered you. Not that I am of a mind to defend him, but you should know that all men aren't beasts."

Just her husband. "Mr. Broadhurst tried to make me like in-intercourse, but I preferred to get it over with." His pinching and mauling had only made it worse. She was incapable. Some women were and she must be one of them.

"I'm not him," said Jack. His thumb moved in a tantalizing circle on her hip.

She felt loose and tense all at the same time. "I know."

He shifted, repositioning her. Concern about his leg flooded through her. She bit back her worry.

"This sin thing." Jack sighed. "My sin must be far worse than yours because I have to experience pleasure to give you a child." He found her free hand and laced their fingers together. He let their joined hands rest against her stomach, which made flutters stir.

"You are not the one who took vows."

He rubbed his thumb across her wrist. "You were a child."

Tingles radiated up her arm, connected with the flutters

in her stomach and moved lower as a growing force. "I was nearly fifteen, not a child."

Although, as she said the words, going on fifteen seemed very young, too young to make decisions affecting the rest of her life. The marriage had been whirlwind fast. Mr. Broadhurst wanted children right away.

Jack brought her tighter against his chest and rubbed his hand down her back. Her bones turned soft.

"Caro, the real sin was selling you to that evil old man."

She tensed thinking of the insult to her father, but she couldn't work up any real offense. Jack only spoke the truth. She had been bartered, but brides had been bartered since time immemorial. Women of her class had a dynastic duty to uphold. They were brokered for power, for land, and for money. Her upbringing had prepared her for that. Only those with nothing to gain or lose could choose freely. She envied the simplicity of his world, where he could marry for love.

She flattened her palm against Jack's chest, relishing the feel of his heated skin.

He sighed again. "And don't you think God would over-look the sin in what we are doing, given that he wanted us to go forth and multiply?"

"I don't know." Would God look so favorably on her when she wasn't thinking of a child? When all she wanted was to be in Jack's orbit? Of course she still wanted a baby, otherwise why would she be here risking everything?

Jack shifted them again, turning more catty-corner on the chair.

She pushed away from his chest. "I am hurting your leg."

"No." He rolled his eyes, but the deep vee between his brows and his squint betrayed him.

She looked down at his leg. His bleeding should be

checked to make it sure it wasn't coming from a rupture to the sutures under his cast. "I have to look at it."

"Caro, I'm fine."

He didn't sound fine. He sounded impatient and angry. He had rather quickly agreed with her assessment of a horrid day. Had something happened when he went to his father's house? Or had he just been frustrated at his physical shortcomings? Or her crying?

"It's going to bother me if I don't," she said.

He tilted his head back against the chair and looked heavenward. "The weight of the plaster just rubbed my foot raw."

She should have checked on him earlier, but unlike the doctor, she didn't have an injection to give him to ease the pain. "Would you like some laudanum?"

"No more laudanum," he said in a resigned voice.

She slid off his lap. Putting his hands on the chair arms, he let her go. His lack of resistance left a bitter taste in her mouth. Kneeling in front of the chair, she pushed back the stained cotton under the plaster splint. With the sporadic loss of feeling he had in his foot, he might not have known how badly the plaster had dug into the top of his foot. Around the oozing sore, his flesh looked clean and smelled of soap. He must have washed it as best he could.

A sigh of relief left her as a strange tightening began low in her belly. Jack had been exhausted, yet he'd taken the time to clean before she came to his room. She couldn't be certain the effort was for her, but most other men would have gone straight to bed.

Reaching down, she grabbed the hem of her nightgown and twisted until she found a seam. Holding the two edges fast she ripped them apart and then with her teeth started a slit so she could tear off a strip all the way around.

As she started to wrap his foot, Jack leaned forward and

caught her chin, tilting her head back. "Just so you know, this does hurt, but do what you need to do."

She pressed her lips together and concentrated on pulling the wrapping tight as the doctor had done. "I cannot like that this happened to you, but I am glad it brought us . . ."

"Together," Jack finished for her. "I had rather different plans to bring us together."

Her heart beat faster. "Plans?"

Jack winced. "Yeah. I had lots of plans."

Finished with wrapping his foot and stuffing material into the gap so the heavy cast wouldn't cause further damage, she tentatively put her hands on his thighs. "Jack, what happened today?"

He shook his head, but the corners of his mouth turned down. He glanced toward the fire and then after a moment back toward her. Threading his fingers in her hair, he whispered, "You're so beautiful."

Her eyes were swollen and her nose was probably red. She lowered her gaze. "I'm not. Especially not now."

The compliment was probably meant as a distraction. A vague disappointment crawled through her.

He leaned forward and slipped his thumb under her chin. He slid his fingers along her jawline then tilted up her face. His brown eyes searched hers. His breath whispered across her lips. Her pulse surged and her lips parted.

This time he would kiss her, and if he didn't she thought she would die. Her lashes fluttered down, the intensity almost too much for her to bear, and then his lips brushed against hers.

"Caro," he murmured. "I planned to go to London and make a fortune . . . so I could come back and be worthy of you."

A whoosh of yearning poured through her. Her eyes popped open. She searched his face for sincerity.

He touched his forehead to hers. "You've always been in-spiration for me to be the best man I can be."

Her heart opened. How could she not love this man? Holding her gaze, he closed the distance between them and drew her into a kiss so gentle it made her ache. His tongue touched her upper lip. Her lips parted and their breath mingled. This was normally the time she wanted to turn her head or push away. Instead she strained toward him.

Jack deepened the kiss, sliding his tongue against hers and coaxing hers into a sensual dance. Her lips tingled and her breath grew short. Her body felt liquid and soft, yet tightened with anticipation.

Jack pulled back.

Feeling bereft, she whimpered. She opened her eyes to find him watching her with his head tilted.

"Was that so horrible?" he asked.

She shook her head and looked away. No, it was wonderful. He was wonderful. Their situation was *not* wonderful.

She couldn't love him, couldn't be with him other than for the next few days. She was married to a man who would hunt them down if she and Jack ran away together. With his cast, Jack would be too distinctive to disappear into the world. Mr. Broadhurst would find them. He had unlimited funds to track them. She couldn't even tell Jack the way she felt. It wouldn't be fair to him and might give him hope for a relationship that could never be.

What she needed from him was a baby. To yearn for anything more would only break her heart and maybe his. She slid her hand up his thighs, feeling the muscles jump under her touch. Her thumbs brushed the male parts of him.

He gasped.

The thin layer of his smalls couldn't disguise the throbbing hardness. She ran her fingers over him. He would be able to continue.

He cupped her face and gently nudged her around to look at him. She watched his eyes darken with passion and a question that pulled her toward a path she knew was fraught with pitfalls. She was too fragile to hide her feelings, too uncertain.

Possibly in the harsh light of day she would realize this feeling was just gratitude for his gentle consideration. Or that she wanted to persuade herself she had finer feelings toward Jack to make this less wrong. Only as she called up reasons she could be in error, she was at the same time trying to build a scenario where she would never have to let him go. A way to hide him in the attics or a cottage to keep him.

Suddenly unable to bear his scrutiny, she rose to her feet and reached for his crutches. She leaned them against the chair.

"Come to bed, Jack. I am truly ready this time."

Jack stared into the fireplace. He had been so close to getting through to her. Now Caroline had moved to the side of the bed and waited for him.

He supposed she was more ready than she ever had been before, but she was still a long way from the sated state he wanted to take her to. He, though, was caught in a welter of desire. He had tasted the beginnings of passion on her lips. Her budding response was a more powerful drug than the morphine.

He wanted to spend hours seducing her, showing her the pleasure to be found in her body, but she was too impatient to accomplish baby making to allow herself to savor the moment. He hovered on a knife's edge of desire. His erection was rock hard. His stones were drawn up so tight they almost hurt. He wanted to get on with it, but then, he didn't want to allow her to shut down her body's response.

Wearily he gathered the crutches and scooted to the edge of the chair. He didn't know if the rules were still in force, but until Caroline released him from his promise, he had to keep his word. No touching, kissing, hugging while engaged in the act. Men of honor always kept their word, and he wanted to be honorable. He wanted Caroline to respect him. He at least wanted that much from her.

He pushed up, positioned the crutches and made his way toward the bed, which seemed far away, even though it was only a few steps. Caroline watched him, and he wanted to tell her to turn around, to not look at him like this.

She was exasperating. When he wanted her to look at him, she wouldn't. He'd been trying to maneuver her on the chair to get both hands free and to watch her face, and she'd taken it as a sign of his discomfort.

"You look tired, Jack. We should finish so you can sleep."

He sighed. The day had been impossibly long. He didn't have the energy to fight her and his desire. "If that is what you want."

He never should have allowed her so much control over their encounters, but then they might not be having any encounters at all if it weren't for his agreement. Why would she choose a poor millworker over a polished gentleman to father a baby?

She glanced toward the door and then back at him. Her eyes glittered in the low light.

"You aren't going to cry again, are you?" The words were out of his mouth before he could stop them.

She seemed to gather herself, straightening her shoulders

and lifting her chin. "I shall endeavor to not make such a ninny out of myself again."

"Caro, it is just us. If you must cry, don't hide it from me. I have sisters, I understand the need for a good cry." He frowned. His sisters went so far as to say they felt much better after a long spate of tears. "Well, I don't exactly understand, but I've seen it enough times to know women cry."

She gave him a tremulous smile and it knocked the wind out of him. She would probably assume his breathlessness was due to the exertion of walking five feet. He never should have let her look at his leg. How could she see him as an object of desire when he was disfigured?

Jack stopped beside the foot of the bed. "You really are beautiful. I've thought so since the first time I saw you insisting on being handed down from the curricle."

Her brows drew together.

"At church." He may have been the only one who was close enough to see her dismay as her husband walked away, the flash of fear on her face and then her resolve. "The first time you attended here."

"I don't remember seeing you there."

He'd been lugging a baby, probably David, who was now sixteen. If he hadn't had his arms full, he would have stepped forward to hand her down. He hadn't really understood at the time, because he'd barely decided he was interested in females, but she, the girl who was not of their kind, intrigued him.

"I thought you were brave." And foolish to be so demanding with Mr. Broadhurst, but the man had turned around and helped her down. At the same time, the exchange sparked something in him.

Jack crutched the remaining distance and leaned his crutches between the bed and the nightstand. Caroline had already put the lid on the crock and placed it on the far bed table. Using the post, he started the awkward struggle to get on the bed.

He wanted to show her the world, to be one together, to simply share the wonder that could happen between a man and a woman. She wanted a baby.

But he had made progress, and there would be tomorrow night, and the night after, because he sure as hell wasn't going to make it to his appointment in London without any money.

He succeeded in getting his backside on the edge of the bed, and from there he used his good leg to push back. He almost groaned from the effort it took. How in heaven's name could he expect her to desire a man who was lame? "Tasks will get easier as I figure them out."

"I have no doubt you will achieve anything you put your mind to," she said softly.

He wasn't sure she was talking about everyday tasks challenging him or if she meant in a larger sense. But he couldn't keep her interest focused. He didn't feel capable of much.

He pushed his drawers off and moved to the center of the space, pulling the sheets and coverlet over his lower half. He turned toward Caroline, who stood beside the bed, gnawing on her lip.

Her hesitation stirred hope.

He lowered himself to his elbows, all the while watching her face. "Caro, if you are ready to release me from the conditions of our bargain, you have only to say the word."

She didn't, though. Her shoulders lifted toward her ears.

"Or not," he added softly, trying not to be disappointed.

"It is late, and you are tired." She stepped onto the rail and then put a knee on the bed. She made climbing in look easy. She knelt beside him, her knees brushing his hip.

Her forehead crinkled in a worry pattern and her eyes darted to him, down to his body, and then away.

He supposed it was to be the businesslike affair she wanted. But that didn't mean he couldn't think of the taste of her lips, or the sweet yielding of her mouth. Next time he wouldn't give her time to think. Next time, when he sensed her resistance waning, he would press his advantage. In spite of his failure to lure her into a more equal pairing tonight, anticipation tingled in him.

Sidling closer, she put her hands on his chest. His skin leaped. Her eyes widened as if his response surprised her.

"I love when you touch me, Caro."

Her gaze jerked to his. Offering silent encouragement and reassurance, he met her wide blue eyes. Then she shuttered her lashes and turned her attention to where she was touching him. She lowered her bum to her heels and traced the lines of delineation on his chest.

Her cool fingers slipped lower and his abdomen quivered under her touch. She splayed one hand and slid it down. His heart raced as her palm caressed his length. Then she curled her hand around his member and rubbed. Desire pounded in him. He watched her slender fingers as she stroked his length. Her hands were white and so soft, the hands of a lady—on him.

His breathing quickly grew ragged and urgency burned through him. Yet, he wouldn't stop this sweet stimulation for the world.

Her lips parted. Her chest rose and fell rapidly. Had he been going about this wrong? Was the best path to awakening her desires to show her how aroused she could make him? Certainly his partner's pleasure always served to send him to new heights.

Yet, he couldn't ever remember wanting a woman so

badly or wanting her to feel pleasure worse than he wanted his own release. Having her and feeling she was holding herself apart was driving him insane.

She drew her hand away and shifted back onto her knees. Bunching her nightgown with its ragged bottom edge at mid thigh, she hesitated. Her nostrils flared and her lips pressed together as if she were gathering her resolve to press on. As she had earlier, she seemed more like she wanted to bolt than to join with him.

He had to remember *not hurting* was the oddity to her. He tilted his head back and stared at the canopy. He didn't want to rush her, but his need for her was making him ache. Waiting for her to join them together had to be one of the hardest things he'd ever done.

"You know, I would never intentionally hurt you." He couldn't even say he wouldn't hurt her, because he had last night. He'd made her sore and swollen. And tonight he couldn't be sure that the honeymoon ointment would be enough. It was soothing, but not a miracle cream.

She shook her head and straddled him. "It wasn't you."

He tensed. If it wasn't him, who the hell was it? He caught her hips because he had to touch her.

Leaning forward, her hair brushed his chest and the heat of her feminine core settled against him. His head spun, caught between sexual desire and wanting to know who had hurt her.

"Caro," he growled. When he left, had she returned to one of the gentlemen?

She made a small sound and wiggled on him.

Heat flashed through Jack and made him shudder with need. He fought to find sanity. He just had to focus on any one of a dozen aches in his body, but all he could think about was her leaning toward him, engaging in his kiss, her fingers stroking his cock, and the desire he'd been so close to stirring in her.

"What are you saying?" he sputtered out.

She tensed all over and stopped trying to seat herself on him.

He fisted a hand in her hair at the nape of her neck and pulled her head back to look at him.

She bit her lip.

He let go, ashamed that he'd just promised to not hurt her and then yanked her head back by her hair. He gentled his voice, although it was lower and rougher than normal. "Caro, what are you saying?"

"When I was in the library," her voice was high and breathy, "I got through the encounter by imagining I was with you."

A wave of tender dismay swept through him. When she emerged from the library, he'd been so disappointed in her. Yet, she'd been thinking of him. But that was neither here nor there. As much as he liked knowing she had been thinking of him instead of the man she was with, it was a distraction. He worked to keep the anger from his voice. "If it wasn't me who made you sore, who was it?"

"I didn't mean to say anything," she said on an unsteady voice.

"But you did. And I know I hurt you last night." Had it only been last night? It felt like a lifetime ago.

She lifted a shoulder. "I didn't want you thinking you had really hurt me. I was only a little tender when I left you last night." Her voice ended on a barely audible squeak.

He knew who had hurt her before he cupped her shoulders and pushed her up to where he could see her face. Blackness fisted in his gut. The man deserved to be drawn and quartered, even though that punishment had been done away with as too inhumane. "Broadhurst."

She refused to meet his eyes. "He's my husband. He has the right."

"No, Caro, he doesn't have the right to"—mark her with his scent as a dog marks its territory—"rape you."

Jack closed his eyes and saw red. Drawing and quartering was too mild a punishment for the man. He should be boiled in oil and fed to the lions in the queen's menagerie. If it was the last thing he did, he would rid the world of that evil man.

Chapter 21

"**I** shouldn't have said anything." Caroline's chest tightened.

Jack's fingers dug into her hips. His jaw was like granite. He started to lift her, but she sat up and let her weight bear down on him. His self-condemnation was so misplaced she'd slipped.

His eyes looked through her. The violence coursing through him seeped into her as if she could absorb his emotions through her skin. She shuddered.

She had to distract him. In his present state, Jack would be no match for her husband. Or at any time in the future. "Jack, I want to stay with you tonight. Sleep in your bed where I feel safe."

"I'll kill him," Jack gritted out.

"No. If he were to die today, I'd be left with nothing. Not the mill, not his wealth, not the house. I need this baby. I need you to help me."

His brown eyes flicked back to her as if remembering she was there, sitting on his lap, their privates pressed together if not yet engaged. "What are you saying?"

"I'm saying I want more than my freedom from him." Her voice was heated. "I could go back home if that was all I wanted. I want all that he would deny me. All that for which I have endured fifteen years of marriage. He will not live forever, but I have to have a baby to secure everything."

Jack's mouth tightened and his nostrils flared.

"You cannot do anything rash. *I need you.*" The word "love" pounded in her brain, but she held it back. Now was not the time. There might never be a time. She reached down and touched his stomach. "I want you."

He manacled her hand, his eyes narrowed. "You want a child."

"Your child, with your smile, your kindness, intelligence, and determination." As she said the words, she knew it was so. No matter whose name the child bore, the baby would always be Jack's, and she would forever cherish this time with him. "You were the first man I thought of when he proposed his wicked scheme. The only man."

His eyes widened. His grip on her wrist relaxed. "Caro."

"With you is where I want to be, even if there never is a child." So much had to fall in line for her to be with Jack: Mr. Broadhurst's inability to father a child, her desire and his for one, Jack's accident, the disagreement with his stepmother. "It is as if the Fates have conspired to bring us together."

He turned his face to the side. "And keep us together," he muttered.

"I wish that could be so," she murmured. "I wish there was nothing left but us in this room and all the rest of the world would go away."

She took the hand that had manacled her wrist. If he wouldn't let her touch him, then . . . She slipped her wrist from his fingers and brought his hand up against her breast.

His fingers cupped her, lifted the weight of her breast and then held steady. He watched her, his brown eyes softening as the anger faded. Heat built in her, coiling and releasing. Impatience too, but he seemed to be waiting for a sign from her.

"Show me. Show me how this should be," she whispered. Her heart pounded, waiting for him to do more than hold her, praying she wouldn't wince if she felt a twinge. She wanted so much to be his in every way. "Please, Jack."

"Do you trust me?" he asked.

"As much as I can trust anyone."

His brow furled, but he said, "Fair enough."

He reached for her left hand, pulled the ring from her finger and hurled the wedding band. It pinged on the wood floor and then hit the wall. "When we are together, before God, you are *my* wife." His voice held a fierce determination.

"Jack," she sighed. They could never be married.

"I know I would have much to gain by such an alliance, but I don't mean it that way." He held her gaze, his brown eyes shining with an intensity that heated her to her toes. He stroked her hair away from her face. "Just you and me, a man and a woman together as God intended. I promise to cherish and honor you for as long as we both shall live."

He had with a single vow taken away her defenses and left her exposed and vulnerable.

"And I would prefer you came to me with nothing, than anything you gained through that bastard. Now, take off your nightgown."

A shiver slid down her spine. She wasn't certain she wanted Jack being demanding, but she reached for the buttons at her neck. He undid the tiny buttons at her wrists and then rubbed one knuckle in the opening she'd made.

Steeling her resolve, she pulled the nightgown over her head. Jack met her eyes and held her gaze for a long time as heat flashed over her face. Then slowly, like a caress, he looked down at her nakedness. Her elbows pressed into her side and it was all she could do to not cross her arms.

"You're beautiful, Caroline. I knew you would be. But you are more beautiful than even I imagined." With the pads of his fingertips, he traced the path his gaze had taken, down the center of her chest, just barely exploring the inner curves of her breasts, down her midsection and to her abdomen. Her skin tingled in the wake of his leisurely exploration. He trailed his fingers across the top of her nether curls and her flesh quivered.

He looked her in the eye again and his nostrils flared. Pulling her down on top of him, he made a soft sound of pleasure. "I have wanted to feel your skin against mine, forever."

He pushed back her hair and stroked the long locks down her back. Slowly, he moved his hands over her skin, exploring, molding, cupping her flesh. He never once grabbed or squeezed, and she relaxed into his tender ministrations.

Just as her body felt liquid and languorous, he rolled her to the side and then pushed her down against the mattress. She whimpered at the space he put between them and reached to pull him back down to her. He slid her hand from his shoulder to his mouth and kissed the inside of her wrist. Tremors of excitement raced up her arm and along her skin.

"I need to see your face," he rasped.

She wanted to duck away, to pull him back into doing the things she knew, but he shook his head and put her hand over his heart. The steady beat fascinated her, and she rested her palm there.

Then he kissed her, first only on the lips. When she thought she'd go mad for wanting more, he deepened the kiss. His tongue danced with hers, coaxing responses that she didn't know she had in her. A tight coiling centered in her core.

After a few minutes he pulled back, stroked his fingers down the side of her face and asked, "Still hate being kissed?"

She shook her head. "Not when it is you, not when it is like that." Not when she loved him.

He smiled and her breath caught. His fingers trailed down the side of her face, down her neck and along the outer curve of her breast.

Tensing, she waited for the inevitable torturing of her nipples, but Jack was intent on other things. He leaned close and whispered across her lips, "Relax, I'm not going to hurt you."

And he didn't.

Every moment was filled with exquisite tenderness as he kissed her until they both breathed like heavy trains chugging out of the station. Her lips grew sensitized until his kiss was like nirvana, on her lips, but also lower in her body, and deep in her soul. With one hand he cradled her to him, while tracing slow meaningless patterns over her skin with the other.

Her breasts tingled, although he only teased the outer flesh with light touches. She too tested the corded strength of his muscles, first in his shoulders and chest, then in his stomach, which leapt under her touch.

He slid lower and explored below her waist. She tensed as he pulled up her knee and rubbed tantalizing circles on the sensitive inner flesh of her thigh. The circles migrated up her leg until he brushed the curls at the apex. Her mind was spinning out of control until she could only think of him, smell him and feel him. She whimpered, wanting . . . wanting more . . . wanting him there.

While pressing his lips to her neck, he slid his hand along her hip, over her ribs, and cupped her breast. The tips had tightened to tight buds, and she arched, thrusting her breasts up into his hand. "Jack," she whispered frantically.

She didn't understand this aching need, or the tight coiling pressure low in her. Reaching down, she brushed the silken softness over iron that marked his erection. He groaned and leaned his head back, eyes closed. The darkness across his cheeks, the flare of his nostrils, the deep sound from low in his throat sent shivers down her spine.

She curled her fingers around his thick rod and stroked. Jack gripped her wrist and pulled her hand away. He tucked his head against his shoulder and sucked in deep breaths. "Too good," he finally rasped.

Shifting lower, he took himself out of her reach. Dropping kisses across her shoulders, he cupped her breast and then bent his head over her. She braced for pain, yet a part of her yearned for his mouth on her breast. He touched the tip of his tongue to her beaded nipple.

A starburst of sensation exploded within her. Her nether muscles clenched as blasts of molten power reached and tingled at the split in her mons.

His breath whispered across her damp nipple, making it tauten, poking up higher as if reaching for his attention. He seemed to be waiting for a sign from her. Threading her fingers through his hair, she pulled him back down to her breast.

Trust, Love, Faith. The words swirled in her head, not really words but concepts all tied to this man.

His lips closed around her nipple and the intense sensation flashed. She looked for the pain, but it wasn't there. He flicked with his tongue, shooting shards of pleasure through her. Her hips twisted and the energy she'd never before experienced built in her.

Jack knew exactly where the intensity burned, and his nimble fingers found the ending place and the source of such intensity. Her legs shook each time he tapped. Allowing her no rest, his finger and thumb closed around the fleshy hood and tugged in the same rhythm as his tongue flicked across her nipple.

Her legs shook and she cried out, "Jack!"

He lifted his head and looked her in the eyes. "Let it happen, Caro. Just come apart for me and let me catch you," he urged, his voice burred with intensity.

She coiled tighter and tighter until she couldn't anymore. Then she fell or shattered or soared, she didn't know how to describe the most exquisite pleasure that built to a place that resembled heaven and then had her tumbling and trembling through wave after wave of bliss.

She only knew it was Jack who brought her to this earth-shattering ecstasy. Jack who was patient enough to let her sensations build, Jack who knew how to touch her in ways that made her body come alive.

He slid up and brought his lips to hers. At first his kisses were gentle, but then grew more urgent. She welcomed the hard probe of his instrument at her feminine entrance, although she could hardly do more than lay in a glorious, mindless, boneless stupor. Her body resisted commands to move. All she could do was hold onto him as he thrust inside her.

She gasped as a new wave overtook her and brought the rapture back to a new dizzying height. "Jack," she moaned.

He lifted and watched her face as he thrust again.

She cupped his cheek. He turned and pressed a kiss into her palm. Then he rolled them until she sprawled on top of him. She tried desperately to gather herself together to provide the motion for Jack—awareness of his weakened state in the back of her mind. He thrust up into her. A new aftershock threatened to make her come undone.

He groaned, and she pressed kisses on the corner of his

lips, his cheeks, and on his neck. His body was hard with tension and she urged him to the place he'd just shown her. Then his face transfixed. He met her eyes as the powerful throbs of his climax had her dissolving in a new spate of pleasurable throbs.

They lay panting with their bodies intertwined in the still room. Caroline didn't know if she could move, her bones felt as if they had dissolved. But every breath Jack drew, she drew one too. Each time his heart beat sounded under her ear, a corresponding thump occurred in her chest. This must be what love felt like, to be so in tune with the other person that their hearts beat in tandem.

His hold was loose but secure. And she'd never felt more complete in her life. She pressed a kiss on the damp skin of his chest. He tasted slightly salty, and she pressed her lips to him once more.

"Caro," he sighed. "Don't get me started again."

Could she arouse him again? But the coals in the fire and the deep stillness let her know it was late in the night. "I know you need your rest."

"You do too, sweetheart." The gravelly tone of his voice wrapped around her like a caress. Was she his sweetheart?

She rubbed her fingers across the firm expanse of his chest. "Is it always like this?"

"You know it is seldom like this," he said roughly. But he leisurely caressed her.

Mr. Broadhurst had certainly never evoked this kind of wanton desire and heated pleasure, but neither had Tremont, Whitton, or Berkley. Was it because she loved Jack?

She raised her head and studied his face. He lowered his lashes, but not before she'd seen the flatness in his eyes.

Her heart jolted.

"Did we hurt your leg?"

He scowled. "My leg is no worse than before."

The connection between them was waning far faster than she liked. A moment ago she felt as if she couldn't separate from him, but now their breathing no longer matched. Their hearts weren't beating as one. A wave of sadness swamped her. Reality would intrude to split them soon enough. The idea of pretending Jack meant nothing to her during the daylight hours ripped at her very soul.

She brushed her fingers across his cheek. Capturing her hand in his, he turned and pressed a light kiss on her fingertips. "Go to sleep, Caroline."

More than exhaustion was going on. He seemed . . . flattened since his return. She had been so wrapped in her own concerns she hadn't probed too learn what had happened to him.

"Jack . . ." She hesitated. "Why did you agree with me about today—or rather yesterday—being a horrid day?"

His eyes popped open, but he didn't look at her and he said nothing.

"You said you went to your father's house. You have always called it home before. Aren't we good enough . . . friends that you can tell me what happened?" They had gone far past being friends, but they couldn't continue as lovers. Not after she conceived anyway.

He stroked her hair back from her face.

Sensing he needed time to compose his thoughts, she waited.

"I had an appointment in London for a job, this Friday." *"Had?"*

He blew out. "I can't make it now." His mouth tightened.

"Of course you can't," she blurted. He wasn't healed. London was hundreds of miles away. "You aren't ready to go gadding about."

Disappointment flickered on his face before his lips lifted in a sad smile. "I know."

Her thoughts whirled, his talk of going to London and making his fortune, his drawings, his unexplained absence at the mill. "Is that where you were the week before the accident?"

"Yes. I took the train from Manchester to London."

She pushed up on a straight arm. His gaze dropped to her chest. A lingering thrill trilled through her, but they had serious matters to discuss, and she was no longer certain of him. Her nightgown was on the floor and her dressing gown was over by the chair. She reached for the sheet to cover her nakedness. But the sheet didn't make her feel less exposed.

He couldn't leave her.

Keeping an arm around her, Jack shifted her to his side.

"It doesn't matter," he mumbled.

But clearly it did. She searched his face, and his gaze slid away.

Her heart twisted.

"What kind of a job?" She was relieved she sounded calm, even though her blood singed her veins.

"Building mill machinery." He shrugged. "Engineering it eventually."

She could fill in what he didn't say: *Designing new equipment, patenting it, receiving the royalties.* "I know you would be good at it."

He met her gaze. "We'll never know now."

This was his dream, his way of rising above the circumstances of his birth. His striving to rise out of the lower orders was part of the reason she loved him. How could she watch him give it up?

If he left for London, she only imagined endless days of her useless existence stretching out forever. She wanted him

near, working in the mill office where she could see him
daily, perhaps show him his child. But how could she do
that to Jack?

He feared his education wasn't adequate to working in a
mill office, and if Mr. Broadhurst ever suspected there was
anything between them, Jack would be in grave danger.

She had to let him go. Worse than that, she had to encourage him to go. She never wanted to do anything less.

Rather than let him see the struggle within her, she sat
up and faced away from him. Pulling her knees to her chest,
she wrapped her arms around them. She wanted to tell him
she loved him, beg him to stay with her, but that wish was
doomed. "I shall send a telegram letting them know you
have been delayed by a mill accident. I'll tell them you can
keep your appointment the Friday after next."

Jack drew in a stiff breath. Caroline's offer hung in the
air between them, a tantalizing offer, but one that would do
him little good. Even if his appointment was pushed back
two weeks, he had no money, no way to get to London, and
little hope of navigating around the city.

Her pale shoulder shifted. "Either I will have conceived
by then, or I will know I have not. Besides, you will be stronger. You are stronger every day."

He closed his eyes. "I can't."

"Yes, you can. I will help you."

He knew she would. If he told her about his life savings,
she would probably replace what his family had taken from
him. Likely it would be an insignificant sum to her. "Caroline, I walked to Manchester. I walked all about London.
Even if I could get to the city, I cannot get around so well
now. It took me well over an hour to get to the village." And
longer to return, not to mention his back had been killing
him the second half of the day.

"I can have you driven to Manchester, and you will have to hire hackney cabs in London," she said on a low note. "Much as I will hate to see you go, this may be for the best."

"I cannot afford—"

"I will give you cab fare. Don't refuse for prideful reasons." Her voice was tight.

If the cab fare was enough for the train, he could figure out a way to make it work. He'd demand the difference from Martha, borrow from his sisters, or sell his soul. This opportunity was everything he ever wanted, except as he stared at the slope of Caroline's shoulders, the knobs of her spine peeking through the dark strands of her hair, and the sweet dimples above her bum, he felt hollow. He wanted to be with her.

It went to her question earlier. This kind of lovemaking was rare and special. Making love to her was like nothing he'd ever experienced before. He had wanted her for as long as he could remember, and that had been aphrodisiac enough.

But her responsiveness had been more intoxicating than any love potion. He'd guessed if a man could ply her sensitive body correctly, sex would be fantastic for her. But to be the only one who'd unlocked her response made him feel like a king, yet humbled him too.

"I shall say I am sending you to Manchester to be seen by a specialist."

Once she allowed him to truly make love to her, he'd been more patient and gentler than he'd thought he could manage. He wasn't sure he could match his efforts when he was well and his urges would be stronger, but damn, he wanted to try. Except now she was all business. Perhaps she was eager to send him on his way when his usefulness was done. "All right."

"Did you even intend to come back yesterday?" Her voice warbled.

He hadn't intended to. He pushed up to sit and reached for her shoulder.

She shrugged away from him.

"You have to understand," he said. "Last night, you took my dreams of being with you and spit on them." He smoothed the dark hair away from her nape and pressed his lips there.

Her shoulders straightened and she leaned forward, away from him. "I'm sorry it was so horrible for you."

"I wouldn't have left the village without telling you." He'd dreaded talking to her. "Besides, I made the appointment long before I agreed to get you in the family way."

"You could have told me."

"Yes, but would you have agreed to be with me if I had?" He pressed another kiss to the back of her neck.

She shivered.

He touched his lips lower, between her shoulder blades. Her head tilted back and she moaned softly. His blood stirred, but he knew better. Even if he hadn't caused it, she was sore. Pulling her back against his chest, he wrapped his arm around her middle.

How could he bear to leave her? "I want to stay with you too."

"It will be best for you to go as far away as possible—" Her voice broke. "If it proves necessary, I can find you in London."

He would have to leave her here with a man who'd killed at least one wife, perhaps two. That, and just being without her, wrenched at him. Even though he'd skated all around declaring his feelings for her, he couldn't hold back the plea. "Come with me. Let me take care of you."

Hell, he didn't even know if he could take care of himself. Certainly he'd be a far cry from providing for her in a manner she was accustomed to. But he'd find a way. "I'll do whatever it takes." He might have to beg, borrow, or steal. He closed his eyes. He'd be in dire straights before he'd resort to thievery, no one he knew had enough to borrow from, and that only left an emasculating choice. "Beg, if I have to."

Chapter 22

Caroline returned to her room just after dawn. She could no longer hold back her tears as she slipped through the door.

Mr. Broadhurst snorted and startled from the chair where he must have fallen asleep waiting for her return. If he ever suspected she was with Jack . . . well, urging Jack to go to London was the right thing, even if it ripped out her heart.

The time with Jack was magical, but it couldn't continue indefinitely. And it broke her heart to tell him she didn't want to think about what could or couldn't be. She rumpled the covers on the unslept-in bed and punched the pillow to create indentations as if two heads had resided there for the night.

Mr. Broadhurst stood with a low groan and shuffled toward her. She stiffened.

"I've already rung for my maid." Caroline planted her hands on her hips. "You should return to your own room."

If she were to go with Jack, live in sin with him, her family would help, but would be tainted by her choice. Until and unless Jack could be successful, the two of them would be poor relations, an embarrassment. If he had to beg, or depend on her family, he would hate it, and perhaps grow to hate her. She would be so little help to him. The scandal would destroy her brother's aspirations. If there were illegitimate children, they would suffer. The list of reasons why it was a bad idea went on and on. But she had desperately wanted to say she would follow him to the ends of the earth.

"Have you been crying?" asked Mr. Broadhurst.

"I hate this. You know how much I hate it." She swiveled so her husband couldn't see her face. She hated that she couldn't be with Jack, now and forever.

He patted her shoulder. "There there. No need to cry, Caroline. It will all be over soon enough."

She didn't want the affair with Jack to end. Now that she found love, she wanted to bask in it forever. Jack's tender touch, his gentle hold, his whispered entreaties, all contrived to make her feel whole, as if she had been nothing but an empty shell for twenty-nine years of her life.

She wished love was the only thing to consider, but to encourage Jack to believe they had a future was foolish. Even if she weren't married, there were still so many reasons they couldn't be together. But she *was* married. A sob bubbled out.

Mr. Broadhurst folded her in his arms, but it was a hollow embrace. She was neither comforted nor warmed by it. Now she knew what a man's hold should be like. When Jack held her, she felt cared for. With Mr. Broadhurst she counted the seconds until she could back away.

"When you have a baby in your arms, it will all seem worth it," he urged.

Would it? Would loving Jack's baby mend the tear in her heart? Would the precious memories of the nights with Jack sustain her through the frigid wasteland of her life?

She took a deep breath. "I want the mill. I have worked hard to learn how to run it." She had worked hard to find a purpose in her life, to have a reason to get out of bed every day, to make sense of why she had been married to this man. "I want a child, but this is awful."

Mr. Broadhurst made a clucking sound. All she wanted was to shove him away, but she forced herself to accept the embrace.

Jack had to go to London. Their only real hope in the future was if he could make something of his life and she could run the mill and be answerable to no one. That was a slim hope.

Mr. Broadhurst continued to hold her, and she remained stiff and wooden in his arms until her maid arrived. As Mr. Broadhurst exited her room through the connecting door, she swore to herself that the first thing she would do after she got pregnant would be to have a lock installed, because she didn't think she could ever bear her husband's touch again.

Jack had to gain respectability and financial solvency. Only then would they be able to be together in some distant point in the future.

"He will see you now," said the clerk.

His heart thumping madly, Jack leaned on his crutches. This was it. The owner of the company had let him sit for a long while.

Perhaps the sitting had been good. As exhausted as he was after crutching through the London streets from the train station, he'd needed to catch his breath. He was still a long way from well, but miles better than he had been the day he went to his father's house. But his frailty frustrated him and had him cursing on more than one occasion that morning. As weak as he was, he had to convince the owner of the company he could work, and work hard. He had to do it not only for his own sake, but for Caroline too.

The last days with her had been bittersweet. The nights were filled with tender lovemaking. Long into the night he'd held her in his arms as she slept.

Still, he was here, and on a path to making a better life for himself, and one day maybe he would have enough to offer Caroline. When they talked of his appointment, she'd always bit her lip as if holding back. But her eyes had said it for her. She wanted him to succeed and come back to her. And a failure would extinguish the tiny flame of possibility that they could ever be together.

Still, Jack wasn't certain leaving her with Broadhurst was the right thing. The man was vile. Caroline's aristocratic family might not provide enough deterrent to keep Broadhurst from harming her. He could have stayed, been a clerk, and seen her every day. But seeing her and knowing he couldn't touch her would be torture. No, he was better off here where the desire to see her again would fuel his efforts to succeed.

He crutched into the office.

The owner stood and came around his desk to shake his hand.

But Jack knew it was over when the man realized he was lame.

Jack had smiled and talked congenially of his designs, showed his schematic drawings, talked of how he had worked as a mechanic for nigh on a decade, but the company owner couldn't seem to focus on anything other than his broken leg.

Nothing persuaded the man to believe he could weld or use a lathe while perching on a stool, or that he might not even need a stool once he was healed enough to walk again. The man had just kept repeating that he needed an able-bodied machinist, not a cripple on crutches.

Jack thought of Caroline and the baby they might have conceived and how desperately he needed to prove himself. He tried to persuade the owner long after he knew it was futile.

Finally, he stopped pushing.

He rose and curled his hands around his crutches to make his way out of the office. The wooden handles cut into his palms, and he wanted to slam the door the door or push everything off the ignorant man's desk, but such actions would not persuade anyone to offer a job.

"I'm sorry you came all this way," said the owner. Jack shook his head as he bent and scooped up his haversack filled with his few belongings that he'd left in the outer office. He had a dangerous second of teetering on his good leg as he swung the pack onto his back and pushed his arms through the straps. Fortunately he didn't fall, but taking care with every motion he made was not easy when his blood was boiling.

"If you would have included in your telegraph the nature of the accident, I could have saved you the trip."

"You're making a mistake," said Jack.

"Do you need money to get back home?"

"Don't insult me. I earn my way," Jack said in a low voice. He should have taken the money, but he grabbed his crutches again and headed outside before he said words he truly would regret. Did that bastard only see a beggar when he looked at a man with only one good leg?

He was so much more, and he wouldn't let this turn him into a charity case. He couldn't. As an indigent, he had no chance of ever having a future with Caroline.

He left the building and gripped his crutches so tight the wood bruised his palms. The panes of the window begged for him to knock the wood right through, but he resisted the destructive urge.

Crutching down the walkway, he stared at the brick facades of the buildings and tried to take stock of his prospects. He could design machinery and build it; he knew he could.

If he'd had the money that was stolen from him, he could have spent a few days looking into other machine shops, but as it was, he didn't have enough for even a meal, let alone lodging. He didn't want to face another prospective employer who would only look at his plaster cast. He was so tired and wretched after the walk from the train station, he likely wouldn't be believed.

Every uneven paving stone threatened to pitch him to the ground, and the afternoon rain turned the byways slick and treacherous. Jack leaned against his crutches and breathed. The sooty London air offered him no relief. The bustle of the city, instead of invigorating him, made him leery of his leg being jostled. The knifing pain in his back began anew.

Why had he ever thought he could make a better life for himself?

Ahead, a tavern sign creaked. He made his way toward the pub and then spent the last of his money on a pint. He couldn't even afford to get drunk, though that wasn't a solution and would only temporarily ease the ache of failure. It wasn't so much that he wanted a beer, but he needed to rest and he needed something in his stomach.

Jack sat in the corner booth of a tavern and slowly nursed the tankard until the buzz of conversation turned into a pleasant sound like the babble of a brook or the relentless waves of the ocean. He folded his arms and leaned into the wall.

The barkeep roused him in the wee hours of the morning to tell him the tavern was closing. Jack blinked, looking around at the empty room. The roaring fire was nothing more than gray ashes now.

He slid to the edge of the bench and started to stand, before he realized he'd left his crutches under the table hooked onto the seat. He scooted back, gathered his crutches, then slid out from behind the table. Without money to afford lodging or cab fare, he figured he'd crutch through the city at his own pace in the early morning hours. After all, he had miles to go and no more excitement and anticipation to fuel him. Perhaps he could make it to King's Cross Station before the train left for Manchester.

A clerk job in the Broadhurst mill, even if it only lasted a few weeks, was better than no job at all. Once his leg healed enough to remove the plaster splint, he'd come back. He needed to regroup, and then marshal his resources. When he was fully healed and had a few pounds to his name, he would try again.

Surely other places would welcome his ideas and his abilities. Perhaps in Manchester he could find work and opportunity.

"What happened to your leg?" The stout barkeep dropped a wet rag on the tabletop and wiped his hands on a dirty towel slung over his shoulder. Wet swipes in lazy *s*'s marked the haphazard cleaning job the man was doing.

"Mill accident," responded Jack.

"I ain't seen you around here before." The barkeep seemed more inclined to chat than do his cleanup.

"I'm from a village in Lancashire."

"That where the mill was?"

Jack nodded.

"Why you in London?"

"I was offered a job." Jack's shoulders lifted, revealing what he didn't want to say.

"Your accident was recent like?" said the man. "You don't quite seem used to getting around."

"Four weeks ago," answered Jack.

"I take it the job didn't work out." The man cocked his head to the side. "You got anywhere to sleep?"

Jack shook his head.

"Tell you what, you wash up all them tankards, glasses, and the tables, then sweep the floor, you can sleep on a bench here." The man's face crinkled. "Can you manage that?"

"I'll manage," said Jack. "Thank you."

It wasn't charity. Then again he wasn't being paid in coin either. But this time he wasn't going to be so foolish as to turn down an offer of help, even though the offer cost the barkeep nothing.

Jack stood on the train platform and thrust out the leaky pewter tankard he'd filched from the tavern. It had taken him the better part of three hours to thoroughly clean the taproom. Sweeping one-handed was a nightmare, not to mention it looked as though the corners hadn't seen the broom bristles in ages. He'd hoped when the barkeep saw how thoroughly clean the room was, he might offer a coin or breakfast, but he hadn't.

As it was, Jack had no choice but to beg for enough money to get home. He consoled himself with the knowledge that the only reason he had to beg was because Martha and his father had stolen his money, but he felt lower than a worm.

He'd resorted to stealing the leaky mug to beg with. The splitting seam wouldn't leak coins, if he got any. All the cadgers he'd seen in London had hats, baskets, or containers of a kind for the money to go into. He'd even seen one hunchback with a hollow wooden statue.

A man in a bowler with an ebony cane stared at him.

Jack lifted the mug.

The man stepped to the side.

Jack lowered the tankard. A few farthings and a penny or two had been dropped inside, but at this rate it would take him days to get enough to get back to Manchester. Sooner or later he'd have to eat. There were more than enough beggars around, ones who had no problem calling out for money. The best of them searched the faces of the crowd and seemed to know just which people to approach. Jack didn't even want to look anyone in the eye.

A blow against his cast blasted pain through his body. He bit back the agonized shriek that threatened, but a yelp still left him. A black cane had struck the blow. Dear God, were there men who had nothing better to do than torment him. He crutched forward, spilling a few coins from the tankard. Helplessly, he stared at them as a small boy darted over to pick them up. Bending down and getting back up wasn't a move Jack had mastered. It was hard enough to get up from a chair one-legged.

"Put 'em back in the cup, boy. They aren't yours."

Jack twisted around to see the man in the bowler with his ebony cane hooked over his arm.

The boy put a few coins in the cup, but kept at least half of them as he darted away.

Puzzled why the man would hit his leg, then come to his aid, Jack asked, "Why did you hit me?"

The man pulled out his purse from his vest pocket. "Just making sure you hadn't put a plaster splint on a healthy leg. You had a guilty look about you."

Furious at the idea that he'd fake his injury, Jack lifted his leg and yanked down his sock, revealing the angry red lines of his scars that disappeared under the cast. "My ankle was crushed."

The man blanched.

Jack closed his eyes and heaved a deep breath. "Look, I'm just trying to get home."

The man dropped the coin he had between his finger and thumb back into his purse.

The clink made Jack sag. He pulled up his sock. "I'm not a beggar."

Only he was. He was just a very bad beggar. He wanted the coin, and he hated that he wanted it.

"You've family to take care of you at home?"

His hackles rising, Jack turned toward the train. "I have a job there."

A ping in the tankard made him start.

Jack lifted it to find Queen Victoria's profile on a half-inch gold coin. A sovereign?

He twisted.

The man in the bowler was walking away.

"This is more than I need," Jack shouted.

The man turned, gave a wave and the ghost of a smile, then sidled between two people and was lost in the crowd.

Carefully, Jack emptied the coins into his palm and then put them in his pocket.

If he didn't spend a lot of the money on food, he might be able to go to the Royal College of Physicians and see if they could give him any help with regaining feeling and the use of his foot before he returned to Manchester.

And as much as he wanted to see Caroline again, he didn't know how he could face her with his disappointing results.

*   *   *

Caroline woke with an uneasy feeling in her stomach, not quite enough to claim sickness but enough so she would have preferred to roll over and go back to sleep rather than face the inevitable day.

She missed Jack, missed him in a way that went deep and bled the colors out of the world. He'd only been gone a fortnight, but it was if it had been years. If she had failed to conceive, they could try again. Wanting to have failed to conceive was a betrayal of her deepest wishes. Yet, there it was, a hope that bloomed in her every morning and was dashed every evening when her courses didn't come. She was more than two weeks late. Almost three.

Her door opened and her maid tiptoed in.

Caroline gave up on getting more sleep. She needed to go into the mill office anyway. She pushed up to a sitting position.

"I brought you some weak tea and toast, ma'am."

Caroline frowned.

"Just in case you're feeling queasy." The maid set the tray on the bed.

Caroline met the young woman's eyes. They both suspected.

She supposed she had been waiting for one sure sign, a day when she knew for certain, but she wasn't sure now. "It could just be the strain of having guests has upset my natural rhythms."

Her maid pressed her lips together and removed linens from the clothes press. Her rigid posture spoke volumes. She knew, and Caroline couldn't deny it any longer. She was with child.

Caroline waited for the joy to overwhelm her, but instead a keening loss at the idea of never again being with Jack took over.

"You been with your husband enough, he'll think it is his."

A jolt of dismay rocked through her, and Caroline jerked. "Of course it is—if I am with child—it is Mr. Broadhurst's."

Her maid flapped out a petticoat. "Mum's the word, ma'am, but you ain't slept in that bed but in the last fourteen days."

Dear God, if her maid knew exactly when she'd started sleeping in her own bed, would she put it together with Jack's leaving? Servants were always the bane of any secret.

"Mr. Broadhurst prefers his own bed. And that is the end of it," said Caroline. Her stomach turned and she pressed a hand to her flat midsection.

"Never fear. My loyalty is to you. Now, eat the toast. It will help."

Caroline nibbled on the toast and then found herself devouring the remaining crust. She was with child. Jack's child. What they shared had been so perfect, a baby seemed the inevitable miracle to spring from their union.

She only wished she knew Jack was safe. She'd wanted to give him the direction and letters of introduction to the caretakers at her sisters' London houses. But the expression on his face when she broached the subject suggested that he thought her offer implied a lack of confidence in him. So she held back, just as she'd held back the declarations of love that sprang to her lips with increasing frequency.

But she regretted her reticence. She might never see him again, and she'd failed to pour out what was in her heart. More than anything, successful or not, she wanted him to come back to her when it was safe for him to do so.

Chapter 23

Caroline looked up from her desk and stared at Jack in the doorway of the mill office. Her breath caught and her heart raced. He looked so good she wanted to spring off the chair and race to hold him.

He smiled, and memories of every tender touch poured through her with molten heat. Her bones melted under the onslaught.

Slowly, she became aware that the scratching of pens had stopped and all the clerks in the office were staring at Jack. He wore a business suit and looked more like a man of moderate means then a mere laborer.

Swallowing hard, she drew back her chair and stood. "Mr. Applegate."

What on earth was he doing here?

Leaning heavily on a cane, Jack limped across the floor toward her. "Mrs. Broadhurst."

Her mouth dropped open.

His forehead veed and his lips pressed together each time his weight landed on his right leg. The below-the-knee plaster cast interfered with the smooth lay of his trousers. But he was walking.

Tears sprang to her eyes. Her emotions seemed to have

gone wayward lately. One day she missed him so much it was all she could do not to sob all through the day, the next she was glad the temptation was removed, and other days she prayed fervently for his success so there was a chance they could have a future.

Jack's gaze shifted behind her. "I've come for the job you promised me."

Caroline turned as Mr. Broadhurst came out of his office. Since she'd told him of her suspected condition, the gentlemen had gone home and Mr. Broadhurst resumed control of the mill, as if her interlude in charge meant nothing.

"Step inside my office and we'll discuss terms of your employment, Mr. Applegate." Mr. Broadhurst returned to his chair behind his desk.

Questions burned in her mind, but she couldn't ask them for fear she would give away her feelings. Instead she ducked her head as Jack moved past her. Was he back because he too found every minute of every day apart an eternity?

Jack leaned against a tree halfway between the Broadhurst house and the mill. The early darkness was nearly complete, and the December air was brisk.

The one bright spot about returning was that Caroline had looked thrilled to see him. Her eyes lit up, her carriage lifted, and she eagerly leaned toward him as if she too wanted to greet him more warmly. But her excitement quickly turned to dismay. She slipped him a note midday asking to meet in front of the house after dinner.

He'd been dreading and anticipating being alone with her, but he didn't know how to answer her questions. Oddly enough, he hoped he'd failed to get a child on her too. He'd failed at everything else.

Even the physicians of the Royal College were unable to do

more than marvel at the ingenuity and advanced treatment of the country doctor who saved his leg when they would have amputated. All they were able to do was give him a new plaster of paris cast that allowed him to walk, warning him his ankle was locked in place and he'd likely need the solid cast or a brace for the rest of his life. Then they shook their heads over his inability to command his toes to move.

The front door of the Broadhurst house opened, allowing a brief spill of light onto the stairs. Then the silhouette of a woman scooted through the opening.

Caro. Even though he couldn't make out her face, and her form was bundled in a long cloak, he knew her.

His heart racing, Jack pushed away from the tree and walked out to the center of the drive.

Looking left and right, Caroline hesitated at the bottom of the stairs.

"I'm here," he called softly.

She walked briskly toward him for a few steps, then trotted, then broke into a full run.

He leaned against his cane, bracing for an impact that was likely to send him to the ground. The cast didn't exactly provide him with the same stability as having two good legs. He'd found he could barely tolerate bearing weight on it for more than ten minutes, but at least his back didn't hurt the way it did when he used the crutches for long periods. But he wouldn't have stopped her headlong hurtle into his arms for the world.

At the last second she drew up. He didn't know if his disappointment or his relief was stronger.

"Jack," she breathed.

His disappointment. He wanted to feel her against him.

Unable to help himself, he reached to brush his fingers across her cheek. "I missed you."

She caught his hand and squeezed. "You mustn't. We mustn't. Oh, why are you here?"

The cold wind gusted, stealing his breath.

Staring at him with glittering eyes, she took a step back and then another.

The space between them was like a dull knife carving out his heart. "Caro."

"We can go to the mill office and talk."

He didn't want to talk. He wanted to pull her to him, to kiss her, and to make love to her until dawn.

She walked faster than he could manage to follow. The office wouldn't exactly provide a soft bed, but it would get them out of the wind. All he could think about was tasting her. His body tightened and his thoughts swirled with memories of the texture of her skin, the softness of her sighs, the eagerness of her hands on his body.

He closed the door behind him as she lit a lamp in the inner office. Making his way through the darkened room, he wove between desks and chairs until he could lean against the door frame and take the weight off his bad leg.

She stood behind her husband's desk and folded her arms. "What happened?"

"The company owner didn't think I could do the necessary work with my leg in a cast." Jack rubbed his face. The man might have been right.

She stepped forward and her hips hit the edge of the desk. "Did you tell him you would eventually heal?"

"He wasn't interested. He couldn't see past my injury to even look at my designs."

She rubbed the upper part of her folded arms. "Couldn't you have tried with other companies? You have other ideas, other drawings."

"No."

Her face fell, and he couldn't bear that he'd disappointed her.

He held out his hand, palm up. "I haven't given up yet. I just didn't have money to stay in the city. I figured being a clerk for a while would give me a chance to save again."

She stared at his palm.

"I'm sorry, Caro. As soon as I have some savings again—"

"What did you do to your hand?"

Belatedly, he remembered that the blisters and raw spots from holding his crutches hadn't entirely healed. He fisted his hand and pulled it back. She came around the desk and peeled open his fingers. She reached for the other hand and did the same.

"The crutches didn't like me much," he said lightly. "Took a lot of walking to get around London." And home from Manchester. He'd hitched rides when he could and crutched when he couldn't.

"I gave you money for cabs."

Jack sighed. "That's all I had to get to the city."

She raised her head and stared at him.

"I saved over two hundred pounds, but my stepmother took it and bought a new stove and paid off the note on the house while I was recovering." His jaw tightened.

"I could have given you more money."

He shoved his hands in his pockets. "I don't want your money. What good is success if another has bought it for you?"

"Jack," she protested. "You should have let me help you. I can give you two hundred pounds. You could have stayed at one of my sisters' houses. The cost would have been negligible to us."

"It's not negligible to me." It had taken him a decade to save two hundred pounds. "I'll be the best damn clerk the

Broadhurst mill has ever seen. I'll earn my keep and I'll save again. I have lots of ideas. I don't have to design mill machinery. I've been thinking about rubber."

He wondered if coating the handles of his crutches would have saved his hands, not to mention coating the tips, which might have kept them from slipping so easily.

Her forehead puckered.

He pulled her against him. She resisted at first, her body tensing, but he let the fight drain out of her before he tightened his hold and pressed a kiss to her temple.

"Just believe in me, Caro. I need you to believe in me. I need to know that you will be mine when I am successful." He wanted her to say that she would wait for him.

She tilted her head back. Then they were kissing and clinging to each other. Even if she wouldn't say the words, her body said it for her. She moaned.

With her in his arms he was home. He could make it through the days of struggling to write and spell legibly, to cram as much learning into his head as it would hold, to hide his feelings from Broadhurst if he had this to look forward to at night.

She made a sound of protest and pulled back. With her hand planted firmly in the center of his chest, she pushed him back. He lost his balance, but fortunately only careened into the doorway while holding onto her arm to stay upright. Steadying his feet underneath him, he regained his equilibrium.

"Jack, we can't do this." Her blue eyes looked bruised and accusatory. "I can't promise you anything. I'm married." She looked down and her voice grew tinny. "I don't need you anymore. I—I'm pregnant."

In that, he'd succeeded. He looked at her belly, but of course she wasn't showing yet. She was going to have his baby late next summer. His emotions bounced around. He was exhilarated. He was disappointed, yet proud. And he was concerned about her. "What the hell were you doing running?"

Her swimming blue eyes jerked back to his.

"You have to care for yourself." He reeled her back into his arms and she didn't resist.

Instead she trembled.

He held her loosely. "I was hoping we'd have to try some more."

She stiffened.

He stroked her arm. "Don't worry. I understand."

"Do you, Jack? Because if Mr. Broadhurst finds out you're the baby's father, I don't know what he'll do. I have the protection of family and a brother who has the queen's ear."

He didn't. He had a family who stole from him.

"I am certain he ordered Mr. Whitton killed after he had been with me. They say a highwayman in a greatcoat and pulled low hat shot him, and I saw a man dressed like that go into Mr. Broadhurst's study the night Mr. Whitton left."

The description niggled at a faint memory in Jack's brain, but he was too intent on the stark despair on her face.

"We have to end this. I can't see you anymore. It's too dangerous." Her voice quivered. "We have to pretend there is nothing between us and that there never was anything between us."

"It's all right, sweetheart." She was breaking his heart, but at least she wasn't rejecting him for being a failure.

"I have to get back, before I'm missed." She didn't move away, though. Instead she tucked her head under his chin and rested against his chest.

"*Shhhh,* just let me hold you a little while," he whispered into her hair. "It seems as though I have been away from you for years, not weeks."

She plucked at his shirt. "How did you get back? How did you pay for your trip if you didn't have any more money than what I gave you?"

Damn, she was going to make him tell her everything. "I cleaned up a barroom."

She leaned back and looked at him.

"I begged." His voice cracked. He struggled for composure, looking at a chipped brick on the far wall. "Being a cripple is good for something. One man gave me a sovereign and it was enough to get me looked at by physicians at the Royal College and get me home." Mostly. "They don't think I'll ever get back full use of my leg."

He hadn't meant to tell her that.

"Oh Jack." She leaned into him and rubbed his shoulder. "They can't know for certain."

"I just thought a job—even a clerk job—was better than begging. When I get stronger—"

She put her fingers in front of his lips. "It's all right. I'm glad you're back. I'm glad you're safe." He could feel her pulling away, even as she shook her head. "I really have to get back."

Letting her go was like cutting off a limb. He'd known this was temporary, that she'd have no use for him after he got her with child.

"I'm staying at the midwife's house, if you need me," he said.

Her forehead furled.

"It is the one place in town you could go without question," he added by way of explanation. And he sure as hell wasn't going back to his father's house. Mrs. Goode hadn't liked the idea either, but she had a spare bed—which he insisted he'd vacate if she had a patient, and sleep on the floor in the apothecary. He promised to man the counter when she was out delivering babies and pay her half his wages. He also told her he wouldn't stay above a year.

Caroline's eyes widened, but she backed away. "It's over, Jack. I will always be fond of you, but I can't be with you in that way ever again."

He nodded. A lame clerk wasn't ever going to be good enough for her. What was worse, he wanted to hate her, but he knew she was right. He'd spend the rest of his life just trying to keep his head above water. If he could keep this job, it would take him another ten years to save two hundred pounds. By then he'd be thirty-eight. It took time to see ideas into fruition. How much time would he have if he didn't do something now?

They left the office. She went her way, he his.

Leaning heavily on his cane, Jack walked to the apothecary shop. He crossed through the store and into the back room, where he found his pack and his crutches.

"Where were you?" asked Mrs. Goode.

"I have to learn how to use this leg sometime," he muttered.

Standing in the storeroom doorway, the midwife pushed back a strand of white hair.

Jack dug out the pewter mug he'd taken from the tavern, crutched to the back door, yanked it open, then pitched the stolen tankard into a refuse heap. So help him God, he would never steal or beg again. And he'd find a way to make something of his life, or he'd die trying.

In spite of Jack's concern, Caroline ran most of the way home. Mr. Broadhurst was an intelligent man. She didn't need him realizing she had gone walking on the first night Jack was back.

She was out of breath when she entered the drawing room, but the running didn't account for the pain in her chest. Jack had asked for her belief in him, but she'd denied him that, just as she refused to admit her love for him. She didn't care that he'd had to beg, except his admission drained the light from his eyes. That part she hated.

For his own safety, she had to break all her ties to him. She had to leave him thinking she had only used him and didn't care for him. If only that were true, she might not feel as if she were only a shell around a hollow core.

"Where did you go, my dear?" asked Mr. Broadhurst.

His question might have sounded solicitous, but Caroline no longer took it at face value. "My stomach was upset, I thought a walk might soothe it."

"Did it?"

Her stomach churned as she moved to pick up her sewing. She'd begun a layette for the baby. "For a bit. The cold helps."

He nodded toward the little cap in her hands. "We should go to London and buy everything for our son."

Caroline put her hand against her flat stomach. What if the child was a girl? What if she lost it? She fought for calm. "It is early days yet, and for now I like the idea of sewing things myself. After all, the finest cotton can be found here."

Mr. Broadhurst's brows lowered speculatively.

Caroline suddenly wondered if the question were a trap. Most of their gentlemen guests, including her brother, had returned to London for the opening of Parliament. Perhaps she should have wanted to see *her lover* again.

She had to distract her husband, and the only thing that might serve was to refocus him on business. "I think we should move my desk into the back office."

Mr. Broadhurst scowled. "Why would I do that?"

"So the transition, when it is necessary, will be smoother. At some point I will need to be in charge until our child is ready to take over operations. Besides, the outer office is a little crowded now."

"Well, that may not last long."

A cold chill ran down Caroline's spine. Did he mean to be rid of Jack as soon as an opportunity presented itself?

Caroline stopped stitching. "I've been meaning to ask you. How did you get your start with the mill?"

"It isn't important."

"I want to be able to answer whatever questions our child has. Did you start small with one loom or did you build the entire manufactory right away?"

"You have never been interested before."

"That's not true. I have asked before, but you have always dismissed my questions." She hadn't pursued it, but now she wanted to understand how one went about building a successful enterprise. She wanted to know for Jack's sake. If she could give him any pointers so he could avoid pitfalls . . . "I just think our son will want to know where he came from. I want him to be proud of your success and know your history as well as mine. Did you work for someone else to learn the cloth business?"

"My mother had a loom. When I came into money, I built the mill." Mr. Broadhurst stood as if her questions made him uncomfortable.

"Why here? Why not in Manchester or near a established town?" she persisted. She knew that Mr. Broadhurst had made money on the village lots, but now their isolation was limiting. Without other industry nearby, they had to continue to employ men while other mills went to female labor forces.

He paced to the fire and held his hands out. "The land

was cheap, not fit for more than grazing sheep. Building my own village gave me more control."

"Would you do it the same if you had it all to do over again?"

Her husband shrugged. "If I had coal mines like Granger, I could employ the men in the mines and the women in the mill and keep the cost of labor down. There are too many cotton mills now, but it was a good thing when I started it."

"If you were to start another industry, what would it be?"

"It's too late for me to start a new industry."

Caroline pressed her lips together, rather than ask again.

Mr. Broadhurst stared into the fire. "It is probably too late to get ahead of the train industry, though machinery of all kinds look promising. Oil and its by-products, especially the polymers and resins, or rubber, are likely to become big profit makers."

A frisson of excitement rolled through Caroline. No one could doubt Mr. Broadhurst's business sense. If he thought it was time to strike with rubber, perhaps Jack was on to something.

Chapter 24

December turned to January. January folded into February and then slipped into a cold rainy March. Jack picked his way toward the mill office. In places the mud turned icy, and if he wasn't careful he'd go sprawling. That had happened on more occasions than he cared to admit. He didn't always know if he'd put his right foot down right, and the brace he wore only helped so much.

"Jack!"

He turned to see who it was.

Lucy skipped up to him and grabbed his free arm. "I've been waiting for you to come calling."

The day hadn't started yet, and her hair was already springing free of her bun.

"Let go, Lucy. I can't walk when you're tugging on me."

"Seems to me you're doing well, working as a clerk and everything."

He turned and assessed her. Her figure seemed fuller than he remembered, softer, rounder. He stared at her stomach. The material stretched tight. Perhaps if he didn't watch Caroline for signs, he wouldn't have noticed the changes in Lucy. His heart sank.

"You know it is silly for you to live at Mrs. Goode's place

and sleep on a cot when you could share a bed with me. If we got married."

He frowned. If it were his baby, she'd tell him. "When are you due?"

Her eyes filled with moisture. "Early fall."

A little after Caro was due, so it couldn't be his. Jack heaved a sigh of relief.

"I'm sorry, Lucy. Why don't you tell the father?"

Her mouth flattened and she looked toward the mill. He followed the line of her sight to a group of men, all of them married. He didn't know which one, but it didn't matter. Out of the corner of his eye he saw Caroline approaching the mill office.

"I can't be late."

"What are you going to do, Jack? Wait your whole life for a woman who'll never have you?"

"I got to go, Lucy." He pulled his arm free. He wasn't waiting so much as biding his time, studying the book he'd bought, *The Origin and Progress of the Caoutchouc or India-Rubber Industry in England*, by one Thomas Hancock. But what the hell was the difference?

For a second Caroline's face revealed a stark yearning to match his. Then she ducked her head and entered the office.

He walked away without another glance at Lucy. If there was the ghost of a chance with Caroline, he wasn't ready to give up. Not when he'd already ordered several sheets of rubber and the chemicals to alter it. He might not be able to afford to start a business, but he could at least experiment with covering the handles of his crutches and padding the brace he wore on his weakened leg. Once he had products, he could go from there.

When he entered the office, Caroline greeted him as she greeted all the other clerks. He was never first or last in her notice. She never did anything to call attention to him.

Later he was engrossed in going over ledger entries, making sure the tallies added up, when his skin tingled. Caroline stood beside him with a sheaf of papers in her hand.

He stared at the ledger, even though the numbers blurred. He couldn't notice the porcelain cast to Caro's skin, or inhale too deeply of her sweet scent. His heart shouldn't be pounding, but it was. She put the papers in front of him and asked a question that she knew the answer to.

"Ma'am?"

She let out a sigh and twisted. "Everyone has gone outside."

He looked behind to discover the office had emptied.

"A caravan with a Punch and Judy show." Caroline shrugged. "I suggested a break to watch."

Jack leaned to see out the window where the clerks and a few of the villagers had gathered around a brightly painted wagon. It didn't matter. He didn't dare leave his work. The few times he'd gone to the production side of the mill to show his brother David how to fix different pieces of machinery, he was careful to get permission, and then stayed late to make up any clerical work.

Caroline reached across, grabbed his far hand and placed it on her belly. "Do you feel that?"

The bulge of her pregnancy was slight but surprisingly firm. It popped under his hand.

Even getting clobbered by a life-size Punch couldn't have erased the grin from his face. That was his baby kicking. "Damn."

"Jack . . ." Caroline's voice quivered.

Had seeing him with Lucy caused her concern? He opened his mouth to reassure her, but then clamped it shut again.

"I need to see you," she whispered.

"You know where to find me."

She hesitated, and he realized he was rubbing her belly. He pulled his hand back.

"I understand if you don't want to . . . if you've moved on." She blushed furiously. "Are you ever alone?"

"When Mrs. Goode attends a birth." Twisting on his stool, he looked past her toward the door. God forgive him, but he'd thought this out too many times. "Molly Chandler is due any day. I will place a lamp in the apothecary shop window when Mrs. Goode goes to attend her."

Her forehead crinkled. He wanted to rub his thumb along her soft skin and smooth the worry away. He wanted to see her eyes bright with desire, not fear. Having her in his arms again would be worth any price.

"You should be able to see it from the upper stories of your home."

The outer door opened and she sprang back.

"I will see that those figures are entered," said Jack.

She nodded and escaped into the inner office as the clerks filed back inside.

Jack shifted his gaze and caught Mr. Broadhurst staring at him.

"Sir," Jack acknowledged. He splayed his fingers to keep from fisting them. He hadn't given the man any reason to sack him, but he didn't trust Broadhurst. And he sure as hell hoped the man hadn't heard him making arrangements to signal Caroline when he was alone.

Caroline felt as if she had been waiting forever to see the light in the apothecary shop window. She looked each evening a dozen times, and it was dark again tonight. She almost was sure she'd missed it, but each morning Jack shook his head before she could find the privacy to ask him.

She sighed and went back down to the drawing room.

Mr. Broadhurst put down his newspaper. "Does not appear to be any signs of war in the States. We are going to be inundated with cotton."

Caroline swallowed hard. She believed she'd made the right choice. "Better too much cotton than having to shut down the mill for lack of it."

Mr. Broadhurst harrumphed.

"It was a gamble either way, sir."

"What are we supposed to do with it? Let it rot?"

"The moors behind the mill could be used for a warehouse. Many of the men from the mill would eagerly take construction jobs. More women could be brought in to work in the mill, and the warehouse could be converted to dormitories for them. But then I don't know what we'll do with the men."

"You have no business sense at all," said Mr. Broadhurst.

Her mouth tightened. "I do not see how war will be avoided with several states saying they will not be part of the United States."

"Fools," muttered Mr. Broadhurst.

Caroline stood. "I believe I shall retire. I am weary."

Mr. Broadhurst watched her as she crossed the drawing room. Perhaps her decision had been bad, and now they would have to spend more money to rectify it. Perhaps she didn't possess enough business acumen to run the mill. Profits were down, costs were up. If all the cotton she'd agreed to buy arrived, they'd be losing money instead of making it.

"I have notified my solicitor that you are expecting."

She stopped and turned. Her heart thumped oddly. Had he claimed parenthood or disavowed responsibility? Who notified their solicitor of a pregnancy?

As if the world had closed in on her, she no longer wanted to be the mouse in this cat and mouse game. She had done what he asked. She had poured her soul into learning the mill, and tried her hardest to make the best decisions for all involved. Still, it might all be snatched away from her at any time.

"I trust you told him how pleased you were." With that she left the room, not looking back to see his response. She simply didn't care what he'd told his solicitor.

After getting into her nightgown, she took one last peek out the front window and saw it, a flicker in the window below the mortar and pestle signboard. Not that she could actually make out the signage, but she'd looked so often out the window, her eyes made a beeline to the apothecary shop.

Her heart hammered and her fingers were clumsy as she threw on clothes, slipped her feet into demi boots, and grabbed a hooded cloak. She locked her bedroom door and flew down the corridor to the servants' stairs, tiptoed down, and went out a side door. Forcing her feet to walk and not run took every ounce of willpower she had. She didn't want to draw attention. No one could know she was seeing Jack.

Her heart was in her throat she scurried down the street. What if he didn't want to be with her?

When she reached the midwife's house she hesitated. She shouldn't be here.

The door opened and Jack stood there. Her breath stole away. He clamped a hand around her wrist, drew her inside and behind him. Leaning out, he looked left and right, then shut the door.

"Did anyone see me?" she asked.

"Not that I can tell. Go in the back, while I get the lamp." He gave her a slight push toward the open door at the back of the small space.

Aware of the bare windows, Caroline followed Jack's command.

As her eyes adjusted to the dimness, she took in the stacked crates, a small stove in the corner, and a narrow iron bedstead against the far wall.

Could she live as simply and as starkly as this? As long as she stayed with Mr. Broadhurst, she could have anything that money could buy, but she was miserable. She didn't know if she could wait for him to die—and it was a horrible thing to wish for. Every time the thought entered her head, she feared God would smite her down with a lightning bolt.

Jack entered the room behind her, carrying the lamp with both hands as he slowly limped over to set the light on a crate near his bed. He turned back and watched her, his head tilted to the side.

She knew he wanted to be a part of her life when Mr. Broadhurst was gone, but did he think of her as separate from the Broadhurst money? Would he want her without the wealth?

Jack stood by his bed, his heart thundering in his ears. He wasn't sure why Caroline had come, but she looked ready to bolt. "I do not know how long Mrs. Goode will be out, but seldom is it less than two hours."

He wanted to make love to her, but she hadn't even pulled back her hood. Her face was shadowed and he couldn't fully read her expression.

The storeroom where he slept was hardly the sort of luxury she was used to. The wooden floors were bare, the walls flat plaster. He slept amid boxes and empty bottles waiting to be returned. Did the simple way he lived put her off?

Not knowing what she would do, he held out his hand.

It seemed to be the impetus she needed as she flew toward

him. He caught her to him and kissed her hard. Yanking free the strings of her cloak, he pushed the garment from her shoulders.

His blood fired as he tasted passion on her lips. She strained against him, mewing softly. Need, want, desire pounded in him. Seeing her every day and denying his feelings had built his cravings for her to an explosive force. He couldn't hold back, any more than he could have leapt over the moon.

He yanked at her buttons as she pushed his braces off his shoulders. Breaking the kiss only long enough to yank his shirt over his head, he struggled to find the sanity to be gentle. Her hands against his skin electrified him. Her lips against his exhilarated him. Her being with him elated him.

Impatient, he yanked down her dress. She wiggled, helping him push it below her hips, where it fell to the floor.

For one heedless second he remembered she needed coaxing and patience and deplored grabbing and squeezing. But he was no longer a man in constant pain with a leg that needed to be coddled. He was hard and urgent for her.

He pulled back, his breath roaring like a bellows. "Caro . . . too long. Can't be gentle."

"I don't care. I want you." Her fingers slid under his waistband and she worked at the button.

Sliding his hand under the material between their chests, he rubbed her breast and bit her bottom lip. She put her hand over his, pushing and curling her fingers around his as her nipple tightened under his palm. He sucked on the sore spot he'd created. She had his trousers open and was easing them down his hips.

Reluctantly, he let go of her and shoved them and his smalls down and unbuckled his brace. He twisted so the two of them fell on his narrow bed. He kissed her deeply. She was like air to a drowning man. He needed her, she was here, and he had to be inside her.

Yet, there was too much material between them. She still wore some white thing that was half unbuttoned at the neck. He grabbed both sides and yanked, rending the material. The baring of her skin made him growl. He slid his hands over her slightly rounded stomach and pushed her legs open to touch her slick folds.

She arched and drew his hand to her breast, while she reached lower and gripped his cock. Heat and pleasure burned in him, and he fought to keep from spilling his seed in her hand.

"I need you," she whispered, and he was lost.

He knew he was probably rushing faster than she could keep up. He wanted her passion burning as hot as his. "Stay with me," he murmured as he spread her legs wider and positioned his cock against her core.

Her hips twisted and she moaned deep in her throat.

He flicked the button at the apex of her folds and plucked at the tightened tip of her breast. Using everything he knew about how she responded, he pushed her toward completion.

"Come with me," he urged against her lips as he thrust inside her.

She moaned and arched and then whispered, "Anywhere," before pulling his head to hers and kissing him.

Anywhere? But he didn't have time to fathom her odd response as pleasure rolled through him. Lost in her scent and softness, he thrust deeply. She wound her legs around his waist, spurring him to completion. The mound of her belly against his stomach only intensified his desire for her. She was his, and they'd created life together.

The passion drove him higher and higher, until he groaned out his climax. She twisted and strained toward him, then cried out as her body throbbed around him, intensifying his pleasure.

Although her response was everything he hoped for, he cringed, thinking he might have hurt her. He pressed kisses on her eyelids and nose. Her eyes fluttered open. "Goodness."

He rubbed his nose against hers. "Goodness?" he teased.

"That was intense."

"I'm sorry." He ran his fingers down the side of her face. "This has been denied me for months and I could not hold back."

Her blue eyes searched his. "I cannot imagine how it could have been better without actually dying."

Smiling, he shifted his weight off her. She moaned a complaint. The narrow bed meant they were pressed close together, her shoulder in his chest, but he didn't want to be far from her. He kissed her temple. "I don't want to hurt you or the baby."

"I think it is my nightgowns that suffer when we are together." She curled into him, tucking her head into the crook of his shoulder. Her arms were still in the sleeves of the garment he'd ripped open. "I am not so easily broken."

He ran his hand over her hip. Her skin was faintly damp, but silky smooth. Now, while he was sated, he should do all the gentle things he'd neglected in his rush to have her. But as he touched her, he realized the fire was not truly banked and required little coaxing to flare anew.

But this time he did touch her gently and slowly, until she quivered whenever his fingers moved. He stared into her face, drinking in her features, measuring each twinge of passion in her expression and memorizing every detail about her, from the flecks of darker blue in her irises to the tiny beauty mark just under her left eye.

As he moved on top of her to join their bodies, she whispered, "I love you, John Applegate. I will always love you."

And again he was lost. His voice cracked as he whispered back his love. Desire tangled with emotion and brought him into her in a way that was beyond bliss. She felt it too as tears leaked out of her eyes and she shuddered into a orgasm so powerful it swept him along with her and blended them into one creature with no end or beginning, but a paradise of the mind and a rapture of their intertwined bodies. He started and ended with her, and a life without her in it would be a barren wasteland.

She slid her hand along his shoulders. "I don't know how to do this, Jack. I can't stand living with him anymore. I want to be with you."

He reared back and looked down at her, finally connecting her "anywhere" with what she meant.

His heart soared. She wanted to be with him.

Then a tiny nudge against his stomach reminded him of the baby she carried.

Reality dug in its claws and shook him. He had nothing, only a few shillings he'd saved from his wages. He couldn't support her, let alone a child. He was a failure. His pathetic experiments that he'd been so eager to show her were drops in an ocean that would need to be filled before he could be considered respectable.

How could they bring a baby into a life of poverty?

"Caro, you have to think of our baby. I wouldn't have agreed to father a baby if I didn't know my child would have a better life. Would have advantages I could only dream about."

Chapter 25

So for Jack it was about the money. Caroline twisted away and sat up, tugging the sheet to cover her nakedness. "You're right. I should be practical for the baby. I don't want any harm to come to this child because I find it hard to endure."

Jack sat behind her and wrapped his arms around her. She would have pushed him away, except his hand curled protectively around her stomach.

He pressed a kiss to her shoulder. "Has something changed? Has Broadhurst threatened you?"

"No. Nothing's changed." Except she could no longer stand the emptiness of her life. What would be best for the child, the cold sterile life filled with things or two loving parents? She knew the answer, but she hated that the world valued wealth and legitimacy more than love.

Jack's fingers tightened and then he splayed them out, gently rubbing them across her belly. His unfettered passion earlier had surprised her, but also lifted her to new heights. When it seemed he couldn't get enough of her, she believed it was because he truly loved her. But it was easy for a woman to delude herself into believing a man cared more than he did.

She just didn't know if he loved her, or he loved the life he could have if she wanted him after Mr. Broadhurst was gone. Or was he truly concerned about giving the best life possible to his baby?

Jack was a good man, and he hated receiving handouts. She didn't know a harder worker. He didn't just treat his clerical duties as tasks to be put aside when the day expired. He learned more than he needed to know, always searching for the why of what they did. And on more than one occasion he'd returned from being summoned to the working side of the mill, dirty from disassembling and repairing the machinery, when it was no longer his responsibility. He thought more like an owner than an employee. He had the right attitude to be successful, he just lacked money and opportunity.

And unless his attitude had changed, he would find being her cicisbeo demeaning. But was it about the money?

"Don't you want the mill anymore?" he asked.

Everything came tumbling out, about how she might have made a mistake ordering cotton from Egypt and the Americas, how the mill's costs were too high because other mills employed more women at three-quarters wages, but there was no other industry in the village to employ men. Her half-baked plan to build a warehouse to give better jobs to the men, and how that was only temporary. Once the cotton was gone there would be an empty building. And if the mill couldn't turn a profit, it was moot anyway.

Jack listened and took her back to her reasoning for her decisions. And made her remember she had a concern Broadhurst had never faced, and she had made a decision she believed in and that might yet be the best.

"Or I may have ruined everything," she said. "If it turns

out badly, Mr. Broadhurst will make sure I never get control of the mill."

"He wants this baby to be his heir, doesn't he?"

Caroline lifted a shoulder. "Only if it is a boy."

Making a sound of displeasure, Jack pushed his cheek against hers. "I would take you away, if I had a thing to offer you, but, Caro, I live in a storeroom. I can't provide for you."

"And I can't cook," she moaned.

"You shouldn't have to. You shouldn't have to come down in the world to be with me," he whispered fiercely. "You deserve so much more."

She took in the room, the narrow stairs leading up to what was probably the midwife's living quarters. Near the bed an upended crate served as his night table. The lamplight fell on a book lying spine up with its pages splayed. He had come a long way if he was reading in bed. She squinted at the subtitle, *India-Rubber Industry in England.* A sheaf of papers probably held his plans.

"My family could take us in."

He sighed and leaned back, away from her. "I never want your family to feel about you as I feel about my family."

She twisted, looking back at him. "But I have earned their support. I have paid for it a thousand times over—or Mr. Broadhurst's money has."

"You have. I haven't. It's not a solution, Caro." He put his hand over his face.

Her family would support her, but there would be costs. "I just hate every minute with him. I used to think kindly of him and that his abrasiveness was just the product of his keen business sense. I worked hard to be fond of him, but I feel dead around him. And it is a terrible thing for me to go to bed wishing for his death, wake up in the morning wishing for his death, so I can feel alive? What kind of a person does that make me?"

"If you are a bad person, I am worse, because there is nothing I'd like to do more than end it for him."

Her heart squeezed.

He gave her a rueful smile. "I think it, but I would not do it. I wanted to be successful like him, but not in that way. Perhaps I am not ruthless enough to be a business magnate."

"Never say that. You are smart and you have good ideas. You will accomplish great things. Even Mr. Smythe is impressed with your understanding and competence. Mr. Broadhurst would have given you your congé a long time ago if you were not upstaging all the other clerks, who had the advantage of education."

"I know. Given my background, I have to show that I am better, to be considered equal." Jack rubbed his face. "I'm trying. I work so hard to get to where I should have been a decade ago. It just seems that every time I take a step in the right direction I am pulled down."

He leaned over and grabbed the crutches leaning against the wall at the foot of his bed. "I have done this with rubber." He showed her where he'd covered the handle sections, the top crossbar, and tips with rubber. "It is not exactly the most lucrative idea I've ever had, but it makes the crutches much easier to hold and less likely to slip. I'm sure this could really help people."

Her heart melted. She hugged him to her.

"And I am working to make my brace more comfortable and better functioning. The rubber, even though it has a sweet smell, can stink to high heaven when I'm heating it. Mrs. Goode is not fond of my experiments. I will have to find a place, buy machinery and supplies before I can truly make anything come of my ideas."

And he was trying to get there on a clerk's wages.

An idea so perfect it was scary came to her. "Jack, would you consider a partnership?"

The door rattled.

"Bloody hell," muttered Jack as he pushed her down and shielded her with his body. "Don't move. Mrs. Goode is back."

The danger of discovery rushed back fourfold. If Mr. Broadhurst ever learned she was with Jack . . .

Caroline tiptoed down the silent hall and retrieved her room key from the pocket of her cloak. Wincing every time it clicked against the metal of the lock, she turned it and whirled inside her room.

It was wrong. A lamp she hadn't lit burned. Her heart jumped to her throat. Dreading what she would see, she slowly turned. The connecting door to her husband's room was open, and he sat in one of the armchairs.

"I provide you with gentlemen and you lay with that ill bred cur." Mr. Broadhurst's low voice cut through her.

"I don't know what you're talking about." She drew herself up. "I couldn't sleep. I went for a walk."

Her mind spun trying to come up with an explanation for locking the doors. How long had Mr. Broadhurst known she was gone?

He closed the gap between them and caught her arms in a bruising grip. "Is that child his?"

"Unhand me."

He shook her until her teeth rattled. "I saw you with him. Not hard to identify a lame man from a distance."

Jack had used his crutches, rather than strap on his brace when he escorted her back after Mrs. Goode went upstairs to her quarters. Caroline's knees buckled. What had she done?

"Is it?" demanded Mr. Broadhurst.

"He reminded me of you, or at least how I imagined you must have been when you were young."

His hand connected with her face with a resounding clap. Caroline spun away with the force of his blow and tasted the coppery tang of blood in her mouth. With her tongue, she probed at her teeth, making sure they were all in place.

"He is nothing but a useless cripple. Our baby could be born with a shriveled leg."

She straightened. "That is the most ignorant thing I have ever heard."

"How could he remind you of me? I was not living in my father's house at his age, I had my own." Mr. Broadhurst paced the room, for once moving fast.

"You said yourself, he is intelligent with good business instincts."

"How could you do this to me?" he demanded.

"I do this 'to you'!" Incredulity exploded out of her. She followed him and poked him in the chest when he turned at the wall. "You did this. You put me in the most god-awful position." She poked again. "No gentleman in the world would have asked this of a faithful wife. You are a knave and aren't fit to wipe his feet."

Her husband stared at her with such coldness, her insides turned to liquid. Oh God, she had to get word to Jack.

"Don't you dare think of harming him."

"I wouldn't dirty my hands." His gaze turned distant, calculating.

His reassurance left her cold. He might not sully his own hands, but he would have no compunction about others getting their hands dirty in his stead. How could she get Jack away from here?

"Oh!" She put her hand to her belly and doubled over.

Mr. Broadhurst didn't make a move.

"Ow!" Caroline reached out, grabbing his arm as if she were in agony. "Something is wrong."

"If you lose that baby, I will have no use for you," said Broadhurst. He shot his cuffs. He had likely never undressed. "I will send for the doctor."

"No! The midwife is closer." She grabbed her belly with both hands. Forcing hard fast breaths in and out, Caroline managed a fairly credible moan. "Send for Mrs. Goode, ple-ease."

Instead of leaving the room to find a servant, her husband walked to the bellpull and yanked it.

When Jack opened the door to Caroline's stricken maid, his heart jolted. He knew he had been too rough with Caroline and now she was having pains and summoning Mrs. Goode.

Mrs. Goode departed with her satchel, and he strapped on his brace and followed. The darkness would cloak him, and if he waited in the shadows just at the edge of trees he could learn the news as soon as Mrs. Goode exited the house.

Oh God, she couldn't lose the baby. It would destroy her. He'd watched her over the last few months. When she thought no one was looking, she would put a hand against her stomach and a Madonna-like smile would cross her face. If he had caused a miscarriage, he'd never forgive himself.

After what seemed like hours, Mrs. Goode finally emerged. She descended the steps and started toward town.

"Mrs. Goode," called Jack, half skipping to try and catch her. "Is Caro—Mrs. Broadhurst all right?"

Mrs. Goode swiveled and stared at him. "Do you know what you're doing, Jack?"

Agony cut through him. "Is the baby . . . ?"

"The baby is fine. Mrs. Broadhurst is fine, except having some sort of hysterics that made her light-headed. For all she is claiming pain in her belly, she isn't cramping or bleeding or showing any signs of a problem."

Jack nearly collapsed on the drive.

Mrs. Goode walked faster. "Her husband never left her side."

Ignoring the pain in his bad leg, Jack hurried to keep up.

"I don't suppose you know anything about the bruise on her face." Mrs. Goode looked over her shoulder.

Dear God, had Broadhurst hit her? He never should have hit her.

"Jack, keep walking with me," said Mrs. Goode in a low undertone.

He looked behind him and could see no reason for her alarm. The house looked the same as ever, imposing, proclaiming wealth beyond what he could imagine.

"She wanted me to warn you that he knows."

Jack cringed. He shouldn't have been so selfish as to allow her to come to him. He should have been content waiting until she was free, even if it took a hundred years. He shouldn't have even been here to risk temptation. He should have been in London making himself worthy of her.

"Do you know what happened to his first two wives?" asked the midwife.

"I suspect they didn't actually both kill themselves," said Jack.

"Maybe his first wife did. I don't know," said Mrs. Goode. "She was miserable she didn't conceive. But within a week of her death, he was engaged to the daughter of the richest man in these parts. I suppose compared to what he has now, she wasn't that well off."

Jack watched Mrs. Goode's wrinkled face.

"Less than a year after he married her, her entire family perished in a fire while visiting. She only got out by jumping

from a window. He was working late at the mill. There were
those who said the fire was too fast to have been an accident.
He built his mansion on the spot, even though she begged
him to move elsewhere."

"I know he brought home the current Mrs. Broadhurst a
few weeks after his second wife died."

"Got too old, she did. Was going through the change. But
was happy as a lark. She liked being rich, didn't like children. No one ever believed she would have hanged herself.
He was working late at the mill then too."

A chill went through him. How much danger was Caroline in?

"Don't fancy my shop and house being burned down.
You'll have to find somewhere else to stay."

Where the hell was he supposed to go? And how the hell
could he leave Caroline with that madman?

Jack turned to go back to the mansion.

Mrs. Goode grabbed his arm and tugged. He ended up
sprawled on the packed gravel of the drive.

"Sorry, but you're not going back there if I have to stand
on you."

Caroline stared in the looking glass. All the purple and
redness of the bruise on her cheek was gone. The tiny remaining yellow smudge was almost completely faded and would
be unnoticeable to most. She needed to return to work today.

She'd already spent a fortnight at home, pretending to
recover from her imaginary almost miscarriage, but really
waiting for the bruise to fade.

Her maid opened her door and carried a breakfast tray
to the small table near the window where the sun was just
peeking in. "Begging your pardon, ma'am. There's another."

"Who is it this time?" sighed Caroline. Her family had

swarmed on her like a horde of locusts. They'd taken one look at her face and burrowed in around her. She had no idea how her family knew to come, but she was grateful for their presence. But each time she asked why they had shown up, they said Robert had sent them. She hoped that meant Jack had gotten to Robert and was safe with him.

First, her mother arrived insisting that she must be with her daughter through the birth of her grandchild. Why she felt the need to attend this grandchild's birth, when she hadn't bothered with the last six grandchildren's births, didn't make sense. Then dragging their husbands with them, the twins showed up within minutes of each other, finishing each other's sentences and insisting Caroline needed to take the air sandwiched between them on an hourly basis. Next, Amelia popped in and insisted they would all have to take an extended shopping trip because "babies needed so many things." Marshaling for battle, Sarah sailed in a few days later.

"Your brother, Lord Nesham, is just arrived," her maid told her.

Finally, she might get some answers. "Have Mrs. Burns put him in the drawing room."

She tilted to look out the window. A lathered horse was being led to the stables. Goodness, Robert must have ridden hard through the night to arrive so early in the morning.

No matter what they said, she was breaking free of her family's cocoon and going into the mill office today. With or without Mr. Broadhurst's support, she would set in motion plans to build a warehouse for the cotton shipments likely to swamp them in the fall. Whether it would be throwing good money after bad or not, the worst thing they could do was be unprepared for its arrival. She didn't know if Jack would accept a partnership to found his business, but she was proceeding as if he would.

Her family's presence meant she hadn't spent one second alone with Mr. Broadhurst and he was forced to act as a gentlemen would. Every night one or more of her siblings decided to have a comfortable coze, sitting on her bed until Caroline fell asleep. But not having a minute alone to reflect on what had happened was starting to wear on her.

She rubbed her hand across the mound of her belly, which seemed to increase each day. Still, each day she went without hearing from Jack was a nightmare.

Forcing down the tea and toast that would help keep her stomach from rebelling, Caroline sat on the edge of her chair. Beyond wanting answers from Robert, she was restless. Her sleep had been fitful and she woke to nightmares of Jack calling and her not being able to get to him in time. Where was he?

She pushed her plate back and went downstairs to search out her brother. Learning he was closeted with her husband in his study, she paced the hall outside.

After a while she tried the door, but found it locked.

Leaning an ear against the wood, she heard nothing. She knocked and then knocked again.

The door cracked. "I said we weren't to be disturbed," said Robert in an imperious voice. "Oh, it is you." His tone softened.

He smelled of horse and looked unkempt. How odd.

Her stomach roiled in response to the strong tang of horse sweat. She put her fingers over her mouth, cursing the weakness the pregnancy evoked. "What are you doing?"

"I needed to go over a few things with Mr. Broadhurst this morning. Go to the drawing room and wait."

Behind him she thought she heard a weak cry.

She rose on her toes.

"Go now, Caro." His voice dropped to a low whisper.

"Jack will be here any minute." Then he shut the door in her face.

Jack would be here? Her heart hammering in her chest, she ran to the front door and opened it. Two carriages were starting down the drive. One she recognized as her brother's, the other was plain and black.

She ran down the steps and bounced. Surely Jack was in her brother's carriage. And he couldn't come here. But oh God, she wanted to see him again. She needed to see him again.

The carriages drew to a halt at the base of the stairs. Like ants escaping an anthill, men wearing black suits and black hats emerged out of the vehicles.

One touched the brim of his hat, but for the most part she was ignored as they swarmed past her. Then Jack descended the carriage steps. His face was determined, but the corners of his mouth lifted in acknowledgment of her as he moved toward the stairs. She wanted to hug him, but she didn't know who the men were.

"It will be over soon, Caro," he said in a low undertone as he pressed a kiss to her forehead.

His fingertips went unerringly to the last of the bruise on her cheek and his brown eyes narrowed.

"He will never hurt you again." He stepped back and glanced toward the door. "Shall we go inside?"

"I've been so worried about you," she whispered.

"We'll have time for talking later," Jack said. He pivoted and walked up the stairs rapidly, like a man with two legs would. His steps had only the slightest hitch.

She dashed at the stupid tears forming in her eyes and followed him.

Two of the men held Mr. Broadhurst by the arms. He was pale and sweaty. His eyes scanned the hall and lit on her.

"Mrs. Broadhurst, send for the . . ." He tilted his head, looking puzzled. " . . . tea trolley. If we sit down in my office, we can reach a reasonable solution." He twisted left and right looking at the men holding his arms. "What was it you wanted to discuss?"

"The conspiracy and murder of Thomas Whitton."

Dear heavens, they were arresting Mr. Broadhurst.

Robert folded back into a corner, his head down. Her mother and sisters stood on the stairs hanging onto one another, their blue eyes big and round in their pretty faces. Caroline had the strongest urge to block Jack's view of them. But he was glowering at Robert, not ogling her beautiful sisters.

"You left me," said Jack.

Robert lifted a shoulder. "I had to make certain his affairs were in order."

Caroline had the oddest sensation the room was tilting. Apparently, Mr. Broadhurst felt it too, because he collapsed, and no amount of shaking by the men roused him.

Then blackness closed in from the edges of her vision, until there was just a pinprick of light, then nothing.

The acrid smell made Caroline retch. She pushed away the hand holding a vile substance under her nose.

"Give her room to breathe," said Jack.

She opened her eyes to find her sisters and mother leaning over her. She scanned until she found Jack behind them. Pushing to sit up, she realized she was on a sofa in the library instead of in the hall.

"Wh-What happened?"

"I'm afraid I've some bad news." Her mother patted her hand. "Your husband has passed away."

That wasn't bad news, but Caroline focused on Jack's

face. His lips tightened. Why would Mr. Broadhurst's death make him angry?

"I'm afraid the shock of being arrested must have made his heart give out," said her mother. "We've sent for the doctor, but he is no longer breathing. I'm very sorry, but if you're feeling better, I need to see to the men from Scotland Yard. And, well, make arrangements for the body." She let her daughter's hand drop. Grimacing, she looked directly at Jack. Then she rose to full height and commanded imperiously, "Come on, girls, let's give your sister a bit of privacy."

Amy leaned close and whispered in her ear. "I've never seen a man move so fast. Then he carried you in here, even though Robert said he shouldn't."

As her sisters filed out, Jack's eyes never left hers. The door clicked behind them.

"Jack," she sighed. Had he really carried her? She looked down at his leg. "Did you fix your brace?"

He lifted his trouser leg and showed her the rubber sleeve attached to the metal bars and leather straps. "I can almost run with it. Still a few kinks, but I haven't had time to work on it."

She smiled. "Where have you been? I've been so worried."

"If you had made it into the mill office, my brother would have given you my letter. He tried to bring it here, but they wouldn't let him see you. He even brought Beth, thinking she might be allowed in, but I told him to put it directly in your hands only."

Caroline put her fingers to the fading bruise. "Mr. Broadhurst didn't want anyone to see my bruise."

"Might have been difficult to explain why he attacked his pregnant wife." Jack pulled his hands behind his back. "I cabled your brother you were in danger, and then wrote him what I knew. Apparently, your father had grown suspicious after your marriage and had the direction of some servants who were working here when Mr. Broadhurst's second wife died. While they made statements about their suspicions, there wasn't enough proof of her murder.

"But after your brother and I compared notes, and you told me about the highway man's description, I remembered a man who used to be a dray driver. The man said he came into some money and quit working, but everyone suspected he still did odd jobs for Mr. Broadhurst. I told Scotland Yard and was able to take them to the man. Lord Langley identified him and his coat. Once the man knew he was to hang, he sang like a canary about working for Broadhurst."

Jack's mouth flattened. "We were coming to arrest him, but your brother decided to rush ahead. I guess he thought it best to make sure there had been no further changes to the will. Said Broadhurst needed to take his medicine."

Her mind spun as she processed the information. She was a widow. Her husband had been arrested for Mr. Whitton's murder and possibly his late wife's. "His medicine," she repeated dully. The foxglove the doctor had warned her about. Robert had been given the warning too. "Robert was probably giving him a chance to keep his name from being dragged through the mud."

"Undoubtedly," said Jack dryly.

When he had a chance to think about it, Jack would realize the scandal would have touched his child too, if a trial took place. She stared at him standing out of reach. She patted the sofa beside her. "Will you come sit down?"

"If I get close to you, I cannot guarantee I will ever let you go."

"Why would I want you to?"

"Just one more thing," he said, taking a step back. "I would very much like to be in a partnership with you for a rubber works, if you do not mind that I focus on medical uses instead of applications that might make more money."

"Of course." She stood to go to him.

He held out a hand, stopping her. Her heart squeezed.

"As long as that partnership is also a marriage. I know I have no right to ask for your hand, but I don't think I could live without you. I love you, Caroline. I think I always have."

"Oh, Jack, what makes you think I would have it any other way? And apparently my family must think it a good thing—or they never would have left me alone with you."

He rolled his eyes. "Family. You will be saddled with mine, because much as I would like to wash my hands of them, I don't think I can get rid of them."

She slid her arms around his waist and looked up at him. "Your family is not so bad. I'm rather fond of Beth."

He groaned and pulled her tight. He bent and pressed a kiss to her temple. "Will I make you happy, Caro? Your brother will kill me if I do not. He said you deserve to be happy after what you have been through. You are a rich woman. There are a lot of better born men, whole men, who would eagerly marry you."

"John Applegate, I love you. I will always love you. And you will always make me happy. I cannot imagine life with anyone else. And it may be a seven year scandal, but I never want to sleep alone again." She flushed as she reached up and pulled his head down to hers. "Now kiss me before I go to the mill and make plans for a warehouse cum rubber works factory."

"Caro, I really think the mill should wait until tomorrow," he said between kisses.

She wasn't thinking about the mill anyway. "Or next week," she agreed.

Epilogue

Caroline rolled on the blanket and stared at the fluffy clouds in the sky. The way the moors rolled around them behind the rubber works, they could have been all alone on this Sunday afternoon.

Jack leaned over her and fed her a grape.

"A penny for your thoughts, Lady Caroline."

She smiled. "Will you ever tire of calling me that?"

"No. I want you to meet the patent people from the United States just so I can introduce you. This is my wife, Lady Caroline Applegate."

"It only means my brother is now an earl." Queen Victoria had decided the romance of a lady falling in love with a millworker as she nursed him back to health far outweighed the scandal of marrying one of the lower orders just a few months after being made a widow. If she knew of the arrest of Mr. Broadhurst, she must not have considered it significant.

Besides, Jack's rubber works and patents were starting to bring in a steady if modest income, and the queen applauded his efforts to expand the use of rubber in medical devices.

"I feel sorry for Mr. Broadhurst some days," Caroline said. "He wanted a son so badly." While their son was christened as a Broadhurst, no one called him by that name. The solicitor had advised them there was no reason they couldn't change his name to Applegate now that the Broadhurst estate was settled. He would own the house and mill when he was older, but other parts of the will conflicted with the marriage settlement and were thrown out. Caroline truly was a rich woman in her own right.

Jack snorted. "The man was a murderer. He didn't deserve a child."

"Mmm," said Caroline, feeling sleepy. This rare Sunday afternoon picnic was a time for both of them to relax away from their demanding manufactories.

"Don't go too far," Jack called to little Johnny. One had only to look at the two-year-old to guess his parentage. He looked so much like Jack, it made her smile.

"So was that shipment the last of the cotton?" Jack stretched out beside her.

Caroline hadn't realized that the extra cotton she'd bought before the beginning of the Civil War in the Americas would turn out to be quite so valuable. She was able to resell it at triple the price, while continuing to buy new from Egypt because she'd been ahead in the game, establishing contracts with growers there.

Her gamble had paid off.

She took Jack's hand and placed it on her flat belly. "What do you think? Will it be a girl or another boy this time?"

"Caro?" His eyes filled with wonder.

That was one way to get him to drop the "Lady" appellation. She shook her head, acknowledging her pregnancy. "I am fairly certain, although it is early days."

Jack slid down and kissed her stomach. Johnny ran over, plopped down, and taking it for a new game, followed suit.

She threaded her fingers into Jack's hair. "I love you."

He put a hand on their son's back and answered in kind. "And I will love you until the end of time."

Johnny pointed at his mother's stomach and said insistently, "Papa kiss."

"That's your new brother or sister in there," Jack told his son.

Johnny looked puzzled and then darted off to chase a butterfly.

Caroline tapped her lips. "Papa kiss."

Jack smiled and inched up to do her bidding. "Next time we plan a picnic, we need to leave Johnny with his nanny."

"Better yet, his nursery maid is coming in a half hour to take him home for his afternoon nap."

"I don't think I can wait that long," said Jack, tracing a finger down the side of her neck.

She slid her hand down his side. "I'm afraid you'll have to."

"Damn," he said as he rolled to his feet, then chased after his son.

Caroline watched her husband trot to rescue Johnny from the big gob of dirt he was ready to stuff in his mouth. At least she hoped it was dirt, but then she was too content to worry overmuch.

Jack grabbed his son and swung him in the air as he brushed the dirt from his hand. She rather fancied a girl, but another boy would be lovely too.

But more than that, she fancied the rest of the afternoon in scandalous bliss in Jack's arms, because there was no other place she wanted to be.

Next month, don't miss these exciting new love stories only from Avon Books

A Scottish Love by Karen Ranney

Shona Imrie should have agreed to Gordon MacDermond's proposal seven years ago—before he went to war and returned a hero—but though she loved him, she would accept no man's charity. MacDermond has everything he could ever want—except for the stubborn beauty he let slip through his fingers.

Within the Flames by Marjorie M. Liu

When pyrokinetic Dirk & Steele agent Eddie goes to Manhattan to investigate a string of murders, he comes upon a shapeshifter, Lyssa, with powers over fire similar to his own. Hiding from brutal memories, Lyssa is reluctant to trust Eddie. But with flames at their fingertips and evil forces at their heels, will the fire between them conquer all?

Beyond the Darkness by Jaime Rush

Shapeshifter Cheveyo walked out of Petra's life when his mission to hunt evil jeopardized her safety. But when he discovers that Petra is the target of a deadly enemy, he struggles to keep his emotions in check as he draws near to protect her. The closer the danger, the deeper the devotion . . . and the deadlier the consequence.

Brazen by Margo Maguire

When Captain Gavin Briggs informs Lady Christina that she's the long-lost granddaughter of a duke, she refuses to meet with the old man who abandoned her as a child. But she knows Briggs needs the reward money and she agrees to go only if he helps her rescue her endangered brother. Peril and treachery await them . . . as well as sizzling attraction, lustful temptation and unanticipated passion.

978-0-06-200304-1

978-0-06-202719-1

978-0-06-206932-0

978-0-06-194638-7

978-0-06-199968-0

978-0-06-201232-6

At Avon Books, we know your passion for romance—once you finish one of our novels, you find yourself wanting more.

May we tempt you with . . .

- **Excerpts** from our upcoming releases.

- Entertaining **extras**, including authors' personal photo albums and book lists.

- Behind-the-scenes **scoop** on your favorite characters and series.

- **Sweepstakes** for the chance to win free books, romantic getaways, and other fun prizes.

- Writing **tips** from our authors and editors.

- **Blog** with our authors and find out why they love to write romance.

- **Exclusive content** that's not contained within the pages of our novels.

Join us at
www.avonbooks.com

AVON

An Imprint of HarperCollins*Publishers*
www.avonromance.com